PRAISE FOR K.J. SUTTON'S FORTUNA SWORN SERIES

"A fantastic urban fantasy series that I highly recommend. Massive thumbs up from me!" —Beckie Bookworm

"If you are looking for a new paranormal series, this is the one for you." —The Book Curmudgeon

"A unique and compelling fantasy series that will grab you right from the start and hold your attention." —Mindy Lou's Book Review

"K.J. Sutton has created a world that is equal parts mesmerizing and terrifying... for fantasy readers who are looking for a little fresh and a lot fantastic!" —Tome Tender Book Blog

"Prepare to delve into a dark and twisted world!" —Perspective of a Writer

"Sutton... managed to create a spin on not only the fae but other supernatural creatures that will fascinate you [and] leave you turning the pages as fast as you possibly can!" —My Guilty Obsession

"The romance tantalizes and teases... leaving the reader begging for more." —This Girl Reads a Lot

"A captivating, fast-paced paranormal fantasy that is sure to sweep you away to a world unlike any o'

DEADLY
DREAMS

K.J. SUTTON

ONCE UPON A TIME
books

ISBN 978-1-0879-0043-8 (hardback)

ISBN 978-1-7334616-1-0 (paperback)

ISBN 978-1-7334616-3-4 (e-book)

This is a work of fiction. Names, characters, places, and incidents either are the products of the author's imagination or are used fictitiously. Any resemblance to actual persons, living or dead, businesses, companies, events, or locales is entirely coincidental.

Front cover image by Gwenn Danae

Typography by Mulan Jiang

Published in the United States of America

ALSO BY K.J. SUTTON

The *Fortuna Sworn* Saga

Fortuna Sworn

Restless Slumber

Deadly Dreams

Beautiful Nightmares

Standalones

Straight On 'Til Morning

Novellas

Summer in the Elevator

CONTENT WARNING

Please be aware this novel contains scenes or themes of PTSD, rape, profanity, sexual assault, decapitation, murder, gore, sex, hallucinations, hospitalization, and kidnapping.

I desire the things which will destroy me in the end.

—Sylvia Plath

PREFACE

There were a lot of theories about what happened when someone died.

I'd been high a few times in my life, and death was fairly similar to that sensation. A feeling of... dreaming. Uncertainty toward what was real, not physically, but of concepts themselves. Time, exhilaration, peace.

Despite the theories I'd heard, I didn't bemoan all the things I should've done or what I wished I had done differently. I did think of the people I loved, but their images were faint, surrounded by wisps of content. They were safe. They would be okay.

With a faint smile, I closed my eyes. At last, I could rest.

And then I died.

CHAPTER ONE

*S*now drifted from the sky as I watched them discover Shameek's grave.

A woman—probably his mother, judging from the streaks of gray in her hair—fell to her knees in front of it. Her shoulders shook with soundless sobs. Slowly, she leaned forward and pressed the top of her head against the gravestone. Carved into its surface, just a few inches above the woman, was an epitaph.

For what felt like the thousandth time, I read the handful of words. *His last act was in the name of courage.* Though I hadn't been there at the time, I could practically hear Collith saying it, almost as if he were speaking right in my ear. He was the one who'd ordered the stone made, back when he'd given the human an honorable burial, despite the Court's displeasure. It had been, perhaps, his first brave decree as a king.

I dearly hoped it hadn't been his last.

From where we watched, so far away that I couldn't hear what the human family was saying, I buried my fingers deep into the bark. I'd hoped the pain would overpower the guilt, but no such luck.

"It wasn't your fault, Queen Fortuna," my Right Hand

1

murmured. Plumes of air left her mouth with every word. She stood beside me. Apparently Lyari had no interest in watching the scene play out, because she faced the other direction, her spine pressed against a tree. She'd been tossing a knife into the air, again and again, and caught it by the tip of that shining blade.

Was my guilt so obvious? Or had my mental wall begun to crumble? A swift check showed that it was firmly in place, however.

"I appreciate that," was all I said. If Lyari knew the guilt I still felt, then she knew that I didn't believe her now. But so much else had changed since the day Shameek had died. My relationship with her, for instance. More and more lately, she treated me with begrudging respect and I actually trusted her. A faerie.

At that moment, a gentle breeze stirred my hair. A few strands blew across my mouth, and I pulled them away, still watching Shameek's mother. *She probably read it first*, I thought. *That goddamn letter.*

There was so much I couldn't control these days. But that letter—ink to paper, letters on a page, words to a dead man's mother—I could control. I lost count of how many drafts I'd written. In the end, it was brief and vague. It contained the coordinates for their son's grave and that he'd died trying to return to them. Ever-cautious and hyper-vigilant, Lyari had made sure that I handled everything with rubber gloves. Literally, because the last thing I needed was to be the suspect in a murder investigation.

Someone else approached the headstone now, bringing my mind back to the present. As a man I guessed to be Shameek's father began to speak, I turned away, feeling like an intruder on their grief. "Let's go home," I muttered, shoving my hands in my coat pockets. Lyari tucked her knife away and followed without comment. We walked in an easy silence. For a few minutes, the only sound was my boots crunching through the blanket of fresh snow covering the forest floor.

The stillness shattered when something moved amongst the trees. Seeing it, my heartbeat quickened. No one else knew we were here—it couldn't be another Guardian or someone in my family.

It seemed Lyari shared the thought, because she began to move in front of me. As she did this, she reached for her sword, which was a constant companion at her hip. It slid out of its scabbard with a delicate ringing. I had weapons of my own, hidden in my pockets, my socks, my sleeves. With a subtle, practiced movement, I produced my new gun, a Glock 43, loaded with holy bullets. I disliked using guns, but they were more effective than knives.

As one, Lyari and I stopped and waited, our stances deceptively relaxed.

Up ahead, the bulky figure came closer, moving through the shadows. A sound like rain drifted through the air. Before I could draw breath to speak, the newcomer stepped into a shaft of moonlight, and the Tongue's deep-set eyes met mine. The beads he always wore flashed and faded like stars.

"What are you doing here?" I asked, frowning. I didn't put the gun away.

I watched his gaze flick down and take note of this. For a moment, the only sound in the forest was a distant *crack*. Probably a branch breaking underneath the weight of the snow. The faerie tucked his hands into the sleeves of the cloak he wore and regarded me with an expression akin to disapproval. His bald head gleamed in the moonlight.

"They are calling for your blood, Fortuna Sworn," he said at last, his voice like an earthquake, deep and rumbling. It felt out of place in the serenity of our surroundings.

"Who are?" I asked, though I already knew. I'd discovered,

during my brief reign, that playing dumb had its advantages—the fae were constantly underestimating their new queen.

"Your people," the Tongue answered, humoring me. The air around us thickened, whether from his power or my own rising emotions, I couldn't be certain. "Those you swore to protect and defend. They suspect you've taken a life, and the tide is turning much faster than your Guardians can handle. One of the attempts on your life *will* eventually succeed."

"For the millionth time, I didn't kill Collith," I snapped. I knew the Tongue couldn't be speaking of Ayduin, since no one suspected my involvement in his death. Yet. Someone—I assumed Lyari—had seen to it the recordings in that passage were erased the night I'd entered the Tralee rooms. "Just as I told everyone else, the Unseelie King will return when his task is finished. I can't say anything beyond that. But you couldn't have come all this way to give me a simple warning. Get to the point, please."

The faerie's jowls swelled as he lowered his chin. "I will help you, Queen Fortuna, because I believe you speak the truth about our king. All I would like in return is an apology."

Whatever I'd been expecting, it hadn't been this. For a moment or two, I just stared at the faerie blankly. Beside me, Lyari made a sound that was suspiciously similar to muffled laughter. "An... apology?" I repeated.

The Tongue responded to this with a single, overly regal nod. "I have dedicated my existence to the crown, Fortuna Sworn, along with every Tongue that came before me. We learn the blood arts, giving our very life force over to the rituals and sacraments, to uphold your decrees and maintain balance. The least you could do in return is show me some respect."

As always, my first instinct was to counter his words with sarcasm or insults. But now a memory surfaced every time I was on the verge of giving in to it—Collith's wide, unblinking eyes. That stream of blood slipping from his nose. The moment

I felt our bond break and fade into nothing. The sound of my own unending screams.

That was what happened when I didn't control myself. That was the result of acting without thinking.

"You're right," I said. I felt both of the faeries' surprise through the bond we still shared. I took a breath before continuing. "I've recently discovered that some faeries are actually likable. I should've formed an opinion of you based on your behavior, not your species. For that, I *am* sorry."

For a moment, all three of us fogged the air with our breathing, sending a strange, swirling pattern to fill the space between us. Finally, the Tongue acknowledged my words with a slight bow. "I forgive you, Queen Fortuna."

His words made my lips purse into a thin line. Forgiveness was never that simple. Forgiveness was never so painless. He was either lying to me or lying to himself. When it came to faeries, it was impossible to tell.

I wasn't sure what to say next, but the Tongue was already retreating. The beads around his neck—I'd only recently learned they were carved from teeth—made that whispering sound. I caught myself wondering how many lives had been lost to make those grisly necklaces. How much blood had been spilled for him to learn his precious rituals and sacraments. However noble he seemed, the Tongue had taken lives and used others for his own gain.

"You're doing so well," Lyari said from the corner of her mouth, as though she'd heard the rumbling thought. "Don't ruin it now."

Being queen sucked.

The Tongue was out of view, anyway. Once it was obvious he was truly gone, Lyari and I turned to continue southward. It was getting colder with each passing moment, and suddenly I wanted nothing more than my warm bed and the sounds of my family around me. Lyari seemed to sense my mood, because she walked faster. How rare it was, I thought, to walk in silence with someone and not feel the need to fill it.

Once again, the serenity was disturbed when faint sounds suddenly filled the woods around us. A moment later, there were minor tremors, like the ground was shaking. Earthquakes were rare in Colorado, though, and my instincts told me this was something else. I slowed to a stop, frowning, and pushed my senses outward. Lyari's sword flashed in the moonlight as she drew it again. There was a line between her brows and a frown tugged at the corners of her lovely mouth.

"Do you feel that?" the faerie muttered, her blue eyes searching the darkness.

Fear crept through the dark and circled me like a wolf. I shook my head, still trying to detect a consciousness with my own abilities. "Feel what?"

"The wind. There's a strange scent…"

I raised my face and sniffed experimentally, but I detected nothing beyond the crisp night and vast sky. Faeries had far superior senses than Nightmares, so I took Lyari for her word. We stood there a minute longer, both of us tense and silent. Slowly, the other female started moving forward, and I followed suit. I half-expected one of Savannah's corpses to lumber out of the underbrush. After watching one kill Fred, then having to burn down my own home to kill the rest, I wasn't ashamed to admit that I was afraid of them. I would bet my entire savings account that Oliver had been keeping more bad dreams away, each one probably filled with the undead.

"What did you smell?" I asked Lyari once our shared sense of unease faded. Still, my voice was hushed, as though someone was listening.

At first, she didn't say anything. She turned her face toward me, and I saw that she was still frowning. A strand of long, brown hair draped across her throat, and at that moment, she had never looked more fae. "Death," Lyari said finally. "I thought I smelled death. But it's gone now."

I was too unnerved to respond. Months ago, I probably would have dismissed her words as paranoia or some faerie trick. But after everything I'd been through—goblins, wendigos, werewolves, sirens, zombies—I had learned the true meaning of fear.

And it wasn't some image I could put in people's heads.

By the time Lyari and I emerged into Cyrus's yard, every window in the house was dark. Someone had left the porch light on, though. It felt like a hand, beckoning me home. Relief expanded in my chest and I allowed a small sigh to escape me.

As we left the cover of the trees, my gaze went to the barn, a hulking shape that stood off to the side. Part of it was destroyed in a fire decades ago, according to Cyrus. Much of the structure was still standing, but the roof sagged, the windows were broken or dirty, and the siding had needed a paint job about twenty years ago. I couldn't understand how Cyrus Lavender— who took meticulous care of Bea's kitchen and his home—could watch it fall into such disrepair. When I tried to ask him, my friend had just turned his face away, that fiery hair of his glinting in the dying light. I'd realized how little I actually knew about the fry cook that had taken us in.

He also had yet to ask a single question about Finn, who came into the house as both wolf and man in regular intervals.

Now, as Lyari and I walked past the barn, I noticed a light through one of the broken windows. I halted instinctively and the faerie's voice drifted past me as she said, "Your Majesty?"

"Collith is in there," I murmured, staring past those glinting shards and into the shadows. Nothing moved, though.

"How do you know?" Lyari asked. There was no surprise in her tone—besides Laurie and my family, she was the only one who knew the truth about the Unseelie King. That he was, in fact, very much alive. Considering how much time she spent at the house, I saw no way to avoid telling her. Unlike the others, though, she asked no questions. Maybe that was the moment I'd started truly liking her.

Seconds went by, marked only by snowflakes and heartbeats. Doubt began to trickle in—maybe Collith was in the house, sleeping like all the rest of our small, broken family. I turned my gaze to that light, a single lightbulb that dangled in the air. As another stillness settled around us like a cloak, there was no sign of Collith, and I couldn't deny the longing that stirred in my chest. The hope that I might catch just a glimpse of him, the faerie that I had been falling for shortly before I killed him.

"It started a couple of weeks ago," I said at last, forcing myself to turn away. Lyari fell into step beside me, this time, instead of following closely behind as she usually did. "Collith took my van, went into town, and came back with all this stuff from the hardware store. Then he disappeared inside the barn for an entire day. All we heard was smashing and breaking. The day after that, all the noises were sawing and hammering. I thought it was good—Collith was *doing* something, instead of spending the day in his room or sitting in that damn rocking chair."

"But now?" Lyari asked, her long-legged strides matching my own.

I let out a breath. It clouded the air in front of my face. "But now I'm worried he traded one hiding place for another."

"Maybe he just needs more time," she suggested.

"Yeah. Maybe," I said. Uncertainty leaked in my voice, though I didn't mean it to. Lyari thankfully refrained from commenting on it, because I didn't want to talk about Collith anymore. A moment later, we reached the edge of the yard. The dead grass was buried beneath a layer of snow. Footprints led from the driveway to the front door, and I knew they were Cyrus's—Emma was retired and Damon hadn't been working at Bea's much, due to the unforeseen event a few weeks ago.

At the bottom of the porch steps, just as I was about to ask Lyari if she was spending the night, I paused. My mind registered the object that my gaze had grazed over in passing. I backtracked a few steps, frowning at the ground.

"What is it?" Lyari asked, keeping her voice low. She touched the pommel of her sword again, and I wondered if she was even aware of it.

I squatted and scraped some snow away with my bare fingers. Ice lodged beneath my nails. "A flower," I murmured, staring at it. The small bloom had a yellow center and dainty white petals. Nestled amongst frozen blades of dead grass, it looked like a lost child in a vast crowd.

I turned my head to see Lyari's expression. She just raised her eyebrows. "So?"

Smiling faintly, I stood up and shook the melted frost off my hand. Her reaction was a blunt reminder of the fact that Lyari was not human—she had never lived among humans, never known a world absent of magic or spells. She knew about seasons, of course, but strange things happened all the time at the Unseelie Court. Why shouldn't a flower thrive in winter?

"So, it's November," I told her patiently, though I was eager to get out of the cold. "There's no way this thing should be alive."

She lifted one shoulder in a shrug. "You know better than anyone that we live in a strange world, Queen Fortuna."

"Damn it, Lyari, I've told you a thousand times. It's just Fortuna, all right?"

The beginnings of a smile lit her eyes, but the faerie didn't allow it to reach her lips. "Your Majesty, I would prefer—"

The entire porch shuddered and a blurred shape came at me. I stumbled back, my heel sliding through gravel, and I hit the ground. Air *whooshed* from my lungs. Lyari started to move forward, her sword bright as a star, but she stopped when the thing on top of me released a long whine. A moment later, a pair of yellow eyes met mine. I blinked, still struggling to catch my breath. After another moment I rasped, "Finn? Are you okay?"

Those wide eyes blinked. Slowly, making a whining sound deep in his throat, the enormous wolf backed away. I knew the guilt would set upon him soon, if it wasn't already, so I forced myself to stand and act as though the fall hadn't hurt.

"You can go," I said to Lyari, barely managing to hide a wince as pain ricocheted up and down my spine. I must've landed even harder than I thought. I would be healed by morning, though— I'd discovered that my bond to the Unseelie Court lent me power. Enhanced my abilities. It was the only explanation for how I'd been changing.

From Lyari's expression, I knew she would protest before she opened her mouth. I mourned the loss of her newfound trust for the werewolf. "He's not stable, Your Majesty," Lyari said, confirming my fear. "If the werewolf slaughters you—"

"Oh, stop. I'm not in any danger from him and you know it."

Lyari and I argued as Finn began the transition back to his human form. We both pretended not to hear the sound of flesh tearing and bones cracking, but as the minutes ticked by, Lyari started to look faintly ill.

Seeing that, I was barely able to contain a smirk. She wasn't fearless, then. The rebellious, deadly Lyari of bloodline Paynore got squeamish at the sounds of a werewolf transformation. Weeks ago, I would have mocked her endlessly for it. Used the discovery as a weapon. It meant something that I didn't now.

The faerie saw my expression and stopped mid-sentence. The breeze drew her hair across her mouth, and she pulled it away impatiently. She said something in Enochian, then probably remembered I couldn't understand her, because she abruptly switched to English. "Why are you smiling?" she snarled.

I was still smiling. "It's just obvious that you really like me."

"I beg your pardon?" Lyari asked. Her expression was so comical that I nearly laughed, but something told me she'd like that even less than the smiling, so I suppressed it.

"You heard me," I told her, then turned away to go up the steps. "For the record, I like you, too. Anyway, I need to get some sleep, because I'm going to work in the morning. You'll just have to trust that Finn won't hurt me—not fatally, at least. You've slept on the couch every night this week. Go *home*."

At the top of the stairs, I faced her again. Lyari must've finally grasped the futility in arguing, because without another word, she whirled and stalked away. As she vanished into the darkness, moving silently, as only a faerie could, I joined Finn on the porch. He was fully dressed, now that Emma and I had taken to leaving him spare sets of clothes in random spots. It had been an interesting week when he'd returned to the house naked after every change. Several times, I'd caught Emma's stares lingering a bit too long on certain parts of his body as he walked by. Finn, having lived amongst a werewolf pack before his time at the Unseelie Court, didn't even seem to notice.

I allowed the silence between us to stretch now, wanting Finn to choose when the conversation began. For too long, he hadn't been given any choices at all. To entertain myself, I leaned on the railing and enjoyed the sight of stars. The sky had cleared somewhat in the time since Lyari and I stepped out of the woods, and the wide face of the moon peered down at us. *Go to bed*, I imagined her saying. It had been a long day after a shift at Bea's and another one at Court. Lately, it had felt like my life no longer belonged to me. Like I had traded one cage for another.

"What was all that about?" I asked after a few more minutes. It had become apparent that Finn didn't intend to address his outburst.

He wouldn't look at me. Instead, he glared at something beyond the yard, as though the trees themselves had betrayed him. The effect was somewhat negated by his long, thick eyelashes, which were the envy of any female that saw them. "You are my pack," he said after a pause that felt like a small eternity.

I frowned, trying to understand. "Yes. We all are, Finn. Everyone here cares about you. Me, Emma, Damon—"

"You are my pack," Finn repeated, more forcefully this time. His face turned toward me. Now his eyes bored into mine, and I knew he was trying to communicate. It probably meant the wolf was closer to the surface than I would ever admit to Lyari. Human words eluded him. All he knew was what he felt, which as a wolf, was even more magnified.

Realization struck me like a sizzle of electricity. *Oh, Fortuna, you idiot.* He was upset because I'd left without him again. Wolves ran in packs. Wolves didn't leave each other behind. It must've felt like he was being rejected and abandoned.

And, though he wouldn't say it, I knew Finn had been feeling guilty since the night I met the demon. He hadn't been there to protect me. To stop me. He might not know the full details of what happened at that crossroads, but like everyone else, he saw the effects of it. The change I'd gone through. Had I laughed even once, over the past month?

"Finn." I took a breath. "I wish I could promise you that I'll never go off on my own again. I'm your pack, but I'm not a wolf —I'm Fortuna. Sometimes, I need to go places alone. It's who I am. I'm also a survivor, just like you, and I will always fight to come home. But it isn't... it isn't your fault if the day comes when I don't. It doesn't mean you should stop living."

Silence wrapped around us as Finn searched my face. I worried my words weren't enough, but they were all I had to give. After another moment, he faced the horizon again. I put my hand on the werewolf's shoulder, thinking how strange it was that I could bear to touch him but not anyone else. Maybe because there was only innocence in my relationship with Finn, and I already knew his fears well.

Almost immediately, his eyes fluttered shut. Etched in the lines of his face, I saw his need. His want. His humanity. There was nothing sexual about it—like most living creatures, he simply needed connection.

After another minute, sleep called to me, and I couldn't ignore it anymore. I gave Finn's shoulder a parting squeeze as I drifted toward the door. The floorboards creaked when I stepped inside.

Just before I closed the door behind me, Finn's hoarse voice reached my ears as he said, "Good night, Queen Fortuna."

Despite everything else that had changed, there was one thing that hadn't.

As usual, I arrived at the dreamscape with my eyes closed. I felt the wind on my face first, along with the scents it carried. Paint, flowers, and the sea. When I was younger, I used to wish that I could put all those scents into a bottle, so I could pop the lid and visit the dreamscape whenever I wished. Now, though, as my nostrils flared and wind blew past my ears, they brought pain. It was a reminder of what I'd done to the kind creature living in my head.

At least he was painting again, though.

With the sense of passing time bearing down on me, I reluctantly opened my eyes. No matter how broken his heart may have been, Oliver's world was still lovely and whole. The twisted oak tree stood nearby, its great arms outstretched, as though to embrace me. The sky was a pale blue, interrupted only by wisps of clouds and colorful birds. In the distance, there was the stone house that had cradled me and Oliver during our childhood. It had eventually become a place where we explored each other, our changing feelings, our sexuality.

But now it felt like a haunted house, filled with the ghosts of what had been and what would never be.

I quickly averted my gaze from it and continued my search for Oliver. There he was, a tiny figure against the horizon. Sitting on the edge of the cliff, as he had been for the past month every time I came, the white button-up he wore looking bright in the afternoon light. I started walking through the tall, golden grass—the summery dress I wore fluttered around me—and sat beside him. I was careful to make sure our legs didn't touch, a fact that Oliver probably didn't miss, knowing me as well as he did. But we were both in perfect denial about what had recently happened between us. Our friendship, for all intents and purposes, had gone back to normal. Well, apart from the fact that we no longer enjoyed a physical relationship. With the exception of Finn, the thought of any male touching me—even Oliver—opened a black pit inside my body.

Once I was settled, he turned his head and gave me a gentle smile. Sun-bleached hair fell into his eyes. "Hey, you."

Guilt filled my throat and made it difficult to speak. "Hey, Ollie."

Tonight, it seemed those four words were all we could manage. The words Oliver had spoken to me on that starry rooftop filled the space between us. *I love you the way a man loves a woman, Fortuna. I want you to be mine, the same way I'm yours.* Though I'd never given him an answer, we both knew my heart longed for someone else. Someone who had barely looked at me since I'd dragged his soul out of the darkness.

It was my need for Oliver's friendship that had made the dreamscape solidify again. His paintings had stopped disappearing and there was no danger of my forgetting him anymore. Not when he held the nightmares at bay and loved me with such a fierceness that, sometimes, it felt like the only thing keeping me from completely shattering.

I must've made some kind of sound because Oliver reached for my hand. I knew he just meant to comfort, but I still couldn't stop myself from jerking away. For a terrible moment, a memory blinded me as it overlapped reality. A night sky high above. Grim, dark trees all around. A man's figure outlined in moonlight.

When I pushed the memory away, I saw that Oliver's brows had drawn together and his eyes were dark with pain. It looked as though I'd stabbed him. "You're scared of me," he said.

I shook my head instantly, gripping the rocky edge with white fingers. "No. I'm not. Oliver, I swear to you, I'm not."

"Then why won't you let me touch you?" he challenged. "You even flinch when it happens by accident. I saw it when you handed me a paintbrush last week."

"I can't talk about this," I said, shaking my head again. I sounded as though I were being strangled.

Before Oliver could say anything else, I pushed myself up and stumbled away. But the memory followed me like a bad feeling. It found its way through the shabby mental wall I'd erected, and within seconds, it filled my skull again. I felt the demon's breath on my cheek. I heard its sounds of pleasure. I saw the dark leaves near his head stir in a breeze.

Oliver's voice sounded in my ear, and it was then I realized that I'd fallen. I didn't get back up. I stayed there, on my knees, with a fist smashed against my mouth to contain the sobs. I stared down at the grass without really seeing it. Oliver didn't touch me, but I felt his presence. I felt others, too—faeries from the Unseelie Court, who'd sensed my pain. The wall standing between us had cracks and gaps, allowing them to peek through. Watching me, the fae whispered and cackled and hissed.

"No," I gasped. I had to keep them out. They couldn't know

where Collith was or what sort of condition he was in—he was too vulnerable to fend off a challenger.

Panic breathed down my neck. Gritting my teeth, I buried my fingers into the earth and focused on the wall. I shoved stones into the holes and plaster into the cracks, again and again, until I was separate from them once more. When the quiet returned, my breathing gradually slowed.

After another minute, I finally raised my tear-stained face.

The cheery daylight had retreated, giving way to the soft glow of dusk. Not because any substantial time had passed, but because the occupant of this world had willed it so. Oliver sat nearby, his arms looped around his knees. His hair looked white in the moonlight. Every part of him was rigid, as though it had taken all his strength not to reach for me.

When our gazes met, his was filled with undeniable anguish. His face had lines where there hadn't been any before, and that sprinkling of freckles I loved so much stood out starkly against his pale skin. "Please let me help you," my best friend said. The wind picked up, undoubtedly from the force of his emotions, and his shirt flapped against his hard torso. "Please."

It felt as though someone had scraped out my insides and left only a shell of pain. My voice was a shadow of what it had once been as I replied, "You can't. No one can."

Oliver opened his mouth, probably to argue, but I didn't want to hear it. Moving with preternatural speed, I pushed myself up and bolted toward the sea. Oliver made no effort to stop me. As I ran, I concentrated only on the sounds of my feet pounding against the ground and my heart beating harder. I stared directly into the sinking sun and thought, *Wake up, wake up.*

I threw myself off the edge without hesitation, arms outspread, head flung back. There was a moment of incandescent, blinding light. I was weightless. I was fearless. I was free.

And then I woke up.

CHAPTER TWO

*a*s I shot upright, a book tumbled to the floor.
It took another moment, maybe two, for my mind to adjust. This was reality. Oliver was the dream. Frowning in drowsy confusion, I looked down at the book resting on the rug. A slant of moonlight fell across the cover. *Moby Dick*. I scowled now, wishing I could shove the novel into a drawer and forget about it completely, but a promise was a promise—I was still trying to keep mine after Oliver had won our bet from the game at his make-believe fair.

A clock next to my bed announced that it was 2:43 a.m. The numbers glowed bright green. I stared at it, straining to hear voices or sounds, but it seemed I was the only one awake. A rare occurrence when I lived in a house full of sad people, each plagued by their own losses and wounds.

Jesus, it's cold. I huddled there on the mattress, wondering if the furnace had gone out. My breath made white clouds whirl through the air. To my left, moonlight still cascaded over the uneven wooden floor, making the rocking chair in the corner look strange and otherworldly.

Since going back to sleep wasn't an option—for now, at least
—I sighed and tossed the covers aside.

Clad in boxer shorts and an oversized T-shirt, I walked past
the bleak, white walls of the room I occupied in Cyrus's house. I
didn't want to depend on my friend's generosity any longer
than necessary, so I hadn't bothered to add any pieces of myself
in here. Everything was bare. A stranger wouldn't know a thing
about me, except that I was a slob. My new clothes littered the
floor, the dresser was covered in books, and the bedsheets were
always rumpled and haphazard.

Though my feet were frozen, I didn't pause to find the slippers I'd recently bought—I was thinking of the others now.
Recent experience had taught me there were monsters in this
world, and not even walls could stop them from reaching those
I loved. Worry pierced my heart and sent it into a frantic
rhythm.

Floorboards creaked beneath me as I moved to check on
everyone. Neither Cyrus nor Emma stirred when I poked my
head inside their rooms. Miraculously, neither did Finn, but I'd
learned that he slept harder on the days he changed form. It was
only within the last week that he finally stopped sleeping in
front of my door at night, and that was because I'd told him I
was tired of tripping over his big, furry body. I studied the
werewolf more closely now, noting the faint pink scars that
marred his handsome face. I also noticed that a month of food
and kindness had caused him to fill out. His shoulders were
broader, his arms thicker, and his ribs were no longer poking
from his skin.

Feeling slightly calmer at the sight of him—a reminder of
how peaceful things had been this past month, give or take an
assassination attempt—I moved on.

At the end of the hall, I poked my head into the room where
Matthew and Damon slept.

My brother snored lightly, deep in the throes of sleep. A few feet away from his bed was the most recent addition to our patchwork family. My two-year-old nephew, who nestled against the bars of the crib we'd just bought yesterday. His pink lips sucked on a pacifier and a stuffed ladybug was tucked under one arm. Sound asleep, despite the strangeness of his circumstances.

Two weeks ago, Savannah left him on our front step with a note taped to his small shirt. *Take care of him for me,* her harried handwriting read. *Tell him I'll be back someday. When it's safe again.*

She'd driven away the moment someone opened the door. We hadn't seen or heard from her since.

It would be up to Damon whether he told his son the truth of what Savannah's note meant. For now, though, he was still acclimating to his new reality as a father. Fortunately, Emma had been eager to help. I wasn't sure how we would've coped without her.

Reassured that my family was safe—although there was still one more room to visit—I turned and slammed into a table resting against the wall. Air hissed through my teeth and I bent to grab my smarting knee. *Every time,* I thought sourly as I hobbled to the living room and sat on the couch. But in a secret, terrible way, I enjoyed the pain. It proved that, no matter how it sometimes felt, I was alive at the very least.

The wind was strong tonight. It pushed against the house and howled with rage, wanting a clear path through the woods and toward new places. I wondered if a blizzard was coming. After a few minutes, I heard something clicking down the hallway. It was the basset hound, Stanley—he must've heard me hit the table. His hackles were raised as he sat near me.

"What's happening, old boy?" I asked softly, scratching the back of his ear. Even inside, something about the pressure in the air didn't feel natural, and my mind chose that moment to remember Lyari's comment in the woods. *Death. I thought I smelled death.*

I was shivering again, but this time, it had nothing to do with the cold. The barn was visible on the other side of the room, through a wide window. My gaze flicked up to the weathervane. It spun violently, a tiny silhouette against the moon.

Then a cry tore through the night.

A flavor burst on my tongue that was now familiar, something cold and metallic. Leaving Stanley, I rushed down the hall and into the one room I hadn't yet checked. Light slanted over the green carpet. It stretched toward Collith's face and made it easier to see the lines that weren't there before. His chest glittered with sweat. He muttered in the relentless grip of his dreams, something about fire and choking air. Roars and red rivers. He tossed and turned like someone in a wild, raging sea.

I ran over to the bed, knelt beside it, and shook the faerie king's shoulder. "Wake up. Hey, Collith, open your eyes. You're having another nightmare."

He shouted as he jerked awake. I was prepared and shifted back just in time. Collith's pupils expanded and shrank as they focused on me. He realized my hand was on his shoulder, then, and drew away from my touch. Tears streamed down his unshaven cheeks. When it was clear that he was truly awake, I perched on the edge of the bed. I listened for the sound of doors opening or footsteps, but it seemed everyone else in this house slept like the dead. The thought caused a flutter of apprehension in my stomach.

Unaware of my own fear, Collith sat up more. The muscles in his stomach bunched. He stared at the far wall, his eyes glassy and tormented. For the past month his brown hair had been growing unchecked, and it hung nearly to his shoulders now. He looked nothing like the lovely, remote king I'd first met.

King. It reminded me that the Tithe was tomorrow. While Collith had been recovering here in the human world, I'd been to Court nearly every day—it turned out that being queen was a full-time job. In the past month I'd hosted the heads of bloodlines at dinners, attended council meetings, made appearances at events and gatherings, and resolved disputes in the form of tribunals. I'd also been dealing with the fallout of absolving the fae's slave trade. There had been three attempts made on my life, all of them thwarted by none other than Nuvian.

When I wasn't doing any of that, or surviving against another faerie who wanted me dead, there was always paperwork waiting. The Never-Ending Pile of Paperwork, I'd begun to call it in my head.

As I focused on Collith now, I realized there were some benefits to the broken bond between him and the Unseelie Court—he was free of the burden that came with wearing a crown. Hopefully, it quickened his healing process. Once he was better, Collith could resume his kingly duties and everything else would go back to normal, too.

But had our lives ever been normal? What did that even mean for people like us?

Thinking of the price I had paid to bring Collith back, of what I'd done to reverse my mistake, my mind shied away from the shame and pain. As always, the demon found me anyway, his leering face popping out of the darkness. *Shall I tell you what my brothers and sisters are doing to your beloved right now?*

"Will you tell me what I dreamed?" Collith asked hoarsely, not looking at me. I refocused on him, grateful for the distraction. He was so close that I felt his breath on my cheek, a spot of coolness that normally would've bothered me in this inescapable cold. I stared at his profile, admiring the curve of his jaw and the way a thick lock of hair fell over his pointed ear. At this angle, I couldn't see his scar, but I didn't like that. The scar was beautiful. The scar was part of his face.

In the next moment, it occurred to me that Collith was still waiting for an answer. Heat touched my cheeks and warded off the chill.

Will you tell me what I dreamed? The pain in his voice should have crept down that invisible connection between us, joining with mine. Even now, weeks after its dissolution, it was strange talking to him without the mating bond. I remembered how, before his death, we'd been able to communicate with just our expressions. Now it felt like there was a brick wall where the magic used to be, and all I could see of Collith were glimpses caught through the cracks.

"I didn't see it," I lied.

I told myself the truth would only cause more damage. The images of Collith's nightmares—they were rank with fear, making it possible for me to see when I wasn't guarded against them—were violent and brief. Flames and teeth. Shadows and blood. Collith wouldn't survive it. He was like those windows in the barn, so fragmented and fragile. One powerful gust of wind, one terrible blow, and even those last, clinging pieces would fall.

Hell was real, and Collith had been there.

The thought made whatever other words I'd been about to say die in my throat. Guilt burrowed in my skin like a thousand wood ticks.

Now that Collith was awake, I moved to sit in a chair near the bed, bringing my legs up so they were against me. I rubbed at my arms and avoided his gaze. The grandfather clock ticked from the dining room. *Tick. Tick. Tick.*

"A storm is coming," Collith whispered suddenly. I looked at him, but his hazel eyes were fixed on the small, round window. The only one his room had. It was too high for him to reach, if he walked in his sleep. He hadn't yet, but Emma still worried.

I frowned and followed his gaze to that black sky. "There wasn't a blizzard in the forecast, but Cyrus is more than prepared for it. He's prepared for everything—a couple of weeks ago, he showed me the bomb shelter he made himself.

There were even shelves of food. So don't worry about a storm, okay? We're completely fine."

Another silence sucked the oxygen from the room. I hated it even more than I hated seeing Collith in pain. I couldn't help but think of what we would've been doing, if I hadn't ruined everything. The people we'd been before would be bantering right now. Playing Connect Four. Making out on the bed. No, doing *more* than making out. Now I felt tainted, ruined, and it would spread to Collith if he so much as touched me.

"Fortuna," he said, startling me.

When our gazes met, Collith didn't say anything else. I still knew what came next, because it had happened this way, every night, for the past month. It was something in his voice, a sort of lilt in the way he said my name. I met his gaze already knowing what I'd find.

Within those haunted depths, a light of pleading shone. "Please tell me," Collith said.

This time, he wasn't talking about his dreams.

It didn't matter that he had asked this question before. For some reason, it never did. I was helpless as my mind went back for what felt like the millionth time. Remembering, no, reliving one of the worst nights of my life.

Still lying on the kitchen table, Collith's eyes shot open.

When I saw this, when I realized he was awake, my heart hammered. Part of me wondered if it was a dream or delirium. I stayed in that rickety chair and stared at him, forgetting how to breathe. Sweat broke out on my palms. Every coherent thought within me went silent.

"Collith?" I whispered finally. The sound of my voice drew his gaze, but he said nothing. Slowly, I stood up. I could sense everyone in the kitchen staring at us in silent shock. I realized how badly I had fucked up. What if the demon brought Collith back in body, but not in mind? What if the demon had put someone else—something else—

inside him? I swallowed once, then twice, struggling to speak past the dryness in my throat. "Are you... all right?"

The faerie king kept looking at me, his expression frozen in confusion, as though he didn't recognize my face.

Then he started to scream.

I recoiled so violently that I fell over the chair and crashed to the floor. Distantly, I heard Emma gasp and Damon say my name. There was no time to respond or explain—Collith rolled off the table, stumbling as he tried to stand, but his legs were like those of a newborn fawn. He fell down beside me and began to crawl. I had the inexplicable, panicked thought that if he reached the door, we would never see him again.

"Hold him down!" I shouted, lunging to seize his ankle. Despite their obvious confusion, the others moved instantly. Collith bellowed, fighting the hands clamping onto him, and I lost my grip. Terror must've lent him some degree of strength—Finn went flying and hit the wall of cupboards—and I realized Collith would overpower them if I didn't do something. The thought of using my abilities on him, though, made me want to vomit. There was only one other person who was strong enough to subdue him. My insides quaked as I took a breath and forced myself to say his name. "Laurelis. Laurelis, we need you."

The Seelie King materialized within moments. He had changed clothes in the brief time we'd been apart, the gold-lined tunic replaced by jeans and a cashmere sweater. His starlight hair was messier than usual, as though he'd run his fingers through it a hundred times in the past hour. I watched his bright eyes land on me first, then move over the rest of the room. Finn, Cyrus, and Damon were still struggling with the faerie I'd brought back to life, while Emma cowered in the corner.

I knew the exact second Laurie registered Collith, somehow, though his expression didn't change. It was something in the king's eyes—a tender sort of disbelief, as though he were half-afraid this was a dream. I knew the feeling. Time seemed to slow, and I felt the unex-

pected prick of jealousy as I saw the depths of Laurie's love. Love that no amount of years, quarrels, or new queens could touch.

Then Collith lunged for the door, and the stillness shattered like thin glass.

He got his fingers around the knob before Laurie moved, who must've seen the lightning bolt of panic that struck me. In the space of a blink, he was across the room, hauling Collith back with no visible effort. His eyes narrowed in concentration while the others burst into action again. Seconds later, Collith's frantic efforts faltered—thank God he didn't seem to remember he had the gift of heavenly fire or the ability to sift—and he stared at the walls with dark, bewildered eyes. His chest rose and fell from the force of his panic. It was my guess that Laurie had made the doors and windows vanish.

After another minute of wrestling, the four males finally succeeded in restraining the Unseelie King. The fight drained from him like water going down a drain. Damon produced some rope from his bedroom, which none of us asked why he had, and soon Collith was tied to a chair. Even as my brother secured the knots, Collith offered no protests. Instead, he hung his head and continued to breathe hard.

Slowly, I got back to my feet. Everything had happened so quickly that I'd remained on the floor throughout the chaos. As I approached, I held my hands out as if Collith were some kind of wild animal. He'd stopped screaming, at least, but there was still no recognition when he raised his gaze. I spoke in calm, measured tones. "You're among friends, Collith. We're not going to hurt you. I'm Fortuna. Your Fortuna. Don't you remember?"

Though I wasn't entirely sure what I was saying, I kept talking. Seconds turned into minutes, and minutes turned into hours. Sunlight shining through the windows, which had begun as a trickle, became a river. Emma and Cyrus slipped from the room without my noticing, but Laurie, Finn, and Damon stayed. There was a distant rumble— probably the mailman—and the steady hum of heat coming through the vents. These were the only sounds in the world, save the uneven cadence of my own voice.

At long last, though, I fell silent. I had run out of words, even the meaningless ones. Nothing I said would reverse the clock or undo the damage. For another stretch of time, the five of us sat in that room without moving or speaking. Questions would come, I knew, but for now, we waited. We hoped. We grieved.

The silence finally ended when Collith started rocking. I reached for him just as he released another new sound—a low keening. I understood, then, and my hand fell to my side, heavy with shame. Inside Collith was a pain so profound that it couldn't be put into words or sobs. Whatever he'd experienced in those hours of death had utterly destroyed the powerful king I once knew.

I'd done this to him. I'd broken him. Tears swelled in my eyes, making everything hazy. It felt like someone had shoved a dull knife into my gut.

"It's going to be okay," I heard myself whisper. Following a faint instinct, I knelt in front of Collith and touched his knee. He went still and looked at my hand with an expression I couldn't decipher. I swallowed the emotion swelling in my throat and added, "I promise."

At the same moment, I caught Damon watching me. There was a tightness to his mouth that revealed how he felt about my words. "You know what Dad told us, Fortuna," he muttered.

Thankfully, Collith didn't seem to hear him. He started rocking again—back and forth, back and forth. I ignored Damon and focused wholly on the faerie I'd sacrificed so much to bring back. Maybe he felt it, because his hazel eyes met mine again. There you are, *I thought with a burst of hope.* My Collith was still in there somewhere. All was not lost. *"Nightmares may be lies, but we don't have to be liars," I murmured, forgetting that we had an audience. "It means that when we make a promise, we keep it."*

Something I said must've reached him. Collith raised his head now, and everyone seemed to hold their breath. Were his memories coming back? Did he recognize us?

Just as I opened my mouth to speak again, Collith's eyes rolled back into his head. The chair tipped from his weight.

He hit the tile with a violent thud.

I pulled my mind back to the present. That had been weeks ago now, and some days I wondered if Collith was still that broken-eyed person who'd been tied to a kitchen chair.

"Would you believe that I doubted it? Before all this?" Collith said, drawing me out of my thoughts. Once again, he avoided looking directly at me. His skin was pearly in the moonlight, all the way down to his waist, where the bedspread pooled around his lean hips. I didn't let myself feel the thrill I used to get whenever I saw him unclothed—it never lasted longer than a moment, and then I saw the demon rising over me, forcing himself inside again and again.

Collith asked you something, I remembered bleakly. "Doubted what?" I asked. My voice was dull.

"I didn't really believe something more existed." Collith uttered a mirthless laugh. There was a hardness to him that hadn't existed before. I'd only caught glimpses of it, but it was there. "I have the proof on my very back, yet I had such trouble believing in what I couldn't see. It's all real, Fortuna. Souls. Heaven. Hell. God. The Devil."

This he said in a whisper.

I didn't know what to say. As I looked away, ashamed of my discomfort, my gaze passed over the alarm clock. I had to get up early for the breakfast shift at Bea's, which meant I needed to get some more sleep. Maybe this time, I'd be too exhausted to reach the dreamscape. I stood up, but I wavered between leaving Collith alone or staying close, offering him what warmth I had.

Compassion and guilt won. I sat on the bed again. Collith was still sitting on the edge, head bowed, his elbows resting atop his knees. I pressed close and wrapped my arms gently around him.

"Don't," he whispered. If he truly hadn't wanted me there, though, he would've shifted or pushed me away. But he stayed in the circle of my arms, his body shaking with silent sobs. I just rested my head against Collith's and breathed in his scent. It was different from before, less fae, somehow. The alluring combination of frost and the earth had been replaced by laundry detergent and pain. As we sat there, a tear dripped off the end of Collith's chin, and I reached up to wipe it away with the tip of my finger.

Just then, another cry echoed down the hallway. One that had nothing to do with the faerie in my arms.

Right on cue, I thought with an audible sigh. Cyrus had been having nightmares, too. Seeing my house burn down had triggered something inside him, or maybe opened a door he had managed to keep shut for as long as I'd known him. Lately, I'd noticed smudges beneath his eyes during our shifts at the bar.

"Are you okay now?" I asked Collith, reluctant to leave him. He just nodded, lowered himself back to the mattress, pulled the bedspread over his shoulders, and turned his back to me. Slowly, I stood and went to the door.

Cyrus gave another shout—he'd wake up the rest of the house, if he hadn't already—so I forced myself to cross the threshold. But I left the door to Collith's room open a crack, just in case he needed me again.

Outside, the wind howled on.

I didn't try to fall back asleep.

As soon as daylight shone through the blinds, I hurried out of bed and got dressed. Within seconds I wore yoga pants and a long-sleeved shirt, my hair back in a long ponytail. Once again, I made my way through the house, cringing with every creak of the wooden floor. Fortunately, no one else seemed to be awake yet.

No one except Finn, whose bright eyes appeared at my

elbow the moment I reached the door. He must've begun the transformation into a wolf while I'd been comforting Collith.

Safely outside—I swallowed a curse when the screen door slammed against the outside wall—I shook my arms and legs, then moved into stretches. Every breath made a frigid cloud. I resisted the urge to go back for a jacket, because I knew I'd be warm soon enough.

When it came time to decide on my route, I looked toward the road, assessing its quiet emptiness, eyeing the smooth pavement. *Too easy.* Some dark, dominant part of me liked the punishment of steep terrain and uneven ground. Maybe even craved it.

Finn disturbed the stillness with a long, eager whine. Taking pity on him, I made my choice. Gravel crunched under my feet as I jogged toward the trees, trying to leave my thoughts behind. Pink and orange spilled across the horizon like someone had poured paint down from Heaven. Not even the beautiful sky improved the sight of the barn squatting on the hill, though. I couldn't stop myself from glancing inside the windows as I passed, wondering if Collith was already inside for the day, but it was utterly still. I muttered a rare, desperate prayer to God, if he was listening, that the Unseelie King was finally getting some sleep.

For the next hour, I ran with a frozen riverbank on one side and trees on the other. Finn kept up effortlessly, visible through the bare branches. An ache started in my side, but I didn't slow or stop. My head filled with the sound of my ragged breathing. The sun-dappled ground occupied the space any thought or memory might've taken. It was exactly what I'd been hoping for, and I ran even faster, as though the Devil himself were chasing me.

But then a shape caught my eye, a tree that stood at the edge of the river and blocked my path. The instant I registered it, I barely managed not to recoil. My tennis shoes slid through a thawed patch of mud, and I flailed as I fought for balance. The incident might've made me laugh in another lifetime. In this one, though, I was only capable of a horrified stare once I'd recovered.

It isn't the same tree, I reminded myself. *That* tree was in the opposite direction, miles away. Watching over a crossroads. But... they looked eerily similar. The same numerous arms, reaching for the sky like some kind of octopus or squid, grappling from the depths. The same looming height. The same evil intent.

Despite knowing this wasn't the place where I'd made my odious deal, I couldn't bring myself to keep going. To pass the tree that seemed to watch me from a face without eyes, silently waiting for its chance to claim me again. Finn must've chased after a rabbit or a deer, because there was no sign of him, and I thought about shouting his name. Searching for him. Following his footprints. Anything to get me away from this place.

Why couldn't I move?

Without warning, the demon's voice sounded in my head. *How charming. You thought I would want your soul. That's not how it works, sweetheart. No, I take something that you value.*

"No," I whispered. For a moment, I tried to cling to logic. I reminded myself that it was daylight, where no demon could walk, and that it had already gotten what it wanted from me. When that didn't work, I finally turned around and ran.

This time, there were no distractions from the monsters in my head. They launched out of the darkness, their yellowed teeth flashing, their mouths frothing. I pushed myself, running even harder, reaching for strength that hadn't been there a moment ago. My body screamed with adrenaline and pain.

Then something leaped from the trees.

I was so startled that, in my effort to stop, I nearly fell. As I struggled to recover, I caught a glimpse of the things filling the air with their snarls and howls. Their fur was dark as Hell, their eyes glowed red, and it was all-too clear every single one of them was on *me*. They thundered down the path and I ran in the opposite direction, heading back toward that nightmarish tree. But my shoes were covered in mud now, unable to find purchase, and I slipped down the riverbank again. Time seemed to slow, and I comprehended that these creatures were the very ones I'd just been picturing.

There was no time to wonder at it—I raised my muddy hands in a pathetic attempt to protect my face as they rapidly closed the distance between us.

In the next moment, Finn was there, slamming into the closest beast. I heard one of them yip, and panic tore through me. Was Finn hurt? The others were still running toward me, though, and I had no weapon.

No weapon? I could hear my father asking suddenly, his voice rife with disappointment. *I've taught you better than that.*

But I haven't made physical contact with them, I tried to argue. *I can't use their fears if I don't know what they are.*

There was no more time, though. I finally scrambled back to my feet. The creatures were upon me, seconds from tearing into my flesh with those gleaming teeth. Reacting on desperate instinct, I threw my hands up, palm out, just as I had done with Savannah. I didn't question it or doubt myself.

My invasion into their minds was so violent and unexpected that the beasts made sounds of pain and went tumbling. Flavors coated my tongue as I felt their strange psyches. These were no wolves, I realized dimly. They were something unnatural, intelligent, and malicious, and I felt no guilt using my abilities on them.

Whatever they were, they had fears. Fears I could use.

The largest beast, the one still glaring at me even as it writhed on the ground, suddenly found itself lost in an unending mist. The one beside it was being attacked on all sides by angels. The third, which had fallen down the riverbank and now lay halfway in water, whined deep in its throat as it watched a figure walking toward it. A figure with golden hair and broad shoulders.

Their terror coiled in my stomach, low and hot, like I'd just taken a shot of tequila. I wanted more. I wanted to get drunk on it. Before I could, a snarl drew my attention away from them. I saw that Finn was still engaged in battle—he looked like he was holding his own, but I was desperate to reach him. Save him. Protect him.

Maybe that was why I proceeded to destroy the red-eyed beasts, one by one, without hesitation or remorse.

As their death-knell cries died away, the baleful lights in their eyes faded, and their twitching paws went still, I turned away. Now an unnerving silence settled upon the forest. I blearily picked my way through the mud and up the embankment. Finn stood at the top, his wide chest heaving. The beast he'd been fighting lay at his enormous feet, its gaze glassy and unblinking.

Once I was certain it was truly dead, I turned my attention to Finn, searching his fur for any sign of blood or broken bones. He would heal, yes, but if it healed incorrectly, it would mean a lot more work and pain for both of us. Besides a cut along his leg, which was already knitting together, Finn seemed wholly uninjured.

I couldn't stop looking at him, though. Something about my werewolf's stance, or the fierceness in his eyes, emanated pride. In that moment, we understood each other perfectly. He was not broken. He had fought back. He had *won*. It was the sort of feeling you only experienced after going to Hell and back. As the silence lingered, I gave Finn a soft smile and said, "Let's go home."

Such a complicated word. *Home*. I didn't think of Cyrus's as ours, and neither did Finn, in all likelihood. That wasn't what made him hold himself a little higher, a little straighter—we'd both learned that home wasn't four walls or the address where all your mail came, but the people you returned to.

Finn and I started to walk away, but it occurred to me that we couldn't leave Fallen where anyone could stumble upon them. Glamour faded after death, if these creatures had even been capable of casting it. Fortunately, being queen came with a few perks. I pulled my phone out and sent a brief text to both Lyari and Nuvian, explaining the problem, along with our coordinates. The service may be spotty at the Unseelie Court, but they'd get it eventually.

Once that was taken care of, I studied the creatures I'd killed, wondering if I should be more upset by my part in their deaths. I could still taste them, though, and whatever humanity those things once possessed had been buried past the bedrock of their souls. All I felt was an exhausted sense of resignation. I'd made a promise, once, and I had meant it. *If you fuck with me and mine, I will return the favor tenfold.*

As we began the journey back—for once, I was grateful that Finn couldn't speak—my mind became a tangle of thoughts. Where had those creatures come from? One moment, they'd been a figment of my pain and terror, and the next they'd been bursting from the trees. Did I… make them appear? Had it been some kind of premonition? And how had I used their fear without needing to touch them first?

Up ahead, Finn's bushy tail swung back and forth. *At least one of us is feeling invigorated from our morning excursion*, I thought with a soundless sigh. Within a minute, the trees fell away, and Cyrus's barn rose up. Finn vanished, probably to begin the transition back to his human form, and I crossed the yard alone.

Once again, when I passed the barn, I couldn't resist looking through the window. At the sight of Collith, who was bent over a benchtop band saw—when had he gotten *that*?—I stopped. For a moment or two, I shamelessly watched. Despite the wintry chill clinging to the dawn, he worked without a shirt on, and the sharp lines of his body looked like a sculpture of marble or stone. His hair, which had needed a trim weeks ago, hung into his eyes and curled against his neck.

Right on cue, Ian O'Connell's face flashed in my mind, and I winced.

As though there were still a mating bond between us, Collith lifted his head and looked directly at me.

Shit. Though it was far too late to pretend I hadn't been staring, I ducked my head and hurried away. Shame coiled in my stomach and hissed like a venomous snake. I had no right to long for him. No right to admire a male I had destroyed in both body and soul. What possibilities or potential that once existed between us had died when I'd killed Collith.

Feeling as though I were on the verge of breaking, I rushed up the porch steps and reached for the doorknob. I heard voices inside, though, and realized my family couldn't see me like this. My hand dropped to my side, and after a moment, I moved away. I lowered myself to the top step.

To keep the memories and thoughts away, I tried to focus on the details around me—the wind in my ears, a single bird calling to the sun, the weathervane creaking. But images kept slipping past my defenses. The red glow of those dog-like creatures' eyes. The gleam of slobber falling from their jaws. The yellowed claws adorning their massive paws.

"What's happening to me?" I moaned, rubbing my face as though I'd been crying. It felt like I should've been, like I wanted to, but I couldn't grant myself even this small reprieve. Another gust of wind went by and found its way through my sweat-drenched clothes. I shivered and flattened my hands against the porch, thinking to stand.

At the same moment, one of the barn doors opened. My head emptied as if someone had pulled a drain stopper out. Everything inside me stood on tiptoe as Collith emerged into the daylight.

He looked nothing like the faerie I'd met at the black market, all those weeks ago. Gone was the self-assured tilt to his head and the gleam in his hazel eyes. In their place was a creature who always looked... tired. There were lines under his eyes, which I hadn't known was possible for an immortal, and he moved cautiously now. As though, at any moment, a trapdoor would open beneath him and he'd fall back into the darkness.

Perhaps Collith sensed my despair, because he didn't walk past as I expected him to. Instead, he lowered himself to the edge of the step and faced the sunrise, as well. His hand was very close to mine, and suddenly every part of me yearned to entwine my fingers in the spaces between his. But I thought of the demon, and I thought of the hatred Collith doubtless harbored toward me, and I resisted.

As surely as rain fell to the ground, though, my eyes went to him again and again. He had recently showered—he smelled like soap and his hair was damp. His skin shone. Worry poisoned my insides when I realized he wasn't wearing a hat or gloves. "You're going to get sick," I told Collith softly. "You're in a weakened state right now."

He didn't acknowledge my words. When I glanced at him for the hundredth time, Collith was staring downward with an unreadable expression. I followed his gaze and realized he must've noticed the flower. It was next to the bottom step, impossibly full and thriving, even as it nestled in a bed of frost.

"It's called a wood anemone," Collith said. His voice was tight. "Usually it's a spring flower."

I frowned down at it, too. "Well, I'd hardly call this spring. Maybe it's the work of a witch?"

But the faerie king had apparently fallen silent again, because my words were met with a lone whistle of wind. For once, he didn't ask about his nightmares or how I'd brought him back. We just sat there, coexisting in the same space, the air around us subtle with grief. All my instincts wanted to avoid it or seek a distraction. Fortunately, I had endured loss before. Pain was like a physical wound—it couldn't be ignored, or it would fester.

"Have you eaten yet?" Collith asked abruptly. I turned my head and studied his expression. After a moment, I shook my head. He stood up and held his hand down to me. I stared at it for a long, long moment before taking it, my fingers curling around his. I waited for the inevitable panic to set in, but there was nothing except the pleasant coolness emanating from Collith's skin.

Suddenly I never wanted to let go.

Damon and Matthew were at the kitchen table when we came in. My nephew sat in his brand-new highchair, making a sopping mess of his cereal. A Cheerio clung to the child's pointed chin, and his skin gleamed in the morning light. His smile radiated innocence. God, he looked so much like Damon it hurt.

Though Matthew had only been with us for two weeks, I knew everyone in this house would lay down their life to protect him. To give him the childhood so many of us never had.

"Maybe he'd be better off with oatmeal or something," I told Damon, trying to make it sound offhand. I opened one of the cupboards to get a clean bowl for myself. Collith slipped from the room, moving as soundlessly as he had that day in the market, when he'd dropped a set of keys into my cage.

"Oh, you're too serious, Fortuna," Emma interjected as she entered the room. A hint of her perfume reached for me, something cloying and sweet. "You should be out having fun. Buy a motorcycle! That way I can borrow it."

I watched her as she spoke, noticing her heavy lids and how the whites of her eyes had gone slightly red. Laughter bubbled up inside me. I disguised it by fetching a spoon from the silverware drawer. "You're high as a kite, Em."

My godmother winked and put a finger to her mouth. As she bent to kiss the top of Damon's head, I started toward the fridge. I was just reaching for the handle when I spotted a jar of homemade jam on the counter, the rim wrapped in twine and a heart drawn on the lid. I wondered which nosy neighbor had dropped it off hoping to see Damon Sworn, who'd been kidnapped and held captive for two years, according to the papers. They weren't wrong, exactly—there just hadn't been any humans involved, and I'd made certain the kidnapper would never take anyone else.

Thinking of everything I'd done to rip my brother out of Jassin's claws, I twisted the lid off, dipped the spoon inside, then viciously shoved all of it into my mouth. The taste of berries and sugar exploded on my tongue, and I'd never found it more unappealing.

While I'd been reliving my first week at the Unseelie Court, Emma had settled into the chair beside Matthew's. I watched as she crossed her eyes at him. Matthew beamed and offered her a Cheerio. What age did children normally begin talking? Shouldn't we have heard him say something by now? Looking entirely unperturbed by his silence, Emma accepted my nephew's offering and kissed his round cheek.

"What would you like to do for your birthday tomorrow?" she asked without looking at me, deliberately changing the subject.

Jam stuck to the roof of my mouth. *Shit.* I was hoping everyone would forget. Luck was finally on my side, though, because Cyrus came through the front door a moment later. He must've just gotten back from taking Stanley for a walk—the leash was still in his hand.

"Good morning, Cy," I blurted, trying not to sound overeager. "Still up for carpooling?"

He'd suggested it last week, in the interest of putting fewer carbon emissions into the air. The fry cook avoided my eyes, absorbed in freeing his dog, and nodded. I got up, trying not to appear overeager, and hurried down the hallway to shower.

"We're celebrating your birthday, Fortuna Sworn!" Emma called after me.

The door clicked shut behind me. I pulled the shower curtain aside and turned the handle as far as it would go. Water burst from the nozzle, pounding against the plastic floor of the bathtub. Steam rose toward the ceiling. With a weary sigh, I undressed and stepped beneath a stream of scalding water.

Maybe this was the day I'd finally feel clean again.

CHAPTER THREE

A half hour later, Cyrus maneuvered his truck alongside the curb on Main Street. It was just the two of us, since Finn hadn't returned before we left the house. The sign for Bea's shone neon-blue in the window, like a strange lighthouse in a sea of concrete and pain. Most people came here to forget that part of themselves.

As my friend killed the engine, a familiar figure walked past. Ariel must not have spotted us, or she would've given us one of her signature finger waves. She pulled the door to Bea's open and slipped inside. I turned to unbuckle my seatbelt, and I caught sight of Cyrus's expression—the fact that he even had one was significant. He still hadn't looked away from the door, either, despite that it had been closed for several seconds now. "Why, Cyrus Lavender," I teased, pressing the button that would release my seatbelt. "Do you fancy our new server?"

My friend's countenance reddened, and he left the truck without answering. Still smiling, I hurried to follow, but apparently Cyrus moved quickly when he wanted to avoid answering certain questions. The weak sunlight bounced off his flame of hair. He didn't look back as he rushed into the bar. I reached the door a moment later, but when I reached for the long handle, reluctance filled the pit of my stomach. I faced the street, thinking to take a moment or two. The sunlight hit my eyes, and I squinted. I saw shapes on the sidewalk, silhouettes of people who'd once stood there. Voices moved through my memory.

No bargain. Not ever!

If a time comes that you should feel differently, all you must do is say my name.

That's going to be hard to do, considering you haven't told me what it is.

It's Collith.

Phantom breath touched the shell of my ear, and of their own volition, my eyes fluttered shut. If I could go back, would I tell that Fortuna to change course? Would I beg her to forget about Collith Sylvyre? Just like Cyrus, I didn't want to face the answer. Turning away, I shoved my hands into my pockets and pushed the door open—I kept forgetting to buy new gloves, since the pair I'd had was now little more than ashes.

The thought dimmed my mood even more as I walked toward Bea's office. Her chair was empty, for once, and I hoped she'd taken a rare day off. Country music played from the speakers overhead while I changed and clocked in. By the time I re-emerged, the breakfast crowd had started arriving. One of the local deputies was sitting in a booth. Not Ian, thankfully. The star on his chest glinted. I hadn't seen Paul in a while—he'd taken some time off while his wife was going through chemo. As though he could feel the weight of my stare, Paul raised his gaze, and I offered a brief wave. He nodded back, just as brief, and then Angela arrived with a plate of pancakes.

I turned my attention to Gretchen Nelson, our longtime bartender and Bea's girlfriend of ten years. She had shoulder-length hair, black-rimmed glasses, and long fingers that made pouring drinks look like a performance. "Is there coffee?" I asked hopefully. Gretchen opened her mouth to respond.

"Don't you just love this time of year?" a cheery voice asked. A moment later, Ariel appeared beside me, sliding a tray of dirty dishes onto the counter. Today her dark hair was divided into two braids, and the style made her look even younger than usual. As I studied her, trying to guess her actual age, I realized that I knew practically nothing about Bea's latest hire. A fact that was entirely my fault, since I'd done little to befriend her.

"What do you love about it?" Gretchen asked gamely, pouring me a cup of coffee. She responded to my grateful smile with a wink.

"Everything! Pumpkin spice lattes, crackling fires, books, Disney movies…"

"You're forgetting scrapbooking and baking," I heard Gretchen reply. My focus was entirely on the coffee, though. Sliding onto a stool, I clamped the mug between my legs to put some cream in. Just as I tipped the small container, the door hinges whined and someone called a greeting to Paul.

At the sound of Ian's voice, I jerked involuntarily, and hot liquid splashed onto my jeans. Ariel made an alarmed sound and said something about ice. I barely understood her words. Barely felt the pain. It felt like I had no control as I lifted my head and faced the man I'd avoided for a month. I knew this was coming, of course, but knowing was much different from reality.

Ian hadn't noticed me yet—his blue eyes searched the room, the same eyes that had smiled down at me all those nights ago. When he spotted Paul, the deputy adjusted his belt and moved toward him. He left a trail of cologne in his wake that sent a shudder through me.

Someone said my name, then, and it was like finding a rope in thick fog. I blinked and realized Gretchen was squatting in front of my stool. She patted at the splotches on my pants with a damp rag. She was still talking, but Ian's presence made it impossible to comprehend any of it. In the next moment, Ariel was back. She pressed something cold into my hand—ice wrapped in a towel. I didn't move.

"Fortuna?" I heard Ariel say from far away.

I'd made the mistake of glancing toward the table where the deputies sat. The commotion must've captured Paul's notice, because our eyes met and a line deepened between his thick brows. Ian followed his partner's gaze. When he saw me, a wide smile stretched across his face. My stomach heaved at the sight of it. *Oh, God. I'm going to throw up at work*, I thought faintly.

More flashes of memory accosted me. Rustling leaves overhead. An empty road illuminated by a single, yellow streetlight. The tiny shape of a bat flitting past.

No. Focus on Ariel and Gretchen, Fortuna. Think about anything else besides the human sitting in that booth. Somehow I managed to tip my head back and look at the women still hovering over me. Feeling as though the air had become solid, I moved slowly and instinctively, putting the ice onto my leg. It did make the burn less painful.

"I need to use the restroom," I said mechanically. I had to get out of this room, away from Ian's unrelenting stare.

Gretchen turned her head, distracted by a customer trying to get her attention, but Ariel gave me a reassuring smile. "Of course. I think I have some extra pants in my locker. I know my legs are shorter than yours, but you can just roll the cuffs up and make them look like capris. I'll bring them to the bathroom, okay?"

I nodded—at least, I thought I nodded—and stood up. Another wave of nausea crashed over me. Ariel frowned and reached for my arm. I was slow to react, but she must've seen something in my expression, because her hand dropped before making contact. The world righted itself a moment later. Letting out a small, relieved sigh, I set the mug of coffee down and left the bar. I felt Ian's eyes on me, tracking every movement. *Don't look at him. Don't look at him. Don't look at him.* It was nine steps to the ladies' room. I counted them silently, needing something to focus on, then I slipped inside and locked the door.

The sounds beyond it became muffled and distant. I turned the faucet on and cupped my hands beneath the stream. Water dripped from my chin and seeped into my collar. I sighed again as I straightened. The wood-framed mirror took no pity on me —the creature it reflected was too thin, her lips chapped and unsmiling. Ghosts peered out from behind her tired eyes. She looked like someone who had been to war, and in a way, maybe that was true. Taunting, cruel, those images slipped past my defenses again. Groaning, I pressed the heels of my hands against my eyes.

There was a gentle tap on the door. I knew Ian wouldn't knock like that, but I was still slow in opening it, reluctant to face the inevitable questions. Ariel brushed past me without hesitation. A pleasant smell followed in her wake, not perfume, exactly, but something floral. There was a pair of leggings in her small hands and a familiar plaid shirt in the other—she must've taken it from my locker. As she closed the door with her back, Ariel watched me pat my face dry with a paper towel. "What did he do?" the girl asked bluntly.

"Nothing." I shook my head and took the clothing from her. "Well, nothing more than usual. But he gets away with it because of who his father is."

For once, Ariel was silent. Her brown eyes appraised me while I changed into the leggings she'd brought, then tied the plaid button-up around my waist. There was nothing sexual in the human's demeanor—rare for anyone in the presence of a Nightmare—and I was too frazzled to think of modesty. When I was finished, she gave me a bright smile.

"You know, we should get drinks sometime," she said.

I tried to smile back, but mine was noticeably thinner. "I'd like that."

She held the door open for me, and we left the bathroom together. The next hour moved at the pace of a zombie. Thankfully, a group of hunters came in and sat in my section. I hurried to fill a water pitcher and set several glasses on a tray. After placing an order in Cyrus's window, Ariel moved to stand beside me. She propped her elbows on the bar and stared in Ian's direction. I was careful not to follow her gaze.

"Some people are alive only because it's illegal to kill them," she muttered.

Though I didn't know Ariel well, it seemed a surprisingly brutal thing for her to say. I didn't respond—it was still taking all my focus not to bolt. A second later, someone must've signaled to her, because Ariel pushed off the bar and rushed away. She put a smile on her face like other people put on clothes. Turning back to my task, I lifted the pitcher with a shaky hand. Water sloshed over the sides and onto the floor.

"Need help with that?" a voice said from behind.

Blood roared in my ears as I faced him. Ian didn't step back. At this proximity, I could smell his cologne and aftershave, along with a hint of sweat. I couldn't bring myself to look directly into his eyes, but the demon had gotten everything else right, from the small scar on Ian's cheek down to his overwhelming scent.

"...from a ski trip," he was saying, ignoring or disregarding my obvious discomfort. "Baby, do you remember meeting Miss Sworn? She's our resident spinster. Too good for anyone in this town, isn't that right, Fortuna?"

My gaze flitted toward the human he was speaking to. Noticing Ian's outstretched hand, she said something to Paul and walked toward us. I did have a vague memory of meeting her, but Ian's new wife was younger than I'd thought. Early twenties, maybe. At first glance, Bella's hair was blond, but brown had started to show at the roots. She wore a sweater with a plunging neckline and jeans that looked one breath away from popping open. Her eyeshadow was blue and glittered under the lights.

At first, she was smiling, the curve of her lips almost painful-looking in its enthusiasm. The longer she looked at me, however, that smile slowly shriveled like a leach sprinkled in salt. I wondered what she saw. A leggy blond, probably, or a dark-eyed beauty.

Buried far beneath the layers of fear, pain, and self-loathing, my instincts stirred. To stalk. To hunt. To take.

"Nice to see you again," I said faintly, worried I might vomit all over Bella's ample bosom.

She thrust her hand out and nearly hit me in the face. I caught a glimpse of her red nails as I jerked my head back. "Likewise! I'm sorry we haven't gotten to know each other yet; Ian and I were celebrating our one-month anniversary," she chirped.

Sorry for your loss, I wanted to say.

To avoid a handshake, I reached for a strand of hair falling into my face, but then Bella's fingers wrapped around mine before I realized what was happening. Her fears hovered just beneath the skin, and dear God, there were so many. Multiple flavors coated my tongue—butter, soap, sweat—and images flooded my vision. Isabella Campbell was afraid of horses, the dark, heights, needles, peanut butter, flying, and countless more. She was the most fearful person I'd ever met.

My power was greedy, even if I wasn't. It dug deeper with its wicked claws. At the edges of her mind, like stars at the edge of a galaxy, were her true fears. *No.* I resisted reaching for them.

The new Mrs. O'Connell said something, but I was too nauseous to comprehend her words. I must've given her a response, because she laughed, the sound like wind chimes. She walked away, her heeled boots like thunder against the wood floor. I swallowed and avoided looking at Ian. *Please follow her. Please leave me alone.*

"You've got an eyelash," his voice rumbled. He raised his thick fingers toward my face. I recoiled, slamming into the edge of the bar. The man lunged toward me, probably to keep me from falling, but I was surrounded by trees now. A wide moon glowed overhead. And Ian was a demon with black, bottomless eyes. He grinned at me, showing all his teeth. He was still smiling as his voice slithered through my mind.

How charming. You thought I would want your soul. That's not how it works, sweetheart. No, I take something that you value.

Between one moment and the next, I was on the floor, my entire body curled into a ball. I squeezed my eyes shut and whimpered a name. All the sounds in the world were blending together, becoming a chaotic song of clinking dishes, frying food, and voices. When a hand landed on my shoulder, I struck out blindly. I didn't want to be touched. Never again.

"I've got her," I heard someone say. There was a sudden warmth against my side and ear. I couldn't move or speak, because the darkness was spinning, and it was all I could do not to vomit. I realized that someone was carrying me. It was a voice in my ear, not an ocean wave crashing against a shore. *Breathe, just breathe,* it was saying. I was so frightened that I obeyed.

Door hinges whined. The arms around me flexed. A moment later, I felt the coolness of a tiled floor against my hand. *He must've sat down,* I thought dimly. I still wasn't ready to open my eyes, though.

"Take your time," that same voice said.

The memories continued receding until all that remained was the light behind my eyelids. I slowly returned to myself, becoming aware the chest I rested against was warm and muscled. Slowly, I opened my eyes. Reality came into focus like the lens of a camera. The face hovering over me sharpened. After a moment, I comprehended that it was Finn's dark, anxious eyes boring into mine, and disappointment sliced through me. Of course it wasn't Collith. He hadn't left Cyrus's in weeks.

"Breathe in through your nose," he instructed, unaware of my thoughts. "That's good. Now out through your mouth. Do it again."

I released another long breath and studied the room. Familiar wooden walls surrounded us—I was back in the restroom, still cradled in the circle of Finn's brawny arms. Noises drifted through the door, a steady hum of voices, and heat spread through my face as I relived the past few minutes. No doubt rumors were already circulating. *Fortuna Sworn is on drugs. Oh, the virgin server threw a jealous fit when she met Ian's new wife. That Sworn girl had a breakdown.*

"How did you know what to do?" I asked finally, shifting off Finn's lap. When the world didn't tilt or waver, I grasped the edge of the sink and hauled myself up.

"My daughter had panic attacks sometimes," he said. His voice was soft.

Slowly, I turned around and leaned on the sink. Finn remained on the floor. I looked down at the dark-haired werewolf, noting the tightness to his angular jaw. I didn't need to ask where his daughter was now—Finn wouldn't be here, in this bathroom with me, if his child was still alive. It felt like the edges of my heart were made of razors, cutting into me with every beat. "Was it Astrid?" I bit out, picturing the sallow-faced female that had threatened everyone I held dear.

Finn kept his gaze fixed downward. "No. Hunters."

"Hunters?" I repeated with a frown. "Did they think your daughter was a wolf?"

"No. They knew exactly what she was. They were Fallen hunters." He spoke in his usual gentle way, but I still flinched. My parents had spoken of such hunters, of course. Warned Damon and I to be ever-vigilant every time we left the house. I'd never met one or heard an account from someone who had, though, and it was easy to dismiss something that sounded like a bedtime story.

Finn stared at the tiles, as if they were the answer to a question or the ending of a story. "They killed my mate first," he said without looking at me. "Came right into the house and started shooting. Katie and I escaped. Not before they shot her with a holy bullet, though. We sought refuge with Astrid's pack. Their doctor tried to save Katie, but it was too late."

His voice made my heart hurt. It was hollow, like someone who had cried every tear, felt every pang of agony, and now there was nothing left. "Astrid wasn't the kind of person to help unless something was in it for her. What did she ask for in return for their doctor's services?" I asked, holding the sink with white fingers.

"You're looking at it." Finn got to his feet. He reached for the paper towel dispenser and pulled one out. "She kept me for a while, to amuse herself, but then the pack needed money for more heroin. Astrid sold me to a faerie passing through. That's how I ended up in the Unseelie Court."

"She's lucky Cora killed her. I would've made her suffer," I muttered. Finn gave me the faintest of smiles and held out the paper towels. I accepted them and faced the mirror. My eyes were red and puffy—I didn't remember crying, but the proof was looking back at me. Sighing at the thought of everyone witnessing my mental breakdown, I dried the remaining tears, then splashed some cold water on my face.

"I brought the van. Want me to drive back?" I heard Finn ask. Another paper towel landed in my searching, outstretched hand. I dried myself off and faced the mirror again. The redness had slightly faded, but there was still a haunted cast to my face that couldn't be washed away. I tried to find the will to fix my apron, tighten my ponytail, and get back to work.

For the first time since starting at Bea's, I knew I couldn't do it.

I forced myself to meet Finn's gaze. Despite the tragic story he'd told me today, his expression was mild as ever. He watched me with the quiet patience of a wolf. "I need to tell Gretchen that I can't finish my shift. Do you mind meeting me at the van?" I asked hesitantly. The gossips of Granby would notice if a golden-eyed stranger followed me around the bar, and they had enough ammunition for one day.

Finn just nodded and slipped through the door, leaving it open a crack. I lingered there, in the quiet safety of the bathroom, for a few more seconds before following him out.

Country music was still floating down from the speakers. The sound of clinking dishes and a myriad of voices was so familiar that I instantly felt calmer, and I was about to walk toward the bar when I heard a voice down the hall. I turned and saw that Bea was in her office—she must've arrived while I was in the bathroom with Finn. It was the perfect excuse to avoid seeing Ian again. I started in her direction, passing the order window as I did so. Cyrus was so preoccupied with his food that he didn't notice, but I made sure the garbages weren't overflowing before moving on.

At the sound of my footsteps, Bea lifted her head. There was concern written in the lines of her face, and at the sight of me, those lines deepened. A cigarette dangled from her mouth, which she quickly put out on the ashtray. I knew she only smoked when she was stressed. Guilt seared through my veins, which was becoming a habit with my boss.

"Gretchen told me what happened. Are you all right?" she asked bluntly.

It was my first instinct to lie, but something stopped me. When were we taught to tuck away pain or uncertainty? Why was it ingrained in us that telling someone the truth was to burden them? "No," I said instead.

Bea flipped her long, graying braid back and folded her hands on top of the desk. I wondered if this was in an effort not to stand and embrace me. She stared down at them, fighting a battle I couldn't see or hear. It felt like several minutes had ticked by when she raised her gaze to meet mine. "You can tell me anything. I hope you know that."

"I do. Thanks, Bea."

She took a breath, as if preparing herself for a confrontation. "I want you to take the rest of the day off."

"I wish I could see the look on Angela's face when you tell her that," was all I said. Bea shook her head just as the phone rang. She picked it up, her other hand still holding a pen, and sighed when whoever was on the other end started talking. As she launched into reassurances that there was absolutely no gluten in our bacon, I removed my apron and hung it up. I fetched my purse from the row of lockers, waved at Bea, and walked down the hallway again. The breakfast rush kept Gretchen and Ariel so busy that neither of them noticed me hurry out the door.

As agreed, Finn was waiting by the van. Neither of us said a word. We didn't need to—at some point, we'd come to an unspoken understanding that, when it was the two of us, there was no need for false smiles or meaningless conversation. The drive home was blessedly uneventful, and we existed in a comfortable silence. Tiny, fluffy snowflakes drifted down from a gray sky. I tuned the radio to a local station, and classic rock floated around us until Finn turned onto a familiar driveway.

The engine had barely faded into silence when Finn got out. He immediately headed for the woods, where he would take the form of a wolf and run, as fast and far as his legs could carry him. He wouldn't outrun the memories, of course—Heaven knew I'd tried—but there was something about the movement. You weren't just standing still and waiting for the pain. Instead, you were fighting back, in the only way you knew how.

I went up the porch steps slowly, thinking about how to fill the day. Maybe I would take a nap and visit Oliver. It had been so long since we'd been able to have fun. Since we'd been able to *laugh*. I missed my best friend. Now more than ever, I needed him.

I tested the doorknob and found it unlocked. The hinges made the slightest of moans as I stepped inside, but the rest of the house was absolutely silent. Damon must've taken Matthew for a walk—he was trying to teach his son about plants that grew in the woods, despite our remarks about how young Matthew was, or that nearly all those plants were dead right now. My brother had always done things his own way, and I was glad that hadn't changed after everything he'd been through. As I took off my shoes, I heard something in the kitchen, a sound so small I couldn't define it. Curious, I peered around the doorway, careful not to make the floor creak.

Collith and Emma stood in front of the sink. The old woman had her arm wrapped around him, and neither of them were saying anything. His head was bowed and his shoulders slumped, as though they held the weight of the world. Once, I'd thought carrying planets was nothing to him.

They must've just finished eating breakfast—dirty dishes littered the table behind them, and the air smelled like bacon. On the floor, beneath the highchair where Matthew always sat, there were over a dozen soggy-looking Cheerios. There were still pans on top of the stove.

As I watched, Collith reached up to rake his hair back. His face was more visible now, his profile in stark contrast against the sunlight. He wore the same expression I saw every time he woke up from a nightmare. It was pain. Pure, naked pain. I'd clearly interrupted a private moment, and I was about to retreat when Collith finally straightened. Pulling away from Emma's grasp, he reached forward to twist the sink handle. Water trickled down.

"You can't fix everything," he said. His voice wasn't unkind, exactly, but there was a sharpness in the words that my heart feel like it was being squeezed.

Emma was unfazed. She handed him a sponge and smiled. "Very true, I can't. That's up to you guys. But I can point you in the right direction."

I wish it were that simple—someone taking hold and guiding us to a better place. I watched the two of them a little while longer, but apparently the conversation was over. Emma found a container for the leftovers and Collith started washing the dishes.

Eventually I tiptoed past, heading toward my room, and it seemed like a small miracle that I didn't get lost along the way.

Later that night, I laid in bed and stared at the ceiling.

Despite how tired I'd felt all day—how tired I *always* felt— sleep eluded me. Seeing Ian again had cracked something open within my mind. Normally I could distract myself or fall asleep quickly enough, but tonight was different. There, in the darkness of night, surrounded by silence, it was impossible to hold them at bay. The memories. They came at me from all sides like battering rams, sending shock and pain through my body. A sob escaped me before I could stop it, and I put my hand over my mouth to contain the rest.

A minute later, I heard the door creak open. *Collith*, I thought with a rush of feeling. Apprehension, excitement, worry. I sat up and shifted my legs to make room on the bed. But the scent that washed over me wasn't Collith's—laundry detergent and a woodsy shampoo. A moment later, Damon's thin arms wrapped around my shoulders. "Hey, Fortuna," he murmured.

I didn't say anything, because it didn't seem necessary. I felt like we were children again, and I'd just woken from another nightmare, my little brother trying to offer comfort. Damon had often been there as I cried myself awake—unlike most children, who liked to crawl into bed with their parents, Damon always sought me when he left his room. Eight-year-old Fortuna had thought it was annoying. Now I wished I'd been kinder to him.

This thought gave me the strength to stay there, in the circle of his arms, when all I wanted to do was shove him away. I had an irrational fear—a phobia that lurked beneath my skin, just like those I touched—that the filthiness all over me would get on him. Maybe Damon sensed it, because he pulled away. I waited for him to leave, but he didn't move. I started adjusting my pillow. I needed to stay busy, somehow, or the memories would come flying back.

"You've even started to move like one of them," Damon said suddenly, leaning over to turn on the lamp. Light trickled over the rug and onto the wooden floor.

I tucked some hair behind my ear and frowned at him. "What do you mean?"

"The fae. You've spent so much time at Court lately that…" He hesitated and shrugged, as if he was only now realizing that I might find his words horrifying. "You're adopting their mannerisms a little."

"I'm sorry, didn't you come in here to comfort me?" I demanded, drawing my knees against my chest. I held onto them tightly and hoped he wouldn't notice. The thought I was becoming like *them*, the creatures I had vowed to destroy, who had caused the world so much pain, felt like a fissure going through me. If I didn't hold myself, everything would shatter.

Damon made a sound like laughter, but there was nothing joyful about it. "Yes, I did. Apparently I don't know how to be a father *or* a brother."

"You've only known about Matthew for a few weeks," I reminded him gently, watching his eyes darken as his mind descended into worry. "You're doing just fine, Damon. Do you think anyone actually feels like a good parent in the beginning?"

"Ours were. Good parents, I mean."

"Yeah. We got lucky," I said with a bittersweet smile. We fell silent after that, but for the first time since I'd brought Damon back from the Unseelie Court, there was nothing spiteful or uncertain about it. As I thought about our parents, a memory resurfaced. "Do you remember Dad's cowlick? Mom was always trying to fix it. It became a habit, and she ran her hand over the back of his head every time they kissed."

Damon smiled. The sight of it sent me soaring—it was his old smile. "He never got annoyed with her, either. He'd just patiently wait until she gave up."

My eyes had that telltale sting in them, a warning tears weren't far off. I blinked rapidly to force them back. Damon and I went quiet again, and the air between us was sober now. Because, while most of the memories were happy ones, the last one was inevitable. It would always be how that part of our story ended, no matter how many times we tried to rewrite it. An image flashed in my mind like a camera. My mother, sitting on the floor, slumped against the wall. *No. Not that one. Please don't make me remember that one.* In my desperation to think of something else, my mind latched onto another conversation I'd had with Damon.

"There's something I've been meaning to ask you," I ventured, wary of destroying this fragile peace between us.

It was probably the uncertain note in my voice that caught his attention. Damon opened his eyes and looked at me. In that slant of moonlight, he resembled our father so strongly it was unnerving. "What is it?"

I made a vague gesture. "It's about something you said to me at Court. 'We just don't belong up there. We never did.' I never knew you felt that way. You always seemed so…"

"Human," Damon finished for me. He tipped his head back

until it rested against the edge of the headboard, then raised his eyebrows. "Was there a question somewhere in there?"

For once, he wasn't being cruel. I hit his leg with the back of my hand. "I guess I've just been wondering if you still feel that way."

Damon didn't answer right away. He stared at the ceiling, a frown hovering around his mouth. Maybe he was remembering all over again that I had taken Jassin from him. I was silently berating myself for being the one to remind him when he finally answered. "I think about it constantly," he said. "What we are. What I wish I could be. I'd toyed with the idea of performing the Rites of Thogon, but then I saw you force Arcaena through them and changed my mind."

"That would do it," I agreed. It was all-too easy to remember that night—I could still picture the line of drool coming out of Arcaena's mouth as she bent over the flagstones. Had that been the beginning of my transformation into a creature that could kill her own mate? Or did it go further back than that? I'd killed those goblins without hesitation. Maybe that was the moment I'd begun my descent, and the fae had nothing to do with it.

Sensing my vulnerability, another memory leaped out of the darkness. I saw Collith's unseeing eyes, staring up at a roiling sky. I relived the pang of horror when I'd realized he was dead. The hole inside me widened, and I pressed a hand against it. I wondered if I would ever wake up someday without that ache in my chest. If I would ever again feel moments of content or happiness. Right now, it was hard to remember those moments. They had happened in another lifetime, to another person.

"Do you have any scars?" Damon asked without preamble.

The question made my brows lower, but I still answered. "Yes."

"It's like that. The pain," Damon clarified. He must've guessed at my thoughts, or read them in my eyes. "At first, it's like you're walking around with this gaping wound in your chest, and it seems impossible that no one else can see it. Every time they pretend not to, you want to scream. But then, if they actually do notice, you don't even want to think about the pain, much less talk about it. Try to explain it. Nothing you do will quicken the process or dull it, either. You just have to survive moment to moment, day to day, until one morning you wake up and it hurts a little less. There are setbacks, of course—you'll have a thought or see something that reminds you of him, and it's like you picked at the scab. But it does eventually fade... into a scar."

Is that what's happening to you? I let the question go unspoken, because I didn't need to ask it. The truth was in my brother's expression, which now bore new lines of sorrow. As though he'd aged ten years in the two he'd been gone.

I let Damon's words go around in my head, and they gave me a muted sense of hope. Part of me longed to tell him everything, all the secret fears hiding in the shadowy corners of my mind. But there was a bigger part of me that worried Damon would never love me again, if he knew I'd made a deal with a demon. He may not have known our parents long, or had much opportunity to learn from them, but loathing demons was in our very blood.

Eventually I just said, careful to keep these thoughts out of my voice, "I thought I was hiding it pretty well."

"Even a blind person could see that you're hurting, Fortuna. I just recognize the scars because we now bear the same ones." With that, Damon stood up.

I stayed where I was. There was a string sticking out from the bedspread, and I started to tug at it. I didn't look away from it as I spoke. "I looked for you so hard. I used to imagine a thousand different scenarios you could be in, and every single one of them was unbearable. Please know that I tried to save you from that, Damon. I did try."

"Of course I know that." Damon shoved his hands into his

pockets, and I expected his shoulders to hunch. I waited for him to become the confused, broken person I'd met beneath the earth. Instead, he stood there, tall and pensive, just like our father. His eyes grew distant. "When no one came to save me, I was never angry or bitter. I was just afraid. I didn't want to die, Tuna Fish."

When that nickname came out of his mouth, I forgot my pain for the briefest of moments. A spot of warmth flickered in my chest and spread outward. "Oh my God. You did *not* just call me that," I deadpanned. I reached for one of the pillows as a warning.

Damon looked at me with a confused expression. It was the same one he'd given our parents, or Dave and Maureen, when he'd wanted to convince them of his innocence. "What's wrong, Tuna Fish?"

I threw my pillow at his head, and my brother ducked. I glimpsed another smile curving his lips just before he stepped into the hallway and closed the door.

With a smile of my own, I curled onto my side and pulled the bedspread over me. The floorboards creaked as Damon returned to his room, and the sound was oddly comforting. For the first time in weeks, the chill that was constantly in my bones had gone. My eyes fluttered. Through the wall, I heard Damon's voice, offering gentle reassurances to his son.

And at long last, I fell asleep.

CHAPTER FOUR

I slept so hard that even Oliver couldn't reach me.

When I finally opened my eyes, daylight shone through the window. Drowsiness still hovered around my mind like a fog, and I entertained the idea of going right back to sleep. I glanced at the alarm clock, mostly to reassure myself I could do exactly that, then I gasped and lurched upright. I was expected at the Unseelie Court in less than two hours, and it would take half that long just to get there, not to mention the time it would take getting dressed. In a flurry of bare legs and tangled hair, I wrenched the door open.

Collith stood on the other side, his hand poised to knock. He opened his mouth to say something, but I beat him to it.

"If I'm late for the Tithe, Nuvian actually might kill me!" I darted around him and dove into the bathroom, where I rummaged for my can of dry shampoo. As I reappeared in the doorway, I sprayed it around my head. I sounded breathless as I asked, "Is Lyari here yet?"

"No, but someone else stopped by earlier. One of the men that's on the cleanup crew for your previous home." Collith held up the ring that had been in my nightstand. I was surprised it survived the fire—I'd guessed it was made from cheap metal. "What is this?"

"It was in the goblins' van." I lifted one shoulder in a shrug while I ran a brush through my snarls. "It's just an ugly ring, what's the big deal?"

"There is power in it. Probably a spell," Collith said, frowning. He studied the jewels more closely.

There was a subtle shift in the air, and a moment later, Lyari materialized in the hallway. She scanned me from head to toe. When she was finished, her blue eyes looked like two chips of ice. "Are you seriously still in your pajamas?" she asked flatly.

Inwardly cursing, I ran past them both and talked as I went. "Does it really matter? I'm changing when we get there, anyway. I just need to get my boots on."

I ran for the pile of shoes in the entryway. Lyari followed on silent feet. After a moment, she opened the front door for me, her mouth tight with disapproval. I resisted the urge to annoy her and jogged down the porch steps without a word. Finn sat near the line of trees, clearly waiting for us. He was in his wolf form, and his gray fur gleamed like metal. Once I reached him, he loped alongside me. His breath joined mine in the air.

Lyari overtook us with several long-legged strides, then walked ahead. After a few minutes, I noticed that she was leading us on a different route than usual. *Smart*, I thought. Unpredictability made monarchs harder to kill.

Knowing that I would be trapped beneath the ground for hours, I tried to enjoy being out here. Beams of fading sunlight reached through the bare branches overhead. Leaves rustled beneath our feet. The air smelled crisp and damp, and my nostrils flared as I inhaled. I did a double-take when I realized I was looking at a person and not a tree. Before the figure ducked out of sight, I caught a glimpse of something long and glittering. A sword. I glanced at Lyari. She must've felt my gaze—she was too perceptive not to—but she kept her focus on the trees around us. "Why are there Guardians hiding in the woods?" I asked bluntly.

The faerie heaved a small sigh, as if she'd been hoping to avoid this. "They're here for your protection. Nuvian's orders."

"Has there been another assassination attempt?" I frowned as I searched the trees again, wondering how many there were. I didn't like having so many fae this close to my family, this close to Granby. Even if their purpose was to guard my life, every creature of the Unseelie Court was on edge. The humans were far too fragile and oblivious—if one of them encountered the lovely, lethal allure of a faerie, I wasn't sure they would survive.

Lyari's expression remained neutral, which undoubtedly meant she was hiding something. "Not that I know of," was all she said.

"So why…" I trailed off as something occurred to me. I could feel Finn's eyes on my face, watching every reaction closely. "Hold on. Does Nuvian *always* have guards following me? Even when I'm home or at work?"

"You are a ruler of the Unseelie Court. How can you expect him to do otherwise?" Lyari snapped, that careful façade finally cracking.

"Because I made it clear that I wanted it separate," I hissed back, stopping to fully confront her. Lyari faced me with a stubborn set to her jaw. "My role down there and my life up here aren't connected. They can't be. The *only* perk of being queen is being able to keep humans safe, to make sure the people I love are never hurt again. Damn it, Lyari."

I swung away, rubbing my forehead. If anyone in town had been hurt as a result of the Guardians being here, it was my fault. Had there been any rumors? Any articles in the paper? I'd been so consumed by my pain that I hadn't been looking for anyone else's. I could order the guards not to harm a single human, of course, but they were faeries—they'd been taking whatever they wanted for thousands of years, without consequences or conscience.

I let out a breath, hoping it would calm me, and walked back to Lyari. My hands balled into fists as I met her gaze. "No more secrets. Not one. If I find out you've kept anything else from me, you will know the true wrath of a Nightmare. Are we clear?"

We stared at each other. I'd never peered so intently into Lyari's eyes, and at this proximity, I could make out the rings within her irises. The silence between us felt dark and cold, like a winter night. "We are clear, Your Majesty," my Right Hand said evenly. A single strand of her hair lifted in a breeze.

Thankfully, she didn't point out that I'd been hesitant to use my abilities since Collith's death. Some of the tension eased out of my body, and I held back a sigh. "Good. Is there anything else you need to tell me, then?"

"No, Queen Fortuna."

I waited a beat, giving her a chance to change her mind. But Lyari just looked back at me and said nothing. Slowly, I turned and started walking again. We were silent the rest of the way to the entrance. Finn stayed closer to me than usual, and every once in a while, his solid warmth brushed against my hip. I didn't spot any more Guardians, but now that I knew they were there, any sense of calm I'd achieved was shattered. Almost unconsciously, I tangled my hand in Finn's fur and left it there.

The moss that once hung over the opening to the Unseelie Court had long since withered and died. The first time I'd stepped inside, I had thought of it as a mouth, black and bottomless. Swallowing me whole. Now I wasn't sure what it looked like to me.

Minutes later, when I finally stepped into Collith's rooms, they were empty. I'd been half-hoping Laurie would be waiting with a mischievous smile and a flirtatious remark. For a moment, I lingered near the door, feeling more alone than I ever had. It was a different sort of loneliness than what I experienced during those days of Damon being missing or the night in the dungeon. Now so much depended on me, so many lives and decisions, and I still didn't know who I could fully trust. Tonight the throne beside mine would be empty again, and the air ripe with suspicion toward me.

Swallowing a weary groan, I forced myself to approach the wardrobe. Finn moved toward the corner, where there was a pile of bones he'd been accumulating. The sound of crunching filled my ears as I chose a gown at random and pulled it on. It was another black one, as that was what I seemed drawn to these days. It was less intricate than the others I'd worn, but no less dramatic. Sleeveless, made from a combination of leather and lace, the bodice looked like it could hide a dozen knives. Like I was ready to fight for my life. This was accentuated by a long slit in the skirt, which exposed my boots and would allow me to literally kick someone's ass if the need arose.

The standing mirror Laurie had brought awaited near the fireplace. I found the small makeup bag he'd left in a drawer and moved toward the glass. After a few minutes of struggling, I settled for liquid eyeliner and a dusting of blush. Makeup wasn't my strong suit. Hair even less so. I ran a brush through the tangles and gathered it into a high ponytail. Combined with the eyeliner, the effect was pretty badass, if I didn't say so myself.

Nuvian was waiting in the passageway when I emerged. His hair hung over his shoulders in golden dreadlocks, framing a face that could inspire sculptures. He wore the armor I was half-convinced had permanently fused to his body, as I had yet to see him out of it. There were so many Guardians behind him that it looked like a bizarre parade.

"Is it just me, or have you added a few more guards?" I said tightly, thinking of the faeries he'd set loose in my world. But that conversation would have to wait—if I challenged Nuvian now, in front of his warriors, it would only infuriate him.

As always, Nuvian stared at my forehead, rather than meet

my eyes. I could never tell if it was an attempt to guard himself against my power or just a snub. "Per request of the Tongue," he replied.

His tone was curt, bordering on insolence, and I knew Lyari would want me to put him in his place. But I was tired—God, I was tired—and I couldn't bring myself to say anything. "Why?" I asked instead. "Because of the assassination attempts?"

Nuvian didn't acknowledge the question. After a stilted moment, Lyari answered for him. "Whenever there is a shift in power, it sends out a call, of sorts," she said, her voice drifting to me from behind. "Creatures come from other lands and dimensions, responding to it. The Tongue's request is a precaution."

Swords clinked and armor creaked as we made our way toward the throne room. I'd become so accustomed to the dirt and darkness that my mind wandered. "I keep forgetting to ask," I said suddenly, remembering the mystery that had been niggling at me for two days. "What were they? The things I killed by the river, I mean?"

Once again, Lyari was the one to answer. "We don't know, Your Majesty. They were like nothing either of us had ever seen before."

Hearing this, my stomach gave an anxious flutter. Had my coronation brought a new species of Fallen to Granby? What if there were more of them?

"Don't forget about the feast afterward," Nuvian said without looking at me. I stared at him blankly for a moment, still thinking about those strange creatures I'd encountered. When his words did finally register, I almost stopped, right there in the middle of the passageway. *Shit.* I'd forgotten about the feast. It was the Tongue's idea, of course—a way to get back into the fae's good graces. Who could stay mad when you were plying them with free food and booze?

There was no chance to respond to Nuvian, because we'd arrived at the Mural of Ulesse. Every time I gazed up at those violent, colorful paintings, it seemed like I always noticed some-thing different about them. My gaze flitted over a scene of redcaps hunched around a table. The artist hadn't revealed whatever they were eating, but I could guess. A sour taste filled my mouth. I ducked my head and followed Nuvian toward the wide, stone doorway.

A faerie noticed us crossing the room and rushed to catch up. "Your Majesty," he whispered urgently, "I'd hoped to catch you alone. I wanted to say, that is, you must know that I'm utterly in love with—"

I directed a single, irritated glance toward Lyari, who instantly seized the male's arm and yanked him back. My Guardian's low, lethal voice faded behind me as I reached the threshold of the throne room.

The sight that greeted us was vastly different than that of a month ago—I had made some changes in this cavernous space, during my brief time as queen. Gone were the tapestries that once hung on the walls, depicting scenes of fae brutality and depravity. In their place were paintings that had just been gath-ering dust in a vast storage room, which I'd discovered after Lyari mentioned its existence in passing. The colorful images ranged from a meadow, to a herd of elephants, to a great tree, to a pair of shining gates.

Down the length of the room, instead of a blood-colored rug running toward the thrones like a river, I'd put rugs of all shapes and hues. The effect was startlingly cozy. I had also ordered vases of flowers to be placed along the walls and vines to be entwined around the towering pillars of stone. None of which the Court's event planner had been too thrilled about, considering I'd freed the slaves who had once done such work for him.

All I had not changed were the thrones themselves. Collith's still rested beside mine, and it had the feel of a ghost, haunting all the rest of us. My own chair, which wore the face of the

Leviathan I'd killed, also felt like a presence throughout my every edict and decision.

As I settled on the hard seat and raised my gaze, I didn't need a supernatural bond to know that a majority of the crowd loathed me—only their fear of my power kept them in check. Well, that, and fear of Finn, who currently rested at my feet like an oversized dog. Except most dogs didn't have the ability to tear someone's arm off or open their stomachs with a single swipe.

I looked out at them without flinching. It had become second nature to hide every thought and feeling while I was on that dais. Giving someone a glimpse of what was in your mind was giving them power, no matter how little. So, as I appraised tonight's gathering of bloodlines, they had absolutely none over me. But they couldn't say the same. I'd noticed that the females of the Unseelie Court—and some males, too, honestly—came to the throne room wearing outfits eerily similar to ones I'd appeared in. However much they hated me, they envied me. I wanted to tell them it was an illusion, that being beautiful or formidable was mostly just… lonely.

To my displeasure, there were also some battered-looking humans amongst the gathering tonight. My mouth tightened at the sight of them. Despite my having freed the Court slaves, many of them remained anyway, probably because they had no other home or it was all they knew. But good had still come of my new law—weeks ago, I'd gone back to that hole where Annika and the child had been living, but found it empty.

At that moment, Nuvian caught my eye, and I gave him a barely perceptible nod. The sooner we got started, the sooner I could go home, get in my pajamas, and polish off that pint of cookie dough ice cream in the freezer.

The steady hum of voices quickly faded, and Nuvian began his usual speech in Enochian. For the first time, I was able to recognize a handful of words. I'd been studying during my breaks at the bar, and in the woods with Lyari, and before falling asleep every night. Nuvian was saying something about tradition.

Just as he finished addressing the Court, an enormous male moved forward. This was a face I didn't recognize, and I struggled to hide the frown pulling at my mouth. When I wasn't learning their language, I had taken to memorizing bloodlines, photographs, portraits, and anything else I could get my hands on. Even fae who didn't live at Court were in the records I'd consumed.

Whoever he was, this stranger emanated menace. Long, ginger hair hung over a gaunt face. He had hard gray eyes, set deep within their sockets. Every part of exposed skin was covered in what I hoped was crusted mud. He looked like he'd just stepped out of a jungle after a disastrous expedition, and judging from the expressions of faeries standing around him, he smelled like it, too.

I waited for him to bow. Instead, he lifted his bearded chin and met my gaze with open defiance. "There are rumors, Nightmare. They're saying you murdered our king," he said. His voice was made of thunder and earthquakes.

There was an instant of stunned silence, and then the room burst into sound.

Shouts of agreement, speculative murmurs, and cries of outrage bounced off the walls. Finn got to his feet, hackles raised and teeth bared. But if the crowd surged forward, neither he nor the Guardians would be able to save me. Panic gripped me by the throat, and my grip tightened involuntarily on the armrests of my throne. If I didn't act now, the fae might begin to suspect that something was wrong with my powers, or my ability to use them. There would be nothing to stop these creatures from taking their vengeance on me or resurrecting the slave trade.

Some of my subjects had already noticed something amiss—

I caught a female staring at me with an intrigued expression. It was obvious even with the strange, golden flakes covering half her face like tinfoil.

Before I could respond to the stranger's accusation, Lyari's voice rang through the room. "You will use her correct title, Thuridan of bloodline Sarwraek," she called.

Sarwraek? I thought dimly. It felt like the blood in my veins had frozen. While the room quieted again, I stared harder at Thuridan. In an instant, I could see Jassin in his features, and I wondered if he was a brother or a son to the faerie I'd killed. This one's face was wider, his mouth fuller, but they had the same coloring. The same cruel glint in their eyes.

"Or what? You'll cut me down?" Thuridan countered, a note of challenge in the words. He lowered his voice—for dramatic effect, of course, as we were surrounded by creatures with supernatural hearing. "I wouldn't put it past you, of course. We all know your mind will break sooner or later. Like mother, like daughter."

Lyari's expression didn't change, but our bond allowed me to feel the burst of pain this faerie's words caused her. In the time I'd known her, I had never seen Lyari so much as flinch, and I didn't like that someone had managed to hurt her now.

Power, dark and eager, slid through my veins.

"What's your name again?" I asked pleasantly, my hold on the armrests loosening.

Those gray eyes refocused on me. There was no trace of fear or desire within their depths as he replied, "Thuridan, *Your Majesty.*"

"How pretty. Now, tell me, do you have a death wish, Thuridan?" The question only made him quirk a brow. I knew this game was dangerous, potentially catastrophic, but a spark of my old self had flared to life and I couldn't bring myself to snuff it out. I leaned forward, feeling tense and coiled, like a snake about to strike. "This entire Court has seen me reduce your kind to mortals or shells of who they once were. So you *must* have a death wish, because right now, you're really pissing me off."

Even if Thuridan wasn't worried about his fate, the rest of the Court was. Their whispers and murmurs filled the cavernous space. I felt their fear, rising in the air like a heady cologne. I wanted to walk amongst them, nostrils flared, and breathe it in. The large faerie turned and took in his people's reactions. When he faced me again, he finally had the good sense to hide his disdain. His expression became a mask of neutrality. "I didn't mean to offend, Queen Fortuna," he told me in a clipped voice.

"Yes, you did. You're surprisingly bad at this game, though. Are you sure you're related to Jassin?"

Thuridan's eyes flashed. "You dare use his name?"

His tone made Finn growl. The low rumble went through the wolf's entire frame and echoed through the air. Unease finally stirred in Thuridan's eyes. I stood up and descended the uneven steps, my long train dragging behind me. At this proximity, the faerie's smell was so overwhelming that it stung my nostrils. Before he could move back, I grasped his chin between my thumb and finger. His fears came to me like old friends, warm and eager. I waited for the guilt to come, too, but once again there was none. Maybe I really was getting better.

"Unless you want to be skinned alive, which apparently is a fear you have, you will get out of my sight," I told Thuridan calmly. There was a promise hidden within my simple words, and from his reaction, I knew he heard it. "Now."

Thuridan looked at me with fear, arousal, and rage warring in his eyes. He jerked out of my grasp and stormed away. His thundering footsteps—very unlike a faerie—felt like the notes of a song that had only just begun. I returned to my throne and took advantage of the Court's distraction, gesturing to Lyari.

She started to move toward me, but a new voice sliced through the stillness.

"His Majesty, Laurelis of the bloodline Dondarte, King of the Seelie Court!"

No fucking way. My head snapped around just as the sea of fae parted. In the next moment, Laurie was there, striding down the center of the room. Three faeries flanked him, one on each side and one behind. The Seelie King had dressed to impress. Around his shoulders rested a feather shrug, the silky-looking feathers glistening black, green, and violet beneath the light of the chandeliers. He wore no shirt beneath, which allowed the entire Court to see his pale, ridged stomach. His pants were dark and torn in several places, allowing glimpses of the muscled legs beneath. Muscles I hadn't been entirely aware Laurie had. A sword hung at his slender hip, long and silver, like a relic from another time.

What the hell was he doing here?

The Tongue hurried forward as I tried to pinpoint Laurie's motives. It was common knowledge that Collith and Laurelis had a dark past—it had never been explicitly stated, but everyone knew the Seelie King wasn't welcome at our Court. The fact that he'd now come twice in so many weeks had set the fae ablaze with gossip. Once more, their murmurs filled my ears.

"This is not how things are done," the Tongue muttered, keeping his body angled toward me to prevent others from reading his lips. His large forehead shone with perspiration. "In years past, His Majesty sent an emissary. Highly irregular that he's come himself."

Laurie halted at the base of the dais. He arched his head back, looking like he was suppressing a smile. "Greetings to Queen Fortuna, Conqueror of the Leviathan, Challenger of the Fearless, and Slayer of the Undead."

That was a new one. I gave Laurie a frown to convey how

thrilled I was with his addition to my accolades. Already I saw faeries taking note of it, spreading it through the rest of the bloodlines. By sunrise tomorrow, every single one of them would know what the Seelie King had said. Even the ones that lived aboveground.

"What brings you to the Unseelie Court, King Laurelis?" I asked, hoping no one else could hear my heart, beating against the wall of my chest like a fist. Laurie was up to something. *Don't make my life more difficult than it already is, you slippery bastard.*

"I've come to propose peace," the silver-haired faerie announced, his eyes gleaming like newly-hewn diamonds.

"Peace," I repeated. It seemed the safest response. My mind was still racing.

"Indeed. Between our two Courts. An alliance forged out of union."

If I'd thought the fae were loud after Thuridan's display, they were deafening after Laurie's. Either I wasn't hiding my chagrin as well as I thought, or the Tongue had learned to read me, because he leaned close again and said, speaking louder than normal to be heard over the din, "King Laurelis is suggesting a mating ceremony between the two of you, my queen."

My stomach dropped. I leaned away from the Tongue's hot breath, swallowing a curse. Laurie wanted to marry me? What did he get out of it? Why make this spectacle? Well, it would infuriate Collith—that was probably reason enough for him.

The Seelie King was still waiting for my answer. Despite how beautiful he was, I'd never wanted to punch his face more. The room was still buzzing with noise. I opened my mouth to remind Laurie that I was already married.

Then someone tackled him from the side.

I was so startled that I couldn't stop myself from jumping. Finn and Lyari formed a shield on either side of me. Guardians were already rushing forward to intervene. Laurie had recovered quickly, as well, and he was back on his feet when I stood from my throne.

I glanced toward his attacker, but it was a faerie I didn't recognize. As the stranger turned to strike Laurie again, something flashed, and I caught a glimpse of the clunky, dulled ruby on his finger. This I did recognize—the ring from my nightstand. For a few seconds, all I could do was stare with incomprehension. After another moment, Collith's remark about a spell on the ring resounded through my head. The pieces clicked together, and I felt my mouth drop open. *Oh my God.*

It was Collith.

Laurie had put it together somehow, too. It was in his taunting grin, which made Collith dive at him again. They rolled across the flagstones like a couple of teenagers duking it out over a girl. Except, no matter how much I wanted to think so, it wasn't me they were fighting over. At least not just me.

Courtiers scattered to avoid the brawl. Lyari shouted something, but I was too preoccupied to hear it, all of my focus on the two fae kings still beating each other to a pulp. Laurie's nose was obviously broken and blood ran from Collith's split lip.

"If you're not going to kill each other, then take this brawl elsewhere," I called, waving my hand in dismissal. As I started descending the stairs, several Guardians finally caught hold of Laurie and Collith and pulled them apart. My indifference was all for show, of course. I couldn't think of another way to diffuse the situation without starting an outright war with the Seelie Court. I wasn't about to have Collith whipped—although *that* would've been ironic—and I didn't want to remind the crowd of Laurie's question. Removing him from the room completely, without insulting his entire Court, was the only way to go.

Halfway to the side door, I stopped. *Oh, right. The Tithe and the feast.*

I turned back, thinking to handle the crowd, but the Tongue

had beat me to it. His deep timbre echoed through the room. Our eyes met for just an instant, and I had the thought, however foolish it was, that maybe I had another ally in the Unseelie Court. The Tongue nodded at me, as if he'd heard the thought, and refocused on his task.

Holding my head high, I followed a line of Guardians through the door and into the passageway. There, and only there, did I allow my shoulders to slump. The chaos of the throne room subsided into a distant sound, like music playing in another room. I automatically started in the direction of Collith's chambers, and it took several moments to realize that I'd buried my fingers in Finn's fur again. Once again, I didn't pull away.

We'd been walking less than a minute when Nuvian materialized beside me. "We should release the Seelie King, Your Majesty," he said without preamble.

I shook my head. "No. Bring them to Collith's rooms."

Thankfully, Nuvian didn't argue—he just vanished from view. The rest of the journey was spent in silence, because I didn't trust that anything I said would stay private. At Collith's rooms, Lyari pushed the intricate door open and entered first. Like the well-trained little monarch I'd become, I stood outside with the other guards. Seconds later, Lyari reappeared in the doorway and nodded.

I brushed past her, sat on the bed, and waited.

A rumble traveled through Finn as the faerie kings arrived. The Guardians behind them guided the two males to opposite sides of the room. Collith still wore the face of a stranger, and someone had bound his wrists in rope soaked with holy water. Laurie's arms hung freely at his sides, probably because tying him up would've been considered an act of war.

"Cut this one's ropes, please," I ordered the guard closest to Collith. The dark-eyed female pulled a knife out of her boot and moved to obey. Her expression didn't betray any hint of incredulity or reluctance. Whatever his faults, Nuvian had trained them well. A moment later, the ropes fell away, and I saw the skin around Collith's wrists was blistered. He didn't wince or make a sound, though—all his focus was on the faerie standing across the room.

"Leave us," I said without looking away. I was glad to see the cut on his lip was already healing. One by one, every Guardian filed from the room, until only Lyari and Nuvian remained. I peeled my gaze from Collith—or, rather, the brown-eyed stranger the spell had put in his place—and met Nuvian's gaze. "I'm sorry, but that includes you, too."

Outrage flashed across his face, and I knew that if I'd made any progress in gaining his respect, it was gone now. Wiped away in a single moment and a few words. But Nuvian didn't know Collith was alive, and if he stayed in the room, that would change. There was no good excuse I could think of that would appease his pride. I watched Nuvian move toward the door, every movement stiff with fury. My shoulders slumped a bit more, as if another weight had been added to them.

"Are you guys thinking what I'm thinking?" Laurie asked the instant the door closed. He raised his brows and glanced at each of us with an impish gleam in his eyes. "Orgy, right?"

Collith made a sound I would've defined as a snarl, if he were a beast instead of a faerie. "I will burn you alive before I let you have her, Seelie scum."

Never, in all the time I'd known him, had I heard Collith talk like that.

"Do you both feel better now?" I asked, standing up. Neither of the males replied or even glanced in my direction. I rolled my eyes and turned toward the wardrobe—I wanted to get out of this damn gown. In the mirror, I caught Lyari's bewildered frown and realized she had no idea that it was Collith standing between us. Without a word, I strode over to him and held out my hand.

His gaze flicked to me for an instant before he removed the ring, dropped it in my palm, and refocused on Laurie. The illusion faded immediately, revealing Collith's austere features. Lyari grabbed her sword and swore.

"You only want her for her power," Collith said, ignoring her. His voice was quiet now, and somehow, this seemed even more threatening.

Quick as a blink, Laurie was grinning again. "Hello, pot. Allow me to introduce myself—I'm the kettle."

Collith uttered a low oath just before he sifted. He reappeared across the room, right in front of Laurie. This time, I wasn't caught off guard—I rushed across the space. Just as Collith brought his arm back to strike, I caught it in my hands, startling him. The ring fell to the floor with a hollow sound and bounced off into the darkness. We stared at each other, our faces inches apart. His cool breath touched my cheek. Power rolled off him in waves, alluring and frightening all at once. It stirred the power within my own veins, a piece of me that had been dormant these long weeks, like someone in a coma. It felt like the rest of the room faded into darkness, leaving only me and Collith, the connection between us crackling like something bright and palpable.

Laurie made a delicate coughing sound.

The stillness shattered like a thin pane of glass. I let go of Collith and stepped back. My face was hot and it felt like a chasm had opened beneath me. I remembered that I was furious at both of them. "*Now* will you tell me what happened between you two?" I snapped, moving to retrieve the ring. This thing was like a bad penny.

Neither of them spoke. I looked back and forth, studying their expressions. Collith's eyes were dark with fury and... pain. It was buried deep, only visible to someone who'd seen it before. When I turned to Laurie, I saw that his face echoed this, along with a hint of defiance.

Maybe Collith's anger was too close to the surface. Maybe he'd come back a little different from Hell. Or maybe he didn't like that I noticed Laurie's pain, too. "He's the one that gave King Sylvyre the spell that's slowly murdering my mother," Collith said flatly.

My eyes widened.

"To be fair, I thought he was planning to use it on you," Laurie countered, giving me no chance to react. He smiled at Collith, but there was nothing teasing about this one. Seeing it sent an instinctive quake of fear through me—sometimes I forgot how powerful Laurie truly was. That was probably by design on his part. He was so pretty, so teasing, like the magician that waved one hand while he worked his trick with the other. Laurie's eyes glittered as he crooned, "Shall I tell her your secrets now, dear one?"

A muscle flexed in Collith's jaw, and suddenly I could sense his fear. It was faint, barely more than a whisper in my ear, but it must've been much more—normally, Collith's mental shields were firmly in place. There was something he desperately didn't want me to know.

Hoping Laurie would go on, I looked at the other king. The knowledge that he was responsible for Naevys's fate didn't surprise me, exactly, but the ruthlessness of it did frighten me. What would Laurie unleash if *I* ever pushed him too far?

I reminded myself that Collith's revelation couldn't be all to the story. However devious and arrogant he was, Laurie wasn't evil. I knew that sort of darkness intimately now.

My mind shied away from the thought like a skittish horse.

Feeling nauseous, I refocused on Laurie, who'd apparently decided to keep Collith's secrets. "Let's talk about earlier. Did you seriously *propose* in the throne room? Thank you so much for dropping another problem into my lap. Now I have to worry about offending your Court with my rejection."

"It was just another attempt to harm me," Collith said through his teeth. "To take something that matters to me."

Silence swelled in the room after he spoke. The words replayed in my head for at least a minute. *Something that matters to me,* he'd said. Present tense.

I kept waiting for one of the kings to say something else. Whatever happened all those years ago, it had resulted in consequences I still didn't fully understand. One moment Laurie was telling me that he wanted to keep Collith safe, and the next he revealed that he'd been the one to scar him. He took every opportunity to taunt and annoy Collith, and yet, he obviously still cared about my mate. *Not mate,* that small voice reminded me. What was he to me now, then? My... friend?

Not exactly important right now, Fortuna.

"I was protecting her," Laurie declared, finally answering the unspoken question hovering over all of us. I frowned at him, and his gaze darted to mine. I saw nothing in those blue depths that could tell me whether he was being truthful, for once. He returned his attention to Collith and added, "Since you're officially 'away' from Court, she appears unclaimed. The wolves are circling her, kingling."

Collith's clenched hands began to glow. "Don't call me that."

"All right," I cut in, sounding as exasperated as I felt. Lyari's grip tightened on her sword and Finn moved slightly in front of me. "I'm not a licensed therapist, so it's doubtful you two are going to resolve this tonight. Laurie, thanks for the half-assed proposal, but no thanks. Collith, you're not fooling anyone, okay? This isn't about me, so next time you feel the urge to steal my jewelry and start a brawl during the Tithe, how about you suppress that urge? Laurie seems like the type of guy who responds to texts pretty fast—maybe try that first."

With that, I finally grabbed a change of clothes from the wardrobe and went behind the privacy screen. There was no zipper or laces, only buttons, and it took a minute to undo each one. It would've been much easier to ask for help, but it had become important to do things on my own, no matter how small they seemed. Eventually the gown pooled around my feet, and the absence of its weight felt freeing. Suppressing another sigh, I reached for the pile of folded clothes.

By the time I re-emerged, wearing jeans and a quarter-sleeved shirt, holding the ring in my fist, Collith and Laurie had returned to their original places on opposite ends of the room. Something in the Seelie King's face shifted at the sight of me. His voice was noticeably lower as he asked, "Are we finally going to get on with that orgy I—"

"I think it's time for you to go," I said quickly. To emphasize my point, I went to the door and opened it. Laurie smirked but didn't argue. He sauntered up to me, the ridges of his stomach moving with every step. I pressed my back against the door, partly to avoid him and partly to let him pass.

"You're wrong, by the way," Laurie said. As he drew even closer, his entire body emanated a delicious-smelling warmth. He pressed his chin against my temple to whisper the next part. One of the feathers on his throw tickled my cheek. "We were most *definitely* fighting over you."

Before I could tell him it had been a waste of their energy and time—two grown males resorting to a fistfight was hardly what I'd call sexy—the silver-haired trickster pulled one of his vanishing acts.

Relief expanded within my chest. This time, I allowed myself a deep, long sigh. In doing so, my palm tightened around something. Frowning, I glanced down and remembered the ring. The gauche jewel gleamed dully. My gaze jerked back to Collith, and I started to demand why he'd come to Court wearing it. But his attention had wandered, and I knew, somehow, that he was thinking about his mother. Toying with the idea of visiting her. Slowly, my ire faded.

"You can't," I told him, talking to him like I would grieving

Emma or cautious Cyrus. "Not unless you're ready for the entire Court to know you're back—even if you wore the ring, you could be overheard or questioned. But I can go see her, if that would make it better."

"All right. Thank you." He looked at me, and though he didn't smile, there was a gentleness in his eyes that felt like one. Something inside me responded to it, and I couldn't think of what to say. Collith spared my dignity by sifting, doubtless going back to the barn he spent so much time in these days.

There were only three of us left in the room now. Since the Tithe and its subsequent feast had been effectively canceled—or more likely, rescheduled—I reached for my coat. As I pulled it on, I raised my eyebrows at Lyari. I hadn't forgotten about what Thuridan said in the throne room. *We all know your mind will break sooner or later. Like mother, like daughter.* "Remind me again why you're hiding the true extent of your power? Knowing you're not a lower caste of fae might get assholes like Thuridan off your back. The cowardly ones, at least."

She just opened the door for me, exactly as she had at the start of the night. I glowered and walked out. Faeries and their fucking secrets.

I didn't tell the Guardians where we were going—they knew the instant I turned right in the passageway. For the third time that night, I walked through the underground world of the Unseelie Court. Its sounds were familiar to me after weeks of time down here. Moans and cries drifted through the dirt walls. The endless rows of torches trembled and flickered. Once, I'd found it all unnerving.

"You have good instincts," Lyari said matter-of-factly, walking alongside me. This part of the tunnel was wide enough for both of us.

I frowned at her. "What?"

She inclined her head in the general direction we'd come from. "Back there. In the throne room—when those two fought, you acted bored. Like you didn't care one way or the other if they survived. You know your weaknesses, and you guard them closely. That's the mark of a strong leader."

"Or maybe it's just the mark of a strong person," I said. My voice was unexpectedly soft. Lyari glanced at me sharply, and when she saw my expression, a storm rumbled in her eyes. I wasn't talking about myself, and she knew it. Despite everything, I wanted to be this faerie's friend. I liked her, damn it.

Lyari was about to respond when her attention shifted. She moved with preternatural speed as she unsheathed her sword. The other Guardians did the same. Finn shoved his body in front of me, and I was so distracted I almost stumbled into the wall. I regained my balance just in time.

"Show yourself," my Right Hand ordered, her eyes fixed on something farther ahead. The darkness was so profound between the torches that I couldn't see anything.

There was a moment of hushed tension, then a woman stepped forward. I sensed some of the agitation around us begin to fade. She looked to be somewhere within her late twenties and early thirties. Beneath the grime, she was beautiful, with hooded eyes and rosebud lips. Like a small, vibrant bird flying amongst sharp-beaked hawks. Her clothing was decent, at least, and a pair of boots covered her feet. The hawks weren't actively trying to kill her.

"Viessa would like to see you this evening," she murmured into the stillness, addressing me directly.

The fact that she left off my title spoke volumes, but I wasn't sure how. There was something in her expression that sent a chill of apprehension down my spine. I strove to sound unaffected as I said, "Tell her I can't come tonight—I have a previous engagement."

The woman stared at me for a few seconds, as if giving me a chance to change my mind. When I said nothing else, she bowed and retreated.

While the sound of her footsteps quieted to nothing, I stared into the darkness, wondering if I'd just sent another person to their death. What if Viessa lost her temper? What if she thought hurting the human would send a message? However much the faerie in the dungeons had helped me, the truth was, I knew far too little about her. Maybe it was time to change that, especially considering she could call in her debt at any time.

But that time was not now. Battling an onslaught of exhaustion, I continued down the passageway, where it would eventually fork. The right path would lead downward, deeper into the earth, where pain and magic clung to life in the form of Collith's mother. As we once again walked in that direction, Lyari didn't comment on Viessa's request. It probably meant she approved my handling of it—nothing good could come of my bargain with a would-be assassin.

Over the past few weeks, I'd come to this place enough times that I had learned the guards' schedules and rotations. I knew it would be Omar and Úna on duty before the door loomed into sight. I avoided the female's searing gaze. "How is she?" I asked Omar, who no longer cowered whenever I came near.

"It's a good day," he told me with a small, welcoming smile. The response sent a ray of light through my heart. I nodded my thanks and passed through the doorway, touching one of the blue flowers as I went. Lyari stayed behind, but Finn's paws made soft sounds against the packed dirt as he followed me.

When I entered the shadow-filled room, my expression was pleasant. It had taken some practice, because no matter how many times I saw Naevys, the horror struck me anew. It didn't help that the ground swallowed her a bit more every day. The first time we met, her face had been untouched, for the most part. Now delicate roots covered one of her cheeks and brittle moss crawled up the column of her throat.

"Fortuna," Collith's mother said in greeting. It was her way of telling me that she knew who I was. Finn lumbered to the corner, where he laid down and peered at us through half-lidded eyes. I smiled at Naevys and dropped onto the loveseat someone had brought into the room—one of the Guardians must've noticed that I always sat on the ground during my visits. The thoughtful gesture unsettled me, and for once, I knew exactly why. Faeries were not kind. Faeries were not generous. Yet they seemed determined to prove me wrong at every turn.

"What shall we do this evening?" Naevys asked, interrupting my stream of thought.

I lifted my head and mustered another smile. God, I was tired. "We can play chess again. Or you can tell me more stories about Collith."

Naevys gave no response—instead, she searched my expression. There was something unnerving about the steadiness of her gaze, as though, like her son, she saw far more than I meant her to. They had the same hazel eyes, I noticed for the hundredth time.

I was on the verge of fetching the chessboard when, without any warning, Naevys started humming. She closed her eyes and seemed to settle deeper into the earth. She didn't say anything else, and I couldn't bring myself to cut in. The melody had caught hold of me. Haunting, bittersweet, like a story that hadn't ended the way it should've, if the world were fair or kind.

As Naevys filled the air with her soft song, my attention began to drift. I shifted in the chair, thinking to lean my head against the armrest, and something sharp dug into my hip. I grimaced and pulled the goblins' ring out of my pocket. Truth be told, I'd forgotten about it again. I watched the dull, red stones gleam weakly in the firelight, but my mind filled with the scene from the throne room. I saw it on that stranger's finger and relived the burst of disbelief when I realized who was truly wearing it.

Witches' spells had side effects. Consequences. Savannah

Simonson learned that lesson the hard way, but Collith knew better. The fact that he'd put a powerful ring on, unaware of what those consequences would be, spoke volumes on his state of mind. Collith was not the cautious person he'd once been. How else had he changed, since I'd taken his life and destroyed both of us? The thought made my stomach churn. I put the ring back in my pocket and refocused on Naevys.

When I got back to Cyrus's, I'd hide it in a place no one would find.

The faerie in the wall still hadn't opened her eyes, but maybe she sensed my agitation—a few seconds after I tucked the ring away, she started to sing in Enochian. Her voice made me think of the sea. Not the sea on a glittering, beaming day, but on one of those chilly, gray mornings when only seagulls and clouds dared to venture close to it.

There were no clocks down here. No way to indulge in the human habit of always knowing how much time had passed. There was only Naevys's lilting song and the sound of my own breathing. In and out, in and out. The tension seeped out of me, until I found myself resting against the armrest, curled into a ball for warmth.

Despite my resolve—I was going to rest my eyes, nothing more, then I'd get up from this chair and begin the journey home—Naevys's song sent me soaring into slumber's gentle embrace.

CHAPTER FIVE

$\mathcal{I}$ awoke to a fragrant breeze caressing my skin. *Oliver*, I thought with a smile. But when I opened my eyes to see the dreamscape, the anticipation was chased away by a sense of foreboding. I frowned as I looked around.

Everything was picturesque as always. A gentle wind swept over the rolling hills, bending the tall grass like reeds in water. The sky was a periwinkle blue, broken apart by fluffy clouds that looked like something from a painting. In the distance, the sea glittered. I stood beneath the great oak tree, wearing a yellow sundress that crisscrossed over my back. All was as it should be, but something had my instincts whispering, urgent whispers that propelled me forward in search of Oliver. He should've been sitting at the cliff's edge, or standing in the doorway to the cottage.

I started walking toward it, moving like a deer in the crosshairs. My eyes darted in every direction and bumps rose along my skin. It felt like something was watching me, like something else was in this dream with me. I could feel its psyche, somehow, spreading through the meadow like a poisonous mist. It was angry. It was dark. It was *hungry*.

I didn't question my instincts, not when it felt like my very survival was on the line. Something must've been wrong with Oliver—maybe he was having a nightmare of his own. As I hurried to reach the cottage, I realized I was too exposed here, with no trees or structures around. There was nothing but my silhouette and open sky. I may as well have been wearing a target.

In the next breath, I dove to the ground, driven by a burst of panic. The skin at my knees and elbows tore. Pain shot through me, followed by surprise—I rarely experienced pain in this world. Oliver didn't allow it. If I tripped, the earth turned into pillows. If I got a cut, my skin knit back together an instant later.

Breathing hard, I raised my head above the grass just enough to look around. Nothing moved. Maybe I was going insane.

"Fortuna?"

I stayed there, frozen, half-convinced I'd imagined Oliver's voice in my desperation. His shoes appeared in front of me, though, and I arched my head back. A face I knew better than my own peered down, his forehead scrunched with concern. His skin was lightly tanned and his golden hair tousled, as though he'd just gotten out of bed. He wore his white button-up shirt with the sleeves rolled up, and it was stained with fresh-looking paint.

A long breath of relief left my lungs. I accepted Oliver's proffered hand and stood. "Damn. I really am losing it," I said, smiling into his cornflower eyes.

Without warning, he bent down and pressed his lips to mine. I reared back, my hands automatically rising to keep him at bay. "Ollie, what are you doing?" I demanded, resisting the immediate urge to run.

Naked branches stretching overhead. A lonely wind winding through the trees. The sound of a zipper coming undone.

I wrapped my arms around myself and tried to push the

images out. I pictured Matthew's dimpled smile, imagined the smell of Emma's terrible perfume, remembered how Bea and Gretchen always swayed together in front of the jukebox. Then, startling me, an image of Collith filled my mind. I thought of that stubborn lock of hair always falling into his eye.

When I finally refocused on him, Oliver was just staring at me, as though my rejection of him had been completely unexpected.

Then something dark crawled into his eyes.

Terror exploded inside me like a blood vessel. *This isn't my best friend*, I thought dimly. I had no idea how something else would've gotten in our dreamscape, or how it was wearing Oliver's face, but that didn't matter right now.

Despite the urge to *run*, to get as far away from this thing as possible, I stayed where I was. There was only a slight waver in my voice when I spoke. "Why don't we go inside?" I suggested, inclining my head. "I'll cook—nothing from scratch, I promise— and we can talk. Sound good?"

The imposter didn't react. When the silence stretched, I decided to interpret it as acceptance. My heartbeat felt like a series of bombs going off as I turned away and started toward the cottage again. I didn't let myself look back to see if the imposter would follow—I was worried he would see the fear in my eyes.

Inside, I headed immediately for the kitchen. My breathing was ragged as I started opening cupboards. The floor, which had creaked for me, hardly made a sound when the imposter entered and crossed the room. Was he a faerie? But how would he be inside my head, my dream?

It felt like I'd forgotten how to breathe. I pulled a box of spaghetti noodles from the pantry, thinking quickly. This person couldn't have innocent intentions—Oliver's absence was proof of that. He was always waiting when I fell asleep. Always. *Oh my God.* My fingers shook as I pulled a pot out from a drawer. What if this creature had killed my best friend?

No, I couldn't think about that right now. Couldn't even consider it. If I did, I would fall apart into a thousand pieces, and I was barely holding myself together as it was.

Only one thing was clear—I needed to kill whoever the fuck was standing in our kitchen.

It seemed impossible the imposter couldn't hear my pulse as he drew closer. I opened a drawer, hoping this would disguise the sound, and reached for a wooden spoon. He moved so he was standing even closer, his chest nearly touching my shoulder. I breathed even harder as my hand passed over the spoon and reached for a gleaming steak knife instead.

In the same breath, I turned and plunged it into the imposter's gut.

He made a sound of shock and pain, but I was already running. I was almost to the door when it completely disappeared. I hit the wall, gasping, and frantically skimmed my hands over the flat surface as if I could find the door by feel. Invading my dreamscape was one thing, but being able to manipulate it? This was no faerie. I spun—the cottage was dimmer, and I realized all the windows were gone, too—and watched the imposter get up from the floor. There was something pouring out of his wound, but it wasn't blood. Instead, it was smoke. Black smoke.

Despite this, his rage-filled eyes were fixed on me, as if nothing else mattered. I knew I needed to move. *Move, Fortuna.* But there was nowhere to go. I stood there, frozen in panic, and a scream clawed its way up my throat.

Just as the imposter took a step toward me, I finally jolted back into motion, aiming for the stairs. They only led to a loft Oliver used to store his paintings, but there was also a window up there. Somewhere. Buried behind the rows and rows of canvases. Hoping this stranger hadn't known about it, I pounded up the wooden steps and heard the thunder of pursuit behind me.

A hand seized my ankle just as I reached the top.

Now I screamed. It felt like something inside me shattered as he wrenched at my leg and pulled me down. For a blinding, disorienting moment, I saw both the imposter and the demon, their faces overlapping above me. They both had the same cruel glint in their eye and self-assured sneer on their lips.

Dimly, I knew I was still screaming. There was a ringing in my ears, and that was all I heard as I thoughtlessly kicked, bucked, bit, and scratched.

Somehow, though, Dad's voice managed to get through the cloud of hysteria around me. *What are you doing?* he asked, calm as ever. Even now, years later, I could see the glint of light reflecting off his glasses. *You're fighting like a human, Fortuna.*

He was right... and I was no human.

Just as I remembered this, I managed to land a kick to the imposter's injury. Hissing, he jerked back. I knew I had one, maybe two seconds to act.

When the imposter had grabbed me, my dress must have been between his hand and my skin, because I couldn't taste his fears. Not yet, at least. Though every instinct I had recoiled at the thought of touching him, I jerked forward and flattened my palm against the imposter's forehead—I was going to fry his fucking brain.

He mistook my touch as an invitation, somehow, and the imposter rose above me. He started reaching beneath the long skirt of my dress, and I waited to feel his fear for exactly two seconds before delving inside of his psyche. The imposter felt my invasion and snarled, flashing Oliver's perfect white teeth. I barely noticed.

It was one of the strangest minds I'd ever encountered—I didn't even know how to navigate it, much less search for what he feared. If he even had any. This was no maze, as it had been with Jassin, or a fragmented collection of images and sensations, as it had been with the Leviathan. Instead, it was the exact smoke I'd seen coming out of his knife wound. If I couldn't find a fear, then I'd leave one like a twisted gift. What was the enemy of smoke?

Water.

You're terrified of it, I crooned to the imposter. *You're worried it will extinguish you. All you can think about is the fear.*

Slowly, I opened my eyes. The imposter was sitting on one of the steps, his back against the wall. His blue eyes stared vacantly back at me. If I'd had another knife, I would've shoved it in the place where his heart should have been. A swift glance around us showed there was nothing I could use as a weapon. I'd stick to the original plan, then. I wasted no more time getting back to my feet. For an instant, I thought about rushing downstairs to see if the windows or doors had returned. But that was unlikely, since the imposter was still very much alive. Decision made, I hurried up the rest of the stairs.

Just as I reached the door at the top, a sound made me pause.

Not possible, I thought faintly. Dread unfurled in my chest as I turned. The imposter was standing up, his eyes clearing, and even the smoke pouring from his injury had slowed. My influence should've lasted hours, at the least. Usually it outright killed the weak-minded.

Fuck. If it couldn't be destroyed, I had to get out of here, then wake up. The rest I'd figure out later—I couldn't think about Oliver right now.

I finally reached for the doorknob, and thankfully, it wasn't locked. I dove inside and turned the deadbolt, breathing in ragged gasps. When I turned back around, my gaze instantly went to the paintings. They were impossible to miss, facing the door as they were. *Oh, Oliver*, I thought, wasting precious seconds to stare at the canvases in the front row. One was nothing but black streaks, as if Oliver had just dragged his paintbrush up and down for hours on end. The painting next to it was the oak tree we loved so much, but it was dead. The horizon behind it was bleak and starless.

Something was happening to my best friend. Something he'd kept secret from me.

There was no time to look at the rest—behind me, the door swung open. What use was a lock against something that could make an entire door vanish?

Moving in a frantic burst, I rushed across the darkened space and started yanking and shoving at the paintings. Dust flew into the air. The imposter was already behind me, reaching for me, but I kept throwing the canvases at him. He grunted and snarled, and this was more disconcerting than if he had been shouting obscenities or threats. *What is he?*

Then, light.

Before I could reach for the window frame, the imposter tackled me from behind and sent us both to the ground. I landed on my side, sending a jolt of pain through my ribcage, but in less than a second I was trying to get up again. The imposter anticipated this and grabbed hold of my wrists. He moved with the swiftness of something supernatural, and as I attempted to wrench free, something white materialized in his other hand. Ropes, I realized with mounting hysteria.

Okay, I thought with deliberate calmness, going still. My heart hammered in my ears and made it difficult to process anything. Maybe it was time to play along… but what if I wasn't able to get free again? As I fought a silent inner battle, the imposter drew closer and began to loop the first rope around my wrists, making the decision for me. I seized the opportunity to study his face. His breath, cold and metallic, puffed against my cheek. Seconds ticked past, thick with silence, and I finally noticed the differences between this creature and Oliver. They may have been wearing the same face, but they were nothing alike. Where this imposter's mouth was tense and thinned, my best friend's was always full and a moment away from smiling. While this creature's eyes roiled with a dark storm, Oliver's shone with love and strength. Even in his darkest moments, he hadn't become anything like this thing in front of me.

Strangely, comparing the two of them grounded me. My mind was once again capable of forming connections and conclusions. *You can't beat it physically,* I thought, still watching the creature work. He was binding my ankles together now. *You can't outrun it. That only leaves one option—trying to reason with it.*

"You can't keep me here," I said at last. "As soon as I wake up, I'll disappear."

Silence was my answer—the imposter didn't even lift his head. With swift, deft movements, those eerily familiar hands worked at a knot. For a disorienting moment, I could only stare at them, struggling to believe the beautiful fingers that created paintings and pleasure could be doing something so ugly.

I'd never forgotten to breathe before, but when my head started to feel light, I realized why. I took a breath, then slowly released it. "Okay," I said. "Maybe I can help you. But in order to do that, I need to know what you want. So... what do you want?"

At this, the imposter raised his golden head. He still didn't speak, but there was an answer in his blue eyes. Me. He wanted me. Terror filled my throat and I braced myself to start struggling anew.

Something moved over its shoulder.

My eyes widened when I registered what I was looking at. It was Oliver—the *real* one. He wore only jeans, because what remained of his shirt couldn't really be called that anymore. My best friend's face was hard, and without an instant of hesitation, he swung a baseball bat directly into the imposter's head. The other male made a strange, disjointed sound of pain, then toppled over.

"He won't be out long," I rasped. "He didn't slow down when I stabbed him or used my powers."

"Don't worry about it. You're safe now." A knife conjured in his hand, and he immediately put it to the ropes. The sharp ridges of Oliver's stomach flexed as he knelt in front of me.

"What do you mean, 'don't worry about it'? Do you know how he got in?" I demanded. Now that our lives weren't in imminent danger, I looked Oliver over more closely, needing to know he was all right. But the sight of him wasn't reassuring—there were cuts all over his body, some half-healed, others still bleeding. Both sides of his face were bruised and swelling. *He's been tortured*, I thought faintly. Apparently the wounds had been deep enough that even Oliver couldn't heal them right away. He was also cutting my ropes, instead of making them disappear. Frowning, I looked at the creature wearing his face, still out cold, and back at my best friend.

Something about this creature makes him vulnerable. I found the thought more terrifying than anything else that had happened tonight. In my mind, Oliver had always been invincible—he could command earthquakes or part the ocean with a single gesture. The notion that he could be harmed, by something other than my own selfishness, made my insides clench like fists.

Just as the ropes around my wrists fell away, the imposter stirred. I couldn't jump up or run, because my ankles were still bound. "Ollie," I said, a warning in how I said his name.

Quicker than my eyes could track, he spun toward his doppelgänger. "If you touch her again, I will *end* you. Damn the consequences," Oliver growled. All I could see was the back of his head, but something in his voice made my breathing falter.

The imposter must've heard the same thing, because he shrank back like a browbeaten child. As he crept away, Oliver turned back to me.

"What are you? What do you want?" I called after the retreating figure, emboldened by my best friend's warm presence. He didn't acknowledge my questions, but I was staring at the shadow his body cast across the floorboards. There was something off about it. Horror sliced through me when I realized what I was looking at. Wings. This creature's shadow had wings.

Before I could convince myself it was a trick of the light, the imposter descended the stairs and out of sight.

"It won't understand you," Oliver muttered, keeping his head bent. He continued sawing at the ropes. "It can only imitate. Did it say something to you?"

"Just my name. Why are you saying 'it'? Why aren't you telling me anything?" The ropes around my ankles loosened and fell. I stood up and the world tilted. Oliver's hand cupped my elbow as I waited for the loft to right itself. I felt high from the adrenaline, almost giddy, but I knew a crash was coming. When I could see again, I fixed a glare on Oliver. "And if he can't understand us, why did *you* talk to him?"

He didn't let go of me—I could feel the warmth of his fingers through the thin cotton of my dress—but he'd never felt farther away. "It's different when I talk to it," he said.

"What? Why?"

"Come on. We should get out of this attic," Oliver said, avoiding my gaze. He put his arm around me, tucking it firmly against my lower back, and I didn't jerk away. Instead, I leaned into the touch, overwhelmed with gratitude that he was alive. Losing Oliver... it was unimaginable.

How fucked up was that?

Rain began to pound against the roof. I followed Oliver down the narrow stairs, pushing every thought away except for what I wanted to know about the imposter.

Downstairs, the air was bitterly cold—Oliver's emotions must've been too strong, for his control to be wavering like this. My summer dress was replaced by pajama pants and a thick sweater. My feet were covered in fuzzy socks. Oliver knew, of course, that I preferred them over slippers.

This small detail felt like a paper cut on my heart. While he went to the kitchen, I settled in one of the plush armchairs and reached for the wool blanket hanging over the back. A fire flickered to life in the grate beside me, and when I saw that I started to breathe normally again—Oliver seemed to be getting back to normal, at least. He returned a few minutes later and pressed a warm mug into my hands. A cautious sip told me it was hot chocolate. Real hot chocolate, not the powder that came in white packets.

Once Oliver was seated in the chair across from mine, I raised my gaze to his and asked the question we'd both known was coming. "What was that thing, Ollie?"

Shadows danced over his face. Though it was unnecessary, Oliver stoked the fire with a poker. It was then I realized he hadn't changed his clothing, as he'd done for me. I had been his only thought, as I always was.

"It's difficult to explain," Oliver said after a notable pause.

One of the logs shifted and sent up a smattering of sparks. My voice was flat. "Try."

But he was silent. I didn't press him, because we both knew the truth was inevitable this time. There was no hiding from what had happened tonight. Seconds ticked into minutes, and I kept waiting.

"It happened around the time my paintings disappeared," Oliver said finally. His eyes were dull with remembrance. As he spoke, he still didn't look away from the flames. "This... terrible pain went through me. All I remember is collapsing face-first into the grass. I couldn't breathe, couldn't think past the agony. When it finally stopped, I pushed myself up and came face-to-face with it. My shadow self."

Damn it. His words made me want to scream. My fault, this was all my fault. I had seen the change in him. I had *known* something was wrong. When that butterfly bit me, I should've confronted him. And when I'd sensed the shadow's presence once, heard the rustle of nearby leaves, Oliver had avoided my eyes then, too. *A deer, I think,* had been his reply when I mentioned it.

"Why does it have wings?" was all I said.

Oliver shook his head. His mouth was a thin, dark slash. "I don't know."

Through the wide window closest to the door, I stared toward a distant copse of trees, sensing the shadow's malignant presence there. Lightning flashed, revealing that my instincts had been right—I caught a glimpse of its shape, out there in the storm. It was turned in our direction. My first thought was to destroy the creature, somehow. But if that thing was part of Oliver, it might kill him in the process, too. *Damn the consequences,* Oliver had said when he'd threatened to obliterate it himself.

Killing it wasn't an option, then.

"Does it want to kill me?" I asked suddenly, thinking of tomorrow night, and the night after that. How would I ever fall asleep again, knowing a monster awaited me on the other side?

"No." Oliver's voice was hoarse, his tone fierce, and I believed him. Thunder rumbled beneath the ground and through the air. This time he didn't look away when our eyes met. Before I could say anything, Oliver went on. "It's like an animal—its instincts are primal. What did the shadow do when you entered the dreamscape? It tried to connect with you. It claimed you. It hid you from me."

If he was trying to be comforting, his words had the opposite effect. I held my mug tighter and said with forced cheer, "Well, that's perfectly creepy."

But Oliver didn't laugh or smile. His sadness so poignant that I was the one to lower my gaze, thinking for the thousandth time that I was responsible for it. That I was responsible for hurting a lot of people, lately. Remorse filled my throat, making it impossible to speak for a few seconds. When I was able to again, it sounded as though someone was strangling me. "Why didn't you talk about what was happening, Oliver?"

He hung the poker back on its stand. Without another word, Oliver got to his feet. I watched him walk to the door, open it, and stride into the rain. Maybe he thought I wouldn't pursue him because it was wet and cold out there.

Guess you don't know me as well as you think. Growling, I set the hot chocolate down on the coffee table and stood up. The blanket pooled on the floor. I crossed the room soundlessly, my footsteps muffled by the thick socks. As soon as I reached the threshold, the rain came to an abrupt stop. This small kindness —Oliver considering my needs, even while I was actively furious at him—only increased my determination to unbury the truth. After glancing around for the shadow self, who seemed to have disappeared, I sought the horizon. There was Oliver, sitting at the edge of the dreamscape, in the same spot he always was.

For some reason, the sight of his familiar silhouette, so slender against the moon, made my ire fade. There was a pair of boots near the door—my size, of course—and I pulled them on. After that, I left the cottage's warm glow behind, walking through damp grass and squelching mud.

As I'd done thousands of times before, I sat down next to my best friend. He kept his attention on the churning sea. White, frothy waves appeared, vanished, and reappeared, almost like an eerie bright-toothed smile. My question hovered between us like a ghost. *Why didn't you talk about what was happening?*

Oliver watched the water as he said, "Probably for the same reason you won't tell me about that deal you made."

My stomach dropped. I stared at his profile, feeling like I might vomit. He knew. Of course he knew. Oliver was many things, but he wasn't an idiot, and there were only so many ways to bring back the dead. I didn't bother trying to deny it. "Did you…" I swallowed and tried again. "Were you watching?"

He threw a blade of grass at the horizon. "I felt it. Usually I can block you out, but your emotions were too strong that night. When you told me Collith had died, then you said he was back, it wasn't hard to put the pieces together."

I didn't miss that he hadn't answered my question, but this time, I let it go. There was a tightness in my chest that wouldn't —couldn't—allow me to ask him again. The silence between us lengthened, until it felt like we were a thousand miles apart, two strangers standing on far ends of this dream world.

"I think I want to wake up now," I said instead. I knew I was running again, but staying would only bring more sorrow.

Oliver didn't reply—he just stared into the storm. The wind ruffled his hair like playful fingers. He looked so alone, so forlorn, that part of me wanted to lean over and wrap him in my arms.

This was *Ollie*. He had been there for every moment of grief, every pang of frustration, every second of uncertainty. He'd loved me as a boney twelve-year-old and loved me as I became a flawed, broken person. Love like that didn't come along often. Love like that was what Fallen and humankind had been killing for, since the dawn of our creation. Yet here I was, causing him unimaginable pain.

I want to wake up now. I want to wake up now. I want to wake up now. I chanted it in my head, over and over, squeezing my eyes shut. Oliver didn't try to stop me. His sadness felt like a knife, buried deep inside me, as the dream faded away and I descended into darkness.

CHAPTER SIX

A week later, Emma came into the kitchen and announced we were eating outside.

"It's kind of cold out, Ems," Damon ventured. He stood at the counter, slicing some carrots for Matthew. My nephew sat in his high chair, making meaningless sounds and staring at his fingers. I'd just started pouring myself a bowl of cereal. At Emma's declaration, I paused.

His response made her eyes narrow. "Children need fresh air every day, Damon. To be frank, you look like you could use some, too. Didn't Matt's mother pack him a coat?"

"Matt?" I echoed, setting the cereal box down. "Is that what we're calling him now? I like it."

"*Matthew* does have a coat, yes," Damon muttered, shooting me a look of warning. To cover a laugh, I made a face at Matthew and handed him a Cheerio.

Five minutes later, I found myself setting some lawn chairs in a circle while Collith got started building a fire. Daylight was fading fast, and he moved with swift grace. I watched him from the corner of my eye, thinking that we hadn't really spoken since the scene he'd made at Court. The goblins' ring was now hidden in my bedroom vent, and Collith hadn't asked about it once.

Cyrus was watching him, too. Or, rather, watching the small flames Collith had coaxed into being. He edged away and muttered something about firewood. Damon entertained Matthew by drawing pictures in a patch of mud. Emma started readying brats to roast. Finn wasn't amongst us, for once, which meant he was probably off on a hunt.

The sun had finished its descent by the time everyone was seated. Finn loped through the trees just as we opened the package of raw brats. Weeks ago, I would've looked at Emma and Cyrus and tried to gauge their reactions to his arrival, but now I just picked up a roasting stick. The humans never seemed to notice that our roommate, Finn, was remarkably absent every time my dog came home. My dog who had, strangely, never been given a name.

But the two of them knew *something*. Emma had seen were-wolves and zombies on the day Fred died, and Cyrus had known exactly what Nuvian was when he came to the house. There was also the fact that both humans witnessed Collith die and come back to life. Yet, despite all this, Cyrus and Emma never seemed worried or curious.

There will be plenty of time for that later, the old woman had said when I tried to tell her the truth. Maybe she didn't want her entire world to change. Or maybe Emma thought she had most of the truth, and she'd explained away some of the things they witnessed that day. Did I have any right to rob her of that? Or did I have an obligation to?

And as for Cyrus, well, he'd always preferred to stay out of things.

The werewolf padded toward me and I noticed blood on his snout. It had been a good hunt, then. Seeing that made a knot inside me loosen. At least I'd done one thing right—despite everything that he'd been through, in his own way, Finn was happy. As happy as someone could be who had lost his entire family.

The fire crackled merrily, reaching for the waking stars with luminescent fingers. Collith had claimed the chair to my left and Emma the one on my right. Damon and Matthew sat on the other side of the flames, with Cyrus between us. The only one missing was Lyari—she must've had plans, for once, or knew I was with Collith. Everyone held a roasting stick, and soon enough the smell of cooking meat filled the air.

I kept glancing around, feeling flutters of childlike wonder. Even now, weeks after Emma and Damon's return into my life, I was surrounded by family and still had trouble believing it. We were safe. We were going to be okay. That's all anyone ever wanted, really. It felt too good to be true.

My gaze landed on Collith again. He seemed unaware of anything beyond the fire, and the hollows of his cheeks looked deeper in the flickering light. I was still staring when he put the beer bottle to his lips. I frowned and turned my focus back to the brat. Maybe the drinking didn't mean anything, or maybe Collith was finally stepping off the precipice he'd been on since his resurrection.

A strange impulse stole over me. I moved slowly but deliberately. Without looking away from the food, I reached over and tugged at Collith's arm. I felt him looking at me, probably wondering what the hell I was trying to do. I tugged again, and he realized what I wanted—his arm dropped to the space between us. I wrapped my fingers around his, more tightly than I meant to, but Collith didn't utter a sound of complaint. He went on watching his own brat as if nothing had changed, his grip cool and gentle.

Matthew lost interest in us and wandered around the yard. Every few minutes, he returned to my brother and showed off his findings. A red leaf, a rock, a fistful of mud. Damon made a rueful sound and tried to clean the toddler's fingers off.

Our small group sat like that for a time, surrounded by frost and a slumbering sky, plumes of breath rising into the air. The stillness was eventually interrupted by my growling stomach. From his spot on the ground beside me, Finn's long ears twitched. He gave me a long, pointed look. "Will you calm down? I don't eat raw meat like *some* people," I informed him primly.

Finn sneezed to communicate what he thought of this. Humoring him, I brought my brat closer and saw that it was ready. Ignoring an unnerving pang of reluctance, I finally let go of Collith's hand to retrieve one of the plates. The faerie king leaned forward in his chair, propping an elbow on the armrest. Easily accessible, I noted, on the chance I wanted to reach for him again. Strands of his hair stirred in a breeze.

"How does it work, exactly?" Emma murmured, startling me. I turned to look at her, but she was watching Matthew, whose delighted giggle floated over to us. "Will he be... like you? Like your family?"

Once I'd recovered from my surprise that she was actually acknowledging our secret, I thought about her question. It was the same one I'd seen in Damon's eyes almost every day. The same one I often asked myself, as well. I couldn't deny it—I liked the idea of Damon and I no longer being the last Nightmares. But if Matthew was one of us, he would pay the price we all did. The constant invasion of other people's privacy. Knowing that almost everyone you met would never see your true face. Always wondering whether someone truly loved you or if they were just beneath your spell. And that was just the beginning.

Of course, there was also the fact that Matthew might be like his mother, which was terrifying in an entirely different way. What did any of us know about how to raise a warlock?

"Actually, I have no idea," I admitted. My brat was tucked into a bun now. Steam rose from it, taunting me, and I searched for the ketchup. It must've fallen out of the plastic bag we'd used to carry out the supplies. "Our kind doesn't usually… intermingle. Mom and Dad never covered it during their lessons, either."

The moment I finished speaking, it occurred to me that Collith might know. He'd been anticipating this, because his voice floated past me before I could move. "He could be either, or he could be both. There's no way of knowing until his abilities start to manifest. There isn't much literature on the topic, unfortunately," he concluded.

Collith didn't seem to be worried about Cyrus overhearing this. I glanced toward the fry cook, dreading the confusion I'd probably see in his eyes—I had hoped to move out soon, once I found the right place, and avoid any conversations about the shadow world that existed alongside his. Thankfully, Cyrus seemed to be lost in thought. He turned his brat over the heat, its brightness reflecting in his eyes. His red hair gleamed even redder, and sitting there like that, he looked like some vengeful god.

Emma made a speculative sound, drawing my attention back to her. The old woman's lips twisted in thought. She didn't seem worried about Cyrus discovering the truth, either. "Can't exactly Google it, I suppose," she mused.

Despite my concern about Cyrus, I started to laugh. At the same moment, I caught sight of something in Matthew's hand, and the laughter at the back of my throat slowly died. Damon was frowning, too. He opened Matthew's small fingers to peer more closely at what he held. "I'm not sure what that one is, buddy."

"It's a wood anemone," I heard myself say. Suddenly I felt very, very cold. I couldn't look away from those gleaming petals in the center of Matthew's palm. It couldn't be a coincidence that the flower kept appearing—plants carried power and meaning, and they were often used in witches' spells. If that was the case for this one, it was highly unlikely it was for protection. But how could I stop whatever was coming? How could I make sure my family wasn't caught in the crossfire during this war?

When I finally managed to look at him, Collith's expression was grim. Before I could ask him if he knew anything else about it, Lyari materialized beside me. All thoughts about the flower faded—for now, at least—and I arched my head back to look at her. Her brown eyes were black in the firelight.

Grateful I was turned away from Cyrus, making it easy to assume I was talking to Collith, I held back a sigh at her expression. "Another one?"

Lyari nodded and stepped back, giving me room to stand. I reached for my new gloves, which I'd abandoned on the ground in order to eat. Collith held my plate as I pulled them on. He tried to give it back once I was finished.

"Keep it," I said, careful to keep my gaze away from his too-thin frame. "I don't want to get grease on my gloves."

The faerie's expression told me he wasn't fooled for a second. I turned away and cleared my throat to get Emma and Cyrus's attention. They couldn't see Lyari, considering if she were to sift in front of them, it would prompt questions I'd been avoiding. They looked at me, and for a split second, I thought I saw Cyrus's gaze dart toward Lyari.

It was dark, firelight and shadows playing across his face—his eyes were nearly impossible to see. Or at least, that's what I told myself.

"I'm going to... a party," I said, hating the lie, hating myself for giving it to them. "Someone who lives down the road is throwing it. Don't wait up for me."

"So many parties lately. Our Fortuna is popular," Emma told Cyrus with a conspiratorial nod.

I rolled my eyes and left the warm glow of the campfire. Finn was instantly at my side, his ears perked forward, eyes bright and alert. Lyari had already started toward the woods. I followed her, scanning the line of trees in search of movement, but Nuvian's warriors were well-hidden tonight. In the past week, I'd only caught sight of someone twice, and it wasn't for lack of trying. It had become a game, of sorts. A way to distract myself from the grim reality that was my reign as the Unseelie Queen.

Tensions had been running even higher since Thuridan's public accusation. The fae were also still feeling the loss of their slaves. I'd lost count of how many tribunals had been called, but whether they were meant to irritate me or simply because the bloodlines were turning on each other, I couldn't say. A council meeting had been set for later in the week, probably to discuss what a terrible job I was doing as their ruler.

When I'd asked Nuvian why I should give a flying fuck what some old farts thought, he charitably reminded me those old farts on the council had the ears of their bloodlines. And if too many bloodlines decided to revolt, I would not survive it. Collith wouldn't have a throne to reclaim, if they put someone else on it.

"Looks like I'm going to a council meeting, then," I'd muttered in defeat.

Now Lyari, Finn, and I wove through the forest of naked trees. The journey had become so familiar that I'd forgotten to be afraid of every sound or shadow. I looked around and didn't see Savannah's zombies, coming at me through the darkness. My mind didn't flash to the night I'd been taken by those goblins. These days, I thought mostly of my runs with Finn, the walks with Lyari, watching Damon show his son an herb or some other useful plant hidden beneath the snow. I would never feel the warm kinship I'd felt before—dark experiences inevitably changed the place where they'd happened forever—but I had managed to make peace here.

It was fully nighttime when we filed through the door and entered the Unseelie Court. In Collith's rooms, I went through the motions of getting ready. I picked out an elaborate gown, put on a layer of makeup, and placed the strange crown on my head. The sapphire came out of its hiding place in my pocket, and I secured the clasp with the confidence of something I'd done many times before.

When I saw myself in the long mirror, the dress had the effect of fire, like the one I'd been forced to leave behind tonight. For this. For the *fae*. The hem was white, but as the dress went on, it transformed from pink, to red, to black. My arms were exposed, which was my favorite feature. I liked my arms—they were well-defined from hours of holding heavy trays aloft. My hair hung free in soft waves.

From his usual spot on the floor, close to the door, Finn huffed his approval. "Thanks," I said with a faint laugh.

Ready at last, I emerged into the passageway and my unsmiling battalion marched me onward. Along the way, I caught one of two Guardians glancing at me beneath their lashes. I hid a faint pang of disappointment. The fae were accustomed to beauty, and I'd been among them for several weeks now—maybe part of me had hoped they'd eventually see my true face.

At least Úna was not amongst them. Her obsession had only intensified since our first meeting, and it was a relief not to feel her eyes boring into the back of my head.

In the doorway of the throne room, I immediately noticed the scent of fried meat in the air. Tonight there was a long table along the right wall—the Tongue's orders, probably, as a way to fulfill our promise for a feast. Honestly, it wasn't a terrible idea. Food steamed on silver platters, and the floor was already covered in scraps and messes. No humans to clean it up, of course, so now it would probably remain there and rot.

I returned my gaze to the gleaming throne waiting for me. Finn had reached the dais already. The fur along his spine stood on end as he sat. By now I had the number of stairs memorized, but I still counted them silently, a way to keep the nerves at bay.

At the top, I sank onto the hard chair and lifted my gaze. *All right. Here we go again.*

There were two figures standing at the bottom of the steps— both of them wore haughty expressions and clothes that boasted wealth. Rings shone on their fingers and the males' hair fell to their slender hips in straight curtains, the mark of faeries that had been brought up at Court, rather than amongst the humans. Looking at them, I knew it was going to be a long night.

My stomach complained again, reminding me that I hadn't gotten a chance to take a single bite of my brat.

As the room quieted, Finn walked away from the dais. I tried to hide my surprise—the werewolf had never left my side down here. He approached the buffet and jumped up, leaning his paws on the edge of the table. I watched him take something, then drop to the floor again. The wolf's nails clicked on the stone floor as he returned to me. There was something in his mouth, but I couldn't see it until he dropped it in my lap.

I stared down at the small, golden thing in my hands. *He brought me a honey bun.* Despite the tension in the air and the number of eyes on me, I couldn't hold back a smile. "Thank you," I whispered to the werewolf.

He sneezed and returned to his spot at the right of my throne. As he sat and faced the crowd, the sight of him sent a gentle warmth through me. The starving creature I'd first met, who had worn a chain as a leash, was gone. In its place was a tall, thick-limbed, bright-eyed beast that even I would hesitate to cross.

Feeling a fresh wave of resolve, I focused on the males waiting for me to speak. The proximity allowed my essence as a Nightmare to wash over them, and while the faerie on the right retained his composure, the one on the left stared at me with glazed eyes. I used their distraction to tuck the honey bun into one of my pockets. "Why have you asked for this gathering? In English, please," I commanded.

They immediately tried to speak over each other.

As I suspected, it was a petty dispute involving money. Struggling to hide my impatience, I made fast work of ensuring they both walked away unhappy. Watching them go, I knew I was collecting enemies like some people collected coffee mugs. I swallowed a sigh as I gathered my skirt and stood. Finn left the dais ahead of me, his nails clicking against the stone.

Just as I reached the bottom of the steps, a child broke apart from the throng and came toward me, holding what appeared to be a jewelry box. She looked like a doll with her pink dress and white gloves. Her brown skin set off her dark eyes, and someone had curled her hair into perfect ringlets. She was the young girl in every horror movie who said something creepy just before the terror began. But I didn't detect any glamour and Finn wasn't reacting to her, so it seemed safe enough to interact. I met the child halfway and knelt on the flagstones, putting us at the same eye level. "Are you all right?"

She looked back at someone for reassurance—probably the female wearing blue silk, lingering at the front of the ever-moving crowd—and faced me again. She said something in Enochian.

"In English, darling," the female called. She didn't seem worried about allowing her daughter close to the evil Nightmare queen, and when I saw that I felt myself soften toward them both.

The child nodded and took a breath. In a high, clear voice she said, "A gift for Her Majesty from the bloodline Daenan."

She curtsied, then raised her head to present the jewelry box. Her heart-shaped face radiated sincerity. Even if her mother's objective was to kiss my ass or gain favor, this girl truly meant what she said. I smiled and reached for their gift.

"Stop, Queen Fortuna!" Nuvian said sharply. He stepped

forward and put himself slightly in front of me. I couldn't see his expression, but there was no softening in his voice as he addressed the child. "There is a hole in your glove, Lady Selussa."

Because of where he stood, I could only see half of the child's —Selussa's—stricken face. An instant after Nuvian spoke, she burst into tears. Sobs wracked that delicate pink-clad frame, and Selussa's mother rushed forward to wrap a protective arm around her. "She didn't know, Queen Fortuna! Have mercy," she cried.

Knowing I probably looked as bewildered as I felt, I turned to Nuvian for an explanation. There were shutters over his eyes as he said, "Lady Selussa is blessed with the ability to bestow death upon anyone she touches."

The Hand of Death. Suddenly their terror made sense. If Nuvian hadn't intervened, my fingers probably would've brushed against the child's as I took the box from her, resulting in my immediate demise.

Something inside me darkened like a stormy sky.

I returned my gaze to Selussa and her mother, who clutched her daughter's shoulders as if I were about to wrench her away and eat her alive. It was a clever game they'd played—using the child had made it impossible to accuse them of outright treachery. I could order the Tongue to work a truth spell on one of them, but Collith's books had taught me there was a reason fae used this as a last resort. Most creatures, fae or otherwise, didn't survive the process. Apparently it was even more grueling than the Rites of Thogon.

And I wasn't sure I could survive another death on my conscience.

Everyone waited for my verdict—most of the bloodlines were gone or still filtering out of the room, but our small drama had caught the attention of a few. I glimpsed a curious-eyed redcap peering out from behind a pillar. A human stood at the table, looking for all the world as though she were there to stack her arms high with food-crusted plates, but she moved too slowly. She'd probably been ordered to eavesdrop by her master.

I put them all from my mind and looked down at Selussa, whose cheeks were streaked with tears. If she had unique abilities at such a young age, it meant she'd probably acquired them through trauma. I wasn't going to be another villain in her story.

"Daenan, you said?" I asked, my voice soft as velvet. The child hiccuped and nodded, the picture of distress. I looked up and directed my next words at her mother. "Rest assured, I will remember your bloodline now."

Recognizing this as a dismissal I'd meant it to be, Selussa's mother instantly pulled her away. I watched them flee, wishing I could justify separating them. As long as the child was within her family's grasp, she would only know corruption and cruelty. I'd probably sent her away to become just like them.

None of these thoughts showed on my face as I turned toward the exit near the dais. With Nuvian leading the way, Lyari and Finn bringing up the rear, we filed through the dark doorway.

Once we were safely out of sight from prying eyes, I stopped. Nuvian noticed immediately and retraced his steps. He stared at the wall behind me, managing to radiate annoyance without dropping his mask of neutrality. It was a fae trait, I realized, and it was exactly what I'd been doing every time I came down here.

Maybe Damon was right. I *was* becoming more like them.

The thought sent a jittery feeling through me, and suddenly I felt uncomfortable in my own skin. I wanted to take it off. I looked up at Nuvian and spoke more sharply than I meant to. "I know that isn't the first time you've saved my life. For whatever it's worth, you have my promise that I will never use my abilities on you again."

The faerie didn't respond, but I hadn't really expected him to. I wasted no time turning my back and hurrying down the tunnel, eager to be back amongst people who weren't trying to kill me. With Finn and Lyari keeping pace every step of the way, I stopped by Collith's rooms to change, then hurried toward the surface. I almost broke into a run twice.

The moment we reached open air, my Guardians spread out. I almost told them not to bother with the pretense anymore, but it occurred to me that I liked Nuvian out of sight. So I said nothing and they melted into the forest like something from a dream. For what felt like the thousandth time in the past month, we began the hike back to Cyrus's through snow and shadow. Lyari walked beside me while Finn trotted off into the darkness.

The night was so still that even the sky seemed to be sleeping. I tipped my head back to see if I could find the moon.

"Soon, Your Majesty, you will have to choose," Lyari said without warning, startling me.

I glanced at her, but she kept her gaze on the trees around us. "What do you mean?"

Lyari stepped over a frozen puddle. Seeing that, I had a flash of memory—my father stepping on a thin sheet of ice, the tip of his dress shoes gleaming. *Doesn't it sound like I'm tap dancing, Fortuna?* I blinked the image back and waited for Lyari to answer. She still pretended to be absorbed in our surroundings as she said, "There's a reason our rulers live at Court, and not in the human world."

I scoffed. "Are you saying I need to give up my family? Leave them behind just so I can keep resolving petty disputes and watch pointless grandstanding?"

Lyari was silent. A stick snapped beneath my boot, echoing through the night like a gunshot, and something about the sound disarmed me. We walked the rest of the way without speaking, and I huddled in my coat, longing for the warmth of my bed. After a time, Cyrus's barn appeared up ahead. In the faint moonlight it was just some faded wooden planks between the trees, but my exhale of relief pooled into the air like clouds.

We'd gotten four steps onto the lawn when, without warning, Lyari whirled to face me. "Is that really what you think of us?" she demanded.

She didn't know it, but Lyari had finally shown her hand—it was obvious she cared what I thought. I stopped, too, and shoved my hands into my pockets. My fingers collided against the honey bun, which I'd completely forgotten about after transferring it from my gown to my coat. An owl hooted somewhere nearby. "No. Not entirely," I admitted. "There are a lot of assholes down there, though."

Lyari's jaw worked. She was so beautiful that she even made a mulish expression attractive. "There are assholes everywhere, Your Majesty," the faerie countered.

"You may have a point." From somewhere nearby, there came the unmistakable sounds of Finn changing forms. Lyari was already swaying on her feet and looked five seconds away from spewing vomit all over me. I fought a smile and pointed at the house with my thumb. "I've got it from here. Pretty sure I can cross the yard without being assassinated."

The sounds paused. Having watched several werewolf transformations, I knew Finn was probably resting. Bracing himself before more of his bones bent and shattered. As the silence returned, Lyari's face smoothed back into its haughty mask. "I thought I'd spend the night."

"Aren't there people you want to see? Spend time with?" I asked bluntly. My mind had gone to all the time she'd spent with me, against her will, because I forced an oath from her in a petty form of revenge. Maybe Lyari saw my sincerity, because something in her expression relented. Then I added, "Hell, go out and get laid, if nothing else. You need it more than anyone."

She glowered at me now, and I couldn't tell if she was serious or not. "You know what? Fine. I hope you're attacked while I'm gone."

"No, you don't," I said confidently. The faerie rolled her eyes and turned away. At the same moment, I remembered what I'd been meaning to ask her since my latest night with Naevys. "Oh, Lyari? Thanks for the chair."

She'd paused when I called her name, automatically resting a hand on that glittering sword. My words made Lyari's brows lower. "What are you talking about?" she called back.

"The one in front of Naevys," I clarified. "Thanks for doing that."

Lyari's confusion faded. She shook her head, the movement barely perceptible in the shadows. "I didn't have anything to do with the chair, Your Majesty. I thought you'd just gotten sick of sitting in the dirt and ordered it to be brought there."

"Oh. Never mind, I guess." A frown flitted across my face. "See you later."

Lyari bowed and walked back into the woods. Watching her go, I wondered why she didn't sift. It could only be that she didn't *want* to. That she preferred the crisp, open air and a vast sky overhead. Maybe the fae had some humanity in them, after all.

Within seconds, she was out of sight. My stomach protested again, reminding me that I hadn't eaten all day. Finn was still silent, which meant he'd either gone inside without my noticing or he was half-naked nearby, trapped between man and beast. I turned around and fixed my gaze upward as I approached the house. The moon directly above me, trapped halfway between this world and the next. Everything was quiet—the air itself seemed to be holding its breath. Keys jangled in my hand and the light sent a soft glow over the night.

Later, I'd think about that moment and wonder what caused me to glance back. Was it a sound? A shadow? No, because I remembered the silence. There were no birds, no wind, no screams. It felt like I could hear my own bloodstream.

Whatever the reason, I did look behind me. The sight made me freeze, my keys dangling from the lock.

The ground was covered in hundreds of white flowers.

At the same moment I saw them, thunder began to shake the world. Frowning, I walked to the edge of the porch and looked up. There were only wisps of clouds overhead. How could there be thunder without any hint of rain? And at this time of year?

Now my gaze snapped to the horizon, where I saw a flurry of movement. I stared blankly at the approaching shapes. After a few seconds, I understood what I was seeing. Horses. Riders. Weapons. They rode through the air like there was solid ground beneath them. I watched the airborne creatures approach and realized I hadn't been hearing thunder all this time—it was dozens of hooves beating at the sky. Hounds bayed and bellowed. Banners flapped in a sudden wind.

The bizarreness of it triggered a memory, and I saw Collith's upturned face, streaked with shadows and moonlight. *A storm is coming*, he'd said. He had just woken from a nightmare and I dismissed the comment, assuming it was the remnants of his bad dream.

It couldn't be a coincidence. Somehow, Collith had known these creatures were coming. He'd caught a glimpse of what hadn't yet come to pass. Why hadn't he warned me?

The answer came at the same moment—it was one of those flashes of intuition that seemed random and wild, but I knew I was right.

Collith doesn't know when he's awake.

At last I understood the strange expression I'd seen so many times after waking him. Confusion. Fear. Collith had been trying to discern between Hell and reality.

But there was no time to mull over this new revelation. I watched the bizarre riders draw closer, frozen with uncertainty.

Should I rush inside and warn my family? Or should I do every-thing possible to keep these newcomers' attention on me? I quickly realized there was no time to warn my loved ones—the figures in the sky had already crested the trees bordering Cyrus's yard. They possessed a speed that even rivaled the fae. I stood on the porch and watched with a quickening heart as the strange visitors landed.

The thunder became an earthquake. I literally felt vibrations in the boards beneath my feet, and it seemed impossible the horses' legs hadn't shattered on impact. I stared out at the yard, open-mouthed, and the proximity allowed me to make out more details.

The horses were like none I'd ever seen before. Massive and rippling with muscle, every single one had a coat of pure white. Seeing them triggered another memory, and this time it was my mother's voice floating through my head as she read aloud from one of her books. *And so they climbed atop their heavenly mounts, banners held high, and rode shouting through the pearly gates.*

The handful of mounts that survived the Battle of Red Pearls had evolved—or devolved, depending on who you were talking to—into kelpies. I'd never thought to question what happened to the rest of those steeds after Lucifer's rebels fell, but now I had the answer.

The herd was still fraught with movement, crushing all those pretty flowers, and they filled the air with their huffs and cries. One of the riders battled for control as his mount tossed its head in wild defiance.

This drew my attention to the creatures sitting atop the heavenly mounts.

Every single one of them wore armor or protective gear, but none of it was the same. I saw the glint of a metal breastplate on one faerie's chest, while a shapeshifter was covered in pieces of hard leather. They looked, I realized, as though they had been picking at the remains of ancient battlegrounds like vultures over a carcass. There was also nothing similar about their species or their looks—I saw a scarred, half-changed werewolf in one saddle and a beautiful vampire in another.

One thing each rider shared in common, however, was the emptiness in their eyes.

Staring at these creatures, and the unearthly scene before me, it seemed impossible that most of the world didn't know magic like this existed.

One of the riders dismounted and came toward the house—she was taller than most females I'd met, human or otherwise. She wore dark leggings and what looked like a brown tunic over them, but the shirt was hidden beneath a piece of metal encircling her middle. It looked thin and rusted, the intricate design whorls or flowers, I couldn't tell which. The skin of a fox hung around her shoulders like a cape. Her exposed arms were tanned and defined, long leather cuffs adorning her wrists. One side of her head was shaved. On the other, the hair was blond and braided back. The upper half of her face was covered in black paint, and maybe that's what enhanced the impossible blue of her eyes. For weapons, a giant bow was strapped to her back and an equally impressive sword hung at her hip.

I recognized her from one of Collith's history books, and apprehension fluttered through me. She was an ancient faerie. She led a band of Fallen called the Wild Hunt.

Gwyn. Her name was Gwyn.

"Well met, Your Majesty," she called as she closed the distance between us. Her voice wasn't what I'd imagined. It was... husky. Young. Like a girl in her twenties, rather than someone born during a time when electricity didn't exist.

Once she was close enough, the faerie held out her hand. Slowly, I went down the steps to meet her. She had to know what I was, and offering a handshake could only mean three things—she was either confident in her ability to shield herself, or wanted me to know she could be trusted, or had the same kink for fear as Jassin once did. There was no risk involved for me, so I wrapped my fingers around hers.

There were no phobias waiting under her skin. There wasn't a single flavor on my tongue. Her mind wasn't a maze, or a place of smoke, or a library. It was a starry sky and open plains. There were no secrets to be found, because there were no shadows or boxes. Nothing hiding or tucked away. All I could learn from invading her mind was that Gwyn had been alive a long, long time, and she didn't think like anyone else.

At first, I didn't understand. I couldn't. It wasn't something I'd ever encountered before, in my long list of victims, but the truth stared back at me without flinching.

Gwyn of the Wild Hunt feared nothing.

Everyone had fears, even creatures like Jassin. The faerie before me was either a sociopath or truly immortal.

I came back to myself, blinking rapidly. Gwyn started to let go, but her thumb lingered, brushing against the delicate skin at my wrist. Butterflies flitted through the small veins she touched. "Sorry, my hand is sticky," I said without thinking, pulling away.

Her lips twitched. "You certainly know how to make yourself memorable."

"Why are you here?" I asked bluntly, unnerved by her and the riders staring at us. All I wanted was to go inside and be warm again.

As if she'd expected a different reaction from me, Gwyn tilted her head. It was a distinctly fae-like movement—I'd seen Collith and Laurie do it many times. "I am here for several reasons, Fortuna Sworn," she said. "One of which being that I wanted to meet you."

I frowned. "Why?"

Her voice lowered, deliberately adding a touch of drama to her next words. "Your name is whispered from every corner. The last Nightmare. The Unseelie Queen."

"I'm not the last Nightmare."

"Perhaps not," Gwyn agreed. Her eyes flicked away. "But I'd hardly consider that sniveling creature worthy of the title."

I followed the direction of her gaze and saw Damon watching us from his bedroom window. He held Matthew in his arms, and the baby's head rested against his chest in deep slumber. I didn't like that Gwyn had seen them. I turned back to the huntress, anger stirring in my stomach like waking hornets. "Watch what you say about my brother."

She didn't bother acknowledging the threat in my voice. Instead, Gwyn inclined her head toward the gathering of Fallen. "Would you like to ride with us?"

Thank God I'd been educating myself on the fae—I knew that to ride with Gwyn meant staying in the Hunt forever, or until death took me from it. "Nice try," I said with more bravado than I felt.

The huntress smiled, and it was that moment I realized she was beautiful. I'd been so absorbed with her fierceness, her otherworldliness, that I hadn't even seen it. She drew closer and a strange smell assailed my senses. Like a skittish horse, I retreated.

"Rest easy, Your Majesty. I have no need of your heart," Gwyn said with another flash of amusement.

"What are you—"

Her fingers brushed my bare breasts. I inhaled sharply, but she didn't seem to notice. "I know the one who wore this before you," the huntress remarked, referring to the sapphire.

Gwyn knew Naevys? I frowned, thinking of all the time I'd spent with Collith's mother in the belly of the earth. She'd never mentioned the huntress, not even when she'd been incoherent. That was either a good thing or a bad thing.

I waited for a beat, hoping Gwyn would go on, but she was done. She studied my face for another moment and then turned away. *That's it?* I wanted to call after her. Something—maybe a rare instinct of self-preservation—kept me silent.

I didn't move as the Wild Hunt lifted into the sky and galloped into darkness. Long after they were gone, I stood on the bottom step, my heart thrumming like a hummingbird. It was the same feeling I got after facing a foe or a monster. But the night was still again, and once it was evident Gwyn had really left, I finally went inside.

Finn appeared just as I was about to close the door behind me. He wore one of the spare sets of clothing I'd hidden for him, and there were bits of gore on his face and hands. His hair was clumped with sweat, dirt, and snow. The werewolf slipped between the narrow opening, his eyes averted from mine, and walked quietly toward his room.

"Finn," I called softly. He paused, turning his head to indicate that he was listening. Weariness came off him in waves—the change was exhausting in and of itself, without the urgency Finn had probably added to it—and somehow I knew he was thinking of his family. Thinking of the last time he'd been too late to save someone he loved.

"You didn't fail me," I told him firmly. "You heard the Wild Hunt arrive, I'm guessing. You couldn't come to me because you were in the middle of a change. It's okay. She didn't hurt me."

"It won't happen again," was all Finn said, then he turned the corner and went out of sight. A moment later, I heard the bathroom door close.

The rest of the house was silent. Emma was probably tired from her recent trip to Denver—packing up the life she'd shared with Fred always made her come back a little sadder, a little quieter. There were no sounds coming from Damon or Matthew, either. I had to pass their room to reach mine, and I paused by the doorway out of habit.

Turning from the window, Damon met my gaze. "Do you know what you're doing?" he asked, his voice pitched low to avoid waking Matthew. He was talking about Gwyn.

"Never," I told him with a rueful smile. "Do you know anything about her?"

Pain flitted across his face, like a shadow cast on the ground by a bird. "I only know what Jassin told me—he was fascinated by her. He said she was the most interesting creature he'd ever met."

"Interesting how?"

Damon shook his head. "If he elaborated, I don't remember."

I was tempted to ask more questions, to keep prodding. It wasn't the right time, though. Shifting my attention to the rosy-cheeked baby in his arms, I moved closer to press a feather-light kiss to my nephew's temple. He smelled like children's shampoo and good dreams. "Good night, Matt," I whispered.

"*Matthew*. His name is Matthew," Damon hissed, but I was already hurrying back into the hallway and out of earshot.

As I moved in the direction of the bathroom, my mind went to Oliver and the dreamscape. What if he'd been wrong about his shadow's intentions? What if that thing was biding its time, waiting for another opportunity to attack? It felt like the simple, beautiful world Oliver and I created together no longer existed —adulthood and pain had warped it into something else entirely. Before meeting Collith at that black market, I couldn't wait to fall asleep.

Now I was afraid to.

At that moment, I noticed the door to the Unseelie King's bedroom was wide open. There was a single lamp on, and Collith sat perfectly still on his bed, eyes closed. I entered without permission, making sure he heard my footsteps, and sank down next to him. He didn't move or tell me to leave. Why did it feel like I was at the starting line of a race? I closed my eyes against the sight of our almost-touching knees, sat up straighter, and tried to focus on my breathing. It should have been easy, in this dim place, with Collith's heart beating steadily at my side.

"Did you know that you can't read in a dream?" he asked suddenly.

I opened my eyes and discovered him looking back at me. "What?"

"I read it on a website," Collith said. His expression was strange. "It said that one way to know when you're dreaming is whether you can read something."

I knew I needed to tell him about Gwyn—God, there was so much I needed to tell him about—but I recognized the look on his face now. Before we said anything else, Collith needed to know he was awake. I uncrossed my legs and searched his room. Like me, Collith hadn't added any personal touches to his space, but there were coloring books and washable markers scattered across the floor. He must've watched Matthew while Damon was in the shower or covering a shift at Bea's. I moved to pick up one of the markers.

Feeling Collith's eyes on me, I pulled off the cap with my teeth and scrawled across the pale skin of my forearm. "Okay, then," I said. "Can you read this?"

"Fortuna misses Collith," the faerie king recited softly. I looked away, my face burning, and studiously ignored his gaze. His voice floated to me for the next part. "Tell Fortuna that he's right here."

This made me turn back. My eyes flicked between his, and for the first time in weeks, I felt... hope. "Is he?" I asked.

Collith didn't answer; he didn't need to. The air felt warmer, reminiscent of the electricity that used to crackle between us. I imagined the rasp of his whiskers against my skin. In that instant, I knew it wasn't Gwyn I'd wanted when her fingers brushed against my cleavage—she had awoken something with her sensuality and her power, but when she touched me, my thoughts had gone to Collith. It was Collith who I wanted to be whole for now. I licked my lips and I watched him notice the movement. His eyes lingered on my mouth. Our shoulders pressed together, even though I didn't remember moving. I could feel Collith's breath on my cheek.

Then I turned my face toward his. It felt like the planet had stopped moving, and even time itself hung suspended. All of it waiting, hoping, staring at the two of us. The entire world wondering if he'd do it, and if I'd let him.

Collith lowered his head and kissed me.

I threaded my fingers through the silky hair at the base of his neck and kissed him back. There was nothing complicated or uncertain about it, no choice to be made. My heart was beating so hard it seemed impossible he couldn't feel the vibrations of it. It was a physical reminder of who I was touching. The taste of him was tantalizing and just as good as I remembered. I'd missed this. I'd missed his tongue. No, the real truth was written on my arm in black ink—I'd missed *him*.

And yet, in the darkness of my closed eyes, like the flash of a strobe light, I saw a face tinted in yellow. A silver pin gleamed in the headlights. DEPUTY O'CONNELL. I pulled away from Collith abruptly, worried he'd see terror in my eyes.

My first instinct was to run, but I remembered the original reason I'd come. *Tell Collith about Gwyn and everything that's happening at the Unseelie Court*, an inner voice urged. I stared at the floor and willed my mouth to form the words that would only add to the darkness that lived in his eyes now.

"I should go to bed," I said finally. Collith just sat there, his hair mussed, his eyes burning. He didn't say anything as I left, but I could feel his gaze on me until I moved out of sight. I started to slow down, instinctively catching my breath, then remembered Collith could hear my footsteps. I hurried into the bathroom and closed the door, grateful to have a barrier between us. *Breathe, Fortuna. Just breathe.*

It took several minutes for my heart to settle into its usual rhythm. Once it had, though, I didn't reach for my toothbrush. I stood in front of the mirror and, to distract myself from what just happened with Collith, I mulled over my conversation with Gwyn. I couldn't shake the sense that I was missing an important detail.

The person in the glass stared at me while I relived every word and touch. Every movement and pause. Finally, I thought about that strange smell drifting off her as she'd come closer, and something clicked in my mind. I remembered how Lyari had faltered, that night in the woods, and tilted her nose to the air. *Death. I thought I smelled death.* Ice crept through my veins, the cold rush of realizing a truth.

Gwyn's face hadn't been covered in paint. It was dried blood.

CHAPTER SEVEN

J was agitated when I finally fell asleep.

For hours I'd laid on my back, arm flung over my head, and stared at the ceiling. My thoughts returned to Gwyn, almost relentlessly, recalling every word spoken and every movement or gesture made. My instincts were like snakes hissing in a nest, sensing a predator near. It would be a relief to dismiss the encounter as a fluke, a one-off, but I knew the truth with a terrible certainty.

Gwyn of the Wild Hunt would be back, and she wasn't finished with me.

As the night stretched, thinning into the quiet darkness that most people slept through, something else kept me awake, too. A voice at the back of my mind, hardly more than a whisper, that kept saying Oliver's name. Reminding me what awaited when I did manage to fall asleep. I wanted to see him, of course I did, but I was also afraid. The entire day, I'd been careful not to think about the shadow being I'd faced.

Whatever the reason—my instincts about Gwyn or my worry for Oliver—when I closed my eyes later that night, I didn't wake in the dreamscape.

Instead, it was a nightmare.

I felt the dirt first, hard against my cheek. I opened my eyes readily enough, thinking there would be an explanation for why I'd arrived at the dreamscape differently tonight. But I opened my eyes to a shadowy, empty place. The walls were made of brick and there were no doors. High above, a circle glowed with moonlight. Bars extended across the opening, preventing anyone who managed to reach it from escape.

The oubliette, I thought dimly. *I'm in the oubliette.*

Before panic could creep into my lungs and make it harder to breathe, I reminded myself it was a dream. It had to be. I turned to see the rest of the space, thinking there was no one else here, and I gasped when I saw the figure behind me. She raised her head.

A sound of horror caught in my throat.

It was Savannah, but she was not a witch anymore—she'd become one of her creations. She reached for me with mottled, withering hands. I scrambled backward, unable to stop myself from crying out. "Someone is coming for you, Fortuna. This aura is dark. The darkest I've ever seen," she rasped.

"Fortuna. Hey, Fortuna."

The voice wasn't Savannah's. I blinked, and suddenly I was looking at Damon. We were in my bedroom, the faint light of early morning pouring inside. My heart slowed, and as I looked around to reassure myself, there was a humming sound in my ear. *Thank God.* I refocused on Damon and realized the sound had been his voice. "Did you say something?" I asked.

"Yeah, I said I was sorry to wake you."

I shook my head, pushing myself up slightly. "Don't be. I should be thanking you, actually."

"Bad dream?"

I gave him a humorless smile. "You have no idea."

Damon studied me, and that's when I noticed the small box in his hand. It was wrapped in Christmas-themed paper. He followed my gaze and cleared his throat. "Oh. Yeah. This will probably be pretty embarrassing for both of us, but I promised Emma I would sing to you—she went to Denver to pack the rest of her things. She'll be back in time for your party, though."

"No," I moaned, scooting back down. "No parties and no singing. Go away. We can both just tell her you did it. But you may leave that gift on the nightstand."

My brother sat on the edge of the bed. He smelled like the bubblegum-scented shampoo Matthew used. "Sorry. Dad was so weird about keeping promises that now I'm weird about it, too."

Ignoring this, I burrowed deeper under the covers, taking my pillow with me so I could cover my ears. His off-tune singing reached me anyway. I came back out, sighing. When it was over I asked quickly, "What did you get me?"

Damon set the box down next to my hand. Fingering the little present, I avoided his gaze. I didn't want to open the present in front of him—the night before had drained me. I didn't think I could pretend happiness or even gratitude.

We both shifted uncomfortably. A sound burst into the stillness, and the baby monitor in Damon's hand lit up. It was Matthew, babbling softly, letting the world know that he was awake. A smile spread across my brother's tired face, and he stood. "I better get started on his breakfast."

I held up the box. "Thanks for the gift... and the song."

"Yeah. Anytime... but not really," he added, his voice filled with soft teasing. I smiled back, but I couldn't help wondering if Damon would've come without Emma pressuring him.

It was the thought that counted, I told myself as I watched him leave. I peeled off the paper and discovered a wooden box. It was decorated in swirls and fake diamonds. The inside was lined with thin red velvet. I flipped it over and found a sticker with a Target label on it, the price marked down to $4.99. Yes, it was definitely the thought that counted.

Damon's voice drifted down the hallway. Knowing I wouldn't be able to fall back asleep, I set his gift on the nightstand and left the sweat-dampened bed. As I adjusted my shirt, which had ridden up my back, I sighed at the realization that I'd need to wash the sheets *again*.

My alarm sounded just as I finished stripping the bed. I turned it off, gathered the bedding in my arms, and left the room.

Over the next hour I started a load of laundry, brushed my teeth, showered, and dressed. I towel-dried my hair and scraped it up into a high messy bun. When I entered the kitchen, Damon stood at the counter, slicing a banana into small pieces. Matthew beamed at me from his high chair. I crossed the room and kissed his silken head. As I went to the coffee maker Damon asked, "Why was your alarm going off, anyway? There's no way Bea scheduled you on your birthday."

"Oh, I take self-defense lessons with Adam." I poured coffee into a travel mug. A thin column of steam rose from the flow. The aroma greeted me a moment later, and my stomach rumbled.

Damon reached for a container of strawberries. "Didn't Dad teach you all that?"

"Yeah. I guess it makes me feel strong." I kept my eyes on the lid I was screwing onto the mug as I added, "Maybe you should look into taking a course."

My tone was too casual. But I had wondered, more than once, how our lives would've gone if I'd just taken the time to teach Damon how to fight. He was so young when our parents died that Dad didn't have the chance. It probably wouldn't have done much good against a faerie as powerful as Jassin... but what if it had? What if we'd never lost those two years?

You never would've met Collith, a voice whispered. The startling truth of it made me frown.

My brother didn't seem to notice anything beyond the

strawberries he was cutting. He popped a piece into his mouth and shrugged. "Maybe."

I was tempted to stay and eat breakfast with them, but I wanted to train more. The nightmare had weakened me, rendered me vulnerable, and I needed to prove that I wasn't. "I'll be back later," I told Damon.

"If you're not back in time for dinner—" he started.

"I'll be back in time for the dinner, damn it," I cut in, glaring at him. I was only half-teasing. My brother suddenly became absorbed in placing the chunks of fruit into a bowl. The moment was so reminiscent of our teenage years that I almost ruined it by smiling.

With the travel mug in one hand and a banana in the other, I dropped another kiss on Matthew's head and left the kitchen. I set both items down on the entryway bench, took my coat down from the hook, and shrugged it on. Keys clinked in the pocket. I shoved my feet into a pair of boots, picked up my breakfast again, and stepped into the new day.

A minute later, I guided the van down Cyrus's driveway. The sky came apart in lovely pieces, without panic or protest. Every sound was distant or muffled, every light small and faint. It felt like I was the last person on Earth. I turned up the radio to blaring, wanting to leave no room for thoughts.

The music was so loud that I almost missed the sound of my phone ringing. Glancing at the Caller ID, I touched the screen and raised it to my ear, reaching for the volume knob at the same time.

"Where are you?" Lyari asked.

"Hello to you, too. Hey, will you ask Nuvian to do something for me?"

She didn't make any sounds of annoyance, but I could still feel it coming through my phone. "Yes, what is it?"

I pressed the brakes at a four-way stop and double-checked

for other cars. "Ask him to investigate why the Wild Hunt is here."

There was another pause between us, but this one was notably shorter. Without warning, Lyari released a string of swear words in Enochian. Some of them I recognized, others I didn't. She ranted in my ear some more and abruptly switched to English. "Where are you?" the faerie demanded again.

My van crept forward. "In life? That's kind of personal, but if I'm being honest, my life is a clusterfuck."

Lyari was definitely speaking through her teeth now as she said, "Physically. Where are you physically, Your Majesty?"

"I'm on my way to Adam's," I said on a sigh, knowing there would be no deterring her. She appeared in the passenger seat before I'd finished speaking. I yelped and jerked the steering wheel. "What the *hell*, Lyari?"

"How do you know the Wild Hunt is here?" she demanded, ignoring my reaction.

As I put my cell phone back in one of the cup holders, I held the steering wheel tighter and counted to five. "Gwyn paid a visit last night."

The faerie's eyes flashed. For once, she looked like she'd actually taken a bath and gotten a good night's sleep. "And you didn't think it was pertinent to tell me?"

"I'm telling you now, aren't I?" I countered. Her nostrils flared, and when I saw how much I'd upset her, I relented. "Okay, I'm sorry. You're right. I've been… distracted."

Lyari made a dramatic show of looking into the backseat. "And where is the werewolf? You know you're supposed to contact me if you need a guard, Your Majesty."

I didn't respond, because this was the part I usually said something I'd regret later. I reached for the volume knob again and filled the space between us with a Denver morning show. I could feel Lyari simmering. She turned her face toward the window, and for the next two minutes, I enjoyed the radio hosts' banter. It was almost possible to pretend I was still alone.

Lyari's voice ruined the illusion. "This vehicle smells foul," she declared.

So much for the air fresheners. I turned on the blinker and it clicked into the stillness. "Yeah, well, it once belonged to goblins who didn't care about things like personal hygiene."

Anyone else might've been curious, but not Lyari Paynore. In her mind, she'd probably gotten the relevant information and considered our conversation over. Something about the thought made me smile faintly. The rest of the drive passed in silence, both of us listening to the radio hosts go back and forth. Once we reached Main Street, I maneuvered the van into a parking spot.

"I will wait in the coffee shop next door," Lyari said, eyeing Adam's building with distaste. Faeries had a well-known dislike of vampires.

"Adam will be heartbroken," I told her. In truth, Adam had asked Lyari to dinner the last time she'd been there. She gave me a look that said, if I weren't the queen, she'd be making a rude gesture right now. I responded with a sweet smile, and Lyari got out of the van. She closed the door harder than necessary. I tried not to laugh as she approached the coffee shop like a storm cloud. With the skill of someone that had been doing it for years, she cast a glamour that made her look like a human girl and went inside.

In a yard across the street, a child bent and attempted to make a snowball, but it wasn't sticky enough. As he kept trying anyway, I adjusted the rearview mirror and wiped the skin under my eyes to get rid of any excess mascara. Once I looked less like a person who had been up all night, I grabbed my gym bag and stepped into the cold.

Less than a minute later, the familiar scent of machine oil and sweat filled my senses. The door clicked shut with a jarring sound. I frowned, wondering why it had been so loud this time. That was when I realized there was no music playing from the speakers. My instincts stood on end like the fur along Finn's spine. I glanced toward Adam's room, remembering the night I'd found broken glass scattered across the floor and my friend fighting his bloodlust.

Before I could decide what to do, Adam emerged from the office. He saw me and froze. "Shit, Fortuna, I'm sorry. Forgot to text you," he muttered, rubbing his cheek with a knuckle. It left a smear of oil behind.

The sight of him sent relief rushing through me. *You're starting to imagine things, Fortuna.* I smiled wryly at Adam's greeting. "Let me guess. You can't train today."

The vampire opened his mouth to respond, but a new voice slithered in the space between us. "Please don't change your plans on my account."

I turned faster than I thought capable and instinctively reached for the knife in my coat pocket. I paused when I saw the person coming toward us. He was the most beautiful black man I'd ever laid eyes on. His eyelashes were dark and thick, making his strange eyes all the more prominent—if it were possible, I'd say they were gold. His jaw was strong, but not overly so, and his lips perfectly full. He also had cheekbones any female would murder for.

"Fortuna, this is my sire," Adam said. His voice was the same as ever, but something in it still made me glance at him.

"Does your sire have a name?" I asked, keeping my expression a blank mask.

The stranger inclined his head. His dark eyes never left my face. "It's a privilege to meet you, Fortuna Sworn. I am Dracula."

If he were human, I'd guess Dracula's age to be in the early twenties.

A thousand questions flitted through my mind like paper planes on the air. My own parents had believed Dracula to be an urban myth. The stuff of gothic literature. If he was real, though, he might have the answers to questions I'd never asked anyone.

Questions about Nightmares, who hadn't always been on the brink of extinction. Statistically, a vampire as old as Dracula had probably met some during the course of his life. Learned about them.

"As I said, don't allow my unexpected visit to affect your regular schedule. Please continue," he said to Adam now. He had a surprisingly melodious voice. I scanned his outfit, realizing that I'd been so distracted by his face I hadn't really seen anything else. He wore expensive-looking leather shoes, jeans, and a shawl-collar sweater. The only detail that seemed out of place, like something a vampire would own, was the cane. It was carved from dark wood and discolored at the edges. The head was made of silver or steel, and it formed the skull of a bird. I couldn't tell if it was a crow or a raven.

When Adam turned to me, his expression gave nothing away, but there was something strange about his movements. They were... mechanic. As if he were a puppet and someone was controlling his strings from high above. Suddenly I wanted nothing more than to turn around and leave. But my friend was already heading toward the mats, and I didn't know enough about the relationship between a vampire and his sire. Or maybe there were vampire politics at play. I didn't want to make things difficult for Adam.

So I stepped onto the mat and faced him. The lack of music was still unnerving.

The vampire picked up where we left off last time I was here. "A good head butt will feel like a cannonball to your attacker," he said abruptly. His cold voice echoed through the room. "Always, always make sure you tuck your chin. That way you're hitting him with the crown of your head. Otherwise you're using your forehead, and that'll just knock you out, which is probably not what you want."

As Adam spoke, I allowed him to guide me through the motions, but there was tension in the way he moved. It was obvious he didn't want me here. Hell, I didn't want to be here, either. Dracula watched us intently, making no effort to pretend otherwise.

I demonstrated. "Like this?"

This earned a brisk nod. "Good. Cup your hands behind your attacker's neck. Make sure your arms are bent. Jerk hard and fast as you pull your attacker's face in, while you're moving forward with the top of your head."

He showed me, and we continued. There was none of his dry commentary or my friendly insults. When the hour was up— both of us casting surreptitious glances toward the clock—I stepped off the mat, containing a sound of relief, and moved to my bag. "I better get going. I'm sure you didn't come all this way to see a self-defense lesson, Dracula."

"Actually, I came to see the new Unseelie Queen," the vampire said. He stepped past Adam, those unnerving eyes fixed on me. Without warning, he tucked the head of his cane beneath my chin and tilted my head back. My hands clenched into fists, but I kept my volatile instincts in check. "The supernatural world always takes notice when there's a new power player."

"I'm not a power player," I said automatically, jerking away.

However young he appeared, this vampire acted like something that had been walking the Earth for a long time. He blinked at me, abrupt and quick, almost like an insect. "You're not? Did you not free the slaves at Court?"

If he was trying to trick me, I couldn't figure out how. "Yes," I said slowly.

"Did you not undergo a series of three deadly trials in order to obtain a crown?"

"Yes."

"Well there you are, then."

"You didn't come all this way just to meet me," I insisted, still trying to see the game board from his vantage point. First Gwyn, now Dracula. Something else was going on, something I was missing, and neither of them was telling the complete truth.

Dracula acknowledged my words with a faint smile that made warning bells clang in my head. "Very good, young one. You are correct—it is not the only reason, no."

Okay. There was being diplomatic, and then there was being a doormat. I looked Dracula in the eye and allowed him to see the monster living inside. "You may call me 'Fortuna' or 'Your Majesty.' Another 'young one' will get you a one-way ticket to my dungeons," I told him flatly.

Amusement glinted in his gaze. "So young. So arrogant. I miss that feeling of invincibility."

"Don't you have somewhere to be, Fortuna?" Adam asked suddenly. We both looked at him. His tone was as detached as ever, but there was something different in his eyes. Deep within the darkness. A warning. *Leave.*

For once in my life, I did what I was told. I spoke over my shoulder as I walked away. "Yeah. I mean, yes. Emma is making this big birthday dinner—oh, God, don't tell anyone it's my birthday—and she probably needs help. Appreciate the lesson, Adam. See you later."

Thankfully, my babbling was cut short by the booming sound of the door handle. I stepped outside and let the door close behind me. The moment I heard it *click*, my heartbeat began to slow.

The sky was clear and reserved now. Everything was covered in a fresh layer of snow. The boy across the street had given up on his snowball, judging from the set of footprints leading back up the front steps. I started walking in the direction of my car, which I'd parked on the street by habit. The air plucked at my loose t-shirt.

Halfway there, my senses prickled, and I knew I was no longer alone. Confirming this, Laurie's scent floated past a moment later. It always reminded me of springtime. I didn't look at him as I said, "You haven't been around lately."

The door to the coffee shop opened. Lyari emerged, a strand of long hair lifting in a breeze. She noticed us right away, but something about our expressions made her pause. "I'll be in the vehicle," she announced. Then she sifted.

I resisted the urge to roll my eyes. *Thanks for making it awkward, Lyari.*

Usually, Laurie would fill the silence with a quip or a come on. But the Seelie King just walked with me, his frame lithe and lovely, even beneath the wool coat he wore. He wore no hat or gloves, of course, as fae were hardly bothered by the cold. His silver head shone in the pale sunlight. Surrounded by snow and our plumes of breath, he looked more otherworldly than ever before.

"There's unrest in my Court," Laurie said, startling me. It took a moment to realize he was responding to the comment I'd made.

"Anything I can do?" I asked. It was a knee jerk reaction, a question I would ask anyone who had just confided in me.

There was an odd look on Laurie's face. It was so fleeting that I had no time to define it. "Not at the moment, but I appreciate the offer," he said. His tone was normal, and I wondered if I'd imagined it.

We'd reached the van by that point. I mustered a smile and rummaged through my bag in search of keys. Lyari was in the passenger seat, but she probably wouldn't unlock the doors for me. She was spiteful like that. "Of course. That's what friends are for," I said, still digging.

I was tired, hardly thinking about the words before they left my mouth, but something about them made Laurie's expression intensify. At the same moment I found the keys, he moved closer to me. I pressed the UNLOCK button and looked up at him, thinking to say goodbye, and the Seelie King brushed his fingers over the gray smudge beneath my left eye. His touch was warm and feather-light. "You haven't been sleeping, have you?"

"I never do," I commented, taking a casual step back. My back hit the van, and Lyari yelped. I would definitely be giving her shit for *that* later.

Ignoring the Guardian completely, Laurie quirked a brow at me. "Seeing as we *are* friends, I should return the favor. Is there anything I can do for you?"

I hesitated. There *was* something I'd thought about asking him for during my sleepless night. *Well, since he's offering...*

"You mentioned, once, that you know a witch," I ventured. I was aware that even as I said it, there would be a price to pay. Maybe not tomorrow, maybe not next week, but there would be. If Lyari was eavesdropping—and who was I kidding, she absolutely was—I would be getting another lecture on the drive home.

Laurie's eyes were bright with interest. "My bloodline keeps several on retainer, yes."

Apprehension flitted through me and my grip tightened on the keys. "Would she know a spell to keep someone out of my house?"

I knew, before he opened his mouth, exactly what he was going to ask. Laurie was too curious not to. "What's going on, Fortuna?"

"The Wild Hunt stopped by," I said, annoyed by the ember of fear that flared in my stomach. Gwyn wasn't like Beetlejuice or Voldemort—talking about her wouldn't make her appear.

Laurie had gone still. Like Lyari, he gave nothing away in his expression, but there was something preternatural about how he stood. Even the slight movements of his chest, as he breathed in and out, had ceased. That was his tell, I realized. I tucked the information away, where I kept all the knowledge I could potentially use to my advantage, if the need ever arose.

"This is bad," the faerie murmured, staring at something across the street. A moment later, his eyes fixed on me again. "This is bad."

"You said that already," I muttered, unwilling to admit how much his reaction had unnerved me.

Laurie moved so that he stood on my other side, his back pressed to the van. He shoved his hands in his coat pockets. "It seemed worth repeating."

"What can you tell me about her?"

His answer was slow in coming. I could practically hear his mind working, those sharp gears turning and shifting. "She's in countless history books and children's tales," Laurie said eventually. "All of it is true. Her prowess in battle is unparalleled. She can't be killed. Then there's that nasty business with the Courts—they found leverage over Gwyn and used it to stop her bloody rampages. I voted against blackmailing her, but alas, I was not king then. My input didn't hold much weight."

"What leverage? Why did you vote against it?"

At this, Laurie looked at me and raised his pale brows. "Because spells are meant to be broken, my queen, and once she was inevitably freed, who would she hunt first?"

I didn't need to think about it. "She would go after the ones that bound her," I said instantly.

"Precisely, and I happen to *like* being alive. There are still far too many beautiful people to ravage." Laurie stared at the horizon, and the light made his eyes bluer. "She can't be here on a hunt; she would've moved on already."

"Dracula is in town, too," I added with a note of false cheer. "We should throw a welcome party."

I saw Laurie blink at my words. His face turned back to mine. "Did you say Dracula?"

"Yeah, why?"

The faerie king opened his mouth to respond, but a car pulled up alongside us, and we both looked toward it. My stomach instantly dropped when I saw the words GRAND COUNTY SHERIFF along its side. A moment later, Ian rolled down his window and gave me a two-finger salute. Though he was smiling, his eyes didn't quite match it. He didn't say a word as the car pulled away, and that made my nausea worse, somehow.

Laurie watched my reaction with narrowed eyes. "Who is he to you?" he asked.

"Just another asshole. Don't worry about it." My voice was slightly off. I reached for the door handle, but Laurie was still leaning against it. I adjusted the strap of the gym bag with rough fingers. "Do you mind?"

Laurie tilted his head and looked at me more closely. "What happened to you, Firecracker? Where's that lovely spark?"

Once again, I hesitated. The lies waited in my mouth, on my tongue, creating a sour taste. Strangely enough, I caught myself thinking about telling Laurie the truth. But Lyari was in the van and we were on a public street. Not exactly ideal circumstances for such a private conversation. I heaved a sigh and pushed the faerie off the van. "That 'spark' went out after all the closing shifts and sleepless nights. No one else seems to worry about how we'll buy groceries, or pay Cyrus rent, or get Matthew the toys that every kid should have. Have you heard of those, by the way? Bills?"

I pointed at the bar to accentuate my point. Laurie looked over at Bea's, and his expression twisted with distaste. "If you need money, my dear, all you need to do is ask."

"That's not what... you know what? Never mind." I got into the driver's seat and closed the door. Laurie stood there as I jammed the key in the ignition and turned it, bringing the battery to life. Remembering the request I'd made of him, I rolled the window down. "About the spell—"

"If she was here for you, a spell wouldn't stop Gwyn. Nothing would." In an obvious dismissal, he looked past me. His next words were for Lyari. "It's unlikely that Gwyn intends to harm the Queen of the Unseelie Court, but don't leave Fortuna alone. Ever. Do you understand?"

My Right Hand nodded. "I understand, King Laurelis."

"If you don't think she's here for me, why do I smell your fear?" I asked bluntly, pulling my seatbelt across me. I twisted the key and the engine grumbled at me before turning over.

"Because she's old, cunning, and unpredictable." Laurie gripped the edge of the window and stepped so close that it reminded me of the night we danced together at that bar in Denver. I pulled a strand of hair away from my face. His gaze followed the movement, then shifted back to linger on my mouth. "And I would… regret losing your company."

By now I knew better than to attempt a response, and right on cue, Laurie performed one of his vanishing acts. I sat there, trying to define the feelings creeping through me. A leaf skittered past. I frowned at it absently, still picturing the Seelie King's solemn eyes.

Lyari said my name, more loudly than usual. I turned to her, blinking, and she looked back with an annoyed glare. "I've been sitting in this foul smell for five minutes," she snapped.

I rolled my eyes and changed gears. As I checked for traffic, Lyari started fiddling with the radio. She couldn't hide a hint of fascination in her gaze. I pulled onto Main Street, listening to different stations blare through the speakers. I barely heard it, really—my thoughts had gone back to Gwyn.

The entire ride home, I stared at the skyline with a troubled frown, wondering if I'd see the silhouettes of galloping horses.

CHAPTER EIGHT

*H*ot water pounded down on me.

The steam was so thick that it was difficult to see. I knew the water was too hot—my skin was turning red—but I closed my eyes and leaned into it. The longer I stayed in the shower, the longer I could delay the impending celebration.

In the darkness of my eyelids, though, I saw everything else I was avoiding. Oliver, Ian O'Connell, Gwyn, Dracula. Their faces went around me like horses on a carousel.

My eyes snapped open, and I stared at the plastic wall of the shower, trying not to make a sound in case there was a certain werewolf nearby. I finished washing my hair and ignored the knots inside me, tightening and loosening with every breath. As soapy water ran into the drain, I turned the valve. Stillness coiled through the air, replacing the steam.

The moment I stepped out of the shower, I could hear Emma in the kitchen, working on the birthday dinner she'd insisted on. My conscience wouldn't let me hide anymore. Sighing, I left the bathroom and headed for my room. Evening light streamed through the window. Water still trickled from my clean-smelling hair. I toweled it dry as best I could, then opened the closet doors to see my options.

Despite the cold outside, and a chill clinging to the air within the house itself, I pulled a dress off one of the hangers. Maybe my time at the Unseelie Court had led to a dependence, of sorts, on masks and costumes. But this one was not nearly as elaborate—it was a black, long-sleeved dress I wore to church services and funerals. I pulled it over my head, and once the material settled onto my shoulders, I saw immediately that it was too big. I checked my reflection in the mirror to see how bad it looked. *Damn it*. No wonder Emma had been force-feeding me every time I entered a room.

Down the hall, I could hear Matthew crying. He'd been battling a cold for the past two days, and Damon was worried he had an ear infection, too. Listening to my nephew's pained whimpers, I added getting health insurance to my endless list of responsibilities. Between our shifts at Bea's and my salary as the Unseelie Queen, Damon and I should be able to make it work.

I knew Emma would lend us the money without hesitation, if we asked her for it. But she'd already paid a high price for loving us. I couldn't take anything else from her.

Suddenly a crash came from the kitchen. I swore and turned my back on the mirror, then hurried toward the kitchen. Emma was picking up a pot from the floor, singing as if nothing was amiss. Hip hop music played from an iPad propped on the table. "Are you okay?" I asked, breathless.

"Why wouldn't I be?" Emma asked, putting the pot back on the stove. Without any warning, she started twerking.

I squealed and leaped back, then bit my lip to hold back a peal of laughter. I reached for the iPad and increased the volume. "*Damn*, Ems! Work it, girl."

As the old woman bent down even farther, her hand brushed against the handle of a spatula, and the utensil flipped onto the floor. Grease splattered across the tiles. Emma swore and moved to pick it up, but I beat her to it.

"Will you *please* let me help you?" I demanded, putting the spatula in the sink. This brought my attention to a bowl of left-over cake batter.

"No. I have at least sixteen birthdays to make up for," Emma informed me, slapping my hand away from it. I pouted and went to turn the music back down. "The food is almost ready, by the way. Please sit down at the head of the table. Oh, and we're using the dining room tonight."

The dining room was, in fact, also the living room. On the left side of the space, there was the couch, the coffee table, and the entertainment center. On the right, there was a long table, stretching along the length of the picture window. It was separated from the entryway by a wall with a wide, arched doorway. We'd never used it, and the fact that we were now worsened my anxiety.

Emma was still waiting for a response. I gave her a weak smile. "You're the boss. Hey, do you mind if I step outside for a minute, before we start? I just need some fresh air."

"Of course, sweetheart. Is everything all right?"

I didn't want to lie to her—*fine, fine, everything is fine*—so I made a noncommittal sound and left the kitchen before she could ask again. I paused in the entryway long enough to jam my feet into a pair of fur-lined slippers, and then I was yanking the door open and stepping onto the porch.

I walked to the railing and rested my elbows on it. As I looked out at the view, the tightness in my chest eased. It was the sort of quiet that only happened in winter, everything sleeping and dreaming. Shadows spilled away from the setting sun, dragging the night after them.

When a car turned into the driveway, I saw it right away because I'd already been looking toward the horizon. I didn't recognize the vehicle, and in a town like Granby, that meant it was a stranger. My instinctive wariness kicked in.

When I caught sight of their faces through the windshield, my stomach dropped like a carnival ride. *No fucking way.*

The engine died and the headlights went dark. Confirming this wasn't a dream, Dave stepped out and slammed the door.

He looked the same as he did the day I left them six years ago. His brown hair was thinner, maybe, but he still had a mustache and wore a puffy vest over his plaid shirt. "For Pete's sake, put a coat on, kid," Dave chided, spotting me on the porch.

Maureen got out from the passenger side, her short legs struggling to close the distance between the seat and the ground. My foster mother—well, technically, she was my adoptive mother —looked like she should be on the PTA board for every local school. Her brown hair, now streaked with gray, had been in a pixie cut for as long as I'd known her. She always wore button-up shirts and whitewashed jeans, despite the eighties being well behind us. Her lips were thin and her nose was a bit too large for her face. But it was her gray eyes that always stood out most, whenever I saw her. They shone with kindness. Even as a child, I'd seen that. It was probably the reason I hadn't ever run away.

Something in my chest tightened at the sight of her, and all at once, I was reliving every argument we'd ever had.

Thankfully, there was no time to dwell on any of it— Maureen was coming down the walkway. *Don't touch me,* I thought, willing power into the words. But it didn't work, because she was already closing the distance between us, reaching for me with her delicate arms. As they closed around me, her phobias seeped from her skin and into mine.

The flavors were familiar, a combination of mint, rust, and the glue that you lick on the seal of an envelope. My foster mother was terrified of heights, mice, and blood. I hadn't seen her since becoming the Unseelie Queen, though, which meant

I'd never touched her with all this magic humming through my veins. I tried to imagine a wall between us. I refused to delve into her mind.

But the power was hungry. It wasn't satisfied with those small fears, and my own desires were of little consequence. Between one blink and the next, I was in Maureen's mind.

There was nothing particularly unique about the structure of it. Her fears were easy to find, like a box of memorabilia that had been shoved at the back of a closet and forgotten. When I realized what was happening, I started to free myself from Maureen's hold. To put distance between us before it opened. But it was as if that dusty box wanted to be discovered—the lid unlatched and the darkness beckoned.

I found a story inside.

It was the story of a girl. A lonely girl, who never missed a day of school and turned in every assignment on time. She showed every graded paper and perfect test to her father, who always came home from the factory looking more tired than he had the day before. He never looked at Maureen as she waited, no, as she *yearned* for his approval.

All she ever got was a vague grunt or a muttered word that bore little resemblance to the praise she'd seen her classmates get from their parents.

The girl was not especially skilled at making friends. She was too shy to approach anyone, and they saw her threadbare clothes as a mark of someone different. Someone who didn't belong.

Years went by, and sometimes, all that kept the girl from looking for a way out of her lonely life was the thought of college. She'd heard that people were kinder there, and quicker to accept. That hope became the bedrock of who she was, the foundation she built everything else on, and the mortar was fear. Fear that she would always feel insignificant or unseen.

When she met David Wright, those thoughts went into a box, where they were only taken out on rare occasions.

All of this blazed through my mind like a wildfire. Two or three seconds later, Maureen pulled away, completely oblivious to the invasion of her privacy. There was no time to recover, because Dave was already leaning in for an embrace of his own. The taste of cloves and coffee coated my tongue now. I knew they were talking and I should probably respond, but my power was claiming Dave's memories.

He was a more complicated man than I'd realized. From the moment we met, he had only treated me with kindness. He hadn't attempted to step into a fatherly role, or spend any real kind of time with me, but he greeted me every morning, asked how I was at the dinner table, and bid me good night any time we saw each other before bed. He paid for my gymnastics classes, my clothes, and my food without a word of complaint. But, secretly, I always thought that he'd only adopted us because it was what Maureen wanted.

Now I knew how badly I'd misunderstood him.

Dave wasn't afraid of the things I usually found beneath people's skin—there were no spiders, no clowns, no heights— and when my insatiable power reached for more, consuming fear like it was an all-you-can-eat-buffet, I learned that he didn't worry about death, or pain, or loss.

What Dave did fear was his own memories.

They followed him and tormented him like poltergeists. Even the smallest things let them in, like bread popping up from the toaster—Dave's mind interpreted the sound as a gunshot, and suddenly he was back there, running through smoke, his boots squelching in mud.

At that point, if Dave didn't distract himself, didn't yank his mind free of the memory quick enough, he would remember watching his best friend's arm blow off. He'd see, for the millionth time, his own red-slicked hands, trying to stanch the blood pouring out of the gap in Owen.

And so he drank.

Dave moved through his life in an alcohol-infused daze. He smiled when he was supposed to, he carried a conversation without much effort, and he was capable of caring about the people that shared his orbit. Like Maureen, and the children, and his brother. But the drink made it all feel far away.

As Dave, too, pulled back, he didn't seem to notice how I cringed.

Probably sensing my distress, Finn appeared in my peripheral vision and whined. He must've been on another hunt. Maureen's eyebrows rose when she comprehended his size. "Did you get a dog? What *breed* is it?" she asked with a hint of trepidation in her voice.

"It's huge!" Dave exclaimed. He held out his hand to Finn, palm-down, who gave it an unimpressed stare.

I still wasn't convinced I was awake. My mind was slow to comprehend their words. "No. Well, yes. Sort of. What are you guys doing here? How did you even know where I was?"

"Damon invited us," Maureen said.

As if he'd been standing on the other side, waiting for his cue, the front door opened. Finn saw his chance and loped inside. At the same time, Damon stepped onto the porch with Matthew perched on his hip. The smile that spread across my brother's face was genuine.

Since Collith's death, Damon had been kinder to me. Watching him smile at our adoptive parents, though, I realized that was all it was. Kindness. Not the warmth he'd shown me before I killed his monstrous lover.

"Who is this?" Maureen asked, looking at Matthew. The excitement in her voice made it obvious that she already knew.

Damon walked carefully down the stairs. He shifted the boy to his other hip. Matthew had the tousled hair and drowsy eyes of someone who'd just woken from a nap. Damon had just started the introductions when another vehicle rumbled up the driveway. This time, I recognized the truck instantly—it belonged to Bea and Gretchen. Dear Lord, how many people had Emma invited tonight?

"This is my son, Matthew," I heard Damon say. I turned my head, catching their reaction to the news. Dave was already grinning, and one of Maureen's hands rose to cover her mouth. Her eyes shone with tears as she reached out with the other to touch Matthew's dimpled arm.

Maureen and Dave fawned over their new grandson while the other car parked. I finally descended the steps to meet my boss and her partner on the walkway.

"Why are you staring at me?" Bea asked, drawing closer. I steeled myself for the inevitable embrace. She must've noticed something in my expression, because she added, "For your birthday present, Gretchen and I won't try to hug you."

I shot her a grateful smile. "Honestly, I'm trying to remember the last time I've seen you outside the bar. You don't look... natural, out in nature."

Gretchen laughed while a line deepened between Bea's eyebrows. "I think I'm offended," she said.

A few seconds later, I introduced them to Dave and Maureen, who still hadn't budged from Matthew's side. The sun continued to lower, but we lingered on the lawn to make polite conversation. Thankfully, Emma appeared in the doorway and called that dinner was ready. Our small party headed inside, where it was warm and bright and the air smelled like marinara sauce.

Saving me from another round of introductions, Emma immediately went about learning names and shaking hands. Finn stretched out in front of the fireplace, his head resting on his paws. I searched the rest of the room, hoping to see Cyrus.

"Holy shit," Bea exclaimed, noticing Finn as she turned.

"Regina mentioned you'd been walking around town with a big dog, but... that is a *big* dog."

"Yeah. He might have some wolf in him," I said offhandedly, moving toward the table. Damon made a coughing sound that sounded suspiciously like a laugh.

I sat down just as Collith came in.

Shit. I stood up so quickly the chair legs screeched. I hadn't thought about how I'd explain him to my parents. Thanks to the Granby rumor mill, everyone had heard about it when Collith called himself my husband. Which meant that, as far as Bea and Gretchen knew, we were still married. Any way I looked at it, Maureen and Dave were going to find out I'd gotten hitched and hadn't told them.

Happy birthday, me.

The low hum in my head sharpened into sounds, and I realized it was Collith's voice. While I'd been standing there, mute with panic, he had apparently introduced himself. He was shaking Dave's hand now, nodding at something the older man was saying. For the first time in weeks, he'd made an effort with his appearance—his face was cleanshaven and he wore a white dress shirt. The sleeves were rolled up to his forearms, revealing strong tendons. His dark jeans looked new. Maureen glanced between the two of us, her expression questioning, but I still didn't know what to say.

Emma came to my rescue. "Please, everyone, sit down," she urged, resting her hand against the small of my back.

Everyone moved to obey. Chair legs scraped over the floor and murmured conversations floated across the table. Damon left to get Matthew's high chair while Emma and Gretchen went to fetch the food.

Within minutes, all of us were seated around a meal comprised of all my favorites.

At a glance I saw spaghetti, grilled cheese, and pancakes. Steam rose from the platters. I sat at the head of the table and stared down the length of it, disbelieving. When had Emma found the time to do all this? And she'd done it for me? I was silent for a few seconds as I struggled to sound normal. "Emma, this looks... amazing. Thank you."

She smiled at me, wrinkles deepening around her mouth and from her eyes. "It was my pleasure, sweetheart. Collith, would you be willing to pour everyone's wine? I completely forgot to do that earlier. Gretchen, would you pass that plate of tortillas to the right?"

There was a flurry of activity after she finished speaking, and over the next few minutes, I loaded my plate with every carb known to man. Just as I had during Emma's impromptu bonfire, I found myself continually looking around the table. It was strange, seeing Emma, Bea, and Maureen together. Like three different lives coming together in a dizzying moment of déjà vu.

They were chatting amicably, the topic having something to do with Bea's bar, but I couldn't focus enough to truly listen. I also kept thinking of the reason I hadn't wanted this party, the reason why I'd hoped to avoid bringing all these people together.

It felt like I didn't deserve to be celebrated.

"The spring semester is starting at CU soon," Maureen said without preamble.

Even before I raised my head, I knew she was talking to me. I was silent for a moment, hoping someone else would intervene, but the only sounds at the table were clinking silverware and Matthew's soft fussing. Both Damon and Emma reached over at the same time to touch him in reassurance.

"Yeah, I know. I've just got a lot on my plate right now," I said finally, poking at my pasta halfheartedly. *No pun intended*, I almost added. Something told me Maureen wouldn't appreciate it.

"A lot on your plate?" she echoed, frowning. "Like what? Making cocktails and pouring beers every night?"

I looked at Bea, wondering what she thought about my foster mother's comments, but she was making a point of thoroughly chewing her food. Gretchen caught my glance and gave me a gentle smile. Her wordless encouragement felt like an injection of calm. I refocused on Maureen and somehow managed not to glare. "There's a lot going on in my life that you don't know about," I said, not unkindly.

But Maureen still interpreted it that way. "And whose fault is that?" she countered, her gray eyes flashing.

My fork clinked against the plate with a harsh sound. "Can we have this conversation another time?" I asked with poorly-concealed impatience. I reminded myself of everything I'd learned about Maureen on the driveway.

Then she said, "I don't see how that's possible, considering you won't take any of my phone calls."

"You know, I'm glad to see *your* education didn't get in the way of—" I started. A knock at the front door cut me off. *Probably for the best.* Holding my fork so tightly that the edges pressed into my skin, I turned my attention to Emma. "Who else did you invite tonight? Wait, no! I've got it!"

Damon and Collith had started to rise. Eager to escape the room, I flew to my feet and darted toward the doorway. "Since you're already standing, you may as well refill my wine," I heard Emma say.

Once I was out of their sight, I stopped and pressed my back to the wall. Air rushed into my lungs, then slowly went out. I did it again. Feeling slightly calmer, I hurried to open the door before the newcomer knocked again.

Laurie stood on the other side.

"No. No way." I started to shut the door in his face, but Laurie flattened his palm against it. His other hand held a bouquet of vibrant flowers.

"I heard there was a party happening." He stepped into the light, and I saw that he was pouting. "My invitation must've gotten lost in the mail."

Chair legs screeched against the floor. I glanced behind me, praying Collith hadn't come to investigate. I spun back to Laurie and hissed, "Yes, I'm sure that's what happened. Why don't you go home and keep waiting for it?"

"Laurie!" Emma exclaimed, coming forward in a rush of perfume. "What a wonderful surprise. I was wondering if we'd ever see you again."

Grinning, the Seelie King brushed past me and bent to kiss Emma's cheek. He pressed the bouquet into her hands. "The pleasure is all mine, Mrs. Miller."

Emma was about to respond when Collith appeared in the doorway. He took one look at our latest arrival and said, his voice dangerously calm, "Get out."

"Collith, that was rude," Emma chided, cradling the flowers in the crook of her arm like a baby. "Laurie was a great help to us when we needed it. He's always welcome at a family gathering."

"Thank you, Mrs. Miller," Laurie said warmly.

Beaming, she took his arm and led him into the dining room. Slowly, Collith and I trailed after them. "Please, call me Emma. There's an empty chair right next to mine. Oh, Lyari, excellent. I was worried you wouldn't get my text."

Startled, I followed Emma's gaze and looked behind me. Lyari stood in the entryway. It wasn't her sudden arrival that made me blink; it was her appearance. I almost didn't recognize my own Right Hand. In place of her armor, the faerie wore jeans and a white button-up shirt. It looked like she had actually put on some makeup, too—her eyelashes were darker than normal and a hint of pink highlighted her cheekbones. Her long hair was loose and curled. Her pointed ears were hidden beneath a powerful glamour that even I couldn't see past. She looked like a college student. Like a *human.*

"Thank you for inviting me," Lyari said politely. Her expression was so uncomfortable I almost snickered, which probably would've earned me a scathing glare.

Deciding to take pity on her, I turned toward the table again. The sight of Cyrus sitting in one of the chairs made me pause. Emotion swelled in my throat—I knew he was here for me. Cyrus Lavender hated gatherings like this. The only reason he managed at the bar was because he had his own space, his safe haven, and no one unfamiliar was allowed to enter it.

I didn't worsen Cyrus's discomfort by thanking him. Instead, I sat back down, noting as I did so that someone had put a leaf in the table. I hadn't even known there was one. Lyari and Laurie got settled, and Emma left to put her new flowers in water. She returned quickly, holding a large vase, and Laurie stood to take it from her.

"Right in the center," Emma instructed him, sitting in her chair like a queen. Laurie's eyes gleamed with amusement as he acquiesced. The flowers ended up squarely in front of Collith's plate. I watched him reach for his wine and down it.

For the next ten minutes or so, we actually managed to have a normal family dinner. Dave asked Bea a question about her truck. Gretchen complimented Laurie on his unique blazer, which had silver spikes around each shoulder. Then Maureen glanced between me, Collith, and Laurie and asked, "So how do you all know each other?"

Silence descended upon the long table. *Perceptive*, I thought. Maureen had always been too perceptive for her own good. Seconds ticked by, and no one answered her. I cleared my throat, stalling for time. "I met Collith at a... flea market. He and Laurie were... childhood friends."

"Oh, we were more than that," Laurie purred, winking at

him. He stabbed a meatball with his fork and popped it into his mouth.

Collith had stiffened. In my peripheral vision, I saw Maureen frown. Emma looked at me, her eyes dark with confusion. She'd never asked about the specifics of my relationship with Collith, but she had probably assumed we were together—he lived with us, I spent more time in his room than my own, and I was constantly staring toward the barn like a lovestruck teenager.

"Seriously, don't you have somewhere better to be, Laurie?" I snapped, glaring at him. "I hear Hell is lovely this time of year."

Too late, I realized how this might affect Collith. He was staring fixedly at his glass, but the hand that held his fork was white. His veins stood on end. Laurie opened his mouth to answer me, and power rumbled through the air. The floorboards groaned and the ceiling beams creaked. Lights flickered overhead. Finn shot to his feet and growled.

Sequestered in another room, Stanley was barking now, and the sound drowned out whatever Maureen said next. Lyari had started to stand up. I caught her eye and shook my head, hoping the movement was subtle enough that no one else noticed. Collith struggled to regain control of himself, but he wasn't looking at his glass anymore—he stared across the table at Laurie.

"Collith," I murmured. His head turned toward me, and our gazes met. Slowly, his irises returned to their usual, lovely hazel. The lights stopped flickering and the house went silent. Finn retreated to his spot in front of the fire, but he kept his eyes on us.

"Fortuna, what on earth is going on?" Maureen demanded after a stilted pause. She looked at Collith and Laurie again, and this time did nothing to hide her distrust. Even as her subconscious rushed to explain the flickering lights and rumbling walls, her human instincts were telling her something was different about them. "Who are these... people?"

I resisted the urge to pinch the bridge of my nose. "They're friends, Maureen. Just ignore anything Laurie says. It's what I do."

"Do you work with Fortuna at the bar?" Dave asked Lyari.

Subtle. Real subtle, I thought. My Right Hand took a bite of her pasta. "No. I work in... security."

"What about you?" Maureen jumped in, her face turned toward Laurie. "What do you do for a living?"

His eyes twinkled. Before I could intervene he said, "Who, me? Well, I guess you could say I'm in politics. What about you, Collith? Think you'll ever get back into politics, or are you just going to hide in the woods for the rest of your life?"

Ah, fuck. I steeled myself for chaos. But before Collith could react, Cyrus made a sound. Everyone turned their heads in his direction. His gaze was bright with distress, and he shook his head as if someone had asked him a question. He rubbed his hands together and started rocking. "I don't like it," he murmured, the words so faint I almost missed them. "I don't like this fighting."

My stomach churned as I understood. Shouts and fistfights broke out at the bar all the time, but Cyrus expected it there. This was his safe place. This was where nothing unexpected ever happened.

"I'm so sorry, Cy," I said. "You're right. We're in your home, and we shouldn't be arguing here. We're done now, okay? Emma, thank you for making dinner. It was delicious."

"But you've barely had any," she protested weakly.

"Believe me, I plan to eat all of it," I reassured her. Thankfully, Laurie was already standing. Without another word, I took hold of his shoulders and steered him toward the entryway. I knew everyone was staring, but I pretended not to notice. Laurie looked like he was trying not to laugh. I opened the front door and shoved him through, then stepped out after him.

The wind teased Laurie's hair. Standing there with his impish grin and tousled locks, he looked like a prince from a fairy tale. Too bad he was anything but. I crossed my arms and glared at him. "You know, you're the reason God created the middle finger."

"I know. Happy birthday, Queen Fortuna." With a rueful smile, Laurie held out a small box, pale blue, about the size of a book. I gave him a look—presents wouldn't absolve him of what he'd pulled tonight—but the faerie king just waited, his crystalline eyes never moving from my face. Sighing, I took the box and tugged at the silk ribbon around it. It fell away, and I tucked it into my pocket before lifting the lid.

The necklace was just like Laurie himself—beautiful and obnoxious. It was a string of diamonds. The jewels closest to the clasp were small, but as they went on toward the center, they got bigger. One of them was the size of a raspberry. Thinking about how much this must've cost made me nervous to even hold it. With my luck, a crow might dive down and snatch the shiny thing out of my hand.

"Why don't you take the money you spent on this and get some therapy?" I suggested, putting the lid back on. I held the box out to Laurie. "I can't accept it."

"There's my Firecracker. I wondered where she'd gone," the Seelie King remarked. Moving in a blur, he brushed a kiss along my cheek. He stepped back before I could jerk out of the way.

"Laurie, don't you dare leave without taking this with—" I stopped when I saw that he was gone. Why did I even bother? I glowered out at the trees, knowing I should go back inside, but unable to move. Not when I knew Maureen was still in there.

A moment later, the front door opened and closed. Someone came to stand beside me, and I recognized the alluring scent instantly. "Don't worry, he's gone," I said flatly, keeping my gaze on the skyline. "Are you ever going to tell me what happened between you two?"

Collith didn't answer straight away. A gust of wind whistled past the porch. "Emma wanted to make sure you got your birthday wish," he said eventually.

"Great. Except that's not what I asked."

Silence met my sullen words. Moving carefully, Collith sat down on the top step. I saw that he balanced a cake in one hand and held a mug of coffee in the other. Swallowing an annoyed sigh, I moved to follow suit. Collith placed the cake between us, along with a card.

I stared down at the birthday cake Emma had made. It was a lopsided affair, but I had no doubt it would be delicious. The candle flames flickered and spit. Wax dripped into the frosting.

"Were you the one who got me the chair?" I asked suddenly, raising my gaze back to Collith. I wasn't sure what made me think of it, but somewhere along the way, the answer had become important. Maybe I just didn't like unsolved mysteries.

He frowned. "Chair?"

"Never mind." In trying to hide a faint sense of disappointment, my attention shifted to the envelope beside me. My name was scrawled on the back in Emma's tiny, neat handwriting. I pulled out the card, and the front was covered in an image of a rat wearing a party hat. The words above it read, *Happy birthday from someone who gives a rat's ass.*

A ghost of a smile touched my lips. I opened the card and a business card tumbled out. As I reached for it, I read Emma's note first. *This might be unorthodox, as far as presents go. I wanted to get you something that would help. If you'd rather have a hat, please let me know.* Curious now, I picked up the small, stiff piece of paper. When I saw what it was for, my smile faded. I tilted the card back and forth, watching how the light glinted off the golden letters. CONSUELO THOMPSON. Beneath this it said, REGISTERED PSYCHOLOGIST.

Like Dave, subtlety wasn't Emma's strong suit.

Sighing, I put the card back into the envelope and returned my attention to the cake. The candles were still burning. For the past two years, I'd wished for Damon's safe return. Now that he was home, and it was clear that birthday wishes really did come true, I didn't want to waste this opportunity. I picked up the cake—it was heavier than it looked—and set it on my lap. I closed my eyes and thought, *I wish that, no matter what happens, my family stays safe.*

I bent over and blew out all the candles with a single breath.

"Would you like to hear a joke?" Collith said. I looked at him, but his eyes were on the horizon. "A faerie, a Nightmare, and a werewolf walk into a bar…"

There was a slur to his words I'd only heard once before, after he'd returned from Olorel. *You're drunk.* I didn't realize I'd spoken the words out loud until Collith held up a coffee mug and replied, "Not for long."

I was frowning. At what point in the day did he start drinking? He'd only had one glass of wine at dinner.

I was about to voice my concern when the door behind us opened. I set the cake aside quickly. Collith and I stood as Emma's voice floated into the night. Dave and Maureen walked onto the porch. The door closed behind them, and they both glanced down at the cake. I started to reach for it.

"Don't worry about it," Dave said, stepping over the plate, smoking candles and all. His wife had already done the same. Dave lingered at the base of the steps while she continued on to the truck. Maureen didn't look back at me.

"She means well," Dave said in his easygoing way. Reprising his role as peacemaker, despite all the time that had passed since I'd lived with them. My adoptive father's eyes went to the figure standing so still at my side. "It was nice to meet you, Collith. Come over for dinner sometime—we'd love to have you, and I know it would make Maureen happy to see more of Fortuna."

"Thanks for coming, Dave," I said quickly, unsure that Collith would respond.

But he surprised me. "It was nice to meet you, as well," the faerie said with a polite smile. He went down a couple steps and held out his hand. Dave shook it, grinning, and nodded at us one more time before turning away.

Bea and Gretchen emerged a moment later, and I glimpsed Stanley slipping out behind them. He lumbered down the steps while we said our goodbyes. Neither human commented on the strangeness of tonight's dinner, and for that alone I almost wanted to hug them. Gretchen held out a long, white envelope and murmured, "Happy birthday, Fortuna."

They walked away before I could open it. I sat back down on the step and watched them climb into Bea's truck. The engine started at the same moment Collith rejoined me. As those bright headlights were eaten by the night, I finally peeked inside the envelope. Somehow I wasn't surprised when I saw it contained cash. A thick wad of it. There was an index card tucked in front of the bills. *Don't even try giving it back,* Bea had written with a black Sharpie.

For the second time tonight, a wave of emotion crashed over me. I put the envelope on top of Emma's card and hugged my knees, thinking about how I could thank them. I knew I needed to help with the dinner cleanup, but I didn't want anyone to see my red eyes. Soon. I'd go inside soon.

Moments later, a small form crossed the yard, and I heard a familiar jangling sound—Stanley's collar. The dog climbed the steps, rested his head on my knee, and stared up at me with droopy eyes. I ran my hand over his head, almost absently, and he released a long sigh of contentment. *Lucky,* I thought at him.

He didn't have to burden Collith with unpleasant news.

"What can you tell me about Gwyn?" I asked without looking at the faerie beside me.

When he didn't say anything, I glanced toward him. His

expression was grim but not surprised. "You've seen her. Which means the Wild Hunt is here."

"Last night," I admitted, seeing no way around it. If her interest in me put the others in danger, they needed to know.

A muscle worked in Collith's jaw. The rings on his fingers flashed as he raked his hair back in an abrupt, agitated movement, and then he swore in Enochian. "When I saw the wood anemone, I dared to hope she'd come for someone else."

I was slow to comprehend his meaning. When I did, though, my heart quickened. "Those flowers grew because of her? Wait, are you saying they mean she *is* here to hunt me?"

Collith gave a single, terse nod. "The wood anemone is a residual effect from a witch's spell, placed on Gwyn of the bloodline Nudd centuries ago. That spell created the Wild Hunt and made Gwyn truly immortal, in a way even the fae are not—she cannot be killed."

"Maybe you're wrong about why she's here," I said weakly. My mind went back to that surreal encounter with the huntress. "Maybe she was just curious about me, like she said."

"I'm not wrong. Believe me, I wish I was. The flowers have become her harbingers, and part of her legend. You're not scared enough, Fortuna. When Gwyn begins a hunt, that's it—she finds and kills her quarry, always. There has never been an exception in all the centuries she's ridden the skies. The fact that you're sitting beside me right now only means that she's allowing you to live, for a reason not yet known to us."

I glanced at Collith's fingers. They gripped the coffee mug so tightly I worried the glass would shatter. "Who are the faeries that ride with her?" I asked.

That stubborn lock of hair had already fallen over his eye. I resisted the urge to touch it as Collith answered. "They are the Fallen with darkest cravings. The ones with endless hunger. Kings of the past could not allow them to roam free in the world. Gwyn holds them in check, doubtless because her depravity runs even deeper than theirs."

Remembering the way those hunters had watched me, tracking every movement like a predator lying in wait, I had no difficulty believing his words this time. "Why would she agree to that?"

Collith met my gaze. "Because above all, she longs for the return of Creiddylad."

If I weren't already riveted to every answer coming out of his mouth, his tone would've caught my attention. There was a weight to how Collith spoke the name. "And who is that?" I prompted.

"Her mate. She was a human who lived at the court of King Arthur." He took another sip of his coffee, his expression tight and agitated. It was probably a safe bet that he was wishing it was something stronger. "Centuries ago, the Seelie and Unseelie Courts came together for a singular purpose—to conceal Creiddylad and consequently put a leash on Gwyn. She was causing such a stir that even the humans had begun to take notice."

It still hadn't quite registered that an ancient faerie was in Granby to kill me. My heart was pounding harder, but short of summoning Gwyn and asking her directly, there was nothing I could do tonight.

Reliving our strange conversation for the dozenth time, I fiddled with the delicate chain hanging around my neck. "She told me that she knew your mother," I murmured.

Even though I hadn't said her name, Collith stiffened. Besides that brief moment at the Unseelie Court, when he'd looked toward the passageway that would take him to her, this was always his reaction when Naevys came up. In all the time he'd been living here, Collith hadn't visited her.

I knew it wasn't entirely to keep the Court unaware of his location or his current mental state—there was something else keeping Collith away from his mother. He wouldn't confide in me, but I could hardly judge him for that when I wasn't being forthcoming, either.

For the hundredth time since Collith came into my life, it felt like he could read my mind. "I see your pain, Fortuna. You walk around, talking and smiling, but it's constant," he said suddenly. The words should've seemed random, but they weren't. Not to me.

I thought I'd been hiding it pretty well, but who was I kidding? The way I cringed at the tiniest noises, how I avoided the dark as though it was a monster, it was probably obvious that something had happened to me. Talking about it wouldn't fix anything, though. Nothing would.

"Look, you have your secrets and I have mine. Okay?" I said finally, looking up at the sky. There was a faint smattering of stars visible.

"If you won't talk to me or one of the others, then talk to someone else. Someone who's trained in helping people."

A sharp sound left me, more bark than laugh. "Are you suggesting I should go to therapy? Did you have something to do with Emma's weird birthday present?"

"What can I do? How can I help?" Collith asked, ignoring this.

His questions were dangerous—they forced me to remember that night. Or tried to, anyway. As Collith waited for an answer, my gaze dropped to his lips. I didn't let myself think about what I did next.

I wrapped my fingers around the back of his head and pulled his face down to mine.

For an instant, he was stiff. Uncertain. But I'd missed the taste of him, and I didn't let his hesitation affect me. I pressed myself against Collith and gently coaxed his mouth open. He softened, then responded with equal caution. We were asking each other a question, both of us scared of the answer.

Why have you summoned me?

Headlights. Rustling trees. Two intersecting roads. Without warning, I broke away. Tears were streaming down my face. "Fuck," I whispered.

I tried to stand up, but Collith caught my hand.

We stared at each other, and I swore I could hear a clock ticking somewhere. If Gwyn truly was hunting me, it was only a matter of time before chaos descended upon us again. Even if Collith and I could leave the past behind us, we still wouldn't have a future.

"It's been a long day. I'm tired," I said, looking down at the blackened candles on the cake. I swiped at my cheeks with my free hand. "Good night, Collith."

The Unseelie King let go of me and I stood up. He rested his elbows on his knees and took another drink of coffee, as if he was completely fine with what just happened. "Good night, Fortuna."

Slowly, feeling as if our conversation was unfinished somehow, I went inside and closed the door.

When I turned around, I saw that the dining room table had been cleared and there were no dirty dishes in the kitchen sinks —the others must've been cleaning while I was on the porch with Collith. I hadn't even thanked Lyari and Cyrus for coming tonight. *Not cool, Sworn.* I started walking to my room, so frustrated I almost groaned out loud.

Finn's door was closed, but the door to Matthew and Damon's room was ajar, I noticed as I went past. "Star," a young voice said, clear as a bell.

I stopped in the middle of the hallway, and a smile spread across my face when I realized I'd heard Matthew's first word. Or, at least, the first word he had spoken since coming to live with us. Just like that, the frustration of moments before completely evaporated.

Damon made a pleased sound. "Yes, those are stars. Really, though, they're peepholes made by the ones who aren't here anymore. Do you know why, Matthew? It's so that they can look down and see that the people they left behind are doing okay."

It occurred to me that two years old might be too young to learn about death, but I wasn't the boy's mother. Maybe my own childhood would've been easier, if someone had told me a pretty story about stars and peepholes. Still smiling, I continued on to the bathroom.

Thinking of childhood went hand-in-hand with thoughts of Oliver. As I went through the motions of readying for sleep, my mood shifted once more, and I silently rehearsed what I would say to my best friend. Our survival was intertwined—he deserved to know what was going on with Gwyn.

My mouth tasted like toothpaste when I tiptoed down the hall again. I changed into boxers and a T-shirt, remembering Matthew's pure voice and Damon's response all over again. After a brief hesitation, I moved my pillow so it rested at the end of the bed, then slid between the sheets. I thought about Collith and hoped that he'd gone to bed with the rest of us.

I fell asleep staring up at the stars.

CHAPTER NINE

$\mathcal{I}$ made an appointment with Consuelo Thompson.

At first, I told myself it was curiosity. When that got harder to believe, I said I was helping my family. If going to a couple of therapy sessions eased their worry, it was a small price to pay. Of course I would go.

But as the appointment drew nearer, I started thinking of reasons why I shouldn't. It was a waste of Emma's money—who'd prepaid for three sessions—not to mention a waste of *time*. My father had tried to help people in the same way, but whenever he talked about his work, there was sadness in his eyes. How beneficial could therapy be if even Matthew Sworn hadn't been able to succeed at it?

In the end, without really knowing why, I got in the van and went to the appointment anyway.

Consuelo Thompson's office was in a small town halfway between Granby and Denver. I drove over pink-tinted roads and passed signs that reflected the beam of my headlights. It was nearly dark when the GPS guided me to a street lined with Victorian homes. I parked alongside the curb and double-checked that I was at the right place. The addresses matched. Frowning, I grabbed my purse and stepped into the night.

The van door closed with a stark sound. I hurried around the hood, my breath visible with every exhale, and onto the sidewalk. There was no one else outside, but up and down the street, lights shone from square-paned windows and cast patterns onto the ground. I went up a flight of stone steps, heading for the green house I'd been led to. My sweater did little to protect me from the winter—why had I only worn a sweater?—and a sudden breeze made me walk faster.

A moment later, the house loomed up. There was a sprawling front porch and hedge bushes along its edge. At the bottom of the stairs, I spotted a sign on the glass door. The elegant script directed Consuelo Thompson's clients onward. I turned right and followed the sidewalk, which glowed from small lights on either side. Seconds later, I arrived at a side door and a second sign that read, *Come on in!*

A bell rang when I stepped inside, and I found myself in the entryway of a waiting room. Lit by soothing lamplight, the space held an uncomfortable-looking couch, a side table, and a bookshelf. There were three more doors, one marked STAIRS and another RESTROOM. The third, I assumed, was the office. Muffled voices drifted through the wood.

I hovered there, feeling like an intruder. But I hadn't come all this way only to leave now. I walked to the couch and sank down onto its stiff cushions. Like anyone in for a wait, I took my phone out. I didn't unlock the screen, though—the answer to my earlier question had come while I was sitting there.

I'd worn a sweater because I was a Nightmare, and I shouldn't need more than that.

Feeling so unbearably cold was all in my head.

The reason wasn't a great mystery—making this appointment had affected me more than I wanted to admit. I folded my arms, trying not to huddle, and raised the phone again. A warning appeared about the low battery. Sighing, I looked around the waiting room for a distraction. The walls were bland as butter. There was a clock on the wall, and I marked each second with a tap of my foot. *Tap. Tick. Tap. Tick.*

In the stillness, my mind inexplicably shifted to Collith. There was so much I could've agonized over or wondered about, but instead I just thought about our recent kiss.

Before I could inevitably remember how that particular experience had ended, the office door opened. Two people came through, a man and a woman. The man gave me a polite smile and went to the outer door. A wisp of cold air slipped inside as he opened it.

I refocused on the woman, and she turned to me, still standing in the doorway. Consuelo Thompson was petite. Her dark hair was secured in a knot at the back of her head, and her cheeks and eyelashes were free of makeup. She wore a white blouse, a pencil skirt, and heels.

When she saw me, I watched her experience the same reaction most people did. But my new therapist had a strong mind —within moments, her eyes cleared and her breathing returned to normal.

"Fortuna?" she said with a subtle, lilting accent. I stood up, and she took a few steps to hold out her hand. "It's nice to meet you. I'm Consuelo."

I did *not* want to know the most intimate details of my therapist's life. "I have a thing about germs," I mumbled, reverting back to the excuse I used in high school.

Consuelo was unfazed. She led me into her office and shut the door, gesturing to the elegant furniture set on one side of the room. "Please, sit anywhere you'd like."

There were two plush chairs facing an elegant sofa. After a moment, I perched on the latter. Consuelo went to a chair, sat down, and picked up a notebook from a side table.

"Why are you here, Fortuna?"

Because of someone with good intentions and no boundaries, I thought about saying. But my usual sarcasm felt out of place in this room. My hands splayed out before me. I stared down at them, and suddenly they were blurring. I blinked and willed the tears to go away. "I'm here because something happened recently. Something with a... man. I'm not handling it very well."

The woman looked at me intently. "What happened?"

I didn't answer. Consuelo Thompson was human—if I told her the truth, a story that involved a demon and someone coming back from the dead, she'd probably have me committed. How was I supposed to explain that night and omit every important detail?

Or maybe, that cruel voice whispered, *you just don't want to talk about it. Because you're afraid.*

Once again, Consuelo didn't seem fazed by my silence, and she waited longer than most people would. A full minute went by before she asked about my family instead. This was an easier topic, and I felt some tension leave me when I told her about the patchwork group of people I shared a home with. Telling her about them led to questions about my parents. Time had made it possible to talk about their deaths, and as I gave Consuelo a halting account of how I'd found them, I stopped watching the clock.

Then she shattered my false sense of security with a single question. "Have you told anyone else about the rape?" Consuelo asked gently.

It was the first time I'd heard that word used to describe it. Unable to meet her eyes anymore, I transferred my gaze to her slicked hair. It was so perfect, as if not one of the strands dared to misbehave. "I told you. It wasn't rape," I said, staring at it.

Her voice could still reach me. "Let me ask you this, then. Did you want to have sex with that man?"

My jaw worked. "No."

"Did you want him to stop?"

"Yes."

"Did he know you wanted him to stop?"

"Yes."

The human paused, looking at me with obvious compassion. "If you heard these answers from another woman's mouth, what would you tell her?"

I turned my face toward the window. There was just enough light to make out the view—snow-covered hills, and a field beyond that. I could also see the steeple of a church in the far-off distance. I wondered what kind of church it was, and what kind of people went to it.

"I'd tell her that she was raped," I said softly.

Consuelo was silent. I waited a few seconds, hoping she'd be the one to venture into the stillness between us, but she didn't. When it became uncomfortable, I turned and looked at her. The moment I made eye contact she asked, "Do you journal, Fortuna?"

Something in my chest loosened. I shook my head. "No."

"That will be your task until our next meeting. Buy a notebook and treat it like a release. Don't worry about good writing or tying anything together. No one is going to see it except you." She stood up and smiled at me, a clear indication that our time was up. "It's just a stream of consciousness meant to let you process your trauma."

Trauma. The word made me frown. But I said something polite back and picked up my purse. Consuelo walked with me to the door, then into the waiting room. I gave her an awkward wave and stepped back into the night, feeling as though I was waking from a dream, somehow. I bent my head and hurried back to the van.

During the drive home, I considered calling Cora or Maureen. But I didn't reach for my phone. Music played from the speakers and I looked out the windshield, acknowledging the ache inside me. Even now, though, I couldn't cry.

My face was still dry when the van bumped and slid down Cyrus's driveway. At the same time I turned off the engine, a cracking sound vibrated through the air. I got out of the van and looked around. *Crack.* Was it coming from the barn? Closing the door gently, I shoved the keys in my coat pocket and started toward those tall doors. I was about to grasp the handle when the sound came again. From the way it echoed, it had to be outside. Frowning, I walked along the side of the barn. I rounded the corner and jerked to a halt, my eyes widening.

Collith was chopping firewood.

Despite everything that his body had gone through, it didn't bear the marks of his pain. Every edge was defined, every plane of skin smooth. His abdominal muscles gleamed with perspiration as he swung the ax. That stubborn lock of hair dangled in his eyes. Collith raked it back in an automatic, absent gesture, and as soon as it was gone he spotted me.

When I saw his expression, the subtle heat in my lower stomach faded and guilt took its place. Collith wasn't out here chopping wood because we needed it; he was doing it because he did. Breathing hard, Collith tossed the ax onto the ground and wiped his forehead with the back of his arm. "Fortuna? Is everything all right?"

"No," I said without thinking.

He appraised me as he took off his gloves. They landed on the ground, one after the other. After that, Collith reached for his shirt, which was resting on a pile of freshly-cut wood. "Would you like to talk about it?" he asked.

An automatic response rose to my lips. *No, I'm fine, it's okay. Good night, Collith.* I didn't say any of that, though. Maybe opening up to a complete stranger had opened a door inside me, because something was different about tonight. I wanted to be the people we'd been before everything fell apart. I walked over to one of the other woodpiles and sat down, then tipped my head back to look at Collith. "Do *you* want to talk about it? About... where you were?"

His eyes were dark as he picked up his coat. He shrugged it on over his sweat-dampened shirt and sat on a woodpile next to me. "You can say it. Avoiding the name only gives it more power. Hell. I was in Hell, Fortuna."

And I'd been the one to send him there.

I folded my arms across my stomach and huddled, trying to hoard warmth. I couldn't look at Collith anymore, so I fixed my gaze on the ground at his feet. The snow was flecked with wood chips. "I know there's nothing I can say to undo it. But I *am* sorry, Collith. So incredibly sorry."

I could feel him staring at me. I clenched my jaw to stop myself from blurting out another apology. When the seconds stretched into a minute, it confirmed what I'd already known— we would never be those other people again. Collith still hadn't responded.

"Okay. Well... good night." I stood up and started walking back toward the house.

"Darkness."

I paused. "What?"

"That was Hell," Collith said. I turned around and looked at him. He was still sitting on the woodpile, his foot propped on a log. He didn't lift his gaze. "An eternity in cold darkness. I couldn't see anything, but there were sounds. Those never ended, either. People screaming, the kind of screaming that makes you want to vomit. Like you're listening to them being torn apart. Then I'd hear one of the demons walking past my cell, dragging a body along behind them. Or what was left of it. Time moves differently in their dimension. It's difficult to explain... it moves slower there, but faster than ours. Once, while a demon was torturing me, he mentioned that I'd been with them for ninety-four years. Ninety-four years of being fucked, skinned, and eaten alive."

Our breath drifted through the air. I could feel a spot of ice on my cheek—no, a teardrop. I couldn't speak past the pain and guilt.

Then, startling me, Collith met my gaze and added, "It also gave me ninety-four years to think about my life. The choices I'd made. I don't blame you for how it ended, Fortuna—I knew the risks when I stepped in front of that witch. But if it helps to hear, I forgive you."

I could tell from his voice that he meant it. Forgiveness didn't remove the pain from his eyes, though. There was still an ache inside me, too. I retraced my steps and, with only a moment's pause, knelt down to put my arms around him. Collith was still for a beat, as if I'd shocked him, and then he tried to pull away. I didn't let him.

Until now, we'd both endured our pain quietly. We'd only taken it out when it wasn't an inconvenience to anyone else. But tonight, I didn't go back to my room or retreat into a chair. I pressed my temple against Collith's, inhaling the annoyingly intoxicating scent of his sweat.

"I'm so sorry that happened to you," I whispered, holding him tight.

There was another beat of stillness, and I waited for Collith to detangle himself from me. Instead, his arms slowly encircled my waist. When I didn't move, Collith buried his face in the curve between my neck and shoulder. Neither of us spoke—there were some kinds of grief that no word or sound could express.

But at least we were no longer alone in it.

The pattern my life had become continued.

Another early training session with Adam, during which Dracula never made an appearance. Another shift at Bea's. Another meeting at the Unseelie Court to discuss a faerie that had been caught on video, drunkenly displaying his ability to affect the weather.

I wore a black pantsuit, but there was nothing modest about it—I hadn't worn a shirt underneath, so a generous portion of skin was exposed down to my sternum. As always, I wore Collith's sapphire around my neck and the crown he'd given me on my head. I'd topped the look off with a deadly pair of heels.

Laurie had taught me well.

Tonight we were in chambers that belonged to the Tralee line. The location was different every time, for the protection of everyone at the table. Unlike most of the other rooms I had seen, the floors and walls weren't dirt, but smooth stone. The furnishings were unapologetically extravagant. Persian rugs, gold-framed paintings, and tables made of solid wood filled the space. There must've been a candle or an air freshener somewhere, because a woodsy scent kept slipping past me in pleasant bursts.

There were eight faeries sitting in the other chairs. By now, I knew all of them. There was representation for every bloodline, and luckily for me, neither Arcaena nor Sorcha had been chosen for theirs. Chandrelle was here, of course.

Finn sat somewhere behind me, and though he wasn't connected to the Unseelie Court in any way, no one dared question his presence. The Tongue was an exception to this rule, as well. While he wasn't actually sitting with us—I couldn't decide if this fact bothered me or not—he stood in the corner closest to my chair. Lyari and Nuvian guarded the doorway, both staring straight ahead, and I almost bought that they weren't following the conversation.

It would be impossible not to, though. There were differing opinions on what to do with the faerie who'd almost exposed our kind, and some of the council members weren't quiet about voicing theirs. Eamon, a gray-eyed male with more doctorate degrees to his name than the number of weapons hidden in my room, which was considerable, wanted to make an example of him in the throne room. A heavyset female named Yarrow argued the faerie's fate should be the same as any other lawbreaker, and he was to be placed in the dungeons for a century or so. I listened to every suggestion without showing my distaste—despite my questionable history with the Sarwraeks, Cralynns, and Tralees, the faeries speaking for them had been civil. And if they could be civil, so could I.

"And what of King Collith? Does he have an opinion?" someone asked in a crisp, familiar British accent. Recognizing it instantly, I turned toward the speaker and hoped he hadn't seen my grimace. Micah of the bloodline Shadi. He'd been a pain in my ass from the very first meeting. I much preferred Shadi himself, a watery-eyed faerie who hadn't said a word during his time at the table. But apparently he'd been convinced to relinquish his seat to this sharp-tongued descendent.

Like all of his kind, Micah was easy on the eyes. Six feet of black curls, olive skin, and five o'clock shadow along a defined jawline. Doubtless his beauty had aided in his quest for power. Unfortunately for him, I wasn't swayed by it—more often than not, the beautiful ones were also the most dangerous.

"The king trusts me to handle all matters until his return," I said evenly. It had become my go-to answer every time Collith came up during these meetings.

The faerie's nostrils flared, and when I saw that I knew he wasn't going to let it go this time. "You are not above our laws, Nightmare," he said through his perfect teeth. "One month ago, we all felt something within the bond between king and Court. I would bet my bloodline's entire fortune that it was his death. You killed him and you're lying about it. There are many sins the Unseelie Queen can commit without repercussion, but murdering our king isn't one of them."

Finn growled, and the Guardians shifted. From the corner of my eye, I saw Lyari's palm rest on the hilt of her sword. Keeping my focus on Micah, I put my hand out in a wordless order, knowing everyone in the room would see it. "Actually, I *am* above your laws," I said with a brilliant smile. "That's the beauty of holding your life in my hands. You're lucky I'm even bothering with these meetings."

"Queen Fortuna—" the Tongue started.

I silenced him with a raise of my brows. Everyone could smell the power rolling off me now. However loathe I was to use my abilities, letting this accusation stand could be fatal. I refocused on the pretty male still bristling with righteous indignation. "May I remind you, Lord Micah, that I no longer need physical contact to learn what you're afraid of? Whatever the state of your bond with King Collith, the bond between you and me is very much intact."

His eyes flickered. It was so quick that I almost missed it. "Do you intend to hold us all hostage with your power, then?" he challenged.

"Why not? It's exactly what you're doing to Gwyn, and look how well that's worked out for you," I countered. At my mention of the huntress's name, a ripple of surprise went through the room. *Shit.* I hadn't wanted to advertise the fact she was here to hunt me. I kept my gaze on Micah and smiled again, hoping to distract everyone. "I saw the results when you had a fair and kind ruler. Innocents suffered and faeries like Jassin got away with breathing. I thought I'd try it my way for a while. Do you have any more questions, Lord Micah?"

"No."

"No, what?" I asked, my tone still cordial. But everyone felt a shift in the room. I hadn't been lying—Micah was a younger faerie, by their standards, and his mental guards were nothing compared to Collith and Laurie's. It was child's play to get past them, and suddenly the hesitation that had been plaguing me lately was no longer.

Micah could still see the room, the table, the other faeries around him... but now he was also seeing a bear. It was massive, a perfect replica of the one Micah met as a child when he'd managed to slip away from his nursemaid. As Micah stared at it, the animal rose on its hind legs and fixed its black eyes on him. Firelight moved over its brown fur and shone on its sharp, yellowed teeth.

Everyone at the table watched a bead of sweat slide down the faerie's temple. "No, Your Majesty," Micah said finally.

To get my point across, I let the bear linger, and the predator in me wanted to continue feeding on Micah's fear all night. This was different from the rushed, desperate encounter with Oliver's shadow. The flavors of Micah's terror were so pleasant and it had been so long—I felt slightly buzzed from using it after all this time.

The memory of Collith's death chose that moment to return.

I blinked and saw his pale, shocked expression, that line of blood coming out of his nose. After another beat, I left Micah's head and took my essence with me.

Nausea gripped my stomach. *No,* I thought with gritted teeth. *You are not going to puke in front of these creatures.* I was about to suggest we end the meeting when Chandrelle said, "There is one more matter I'd like to present to our vivacious queen."

I suppressed a sigh. "Go ahead."

"You mentioned Gwyn. This cannot be a coincidence, as one of my descendants informed me she's made camp near one of our doorways." She paused, probably giving me a chance to explain. I remained silent, my face expressionless, and hoped no one could hear my racing heart. After another moment Chandrelle continued, "She hasn't attempted to enter, but it has been eighty years since the Wild Hunt returned to Court. It's common knowledge that Gwyn's... cooperation with us isn't entirely willing."

"I can't imagine why," I said dryly. The Tongue shot me a sharp look.

Chandrelle acted as if I hadn't spoken. "I'd like to suggest a celebration. Gwyn and her riders will be the guests of honor, of course, and the theme of the food and decor will be Welsh."

The Tongue's hot breath touched my ear. Despite his bulk, he'd moved silently. "Creiddylad was born in the British Isles."

Now I understood the irony of calling it a celebration. Chandrelle was clever, I'd give her that. Throwing a party in Gwyn's name would reassure the bloodlines that she was still on a leash, while at the same time reminding the powerful faerie of what they held over her. The Welsh theme was just a way to create the pretense of welcome... or maybe push the knife in a little deeper. It was probably something I should've suggested.

Suddenly I realized the table was waiting for my response.

"I don't see why we shouldn't." Even as I said the words, I tried to think of a reason. What if this supposed celebration only pissed Gwyn off more, and she did something drastic? What if she used the opportunity to kill me?

She could've done that already, logic pointed out. That was true. Collith believed there was a reason she hadn't moved against me yet. Maybe I could discover why at this feast.

Despite my unenthusiastic response, Chandrelle accepted it. As she continued discussing the upcoming party, I felt something push inside my mind. Before I could panic, the Tongue began to speak. His voice had a distinctly oily feel to it. *Micah is right, isn't he?* he asked. *The king did die. But he was brought back, somehow. That is how your voice rings with truth when you claim he's alive, and why we never feel him anymore. But what of your mating bond? Did that survive?*

I didn't look in his direction. I didn't answer. We might've gotten more friendly lately, but that didn't mean I trusted him. The Tongue knew he was right, though, because I felt his certainty as he retreated. Then I was alone in my head again. Chandrelle's voice became louder, as if I'd just tuned in to a radio station.

Anxiety rushed through me. Would the Tongue use his new knowledge against us? What if his display of benevolence after Shameek's funeral had been an act? I clenched my hands, grateful they were hidden beneath the table.

I tried to catch the Tongue's attention as everyone left the room, but he appeared deep in conversation with Eamon. *Damn it.* I wiped the frustration from my face and turned to acknowledge Yarrow, who had been our hostess for this meeting. She swept into a dramatic curtsey, her ringlets bobbing, and told me sweetly that it was an honor. Another excellent liar —not a single muscle in her face twitched as she said the words.

With Nuvian leading the way and Lyari bringing up the rear, Finn at my side, we filed out the French doors someone had gone through a lot of trouble to install down here.

The instant we were in the passageway, Nuvian whirled on me.

"Are you trying to make my job harder?" the faerie snarled. He put his face so close to mine that I could smell him, a combination of sweat and leather. Apparently he'd taken my promise to heart, because the fear I could usually sense around him was gone. Lyari appeared next to me, and Nuvian's gaze darted to her, taking note of this. Something like surprise shone in his eyes.

"Oh, relax," I snapped, losing the last of my patience. "Most of them are too cowardly to actually make a move against me."

For a moment, Nuvian was silent. The air thickened with his anger. Another whisper of unease went through me, and I lifted my chin to hide it. "This is a dangerous game you're playing,

Nightmare," Nuvian said at last. "I'm good, but even I can't protect you if there's an uprising."

The fight seeped out of me. It was obvious in my voice as I said, "There won't be. As I've told you before, Collith is coming back. I just need to buy him a little more time."

The faerie's doubt was like a perfume. I turned away, closing my ears to whatever response he gave. I considered paying a visit to Nym or Naevys, but I'd had enough of faeries today. Even the ones I liked. I started in the direction of Collith's rooms, my fingers brushing the ridge of fur along Finn's back.

Ten minutes later I emerged from behind a privacy screen, wearing jeans and a long-sleeved shirt. Lyari automatically moved toward the door again.

"We're not leaving quite yet," I told her, walking over to the small room that housed Collith's book collection. Finn stayed in his spot, but his bright eyes tracked my movements.

The smell of dust and old paper greeted me as I stepped over the threshold. There was no form of organization to Collith's library—not alphabetical, or by subject, or even date—so it didn't matter where I looked. I started toward shelves in the farthest corner. *Gwyn of the bloodline Nudd*, Collith had said when we spoke the night of my birthday. Maybe my survival was in the story of her bloodline.

Lyari watched from the doorway. "What are you looking for?" I heard her ask.

"Anything I can get my hands on about Gwyn," I muttered. There was a leather-bound tome on the bottom shelf. I pulled it out, using both hands because of its substantial weight, and opened it to a random page. The spine creaked like the bones of an old person. *Damn it.* It was just a record of the Court's finances, dating back to 1877. This could be useful the next time I had trouble falling asleep, though.

Seconds ticked by and Lyari didn't respond. Her continued silence made me turn, and something about her expression betrayed her doubt. "You think it's pointless, too," I stated. It wasn't a question.

For the first time since I'd met her, Lyari hesitated. From how slowly she spoke, I knew she was choosing her words carefully. "No one has ever survived the Hunt, Your Majesty."

"Then why bother guarding me, at this point? If it's so inevitable?" I demanded, holding the book tightly. The fact that Lyari—fierce, proud Lyari—was willing to give up sent a bolt of terror through my heart.

The faerie opened her mouth as if she was going to answer, but nothing came out. After a moment, her mask slid back into place and she looked like the other Guardians. Alert. Cold. Disinterested. "Are you finished here?" she asked instead.

I knew if I stayed, Lyari would stay, too. She would pass the hours standing ramrod straight, listening for potential threats, even though the room was protected by a spell. I'd probably be back tomorrow, anyway. A sigh stuck in my throat as I put the enormous book back. "Finished for now, at least. Let's go."

Finn looked asleep when I walked out, but the instant he heard my footsteps his eyes snapped open. He got to his feet and followed us to the door. It opened with a slight scraping sound. There were two Guardians in the passageway, and neither of them moved or blinked while we passed.

More time passed in the dark, but it was unmarked by urgency or conversation. The torches crackled and our shoes made soft sounds against the dirt. It wasn't until we reached the surface that I faced Lyari again. We stood just beyond the door, in a smattering of shadow and dying sunlight. Finn must've spotted something in the trees, because he was off like a shot. "Nuvian has guards out there, right? Waiting to follow me home?" I asked.

"Yes," my Right Hand said curtly. She already knew what was coming.

"Then why you don't you—"

"—take the night off," Lyari finished. "Did you miss the part where I promised the Seelie King I would never leave you alone?"

"Okay, your first mistake was promising Laurie anything. But between Finn and a dozen faerie warriors, I'll hardly be alone. Look, it's been one hell of a week. After meeting an ancient huntress who's been sent here to kill me, enduring that disastrous birthday dinner, and going to my first therapy session... I just need to process. I want to walk through the woods and forget that I'm the Unseelie Queen for a while. Will you let me do that?"

She didn't approve, I could see that plainly. She was Lyari, a faerie who valued being strong above all else. But I thought there was strength in admitting that I'd been affected by the past few days.

Maybe some part of Lyari secretly agreed, because she made a weary sound of defeat. "I will check my phone every hour—" she started.

"I'm living with a werewolf, a Nightmare, and a faerie. If anything happens, I'm sure we can manage."

Lyari didn't bother to say goodbye; she just glared at me and sifted out of sight. I turned around and scanned the trees, but Nuvian's warriors were on top of their game tonight. Nothing moved, not even my werewolf. For the first time in days, I was beneath open sky with no one else around. Dusk shone through the spaces between dead branches. I walked over leaves and ice, staring toward that fading light. I knew I needed to consider the real possibility that Gwyn might kill me. Not right now, I told myself. Right now, I would watch the sun complete its journey, and try to enjoy my own.

But less than a minute later, a sound reached my ears—a cry that was not human. My head swiveled, and beneath a nearby aspen, I spotted movement. There was something small and struggling at the base of the tree. Wary of fae tricks, I edged closer on silent feet, keeping my breathing low and even.

When I saw it was a fox, the dread left me in a *whoosh*. I hurried over to it, straining to see in the thickening darkness. Shock vibrated through me when I saw the reason for the creature's mewling—someone had set out a trap, and one of its paws was caught in those cruel, glinting teeth.

As I approached, the fox had gone completely still, save for the rapid breaths it took. When the silence grew long, it let out a faint whine. This jarred me into action, and I got down on my knees. The fox recoiled, but the trap stopped it from going anywhere and it shrieked with pain. I guessed from its size that it was young, and I could see ribs moving beneath the thin, dirty fur.

Focus, an inner voice instructed, sharp as a whiplash. I turned my attention to the trap. Within moments, everything else faded away. The trap's design was uncomplicated, with two jaws, two springs, and a round trigger in the middle. It was made of rusted metal and secured to the ground by a chain.

Speckling the dirt and snow around this chain were ruby drops, and it was clear that the fox had been trying to pull free for quite some time. I knew that if I didn't succeed in one attempt, I could cause more damage to its mangled leg. I put my hands close to the jaws in order to achieve the most leverage, and the fox lunged at me as soon as I was within reach.

"Fuck." I jerked back and held my hand against me. Its bite had been startlingly vicious and strong, reminding me that this was not a pet, but something wild and afraid. Though I trembled from the pain, it didn't deter me—once we were past puberty, Fallenkind didn't need to worry about things like rabies or getting sick. I put my hand back on the trap, and this time the fox remained frozen, quivering in fear. I took a brief, bracing breath and applied force to the springs.

The teeth sprang open. The fox instantly veered for the

safety of trees and shadows, but it stumbled on that injured foot. I caught it without thinking. Claws latched into my skin. Agony radiated through my chest, but I didn't care—the fox now clung to me as though I were a ship on a raging sea. I reveled in the feel of its heartbeat against my palms. Its poor paw dangled uselessly to one side, and the fox tried in vain to lick it.

"This pain is temporary," I whispered. Its golden eyes watched my mouth with interest. Encouraged, I got to my feet and started back toward the house, releasing a string of words the entire way. The fox learned about Granby and Bea's. When I ran out of things to say about these, I told the creature about my childhood dream of becoming a veterinarian. All the while, Finn wove through trees and pockets of darkness, his bright tail swishing. I was so focused on the fox that I hadn't noticed him coming back.

Minutes later, I was home. I struggled to hold the fox in one arm as I fumbled with the doorknob. Finn stood on my other side. He was still in his wolf form—turning back wasn't a swift or tidy process—so all he could do was watch. At last, I got the door open and hurried inside. My werewolf brushed past me, the tips of his fur covered in snow, and plopped down on the living room rug. His tongue lolled to the side. I kicked my boots off, and the smell of recently-fried taco meat wafted through the air.

Clattering sounds came from the kitchen. I went to the doorway and watched Emma, who hummed a jaunty tune while she filled the dishwasher. She didn't notice me, but it would've been impossible not to notice her—in the handful of hours I was away, Emma had died her hair orange. Presumably, she'd been going for red, but the result was candy corn orange. I almost burst out laughing. Instead, I pressed my lips together and waited for the old woman to turn in my direction, wary of scaring her. The fox was not feeling so patient, however, and stirred restlessly in my grasp. The movement disturbed its leg, and the small creature yipped.

Emma screamed and spun around. With one hand she brandished a wooden spoon and the other pressed against her chest. When she realized it was me, Emma let out a strangled gasp. The spoon fell against her thigh as her arm dropped. "Oh, thank God, Fortuna! I thought you were a serial killer. There are leftovers in the fridge if you're hungry. What's that?"

She'd noticed the bundle in my arms and came closer to investigate. When the fox yipped again, Emma jerked back, her eyes round as saucers.

"Don't worry, I didn't get us a pet fox. I found it in a trap. There's a place nearby called the Greenwood Wildlife Rehabilitation Center, and I thought I'd head there in the morning." Adjusting my hold, I glanced toward the living room—the TV was off and, for once, no one sat on the couches. Cyrus was probably at the bar, and Damon had undoubtedly fallen asleep while he was convincing Matthew to do it. "Is Collith here?"

Emma walked to the table, where there was a joint resting on a plate. She picked it up and took a lighter out of her pocket. "Yes. He's in his room. I'll be outside if you need me, honey."

I caught her peeking at the fox again as she passed. I crooned nonsensical words of comfort to its whiskered face, then walked carefully down the hall toward Collith's room. We were long overdue for a conversation about the Unseelie Court. These past few weeks, I'd been keeping things from him— namely, the fae's suspicion that I had murdered their precious king.

They weren't wrong, but that was beside the point.

I'd wanted Collith to heal on his own time, without any pressure or obligation. But he needed to know what was said at tonight's council meeting; something told me Thuridan and Micah's accusations were only the beginning.

When I arrived, Collith's door was open and there were no

lights on. Had he gone to sleep already? I stopped in the doorway and peered into the darkened room.

Collith sat on the floor. His back was to the bed, his legs stretched out before him, and his eyes were closed. There was no moonlight coming through the window, but light shone from behind me. It slanted over the carpet and onto Collith's jeans. He wore nothing else.

"Meditating?" I ventured.

"Trying to," the Unseelie King said. His eyes were still closed as he asked, "Would you like to join me?"

I glanced down at the creature in my arms. "Uh, maybe next time."

The fox whined, then, and Collith's eyes snapped open. He saw the bundle I was holding and raised his eyebrows. "What do you have there?"

"Look, honey, I got us a new pet!" I chirped, leaning down so Collith could see. It was obvious from his expression that he couldn't decide if I was joking or not. Before I could mess with him a little more, the fox started squirming again. Its sharp cry of pain pierced my eardrum. Wincing, I straightened and took a few steps back. "It has a bad leg. I'm taking it to a wildlife center in the morning."

"Fortuna and her strays," Collith murmured. There was something in his voice I didn't understand.

Clearly tonight wasn't the time to have a conversation. I tried to hide my frown as I said good night, but Collith had closed his eyes again. He didn't say anything else. I left his room and tiptoed down the hall again. In the bathroom, I took Cyrus's first aid kit out from beneath the sink. The fox didn't make another sound—it just watched with yellow, unblinking eyes. Holding a white plastic box in one hand, I finally headed for my room.

"This one is mine," I whispered to the small creature, pushing the door open with my foot. "I know it's a little plain.

Maybe I should add some color for Cyrus, before we move out, huh?"

Its ears twitched, as though the fox were truly listening to my meaningless string of words. Steeling myself for the possibility of getting bit again, I set the first aid kit down on the bed. Just as I undid the latch, I heard the front door close. I thought it was Emma coming inside after a smoke. But then I saw Collith through the window, crossing the yard in urgent long-legged strides. He went into the barn, and a moment later it flooded with light. I caught a glimpse of his brooding expression. Even after he was gone, I stared at that bright pane of glass, wishing I could use our mating bond to know what he was feeling. The mating bond that no longer existed. Because of me.

The fox released a sound very much like a sigh.

As I turned away to open the first aid kit, I let out a sigh of my own.

CHAPTER TEN

I stayed up all night with the fox.

In the morning, I got ready before the rest of the house even stirred. I stepped onto the porch, carrying the fox in a cardboard box, and started at the sight of Finn.

He sat in one of the rocking chairs. Though his face was unreadable as ever, I got the impression that he was making a point. It was the first time in days he'd left his wolf form, and I caught myself examining him with a critical eye, hoping to see more changes from the starving creature I'd first met. "Ready to go?" was all I said.

He got up and followed me to the van.

With Finn in the back and a fox in the passenger seat, I drove the small animal to Greenwood Wildlife Rehabilitation Center.

It was harder than I thought it would be—walking away. But I did it feeling better than I had in ages, having saved a life, for once, rather than taking one.

Finn and I were silent on the drive back. It wasn't from a lack of interest, on my part, but rather the desire to let him choose whether or not to speak. As we passed the sign welcoming us to Granby, a floral smell emanated from the vents

—I'd gotten another air freshener to overpower the stench of goblin. My grip on the steering wheel was tight, a habit I'd developed since being run off the road by one of Astrid's werewolves. Every experience I'd had these past few weeks had marked me, scarred me, even if most of them weren't visible on my skin.

"How do you do it?" I asked without thinking. "How do you keep going after what you've been through? How do you get through each day?"

The werewolf at my side—he'd switched back to the passenger seat, now that the fox was gone—didn't answer. Three minutes went by, and when he did speak, I'd half-forgotten I had even asked him something. "You become both beast and prey," Finn said in his gravelly voice. I darted a sideways glance at him, wanting to see his expression, but he kept his gaze on the road. "Equally fierce, neither quite wild enough to be rabid, nor quite tame enough to be touched."

I waited for him to continue, but apparently, that was all he had to say. *No one talks like that*, I thought. As though poetry was a language all its own. But Finn's words made me realize how little I knew about this person. How few conversations we'd actually had. Was he a writer, in his previous life? A teacher? Despite what had happened to his mate and daughter, was there a family still looking for him or hoping for his safe return?

A war raged in my heart—I wanted to ask him, to know him better—but then we reached town and it felt like the opportunity had passed. The businesses of Main Street appeared on either side. Open signs competed with the vibrant light of a new day. My gaze went to Bea's first, as it always did, and moved across the street. The restlessness was back in my veins, filling me with the desire to fight, move, avoid.

"I think I'll head to Adam's," I said. "Do you want me to drop you off at the house first?"

Finn didn't answer, but the silence was weighted now, full of his stubborn refusal to be left behind. I smiled faintly and turned on the blinker. Within a minute, I parked the van in my usual spot and reached for a bag I kept in the backseat. Finn got out and strode toward the line of trees beyond the street, where he would undoubtedly change forms. I watched him go, wondering whether I would do the same, if I had the option. What a relief it would be, to howl at the sky and face the world with sharp teeth. To actually be the animal that lived inside all of us.

I let out a brief, wistful sigh and left the warm van. I jogged down the sidewalk and pulled the door to Adam's shop open.

As usual, there were no customers in sight. Only two suspended vehicles and rock music floating through the air. "Adam? Are you here?" I called, walking toward the bathrooms.

"Your Majesty. What a pleasant surprise." The voice came from behind. I spun and rose my hands instinctively, simultaneously prepared to fight or inflict terror. My gym bag bounced against my hip. Dracula stood in the office doorway, his lovely lips curved into a polite smile. "I apologize. I didn't mean to startle you."

"Where's Adam?" I asked, knowing he could hear how my heart had accelerated. I was alone with one of the oldest, most powerful vampires in existence. Why hadn't I thought to text Adam before coming?

Dracula inclined his head. "I believe he said something about a coffee shop."

"Okay. Thanks." I started to turn away, but the vampire's silken voice reached for me again, wrapping around my mind like delicate ribbons.

"May I offer my own considerable expertise?" he asked. When I faced Dracula again, he bent into a slight bow, the movement like liquid. "After all, I *am* the one who trained Adam."

I hesitated. In another lifetime, I probably would have

accepted without thought, driven by my desire to learn. But the world of Fallen had endless shadows, countless pockets of darkness, and now I knew what lurked within them. My mind went to Dracula's motives for offering his time and efforts to someone he didn't know. Did he hope to have my heart? My throne?

I glanced at the vampire's hands. They were uncovered, which meant that if I trained with him, I would be able to discover those answers under his skin. Not only for my sake, but for everyone I cared about. Bea, Gretchen, Ariel—none of them knew the truth of what else existed in the world. They were vulnerable, especially if Dracula was a creature who placed no value on human life.

The ancient vampire had remained silent while I debated. But I could feel his eyes on me the entire time, disconcerting in their steadiness. As though he were a jaguar, sitting up in a tree, peering down at some small-boned creature and lazily contemplating whether or not to descend. "That would be great," I said at last. "I just need to change."

"Of course. Take your time."

Without another word, Dracula strode toward the mats Adam had laid down in a far corner. He wore a cream-colored vest, which came off as he faced me. He stripped off his filmy shirt next—I wasn't ready for the sight of him. His dark skin gleamed beneath the florescent lights, the planes and edges of his stomach like something from a sculpture.

"Do you not know where the facilities are?" Dracula questioned, his golden eyes moving toward the bag I still clutched.

Heat rushed to my face. "Sorry. I got... distracted. I'll be right back."

As I hurried toward the bathrooms, I could've sworn I caught a faint smile curving Dracula's lips. I closed the door and released a breath of relief, meeting my own gaze in the mirror. The person trapped inside the glass looked human. There were smudges beneath her eyes and her skin was the color of grief. I looked away from that sad creature, dropped my bag on the floor, and started taking off my jeans.

By the time I re-emerged into the shop, Finn had apparently finished shifting—I must've taken longer than I realized. He was on the floor, much closer to the mats than usual, and watched me approach without blinking. "How did you even open the door?" I asked him. Finn just looked back without expression. His whiskers twitched.

Dracula was right where I left him, and once again, it felt like there was something unnatural about his stillness. Those golden eyes tracked my movements with such cold calculation that it sent a quake of fear through me. I took my time putting the bag down and stepping onto the mat.

I'd barely had a chance to face the vampire when he flew at me.

In less than a second, it was obvious Dracula was faster, stronger, and far more brutal than Adam. I parried his blows, moving just quick enough to protect myself, but I couldn't land any hits of my own. After another minute, my breathing was hard and there were beads of sweat on my forehead. Dracula, however, didn't even look winded. He spoke as we moved in blurs.

"Your biggest strength is the ability to be both light-footed and agile," he informed me, sweeping his leg. I leaped over it and lifted my arm, which connected with his and sent a tremor through my bones. "By utilizing this, your opponent is likely to exhaust themselves. It's also likely they'll become overconfident and leave an opening."

"Oh, like this one?" I asked, breathless.

Our skin had only made contact for an instant, but that was all I needed. Before the vampire could react or respond, I was inside his mind. There was a wall, of course, which I'd expected

—I shattered through it with all my newfound strength as the Unseelie Queen.

Distantly, I heard Dracula gasp. Felt him try to push me out. Lives depended on me, though, and I needed to know everything about this creature that had come to my home.

Flavors coated my tongue as I straightened. I panted—a reflex more than anything, as there was no need for air in a place I didn't actually exist—and looked around quickly. For a moment, I wondered if I was hallucinating. But I knew I was inside Dracula's mind. I could feel him trapped within some in-between place, slamming at the wall I'd built with him on one side... and me with all of his secrets on the other.

It was the most extraordinary psyche I had ever seen. I stood in a library, and the ceiling was several floors up. It was covered in the same paintings as the Sistine Chapel. Every shelf within sight was filled. Unlike Collith's collection, there was nothing untidy or chaotic about these. Every volume was neatly shelved, tucked between other books of equally impressive organization. There seemed to be no end to the room—in both directions, it stretched as far as my eyes could see. Was this what my mind would look like, if I'd been alive as long as Dracula?

There was no time to think about it. The walls groaned, and my hold on Dracula's mind almost slipped. I ran to the closest shelf and opened a random book. The pages were blank. I frowned and flipped to the middle, but it was more of the same. Not a single image or word, just empty paper.

I put the book back, then grabbed onto the shelves for balance as the library shifted. Pain vibrated through my head at the strength of Dracula's blow. I tried to focus on the spines of the books, which made it easier to think about why I couldn't find his fears. *Maybe you're going about this all wrong.* Dracula wasn't a typical creature with a weak mind, but that's how I was treating him.

Gritting my teeth against another wave of pain, I searched

for a different book. One that would give me useful information in the diminishing time I had left.

After a minute of this, I arrived at a leather-bound book that felt heavier. The entire room started to shake, and tiny bits of rubble fell from the ceiling. "This is an important one, huh?" I muttered, eyeing the pillars and beams around me. Hopefully they'd hold against an enraged, ancient vampire. *Okay, here goes nothing.* This time, when I opened the book, I didn't think about Dracula's fears or his weaknesses.

I thought about blood.

The one thing that could affect any vampire, no matter how old or controlled they were. It was entwined with every thought and every memory. The master key to every lock.

It worked. I got a glimpse of elegant, blinding words scrawled across the pages, and then I was falling.

I opened my eyes in a land of tufted grass and distant mountains. No, I corrected myself, this was not my body or my memory. Bako—that was his real name—was on his back, staring up at a blue sky. In his peripheral vision, he could see the bodies of his fallen comrades. The ones that had been clinging to life, filling the air with their moans, were mostly silent now. Despite his waning strength, Bako kept one of his hands pressed against a gaping wound across his stomach. He knew if he were to stand, all his innards would spill out. In his other hand, he still clutched a sword. It gleamed in harsh sunlight as his breathing slowed.

Night descended like a cloak, making the field of bloody, dead soldiers less tragic somehow. Still, Bako fought to stay. He stared up at a crescent moon, thinking there were worse ways to die. But he still feared the unknown, and that fear was why I'd been drawn to this book. This moment. Bako's thoughts were not in English, but I was experiencing everything from his perspective—I spoke whatever languages he spoke and understood them.

"You fought bravely," a voice said suddenly.

Bako's eyes flicked toward the shadow approaching him. It was too dim to make out a face, but it was round and pale. He watched it loom nearer and nearer, until he saw it was a woman. She halted beside Bako's prone form and added, "You have a choice to make, warrior."

In spite of myself, I was intrigued, and I wanted to watch more when the memory began to fade around the edges—Dracula was finally succeeding in pushing me out.

Damn it. I still didn't know his intentions or his weaknesses. I squeezed my eyes shut tighter and held onto his mind with every scrap of endurance I could find. He pushed and I pulled. Agony rippled through me, but I found the strength to keep grabbing at books. I'd gotten the hang of it now, and it only took a moment or two to sink into the pages. I saw flashes of his life, spanning over centuries, rife with death and pain. But where were the screams and the jolts of fright? Almost everything in these books had occurred after Bako died and Dracula was born. It was as if he viewed the world through a sheet of unbreakable glass. Emotions were muted. Nothing was frightening or unexpected.

All at once, I understood.

Dracula didn't have any small fears, none of the phobias that everything else had, but maybe that was the difference—he was no longer alive. Just as Nightmares were cursed by their beauty, and werewolves by the pain of their transformation, that was the curse of being a vampire. They didn't feel the urgency of the living. So little mattered to them. Adam still seemed to care about things, but something told me he hadn't been a vampire as long as his maker.

A huge piece of the ceiling crashed down nearby. I jumped and frantically kept rooting through Dracula's enormous collection, keeping this revelation in mind. *I need to go back further. I need to find more of Bako's memories.*

I decided to return the book in my hands and run to a different shelf. Just before I slammed it shut, I found it toward the end and froze. Fear. It was buried deep within a memory I had no time to observe.

Suddenly I knew the thing Dracula dreaded most. The moment a powerful vampire had shaped his entire existence to avoid.

He feared failure.

But failure of what?

Agony screamed through my head as Dracula rammed into me again. This time, I lost my grip on his psyche. The crumbling walls, the chipping painted ceilings, and all those colorful books rushed away like Alice down the hole.

I snapped back to reality and staggered on the exercise mat. My temples pulsed. Once my vision cleared, I lifted my head and expected to see Dracula coming at me in a fit of rage. But the vampire stood eerily still again, hands shoved into his pockets, and regarded me with a strange expression. His muscles gleamed beneath a dewy layer of perspiration. "You are breathtaking," he murmured.

"Good thing you don't need to breathe, then," I countered sweetly. In the next instant, I rolled, stood, and brought my fist up to hit him under the jaw. I put so much force behind the blow that Dracula stumbled. He caught his balance an instant later, of course. Blood ran from the corner of his mouth, but as he faced me, he smiled and revealed straight, white teeth.

Then he straightened and dipped into an elegant bow. "You are as formidable as you are lovely, Fortuna Sworn."

His body language made it clear he wasn't going to attack. I noted that Finn was standing at the edge of the mat, his fur standing on end. I kept my eyes on the vampire, though, certain he was trying to trick me. Seconds ticked by and he still didn't move.

However infamous he may be, it seemed Dracula was like

everyone else when it came to a Nightmare's influence. Vaguely disappointed, I dropped my hands and moved to get a towel from my bag. I heard Dracula move and reacted a beat too late. He used his forward momentum to slam into my waist, effectively folding me, and we both went down. The vampire flattened the length of his body—which was surprisingly heavy—along mine, and trapped me to the floor.

I heard Finn snarl. Dracula muttered something in another language and he jerked. My werewolf must've bitten him.

"My back was turned," I managed. My voice trembled, not from desire but panic. Finn's snarls stopped and Dracula went still. I didn't look at either of them—instead, I stared up at the ceiling. It felt like beetles were crawling over my skin. I wanted to scream at Dracula. I wanted to beat him with my fists until his weight was gone. He must've seen something in my face, because in the space of time it took to blink, he was back on his feet. I stayed where I was, trying to contain the chaos inside of me.

Finn hovered near me as the vampire put his hand out. His palm was covered in scars and lines, and I had a strange burst of memory, an overlapping image of Savannah bent over my hand and running her finger along my fate line. "Your lesson of the day," Dracula said, bleeding freely from the wound in his leg. "Never expect your opponent to fight fair."

My mouth tasted like ashes. I slowly sat up and studied him, wondering if the vampire could possibly be as kind as he seemed. While I'd been in his mind, I got a sense of who he was. The essence of Dracula. To my surprise, it hadn't been evil, per se. Mostly it had been... gray.

After another moment, I accepted his proffered hand. It was warm, just as I knew it would be, but I was surprised every time. Romance novels and movies depicted vampires as cold, dead things. It was true that they were formed from death, but a real vampire had a never-ending fever, a side effect or result from the resurrection process. Their skin was always heated.

I walked toward my bag again, and Dracula made no move to stop me this time. With every step I took away from the mat, I felt more normal. Whatever the hell that meant. I took out a hoodie and pulled it over my sweaty tank top. When I started walking toward the exit, Dracula appeared next to me, followed by a small gust of air. Finn growled and pressed against my leg —he didn't like how quickly the vampire could move.

"Easy, warrior," Dracula said. "I don't intend to harm your queen."

I didn't stop, but my eyes narrowed at his wording—it had become a habit from spending so much time with the fae. The vampire hadn't said to Finn, *I will not harm your queen.*

Maybe there hadn't been any double meaning to his words, or maybe it meant I had one more name to add to that ever-growing list of enemies. A memory resurfaced, one that was always floating nearby when I came to Adam's. *I can't train right now. I might hurt you,* he'd said that night.

One thing urban legends got right about vampires, as evidenced by my success while I'd been invading Dracula's head, was the bloodlust. If Dracula had promised not to harm me, I would've instantly distrusted him.

At the door, I faced him again. My gaze flicked down to his bare chest of its own volition. When I looked back up, the vampire was smirking. It was so boyish, so disconcertingly *normal*, that I decided to take a risk. I still chose my words carefully—one, because I didn't want to offend a creature as powerful as Dracula, and two, because it wouldn't be smart to reveal how badly I wanted his help. How badly *Oliver* needed his help. "Being a vampire, I assume you've been around a long time," I ventured.

His eyes gleamed with amusement. "That is a safe assumption, yes."

"Then you might have information on Nightmares." Saying it out loud felt like a risk, somehow, as though I were showing this ancient vampire where I was most vulnerable. But I'd already come this far. I swallowed and forced myself to continue. "You might've heard facts or myths that have been lost through the ages."

"Is there something in particular you're seeking?" he asked. His tone was polite, with no hint of curiosity, as if he knew I'd shut down at any sign of speculation. I could still hear the question, though, even if he didn't say it out loud. *Why would the Unseelie Queen be asking about her own species?*

There were two things I sought, actually. I wanted to know whether the bond with the Unseelie Court would keep changing my powers, and I also hoped for information about a Nightmare's dreams. "I'd like to know more about... our abilities," I said finally. Guess I didn't trust him *that* much.

Dracula was silent, probably expecting me to expand upon this, but I met his gaze and said nothing else. The truth about Oliver hadn't passed my lips since I was a child, and back then, I'd been sent to a psychologist several times to discuss my 'imaginary friend.' It went against all my instincts to speak of him now.

"I will reach out to my contacts," the vampire said after another moment.

Hope filled my chest, making it feel tight. I didn't thank Dracula—he wasn't a faerie, but I wasn't comfortable saying those words to anyone outside my family these days. I offered my hand instead. Dracula didn't attempt to kiss it, like so many of the fae courtiers. He shook it with a firm grip, and just as it was with Collith and Laurie, I felt nothing beyond the touch of his fingers. "Until we meet again, Queen Fortuna."

As I pushed the door open with my back, I gave him a single nod in return, then I was outside and gone. Finn ran down the sidewalk, making the pastor's wife shriek and flatten against the window of the antique store. I bit back a smile and hurried past.

Fresh air filled my lungs, making it easier to breathe. I let out a breath as I unlocked the van and slid behind the wheel. Finn jumped over me and landed gracefully in the passenger seat, which was already covered in his fur. It felt as though he'd been in my life for years, rather than weeks.

Once I'd pulled onto Main Street, I pressed the button that would lower his window. The werewolf shoved his great head through the opening and his tongue flopped out.

Ten minutes later, I was parking the van again, this time in Cyrus's driveway. The brakes let out a long whine. My friend's truck was gone, usually a reliable indication that he was at Bea's. I turned the key, pocketed it, and reached over Finn to open the door for him. He bounded into the trees with a string of yips and snarls—a fat squirrel scuttled up a tree to escape him, chittering with obvious panic.

Careful to avoid hitting Emma's car with the door, I shifted my legs to the side. As usual, sounds drifted from the barn as soon as I stepped into the open. Collith was back to fighting his demons, and I still had some of my own to face. This thought was at the front of my mind when I entered the house.

Damon and Matthew were in the living room, playing with the child-sized plastic kitchen Emma had bought last week. The History Channel played on the flat screen. I scanned the rest of the space, but there was no sign of Emma. Since her car was still in the driveway, she was probably at Fred's grave again.

I still had some time to burn before heading to Court for Gwyn's supposed welcome feast. Remembering the task Consuelo had given me, I took a brief shower, pulled on the first set of clothes I found in my dresser, and padded into the kitchen in search of a notebook. Then I returned to the living room, where Damon and Matthew were still playing, and flopped onto the couch.

My hair dripped water on the cushion I was sitting on. I wrote the date in the upper right-hand corner, then waited for the words to come. What else had Consuelo said? *It's just a stream of consciousness meant to let you process your trauma.* Okay, so I was supposed to write about that night? How I felt about it? Or maybe just how I felt right now?

There was a slight possibility I was overthinking it. Whatever the reason, no matter how long I sat there, the paper remained blank. I clutched my pencil so hard two of my knuckles cracked, and I pursed my lips as I looked at it. Nothing came to me.

An hour went by. Then two.

"The Eskimos traveled for fifty miles in the freezing snow to get to shelter..." the TV droned. Matthew babbled softly, as if he was responding. A bubble of spit formed at the corner of his mouth, and Damon wiped it away with the ball of his thumb. There was such a tender look on his face that it hurt. Why should it hurt that my brother had found happiness?

With frustration rising within me, I put my pencil harshly to the paper. *Roses are red, violets are blue. Something is wrong with me, and I don't know what to do.*

"There," I muttered, glaring at the poor little poem.

Seconds later, Lyari shimmered into view. "Ready to go?" she said by way of greeting. Her armor looked as though she'd buffed it with oil. Her hair was pulled back in thick braids.

Thank God. I nodded, abandoning the notebook on the coffee table with undisguised relief. I caught Lyari glancing toward it with obvious curiosity before she schooled her expression back into its usual scowl.

I took my coat off the hook on the wall and moved to the door. Finn must have been hunting, because he usually appeared when he heard my footsteps. *Good,* I thought. If he were here, he'd want to come to the feast, and I still hated exposing him to the creatures and the place that had brought him so much pain. "Good luck tonight," Damon called.

I paused in the doorway and looked back at him. I snapped a mental picture, on the likely chance that something went terribly wrong at this feast and I didn't come back. The plastic kitchen, Matthew standing in front of it, Damon sitting beside him. "Thanks. We'll need it," I muttered. "Matt, cook some food for me while I'm gone."

"*Matthew*. We're calling him *Matthew*, for the love of—"

The door closed with a thunderous sound. I was grinning as Lyari and I set off into the night.

During the past month, we'd made this journey so many times that we had created a path, of sorts, through the snow. Come spring, the earth would probably be beaten down. As had become our custom, Lyari and I walked without speaking. Weeks ago, it would have been tense and full of unspoken jabs or insults. But somehow, without my really noticing, it had become something different.

"Hey, what can you tell me about Thuridan?" I asked suddenly. My voice felt harsh in the frost-laden stillness.

"Well, he certainly wasn't the brute you saw the other night. For most of his childhood, he was called the Runt. His parents and siblings were cruel to him." There was something in Lyari's voice that hinted she was still bothered by these memories. "He left Court many years ago and hasn't been back since—I heard a rumor that he settled somewhere in Australia. He must've come to the Tithe because he heard of Jassin's death. I almost didn't recognize him."

"Were you friends?"

"Maybe. I thought there was..." She faltered—something I'd never heard her do before—and a moment later, her expression settled back into its usual hard mask. "Obviously I was wrong."

We arrived at the Unseelie Court shortly after that.

Once again, there was no sign of Laurie when I walked into

Collith's rooms. Though a part of me was grateful, it did mean I was on my own for the gown and makeup. I briefly considered asking for Lyari's help—especially considering how much she'd loathe it—but the thought of us picking out clothes together, like girls at a shopping mall, was too strange. I moved toward the wardrobe and pulled the doors open. My gaze went to the dresses at the opposite end of the bar. They were ones I'd already worn at Court, and therefore, according to Laurie, permanently retired.

For a few minutes, my focus lingered on the gown made of sticks and spider webs—still stained with my blood—and I couldn't think of anything but Collith. How I'd hated him, in that moment, as the cat o' nine tails came down on my back again and again. That was when I had made a vow to resist him forever.

Then, later, Collith had revealed what had been going on in his own head during that terrible night. *I made sure to feel every single lash*, he said.

It was so twisted. So dark. So noble. So entirely Collith.

There was an ache in my chest now, as though the string that had once been connected to Collith was tugging at the air, still searching for him. Blinking rapidly, I hurried to pick out a gown, so I could escape this room and all the memories it contained.

Tonight I wore gold. There was nothing whimsical or delicate about it, though—the material looked like armor, as if a goldsmith had melded it perfectly to my body. It outshone even the sapphire.

In front of the mirror, I tamed my hair into something that resembled a chignon. Next I tucked a golden net beneath the crown, hiding the upper half of my face beneath its glittering strands. It didn't look right, so I took the net off and rummaged through the makeup drawer. I found a cylinder-shaped container of gold powder, which I dusted on the swell of my breasts and most of my face, creating a startling effect that I liked.

There didn't seem to be any gold lipstick or gloss in the supplies Laurie had left me, but there were at least five tubes of red. I hurriedly put a layer on, smacked my lips, and moved toward the bed. I shoved my feet back into the boots and walked toward Lyari, who was already opening the door. I started turning right, as we always did.

"Not that way," Lyari said suddenly, making me jerk to a halt. "We're not going to the throne room."

Before I could ask anything else, she veered to the left, startling me. Swearing, I hauled up my skirt and hurried after her. "Where are we going, then?" I demanded. I could hear the subtle sounds of footsteps behind us—Nuvian or some of his Guardians, no doubt.

Lyari didn't answer, probably because she knew how much it would annoy me. We were heading back to the surface, I realized after a minute. It was only until we were walking down the tunnel closest to the door, the path slanting upward, that Lyari finally spoke. "Imagine a clearing," she instructed. "It's surrounded by enormous trees and wildflowers are everywhere. It should be nearing sunset there. I'm standing next to you. Now walk forward, and don't lose that image."

I walked forward with my eyes closed, and I could hear Lyari keeping pace with me. The moment I felt air on my face, I opened them.

Wherever we were, it was pleasantly warm. A bonfire, smoldering under a blush-pink sky, was the only landmark in sight. Everything else was tall grass and pretty wildflowers. Beyond these were trees, as far as the eye could see. There were mountains in the distance.

"Welcome to your first faerie revel," Lyari said.

I shook my head, still searching the grass, the trees, even the horizon. I'd been to a faerie revel once before, in a dream. This empty place was nothing like what I'd experienced with Collith. "What are you talking about? Where is everyone?"

"Look again," Lyari ordered. When I shot her an exasperated glare, she just raised her eyebrows expectantly. Glowering, I refocused on the clearing.

As I scanned the tall grass, another memory chose that moment to resurface, and it felt as unstoppable as a breath. Collith's chest pressed against my back. His tempting, familiar scent surrounded me. His lips brushed against the shell of my ear as he whispered the secret to finding another dimension. *The trick is to expect more.*

The ache was back. I opened my eyes, not realizing I'd closed them, and looked out at the clearing again. Something was different this time, maybe because the memory had opened my mind and left it vulnerable. The grass and shadows shimmered like a mirage in the middle of the desert. Then, between one blink and the next, everything changed.

I gasped, unable to contain the sound of wonderment. I was faintly aware that Lyari was smiling—it was such a rare occurrence that I knew I should glance at her, just to see what it looked like—but I couldn't tear my eyes away from the sight before us.

The entire scene looked like a painting. Bonfires reached for the sky, placed sporadically throughout the clearing. Fae children chased each other, their laughter filling the air like bells. Some of them clutched streamers in their small hands. One of the courtiers here must've had a preternatural affinity with animals, because I saw a doe wandering through the crowd and a mountain lion batting at a female's skirt. She snatched it away from its paw and hissed her displeasure.

"The feast has already begun," Lyari muttered, her eyes on the piles of food. "They didn't respect you enough to wait."

I was so absorbed by our surroundings that I didn't respond. Near the flames, where the light bounced off their bare skin, there were faeries dancing. Some were completely naked. The Wild Hunt was already here, I noted, recognizing several faces among the dancers.

These creatures moved with an abandonment that had been forgotten everywhere else in the world. They didn't fear being watched, or mocked, or seen. As I watched, one of them tilted his head back and howled. I followed the sound, dragging my eyes upward. Overhead, there was nothing but stars and smoke. Despite the lingering daylight, a full moon was visible, gazing down at us with the serenity of something that had existed for a long, long time.

Without warning, Collith's voice sounded in my head again. A memory from another night like this, when I'd found myself drawn to the fae instead of repelled by them. *It's like a flower growing amongst the wreckage. Something beautiful hidden in the ugliness. Worth saving, don't you think?*

A breeze slipped past, fragrant with the scents of crushed grass and burning wood. We walked by a faerie sitting cross-legged in the grass. There was an instrument balanced on his velvet-covered knee. It was similar to a guitar, but smaller, and I had never seen its likeness before. Seemingly unaware of our scrutiny, the faerie strummed his fingertips lightly across the strings, a curtain of greasy bangs hanging over his eyes. "A face lovely as rain, but this queen has claws and fang... even sharper than those of the dragon she slain!"

I barely had a chance to wonder if the faerie was singing about me when he began crowing my name, over and over, and I quickly moved on. Lyari's armor made soft sounds as she followed. I wasn't sure where we were going—probably the strange-looking throne at the other end of the festivities.

In the next moment, I forgot about the throne as I tripped over something in the grass. I managed to find my balance, probably because of Adam's training, and twisted around to see what it was. A wine bottle gleamed in the firelight. After a moment, I realized it wasn't the only one—they were everywhere.

"There are no more humans to attend us," Lyari said by way of explanation.

"Children," I muttered, continuing on. "You're like children."

As we passed another bonfire, I faltered at the sight of a large cage and the massive bear it contained. He looked as alone as I felt. Faeries squeezed their faces through the bars surrounding his place in the world. They gawked, whispered, pointed. The bear ignored them, his eyelids fluttering in his sleep, as if he dreamed of a different time. But as I stood on the other side of the gawking crowd, watching the bear dream, it occurred to me that we were all trapped in cages and none of us knew it.

"What occupies your thoughts?"

I started at the voice so close to my ear. When I turned, I saw brown eyes looking back at me, crow's feet extending from their corners. The female wore red lipstick like mine, hoop earrings, and her hair hung down her back in thick waves. Witch, I guessed. Like Nightmares, they were one of the few species of Fallen that aged, albeit still much more slowly than humans.

"I was toying with the idea of letting this bear loose," I informed her, startled by my own honesty.

The stranger's lips twitched. "Excellent. You lift the latch while I work a spell that traps them all in this clearing."

It was a dangerous game she was playing, and we both knew it. She was trusting that I wouldn't have her seized or killed for such a treasonous suggestion. I rewarded her with a warm smile. "What brings you to the Unseelie Court, ma'am?"

She groaned. "God, did you just call me 'ma'am?' Thanks for making me feel my age."

"Sorry. I'm still pretty new at this whole queen thing."

"Actually, I've heard that you've adjusted to the crown amazingly well," she countered with a gleam in her eye. "Or so my niece once told me. I believe you know her. Savannah Simonson?"

It felt like every nerve ending in my body flared. If this witch was here for revenge—after all, I *had* tried to kill her niece—I was in trouble. I cast a furtive glance toward Lyari, hoping she would see something in my expression. But my Right Hand stood a few feet back, scanning every faerie that wandered near me. I refocused on Savannah's aunt and spoke quietly. "Look, I don't—"

The witch waved a hand, her rings glittering in the low light. "Don't worry, I'm not here for Matthew. Or to take my vengeance on that Nightmare for breaking Savannah's spirit."

She was talking about Damon, I realized. Blaming my brother for her niece's descent, as though he'd had any control over being taken by a faerie from the Unseelie Court. As though he'd had anything to do with Savannah's reckless spell going so terribly wrong. "Then why are you here?" I asked, my voice notably cooler now.

If the witch heard the shift in my tone, it didn't bother her. Her demeanor remained open and friendly as she answered, "I'm trying to find Savannah, actually. She seems to have vanished. Her cell phone is dead and her house was abandoned. No scrying spells have worked."

"I can honestly tell you that I have no clue where Savannah is. She left a note saying she'd 'be back someday,' and that was the last we heard from her." I hesitated. "Are you... like her?"

"A necromancer?" the witch asked bluntly. "No. I tried to undo her mistake, but my abilities come from the earth. Savannah channeled something a lot darker when she completed that spell."

"I didn't know she was doing that kind of magic. If I had..." I pursed my lips. Whatever regret I might have felt vanished when I remembered how she'd betrayed us to Astrid, and the part she played in Fred's death. She was the reason that Emma spent so much of her time sitting on a grave.

The witch turned away from the bear and faced a throng of dancers. She kept her eyes on them as she said in a conversational tone, "Oh, magic. I hate that word. It's originally Enochian, did you know that? Translated, *magick* essentially means 'power.' But then humans started using the word and it became ordinary. Trivial. Fairy godmothers, children's tales, spells that rhyme."

There was a faerie on the outskirts of the festivities, painting on a canvas. His long, thin arm moved in frantic strokes. It was me and Collith, I realized. The artist was so skilled I could already see what was forming on the white surface. The king and I stood in a dark wood, facing each other. My hand rested on his chest, just slightly, and there was an expression on my face I'd never seen before. Hope, maybe.

"If I were you, I would let him go," the witch said.

I looked at her and frowned. "I'm sorry?"

As she spoke, there was a hazy cast to her eyes. I'd seen the same look in her niece's eyes at the bottom of a damp oubliette, and by the time the witch spoke again, I already knew this was a Telling. "You are beautiful, Fortuna Sworn. Beautiful women tend to cost men their lives. Anyone who loves you will pay a price. It will cost you, as well."

I didn't know what to say. As the witch's eyes cleared, I glanced around for Lyari again, hoping to use her as an excuse to leave. That was when I remembered I was a queen and I didn't need excuses.

"Good luck finding Savannah," I said, turning back to the shorter female. I mustered a polite smile. "Anyone dumb enough to piss off a witch deserves what's coming to them."

She smiled back and started walking backward. "See? You were born to be a queen."

"I didn't catch your name," I called.

"Mercy Wardwell," she called back without hesitation. She paused to give me a deep bow. I searched her expression for any sign of mocking, but I found none. "It was a pleasure to meet you, Your Majesty."

Giving me no chance to respond, the witch turned away. I watched her slip through the crowd, graceful as a faerie. I reached down to yank at my skirt and continue walking, but something dug into my palm. Startled, I raised my hand to see what hadn't been there a few seconds ago. It was a business card. Only two lines had been printed on the creamy, stiff paper. *The world of magick is dark, and no one goes into it willingly,* it read in small block letters. Beneath this was a phone number.

Witches, I thought on a soundless sigh.

Tucking the card into the bodice of my dress, I turned around to face Lyari. Her gaze was directed elsewhere. I followed it and spotted Thuridan immediately, standing several heads taller than anyone else in the clearing. Lyari had caught his eye, too, apparently—his expression blazed with an intensity that made me suspect there had once been something more between them. And still was, if their lingering stares were any indication.

Interesting, I thought, tucking the revelation away for later. I could hardly blame Lyari, though—Thuridan had bathed since the last time I'd seen him. When his face wasn't lined with malice, and his eyes shone with desire instead of hatred, he was undeniably appealing. Like most of his kind, Thuridan had high cheekbones. His jaw was angular and strong, contrasting with his full lips. His hair, which had been shampooed and cut, curled against the back of his neck in tawny curls. Most of his mouth was still covered in a beard. Maybe, for Lyari's sake, I should use my queenly authority and order him to shave his face. For my own entertainment, I'd also make him shave everything else, too.

"Good evening, Your Majesty."

I wasn't surprised by the sound of her voice, but I did go still. "Gwyn," I said simply.

It was an insult, in a way. To use a faerie's name so simply, so intimately, indicated a bond or a lack of respect. Gwyn's pleasant expression didn't shift at my greeting, though. She merely folded her hands behind her back. With the firelight flickering over the smooth planes of her face, and the moonlight making her golden hair white, she had never looked more otherworldly. There was no blood hiding her features, but there was makeup caked over her eyes in a black strip.

"Would you care to dance?" she asked.

I kept my eyes on Lyari and Thuridan. "No, I wouldn't."

"Gracious," the huntress murmured after a moment. "It's been a long time since I've felt the thrill of rejection."

"What can I say? I prefer my lovers to be born within the last century. It's why I could never get behind Edward and Bella as a couple."

Despite my blasé tone, the rest of me was tense. But Gwyn didn't lash out or reach for her sword. Her mouth twitched and she followed my gaze to Lyari. "Queen Fortuna, am I to understand that you're calling me *old*?"

I lifted one shoulder in a casual shrug. "Well, you know what they say. If the dentures fit… excuse me, I believe I'm being summoned."

Lyari was still deep in conversation with Thuridan, so I made a show of walking toward Tarragon. The muscular faerie noticed me and, to his credit, surmised the situation immediately. "I apologize for interrupting," he said by way of greeting, speaking just loudly enough for Gwyn to hear. I turned around to see her reaction.

She gave me a look that said, *You've won this round.* I couldn't stop myself from letting out a breath as I faced Tarragon again. I was about to construct an explanation for that little performance when Lyari appeared between us and demanded, "What did I miss?"

Tarragon quirked a thick eyebrow at me. "I believe Queen Fortuna denied Gwyn's request for a dance," he said.

"Are you trying to get yourself killed?" Lyari hissed, staring at me with a combination of disbelief and exasperation. "Sooner, I mean?"

"On the contrary." I resisted looking toward the huntress again, because I knew she'd be looking back. "Gwyn finds me fascinating—wouldn't you want a person like that to stick around? Even if it was just to stave off the boredom of immortality for a little while?"

Tarragon observed our exchange silently, and though his expression didn't change, I could've sworn amusement gleamed in his obsidian eyes.

"I don't like it," my Right Hand muttered. "You're playing a dangerous game."

I smiled faintly, staring out at the clearing of faeries before me. "I'm just playing their game, but better."

I could feel Lyari watching me instead of the revel. A sensation pulsed down the bond between us—a sense of unease. I opened my mouth, but before I could say anything, a cry rose in the air. Something about the sound made me think, *Human.* Without a word to Lyari or Tarragon, I hauled up my massive skirt and started in the direction it had come from.

Within a minute, I spotted a group of fae males standing by one of the bonfires. With the flames reflecting off their smooth, perfect faces, the scene looked like some dark painting I might find on the wall of a decrepit, abandoned house. Something held their attention, and they'd formed a circle around it. I drew closer, keeping my eyes on the spaces between the faeries' bodies, and I caught a glimpse of her. A human girl, her face streaked with tears, her mouth opening to form another cry.

It took me another moment to realize what the males were

doing. Every time she flew across the circle and landed in a different set of arms, there was a blur of movement, and a piece of her clothing tore free. In typical fae cruelty, their game was both psychological and physical.

I pushed through them and snarled, "Get your hands off her."

They turned their faces toward me, and most of them looked amused. I focused on the one who still held the girl. "I told you to let her go," I said.

"Or what?" he asked, sounding genuinely curious.

The simple question made me falter. I stared at him, and he looked back with a taunting smile. The sides of his head were shaved, and the top was styled into a blue mohawk. Silver hoops lined his ears, all the way to that pointed tip, and his pale body was encased in leather.

For the most part, only fae youth—*youth* being a relative term, as their lives spanned centuries rather than decades—wore modern clothing. During my brief reign, I'd grown to hate the younger faeries more than the older ones. They had the arrogance of gods with none of the wisdom.

"Are you the one who brought her?" I asked finally.

"Yes." He flashed a grin. "But she was more than willing, Your Majesty. I have broken no laws."

The girl he held made a sound of defiance. She was even younger than I thought, probably fourteen or fifteen. She had brown hair that fell to her shoulders in dirty clumps. The skin around her wrists and ankles was torn and bleeding. The rest of her was covered in bruises. Some looked fresh, but there were others fading into yellow and violet. This girl had been his captive for a few weeks, at least.

Every face in the clearing turned toward us. A tight knot of anxiety formed in my stomach. Behind the wall I'd built between myself and the faeries of this Court, I felt their curiosity. This was the first time my new law had been broken, after all, and I'd made many dark threats toward those who dared defy me.

My first instinct was to have the Guardians deal with it. But when I saw the thin slash of Lyari's mouth, who stood at the front of the crowd, I knew that wouldn't be enough. She was worried.

As I worked to conceal a lightning bolt of terror that shot through my heart, I turned back toward the human. Her survival probably depended on what I did next. There was no other way. Steeling myself, I took a step closer to the blue-haired faerie, planning to grab his wrist and destroy him. Destroy both of us.

Then his cheek split open.

For a moment, I didn't react. My mind couldn't accept what my eyes were seeing. The faerie stared back at me, open-mouthed, and a line of blood ran down from the fresh gash in his face. "What—" he started.

His eyeball popped out.

Somewhere else in the clearing, a shrill scream rose up. I stopped hearing things after that; I was too horrified, too consumed by what was happening in front of me. *Look away, look away,* I kept thinking. But I couldn't seem to move. It was as though my brain had forgotten how to send signals to the rest of my body. Wide-eyed with horror, I watched the blue-haired faerie die.

It wasn't much different from what werewolves experienced, some part of me observed. His body twisted and contorted, the skin tearing and forming into bark. Branches sprouted from his ribcage, and the faerie was still screaming until his mouth was overtaken.

After he'd finally gone silent, and the place where he'd been standing now filled with a tall, swaying, lovely tree, no one spoke. I knew I was in shock as I turned, trying to find the cause of his abrupt transformation. My gaze landed on a child perched atop a faerie's shoulders. I followed her gaze downward. There were flecks of blood on my chest and neck. I looked out at the revel again and sensed their fear. *They think I did it*, I realized distantly. I found a familiar face in the crowd. It took me an extra beat to realize it was Lyari.

Subtly, so subtly that I almost missed it, she inclined her head. When I just stared at her, uncomprehending, Lyari's voice appeared along the edge of my mind. *Say something.*

Right. This was all a show, and the final curtain hadn't come down yet. I still had a part to play. Was I shaking? Could they see it? I lifted my chin and displayed the gore splattered all over me. "Did anyone else think it was all right to break our law tonight?" I called. It felt like a miracle that my voice didn't waver.

Silence hovered through the clearing. The only movement came from the children and the flames. Everyone else looked like a statue made of flesh and bright colors. Once it seemed they were sufficiently terrified, I found a Guardian—there were always two or three nearby—and directed my next words at her. "Bring this human back to her home. If anyone tries to harm her, kill them immediately."

My blunt order finally broke their silence, and reactions filled the air now. Angry shouts or hushed disbelief. The Guardian helped the human to her feet, failing to hide a grimace of distaste, and the unlikely pair headed toward the edge of the glamour. Someone must've signaled the musicians, because the cheery sound of a fiddle played through the night. A moment later, more instruments joined it.

Lyari walked over to me and stood at my side as the revel slowly resumed. I waited until no one was looking in our direction anymore. It took longer than usual. "Go ahead," I muttered at last. "Say it. I know you're dying to."

Her dainty jaw flexed. Every word was clipped as she replied, "Council members are questioning you. The courtiers started the feast without you. And when that arrogant pup challenged you, the Unseelie Queen, you hesitated. That was not the ruler I serve. That was… someone else entirely."

I knew it should matter to me, what she was saying, but every word only made me want the crown less. Part of me wished I could set it down in the grass and walk away. "I thought you said I was good at this," was all I said.

"I said you have good instincts." Suddenly Lyari was glaring at me. "Do you think you're the only creature to know real pain? Why should you get the luxury of falling apart, while the rest of us pick up the pieces and press on?"

I was about to respond when there was a prickling sensation at the back of my neck. I spun, thinking there would be something behind us, but the only movement was farther off. I recognized her clothes and her short frame. Mercy was walking away, leaving a trail through the tall grass. In a flash of intuition, I knew. I just knew she was responsible for the grisly scene that had just occurred.

"Did you do that?" I asked, raising my voice to span the distance between us.

Mercy turned around. Unlike the Tongue, who always seemed pale and drained after every spell, Savannah's aunt glowed with vitality. Her eyes were unnaturally bright as they met mine. "I don't like bullies," the witch said.

I glanced over my shoulder, wanting to make sure I hadn't imagined the tree. There it stood, dangerously close to the fire, its blue leaves fluttering in a breeze. From this vantage point, one of its branches looked like an arm, bent into a cheery wave. Unnerved, I turned back to Mercy with my eyebrows raised. "Earth magic, huh?"

Her red lips curved into something that wasn't quite a smile. Standing there, she was the epitome of those fairy tale witches she lamented. Beautiful, immortal, and powerful. "We are

Fallen, sister," she reminded me. "There's darkness in that, no matter what form our power takes."

A whisper of instinctive fear drifted down my spine. Mercy Wardwell was powerful—even more powerful than her niece—and I recognized a potential threat when I saw one. If this witch ever went dark, people would die. I had no doubts about that. "Well, I appreciate it," I said evenly. "I know you did that to help me."

Some of Mercy's intensity faded, and suddenly she looked more like the ordinary, middle-aged witch I'd met earlier. She held her shawl tightly against herself. "I sense the road ahead of you is long and dark, Queen Fortuna. Choose your steps wisely," she warned.

Gee, thanks, I almost said back. Luckily, Mercy was already walking away again. With every step she took, it felt like another layer of exhaustion sank into my bones. There was the familiar sound of creaking armor as Lyari shifted, reminding me she was there. "I'm going home," I said dully, starting in the same direction Mercy had gone.

The revel wasn't over—the literature I'd read claimed they could last for days—but Lyari didn't utter a single argument. She fell into step beside me with one hand resting on her sword, as though to warn off anyone who considered approaching us. Maybe I needed to start carrying around a sword, too.

I could pinpoint the exact moment we stepped over the glamour's boundary, because the noise behind us stopped. All the lights and shadows from the bonfires vanished. In the silence, my mind went back to the conversation we'd left unfinished. *Do you think you're the only creature to know real pain?*

If I didn't bring it up now, I probably never would. I cleared my throat. "Hey, about what you said earlier—"

I cut short when I lifted my head and saw Úna, standing in the doorway that led to Court. She instantly fixed those emerald eyes on my face. Her expression was… hungry.

Nightmares had this effect on people sometimes. It was rare, but it happened. I remembered, when I was a child, thinking how creepy it was that our neighbor Mr. Nesbitt followed Mom with his eyes. Unless they crossed a line, there was nothing else to do but avoid them and discourage them.

"You must come now, Your Majesty," Úna said, her voice low and urgent. "It's Lady Naevys."

CHAPTER ELEVEN

I heard Naevys before I saw her.

Her voice bounced harshly off the earthen walls of the corridor. The words were still too far away to understand, but she sounded... enraged. In all the hours I'd spent with Collith's mother, never once had she raised her voice or revealed any hint of anger. Truly alarmed now, I paused long enough to gather my dress, and then I broke into a run. Lyari's feet pounded behind me, her breathing faint and light, as if she ran in heavy armor every day. The shouting got louder and the passageway brighter. Within a minute, two flames appeared at the other end, the torches that burned on either side of the door to Naevys's room.

That door opened just as we arrived, and Wistari—the dark-skinned faerie I'd met the first time Collith brought me down here—slipped through. He raised his head and spotted us. Normally he greeted Naevys's visitors with a pleasant smile and an optimistic remark. Tonight, however, the set to his mouth was grim and his eyes were dark.

"Is she asleep?" I asked. The sounds from behind the door had gone silent.

Wistari shook his head. I noticed, not for the first time, how the hair at his temples was slightly gray. It always made me wonder if the fae's appearance reflected how old they felt, rather than the specific number of years they'd spent on this earth. "We sedated her," he said gravely. "It was for her own safety."

While he was speaking, a second faerie stepped into the tunnel. She was a female I'd seen before, but our only interactions were nods and bows. Her black hair was styled into a pixie cut and she wore bright, red lipstick. She returned to her post across from Wistari. I glanced from her to the door, feeling thorns of apprehension sprout from my heart. "May I go in?" I asked, as though I was a child. I wanted to kick myself as soon as the question came out.

"You are the queen, Your Majesty. You may do whatever you like," Wistari told me, accompanying his words with a fleeting smile to soften them. I gave him a wavering smile back, keeping my own just as brief, and walked past. I paused inches away from the door, tracing those blue flowers with my eyes. I'd hoped doing this would block out the voice in my head. The one whispering, over and over, *You don't belong here. You have no right to offer comfort when you're the one who took her son.*

The whisper only got louder. Grimacing, I pushed the door open and eased through. It shut with the scraping sound all doors at the Unseelie Court made—none of them had doorjambs. When I turned and saw Naevys, the voice inside me fell abruptly silent.

Her head was tipped forward, her eyes closed in a drug-hazed slumber. I crossed the room, hating how loud my footsteps sounded in the stillness. When I was close enough, I noted the gray cast to her skin, and my stomach tightened. Half of her face was covered by a curtain of hair, and I reached for it, thinking to tuck the strands behind her ear.

Naevys's head snapped up and her eyes latched onto mine.

"All those centuries," she spat as I reared back. "All those opportunities to evolve and improve yourself. And what did you do with them? *Nothing*. Your corruption is a disease. I won't let you spread it to our son. I won't."

Her body jerked, as if she were trying to lunge at me. But she had been part of the earth for too long—she was part of it now. All she managed to do was yank her hand forward, like the movement of a broken wing. The action caused a layer of skin to tear off her bones. She released a sound that was between a bellow and a shriek, and her efforts became more frenzied. That hand kept flapping uselessly.

"Naevys, don't," I managed, numb with horror.

Suddenly the faerie went rigid.

I looked up at her with wide eyes, hardly daring to hope that the Guardians' sedative was still working its way through her. I didn't release the breath in my lungs, as if even the sound of my soft exhale would revive her. Naevys stared at something behind me. The muscles in her face were slack. I followed her gaze, but the room was empty. Nothing moved except the torches, and the shadows they sent dancing across the dirt.

A thin whisper floated to my ears. "She still has good inside her. Remind her of that."

I whirled back around, but Naevys's expression hadn't changed. It seemed impossible that she'd spoken, and suddenly I was questioning my own sanity. "Naevys? Do you know who I am?" I asked cautiously, stepping closer. "Are you talking about Gwyn?"

The moment I said the huntress's name, Naevys pierced the air with a long scream, and I clapped my hands over my ears. There was something sharper about this one, more afraid. I'd never touched her—I shouldn't have even been able to sense it—but Naevys was part of the Unseelie Court. Because of our bond, I could taste her fear in the air and in my mouth.

There was nothing I wanted to savor about this faerie's

terror. Images started coming at me, and within seconds, I put it together—she was reliving the moment Laurie's spell claimed her.

The memory was like quicksand. I sank into it, and struggling only made it stronger. Colors brightened, surroundings solidified, until I was in the memory alongside her. I could still hear Naevys screaming, but it was muffled, like she was on the other side of a wall.

Her death began with a single, delicate root. It stuck out from the dirt, no larger than a slender rope. One of the Guardians sidestepped it. As Collith's mother walked past, it reached out and touched her shoulder, like the barest brush of someone's fingertips. She noticed, of course, but dismissed it in her haste—she was late for a luncheon in Paris. Naevys had been meeting with Lady Mirthal for months, planting seeds with every conversation, in an effort to turn the tides against Sylvyre.

Then another root grew from the passageway wall, this one thicker, more insistent. It wrapped around Naevys's ankle with a grip that made her gasp. All thoughts of her luncheon vanished. She stopped and looked down, frowning, but the spell gave her no time to panic or pull free—more roots shot out, this time with enough force to make part of the tunnel crumble. Naevys started screaming. Her Guardians had already surged forward, and their swords flashed as they hacked at the roots. But there were too many of them, pouring from the ground with the inevitability of an ocean wave. The tangle, which was so thick and swarming that all the Guardians could see of Naevys was her head, slowly pulled her into the wall. She felt some of the vines burrowing inside her, then through her.

The last thing she saw was Sylvyre, standing in front of her, looking as satisfied as a well-fed cat.

Naevys would never know if he was planning to speak, to

provide an explanation for this betrayal, because she passed out from pain and terror.

The memory went dark, too, and I saw my chance. Clumsy with desperation, I tore myself out of Naevys's mind and threw up a barrier between us. She didn't fight me. Back in reality, my head already throbbing, I turned in time to see Wistari, the black-haired female, Lyari, and Úna spill into the room, weapons drawn and teeth bared. When there was no enemy to fight, they all looked to me for an explanation. I was frozen, my thoughts slow and dull as a result of what I'd just seen.

"She needs Collith," I said, more to myself than them. Too late, I comprehended that I'd spoken out loud. But the words were in the open now, and I felt the Guardians watching me. I heard the whispers of their thoughts. *If the king isn't dead, what's stopping him from visiting his mother?*

They didn't trust me. I could see it in their eyes. Strangely enough, the realization hurt.

Naevys was stirring again—my attention snapped back to her, and she started muttering in Enochian. Her brows were furrowed, as though she were deep in thought. Or another memory.

I want to go home. The thought came out of nowhere, but it struck me as only a truth could. Suddenly I longed to leave this sad room, see the warm glow of windows through the trees, step into a warmth that smelled like evergreen and coffee. And maybe a little like wolf, too.

Standing there, I thought of reasons why I should give in to the impulse. I was already sleep-deprived from staying up with the fox. I needed to get out of this dress. Emma might worry. The smart thing to do was return home and go to bed.

But there was a bitter, undeniable truth that kept me from turning away.

Naevys was dying.

My mind flashed back to my own mother, lying slumped in that hallway. Her last moments had been made of pain and fear. There was no way of knowing if Naevys would fade tonight, but no one should die alone, especially not a person as good as her. And the one who should've been here was far away, because I'd sent him to Hell and he hadn't come back the same. In a way, her son was still dead.

The chair—the origin of which was still a mystery—was still there. I looked down at it for a moment, already wincing at the thought of sleeping on those hard armrests. I raised my gaze and looked at Lyari, whose resigned expression probably matched mine.

"Will you bring me some reading materials? Preferably something about the Wild Hunt? Oh, and a change of clothes?" I added, hoping none of my weariness slipped into my voice. The faerie bowed and retreated. While everyone left the room, I dropped into the chair and heaved a silent sigh.

It was going to be a long night.

Hours passed in the dark. I waited until Naevys succumbed to sleep, but it had become clear I wasn't going to get any of my own. Not in a chair, at least. Once Naevys's eyelids stopped fluttering and she'd gone completely still, her breathing faint and steady, I got to my feet and tiptoed to the door.

Úna was the only Guardian in the passageway when I emerged. Unease crept through me, but I kept it from my face. "Where's Lyari?" I asked briskly, pretending to look for her so I could avoid eye contact.

"Her shift ended three hours ago."

I stared at Úna, who stared back with heat in her eyes. Lyari wouldn't leave without ensuring there was someone to walk me home. *Fuck.* I swallowed the curse and prayed I was wrong. But when I turned, walking away without another word, Úna's boots crunched over the dirt. She was following me.

Mentally, I rehearsed what I would say if she tried to make a romantic declaration. Úna didn't seem like the kind of person who'd take it well, so none of the usual excuses felt right. We made our way upward, and minutes ticked by. Úna didn't utter a word. By the time we reached the tunnel that would take us to the door, I was half-convinced that I'd been worried for nothing.

Then she grabbed my arm.

My training wasn't fast enough for Úna's passion. She hauled me against her, and I felt her palm cup my cheek. "You're so beautiful," she breathed. "A goddess among mortals."

Panic and training fought for control over my body. "Okay, Úna, I'm going to give you one—"

Her face descended toward mine. Realizing what she was doing, I jerked my head to the side and Úna's lips smashed against my cheek instead. I felt something wet—*her tongue*, I thought with a rush of revulsion—just as I wrenched free. "Get *away* from me," I spat, swiping roughly at her saliva.

A desperate sound burst from her, and once again, the faerie moved so quickly I had no chance to recoil. I screamed, struggling against her. Úna was stronger. She pushed me against the hard, unrelenting wall of the passageway. "No, stop!" I managed, twisting my head to the side. Where were the other Guardians?

She growled, clutching my wrists in one hand and gripping my face with the other. There was no confusion as to what her intent was—I could feel all her desire and cruelty in the way she smothered me with the entire length of her body. My struggles felt like nothing against her brute strength.

"But I love you. God, if only you knew how much I love you. Just let me." With every word, her accent thickened. Her hold on my jaw was tight, too tight. I tried to say her name, tried to reason, but her mouth crushed mine so hard that I was only able to make a strangled sound that no one heard.

Then, I bit her.

I sank my teeth so hard into her flesh that I felt them grind together. Úna screamed and jerked back. She pressed her hand to her lower lip. Drops of blue blood were already staining her armor. For a second she just stared at her wet fingertips, and I stood there panting. Then her eyes narrowed and flicked back to my face. "You *bitch*."

She hit me, a swift blow that sent me reeling. I cried out and slammed into the wall again. My vision went splotchy, back and forth from shades of light to dark. Stumbling, I swung blindly. I'd put more weight behind the throw than I'd thought, and my knuckles grazed Úna's jaw just enough that she staggered to one side.

She laughed.

Before I could react she was on me, pinning me a second time. Now I dug my nails into her face, trying to shove it away. Úna let out a cry of her own. She grabbed my wrist and yanked. I gasped in pain, and suddenly I was back in those woods. Ian O'Connell was everywhere, his face, his scent.

No. This is not going to happen to me again.

With that single thought, my terror hardened into anger. My weapons were out of reach, so I raised my other hand and punched Úna in the throat. She stumbled back, choking, and I didn't give her a chance to recover. As I came down on her like one of the furies from Mom's stories, I didn't use any power. I didn't ruin her mind with her own fear.

I just kicked her fucking ass.

At some point during the beating, I started seeing the demon's face where Úna's should have been. With every punch, I was hitting that thing I'd met at the crossroads. With every kick, I was striking the monster that sent me to the brink of insanity. What I lacked in supernatural speed and strength, I made up for in ferocity. Úna never got the chance to retaliate or defend herself—I was a tempest, a god, a wound. Eventually the faerie fell and couldn't get back up. I raised my leg, preparing to stomp on her, but something stopped me. A memory.

Choose mercy, Fortuna.

I put my foot back on solid ground and glared at Úna, as if it was her fault that I couldn't bring myself to kill her. It was then I noticed her body was stretched across the passageway, blocking the way I needed to go. Gritting my teeth at the thought of touching her, I leaned down and grabbed Úna's ankles. *Damn, she's heavy.*

As I moved her, I talked.

"I read a journal recently. Found it on one of Collith's shelves. In an entry toward the end, the owner wrote about his brother's banishment. A faerie named Marlevaur—that's a mouthful, huh? Well, the Tongue did a spell, and ol' Marlevaur physically couldn't enter the Unseelie Court anymore. Apparently being separated from other faeries for too long, or spending too much time near technology can affect your immortality. Marlevaur's body started decaying. Teeth breaking, skin sagging, all of that perfect youth just… gone. He turned to drugs to ease the pain of being exiled. But they weren't enough. Marlevaur was so desperate for power that he started killing other Fallenkind for their parts. If he had no use for something, he sold it at a black market. Eventually he became the first goblin. Fascinating, isn't it?"

I lowered myself to one knee, and I waited until her gaze met mine. Both of her eyes were swelling shut. "You are henceforth banished, Úna of bloodline Daenan. You will live long enough to watch yourself devolve into a creature that won't be accepted, no matter where you go. Then, you'll die. If I ever see you again, I *won't* choose mercy. Understand?"

She nodded. It was slight, barely more than a twitch of her

chin, but I saw it. That was good enough for me.

For once, I was entirely alone as I returned to the surface. As I walked, I pulled my phone out of the bodice. The bright glow of the screen seemed out of place in the medieval-looking passageway. I allowed the camera to see my face, and then the apps appeared. Now I just needed a signal.

Stars greeted me at the end of the tunnel. Still holding my phone, I emerged into the open, and I was surprised to see it was still nighttime. I sent Nuvian a text, informing him of Úna's banishment—he'd see it the next time he went to the surface. By then, Úna would be long gone. Hopefully the Tongue wouldn't need her physically present for the spell. I probably should've done some research on that beforehand.

Speaking of Nuvian, where the hell *was* he? Or the other Guardians?

If there were any of them in the woods, they stayed hidden while I journeyed home. The wind was angry tonight, just like me. Snowflakes rushed through the air like incensed white bees. It seemed there was a price to pay for its shimmering beauty, for snow couldn't exist without the freeze.

For a few minutes, I just stood there. I knew it was just the adrenaline, but I felt... stronger. Better. As though, by fighting Úna, I'd reclaimed a piece of myself.

I was smiling when I emerged into the yard.

As usual, the porch light was on. I kept my eyes on it and jogged the rest of the way home. After I'd unlocked the door, I closed it behind me and pulled off one boot.

Muffled sobs drifted through the stillness.

I paused, startled, then hurried to get the other boot off. My socks muffled my footsteps as I went down the hall.

The instant I opened his bedroom door, the sound of Collith's pain stopped. I didn't believe for a second that it had passed—that wasn't how pain worked. Instead, we tucked it away, where it was forced to be quieter and where we hoped it wouldn't bother anyone.

It took a few seconds for my eyes to adjust to the darkness. I reached out blindly, picturing Collith on his side, as he so often was during his nightmares. Instead of a shoulder, my hand landed on the muscular swell of his chest. I barely noticed—the skin against my palm was hot. Fear ruptured through me, but it was mine, not Collith's.

The faeries of the Unseelie Court ran cold. That was how evolution had made them, and there weren't exceptions. They didn't get sick, either, which meant that Collith was doing this to himself. Destroying his own body with the power of his mind.

He was dying right alongside his mother.

"Go away," the king rasped when I left my hand there.

I pulled away, but I didn't leave. Now that I knew what he'd been through, I couldn't. Collith either gave up or stopped caring, because he was silent after that. The stillness became so loud, so ringing, that I could hear my own heartbeat. I knelt at Collith's side, even after it started to hurt and the cold sank into my bones. Eventually Collith's breathing deepened and it was clear he'd fallen asleep.

Just as I had with his mother, I stayed. Time passed in our small corner of the world, and I didn't look once at the alarm clock or out the window. My mind rewound and played back everything that had happened since the sun set. It lingered on the part with Úna.

"I saved myself tonight," I told Collith quietly, skimming his forehead with the back of my wrist. His skin was slightly cooler, and I let out a breath of relief. "That's how I know you can do it, too."

Collith didn't reply, but that was all right. Conversation wasn't why I was here.

For the rest of the night, I stayed. Through every shudder

and bad dream, I stayed. I stayed until Collith's demons knew he wasn't fighting this battle on his own.

I stayed until the dark wasn't quite as dark anymore.

CHAPTER TWELVE

*M*orning crept over the horizon.

I was already awake and waiting for it. My blankets and sheets were tangled and damp from my restless night. The moment the alarm clock on the nightstand went off, I threw them all aside. I didn't work at Bea's today—she'd been scheduling me less since my very public breakdown—but I had other ways to pass the time. Other ways to keep my mind occupied. I pulled a clean set of workout clothes from the dresser and put everything on as if I were late.

In the hallway, I discovered that Finn's bedroom door was closed. He wasn't in front of mine, which meant he'd probably changed forms and was sleeping it off. If Lyari found out I wasn't being guarded, she'd be furious. *Guess it's a good thing Lyari won't find out, then.* The thought of more time alone was too tempting to resist. I tried to avoid the creaky spots in the floor as I made my way outside.

The air was strange when I stepped into the open. Charged. It wasn't snowing, but it felt like the wind carried bits of glass on it, hurting every part of my exposed skin. Even this wouldn't deter me from a run. I jogged down the steps, and the instant I reached the bottom, I saw them. My eyes widened and I froze, partly in terror, partly in awe.

The Wild Hunt was airborne. The riders and steeds ran through the gray expanse above, manes flying and weapons gleaming. Where there should've been the sound of pounding hooves, there was only the wind, whispering ancient secrets in my ear. They looked so free, so limitless. They didn't think about things like paying bills or sitting on thrones. No one could hurt them. No one could touch them—not even faeries or demons. My heart ached at the thought, and suddenly I pictured myself among them, my smiling face turned toward the horizon, seeking sunlight and warmth. Our whoops filled the air and so did we. Simple rules like gravity meant nothing. I held the reins tightly, my knuckles sharp and white, as though I'd never let go.

Something moved in the corner of my eye, and the daydream vanished. *Gwyn.* Thinking she was trying to get the jump on me, I recoiled, a cry rising to my lips. But the faerie wasn't even looking at me. She directed her gaze toward the sky, just as I had, and made no attempt to close the distance between us. I didn't relax, though. Not for a second. "Lovely, are they not?" she asked in a conversational tone. A strand of golden hair blew across her lips.

"Yes," I said, looking at the riders again. "But still not worth the price."

I wasn't sure how she would react—apprehension fluttered through my stomach as I said the words—but Gwyn just kept her gaze on the rousing horizon and smiled. There was something bittersweet about her expression.

"There are days I agree with you," she replied. "When I asked the witches to perform the spell that made me what I am, none of us knew what the side effects would be. Nature always finds a balance, of course. I knew that, and I was prepared for the consequences. I thought becoming the ultimate huntress would lead me to Creiddylad. Alas, it didn't work."

The riders began their descent. As the horses hit the ground, many of them snorting with obvious displeasure, I faced Gwyn again. A sound like thunder rumbled through the yard. "Do you tell all your quarries this?" I asked. Though my insides quaked, there was no waver in my voice. *Thank God for small favors.*

Gwyn met my gaze. Her eyes were lined in kohl, which made the blue of her irises look brighter. "No."

It suddenly occurred to me that the riders' landing may have woken my family. I cast a furtive glance toward the house, searching for any lights—I didn't want them to see Gwyn or her dark followers. That would lead to questions, which I would have no answers to. The tight sensation in my chest eased when I saw only darkened windows staring back.

"Have you begun preparing them?" Gwyn asked, probably noticing how my attention had wandered, even if it was just for a moment. Something told me there was very little she didn't see.

Anger, hot and unexpected, flowed through my veins. I gave Gwyn a bitter smile. "And how do you suggest I do that? How, exactly, does a person 'prepare' her family for her upcoming murder?"

The faerie smiled, too, but there was nostalgia in the way her lips curved. "You're so young. Speaking to you makes me remember. How long it's been since I've cared about dying."

"I'd be glad to put you out of your misery," I offered without thinking.

Gwyn appraised me. "You truly mean that. If I asked, you'd cut me down, right here and now."

It was my first instinct to deny it... but then my mind flashed to Ayduin. I saw his eyes widening, pictured the knife jutting from his body. My grip on it had been so firm, so unapologetic. I remembered how steam had risen between us as his body reacted to the holy water.

"It's not like I go on killing sprees," I snapped. It was easy to forget my fear of Gwyn in the face of this new worry—that she and I shared something in common. "I just rid the world of assholes, if a prime opportunity happens to present itself."

The huntress smirked, and I knew she didn't believe me. Her next words confirmed it. "There's a darkness in you, Fortuna Sworn. 'Tis a pity I have to end your life. It would've been so entertaining to see how much that evolves."

"Fine," I said with a shrug, trying to hide my pang of fear. "If you're going to kill me, the very least you could do is reveal who sent you."

"That's not how this works, my lovely queen. What would you give for that information?"

An incredulous laugh stuck in my throat. *Fool me once, shame on you. Fool me twice, shame on me. Fool me three times, and you might as well just remove my head right now,* I thought. The day I made another bargain with a faerie was the day God sent a messenger to let the Fallen know all was forgiven, and we could come home.

My hands clenched into fists, and because my arms were folded, the movement was obvious. I knew I was showing too much emotion and playing right into Gwyn's hands. If Lyari were here, she'd be glaring daggers at me.

"Should we just get this over with?" I asked, willing my eyes to be as cold as I felt, standing there in the early morning.

"I am not here to kill you. At least not yet," Gwyn added, almost like an afterthought. "I thought a demonstration was in order."

Dread felt like a heavy stone in my stomach. "A demonstration of what?"

Rather than responding, Gwyn turned away from me. One of

her followers seemed to interpret this as a signal of some kind, and the cluster of horses and riders shifted. After a moment, a tall figure emerged. He was one of the loveliest faeries I'd ever seen, his pale skin a stark contrast against his dark hair. I had to force my gaze away from his face to take note of the rope he was holding. When I followed the length of that rope and saw what was at the end of it, the dread in my stomach changed to panic.

"Your Majesty, I'd like you to meet Mizuki of the bloodline Ito. She is a courtier of the Seelie Court," Gwyn said. Her eyes gleamed with undeniable anticipation.

When I saw that, it felt like the ground dropped out from beneath me. I was weak. I couldn't save anyone. But something told me Gwyn's *demonstration* would make me want to try anyway.

A moment later, the dark-haired faerie threw the female— Mizuki—at my feet. Her gown was in tatters and long, dark hair rested on her shoulders in snarls and knots. Her face was unrecognizable. Not because I had never met her before, but because it was a mass of bruises, cuts, and swollen skin. Both of her eyes were so damaged they couldn't open.

The Hunt didn't always ride through the sky, because it was obvious they'd dragged her behind the horses all night. Not even her accelerated healing had been able to keep up.

"What was her crime?" I asked tightly, unable to tear my eyes away from Mizuki. She didn't have enough strength to lift her head, and her breath came in faint rattles. Unless a healer was summoned, she wouldn't live much longer. Her body had endured too much during the long night.

Gwyn lifted one shoulder in a shrug. "Angering the wrong person, I suppose. Someone who could afford my fee."

"So you're not a huntress," I said, desperately trying to think of how to help Mizuki. The sight of her reminded me too much of myself, bleeding in that dungeon, surrounded by endless darkness and pain. I lifted my chin and glared at Gwyn. "You're just a mercenary."

The faerie made a soft sound, something partway between a sigh or laughter. She lowered her chin to her chest, wearing a thoughtful expression now, and began to walk. She was circling us, I realized, like a predator toying with its prey. I waited for Gwyn to speak, but she remained silent. Probably waiting for one of us to break or bargain with her. Losing my patience, I bent down to take Mizuki's hand.

"Don't," the dark-haired faerie said, his voice sharp with warning. I paused, and I hated myself for it. A month ago, I would've completely ignored him and helped Mizuki to her feet. Now I watched my fingers curl into a fist, and I straightened. Mizuki didn't see any of it—her face was pressed to the frozen ground, not out of relief or submission, but the inability to hold herself up. A trickle of blood ran into the snow. I caught myself staring at it and wondered if there was someone hoping for her safe return, at this very moment.

Gwyn stopped at my back. I felt her presence like a child senses a monster in the closet, watching from the deep black, its malicious intent filling the air. More than anything, I wished I were young again just so I could call for my parents. Fear swelled in my throat. Even now, my mind worked desperately to think of something I could offer or trade for Mizuki's freedom. But how could I save her when I couldn't even save myself?

"Would you like to know what they always ask for? The ones I hunt?" Gwyn whispered in my ear. Her breath swirled through the dawn. Apparently it was a rhetorical question, because she didn't give me a chance to respond. "They beg for more time."

She stepped back and I heard the unmistakable sound of a sword being unsheathed. Gwyn's armor creaked as she moved to stand over the faerie still bleeding into the snow. For one of the few times in my life, I didn't know what to do. Horror and helplessness rendered me unable to move, unable to speak. Every instinct in my body screamed to look away, but I couldn't. Even now, as Gwyn put herself into an executioner's position, I tried to think of how to stop this. *Please, God, no more death. No more blood on my hands.*

Despite Gwyn's words, Mizuki didn't beg. Instead, she tried to stand. Her legs gave out before she could fully push herself up, and she made a small sound of pain. I started forward, thinking to lend her my strength, but the dark-haired faerie touched the hilt of his sword in a silent warning. Fury burned through me, and I imagined drawing the gun I hadn't brought and shooting him in the face.

"For whatever it's worth, I commend you for facing your death honorably," Gwyn said to the faerie at her feet. There was no regret or reluctance in her expression—only mild interest, like a great cat peering down at the animal pinned beneath its paw.

I looked away as she brought her sword down.

Either her sword was sharper than it looked, or the huntress was incredibly strong, because it only took one blow. A jarring, wet sound burst through the stillness. I didn't see Mizuki's head hit the ground, but I saw a spray of blood stain the snow around my shoes. My stomach heaved, and I knew I was moments from vomiting. I spun and stumbled away. There was a prickly sensation in my throat and an acrid taste on my tongue. I stood very, very still, eyes squeezed shut, and willed the nausea to pass. That terrible sound echoed through my memory again and again.

Weak, a cruel voice whispered. *You're so weak.*

I could feel all those eyes boring into my back. Ancient. Cold. Judging. I took a brief, shuddering breath before I turned toward Gwyn, being careful to keep my gaze on her face. She looked back at me... and grinned. Her straight, white teeth glowed in the sunlight pouring over the trees. I wanted nothing more than to tear through her mind and locate the fears she kept so well-hidden. I wanted to see the huntress on her knees, tears streaming down her face, begging *me* for more time. While I glared at her, another hunter came forward and handed Gwyn a rag. She used it to clean her sword.

"What was the point of all this? Is more time a possibility?" I rasped as she drew near again. The dark-haired faerie moved to retrieve Mizuki's head, but I didn't so much as glance in his direction. My mind didn't need more fodder for bad dreams, and Oliver had enough to worry about these days—he couldn't handle yet another nightmare to keep out of the dreamscape.

"Perhaps," Gwyn said, halting once she was close enough to touch. She smelled like a campfire.

I found the courage to raise my face. At this proximity, her perfection was only more prominent. Her features weren't dainty, like Lyari's, but the strong lines and startling colors only lent an ethereal quality to her ferocity.

"Nothing comes free with the fae," I said. Surprisingly, my voice was steady. "What do you want in exchange for not killing me right now?"

Gwyn tilted her head, pretending to consider this. Her tone was speculative as she answered, "You are Queen of the Unseelie Court—you have access to the old ones. The heads of the bloodlines. Command them to divulge where they hid Creiddylad, then come here in three nights' time and tell me what they said. I can't call off the Hunt, but I can delay it. You could have years to live, instead of days."

Silence wrapped around us. Faeries were excellent liars, but their large, vibrant eyes usually gave something away. I searched hers while I thought about her proposal. "This isn't something you've just thought up. This is the reason you haven't killed me yet."

She didn't confirm or deny it. "Do we have an agreement, dragon slayer?"

"Don't call me that."

The faerie clicked her tongue. "You're so concerned with names and labels. Haven't you figured out yet what truly matters?"

Another rhetorical question, because she was still waiting for an answer to her proposition. Making bargains with the fae never ended well for me, and for once, I didn't say the first thing that popped into my mind. "Look, I need some time to—"

"No," Gwyn said, shaking her head. "I'm not interested in letting you stall or delay. As the humans say, it's now or never, my lovely queen. And I'll do the honorable thing by telling you that there's no need for silly blood oaths or magical ceremonies —a promise made to me in any form is binding."

I didn't want to admit it, but her demonstration had affected me. Facing death was one thing; knowing exactly how it would be done was another. I couldn't resist a glance toward the spot where Mizuki died. There was a bloody stain on the snow, the blue already turning black. Someone must have come and taken her body, because it was no longer there.

"Fine," I said, forcing myself to meet Gwyn's piercing gaze. "We have an agreement."

"Excellent. I shall return in three days' time." Her expression didn't change, but I still felt like I'd just made a terrible mistake. Gwyn swung away, and she walked over the bloody spot in the snow without slowing. She bellowed into the stillness. "Hunters! We ride!"

She jumped into an empty saddle with effortless grace. Her horse tossed its head and the air erupted with more thunder, cries, and snorts. Within seconds, the Wild Hunt ascended into the sky. They made it look effortless. I stood there as they vanished into the horizon like a flock of strange birds.

The silence returned, settling over the yard like a fog. I shook myself, trying not to think about the ramifications of what I'd just done, and turned my back on that bloody spot in the snow. Remembering how furious Lyari had been the last time I delayed telling her something about Gwyn, I pulled out my phone and typed a brief text. If she was at Court, she wouldn't see it until she returned aboveground. *Made a deal with Gwyn. We need to find Creiddylad. Explain more later.*

Right now, though, I needed to find Collith. It seemed likely that, out of anyone, the Unseelie King would know where Creiddylad was. Pocketing my phone, I turned around and hurried up the steps.

It started ringing at the same moment I reached for the doorknob. I pulled my phone back out, knowing whose name I'd see on the Caller ID before I looked at the screen. "Good morning," I said, bracing myself for a lecture.

"Nuvian branded two Guardians this morning," Lyari said instantly.

I frowned, turning away from the door in case anyone could hear me. "Why the hell would Nuvian brand anyone?"

There was an impatient sound on the other end. "It's like a human soldier getting a dishonorable discharge. Nuvian brands a Guardian with the Enochian symbol for shame, and they are a Guardian no more. They will carry that shame with them for the rest of their immortal life. All Nuvian would tell us was that they committed treason and Úna is banished. Now he's in such a foul mood he won't talk to anyone. What the hell happened last night? Where are you?"

"I can't say for sure, because I wasn't there for parts of it, but if I had to guess? I'd say that Úna bribed the Guardians that were supposed to be watching me. She wanted to get me alone so she could..." I clenched my jaw, unable to say the rest. Lyari was silent, which meant she'd already put it together. We stayed on the phone, even as the seconds marched past and neither of us spoke. Finally I cleared my throat and added, "Did you get my text?"

She matched my brisk tone. "I haven't looked at any messages yet. I called you as soon as I reached the surface."

Once she saw it, we'd probably be having an even longer conversation. One I'd have with her later, because I wanted to find Collith before he went into the barn for another twenty-four hours. If he wasn't in there already. "Okay, well, once you read it, take some deep breaths and wait for at least an hour before you call me back."

"Why can't you just tell me what you—"

Hanging up, I hurried back into the house and locked the door behind me. It would do nothing to keep Gwyn out, but it made me feel better, so I secured the chain for good measure. *Collith will probably be in his room*, I thought. I started walking toward the back hallway.

I jerked to a halt when I saw Emma. She stood in front of the sink, a spot which provided a perfect view of the yard. Her skin was aglow from the sunlight streaming inside. Her wrinkled palms cupped a coffee mug that said, FUCK THIS SHIT.

"Good morning," she said with her customary smile. "How did you sleep?"

She didn't see anything, I thought with a rush of relief. I murmured a greeting back to her and moved toward the coffee maker. I took a mug of my own out of the cupboard. The thought of trying to eat after the encounter with Gwyn made my stomach churn, but coffee might be just what I needed to paste on a mask of optimism.

Emma leaned against the edge of the counter. Light shone through the threadbare fabric of her pink robe. "Who were those people? Friends of yours?" she questioned, tilting her head.

I went still. My heart, however, went into overdrive. "What people?" I asked carefully, putting the coffee pot back.

"All those bikers," Emma answered, raising her gray brows. "Do you think they'd be willing to take me on a ride?"

"No." I said it too quickly. Even I heard the note of panic in my voice. I cleared my throat and held my coffee tighter, seeking comfort in its warmth. It made sense that Gwyn glamoured the Hunt—most humans would take one look at their gruesome faces and run. "Emma, those aren't nice people. Promise me you won't go with them. Please."

She gave me a puzzled frown. This was the part where Maureen, my adoptive mother, would've demanded explanations or reasons. But Emma Miller just said, her voice ringing with trust, "All right. I promise, sweetheart."

I let out a breath and my heart slowed. "Thank you."

The old woman studied me, her brown eyes alight with concern. Whatever she saw in my expression made her decide not to pursue the topic. She pushed off the counter in a surprisingly limber movement. "The house sold, by the way," she said as she poured more coffee into her mug, steam rising toward her face. Its rich aroma filled the air. "We should celebrate! Are you free tonight? How about we make some margaritas?"

I didn't answer, because her words were going around in my head. *The house sold.* She was talking about the home she and Fred had shared in Denver. It meant she was staying here, with us, for good. All this time, I hadn't told Emma the truth of what I was—what Damon and Finn were, what Matthew probably was, once his abilities manifested—because I'd been afraid having knowledge of our world would endanger her. But not knowing was putting her in even more jeopardy. If Emma was truly going to be part of this family, she needed to be aware of what she was up against. Who our enemies were and what they were capable of.

The conversation with Collith would have to wait.

"Emma, will you sit down with me?" I asked, trying to hide how nervous I was. "I think it's time we finally had that talk."

Once again, something in my voice made her pause. After a moment, the old woman went to the cupboard where Cyrus kept the liquor. She opened it, took out a bottle of Kahlúa, and plunked it down on the table. She sat down and gave me a smile that said whatever I was about to tell her wouldn't change anything. "Okay, ready."

I took a breath... and went back to the beginning.

Reeking of coffee and deep-fried food, I trudged into the house.

It was mid-morning, the day after I'd made an agreement with Gwyn of the Wild Hunt. Things at the bar had been slow, so Bea sent me home earlier than usual. I couldn't deny that I didn't mind the extra time at home. If this kept happening, though, it could delay finding a new place.

Not that it would matter if I didn't find Creiddylad. A search I still had no idea where to start.

As I closed the door, I was faintly surprised to see Collith sitting at the kitchen table. Any thoughts about finances blew away. He wore a black button-up that was covered in sawdust, and there was a streak of something along his left cheekbone. A cup of coffee rested next to his hand. "It's good to see you. You look tired," the faerie king said.

"Why, thank you," I deadpanned. I took off my coat, hung it off the back of the chair across from him, and sank down onto the chair myself. "I'm glad you finally left the barn. I need to tell you something."

Collith stood up and moved toward the coffee pot. "Very well. Is this the sort of conversation that requires liquor?"

"Isn't that the case with most of our conversations?" I asked, only half-joking.

I heard the clink of silverware against glass. When Collith turned back, he held a coffee mug similar to his. He set it in front of me without comment, and I saw instantly that he'd added just the right amount of cream. I pulled the cup close to me and cupped it in both palms, as if the warmth could ward off my fear. "Gwyn paid another visit yesterday. She offered me more time," I told him.

"In exchange for what?" Collith asked instantly, returning to his chair. Before I could answer, he shook his head. "Wait. Of course. Gwyn wants Creiddylad—that's what she's always wanted. She's been clever, I'll give her that. When she heard the new queen was a Nightmare, she probably made herself available to a courtier with a known grudge against you, in order to secure the immunity of the Hunt. She'd also be able to find you wherever you were, wherever you went."

The intricacies of Gwyn's plan didn't interest me. Not when it displayed a vast patience and intelligence that I didn't possess, making it clear I had no chance of outmaneuvering her. "Do *you* know where Creiddylad is?" I ventured, daring to hope it could be that easy.

His jaw was tight. "I don't."

I hesitated, then forced myself to say, "What about Naevys? She has a history with Gwyn. Out of anyone, she might be our best—"

"No." Collith was already shaking his head, and there was a storm brewing in his hazel eyes. "It was because of her connection to Gwyn that the council didn't trust my mother. They never would've told her where Creiddylad is."

It made sense, but it also meant that finding Creiddylad wouldn't be easy. If I even wanted to find her—the consequences of giving Gwyn what she wanted were vague but worrying. If the Wild Hunt no longer answered to the faerie courts, how far would they go with that freedom? Would they slaughter humans in the streets? Expose our existence to all of mankind? I stared down into my coffee without really seeing it. "Why hasn't she done this to you? Or to your father?" I asked tonelessly.

The mention of Sylvyre made Collith's lips thin. "It's public knowledge the Seelie and Unseelie rulers know nothing of Creiddylad's location. We aren't even told who guards the secret, to avoid being put in the exact position you're in now."

"She knows the effect fear has on people," I said slowly, thinking of the predatory gleam in her eye. "She knows I could get the information I wanted from them. Easily."

My gaze fell on Matthew's highchair. Suddenly I wondered why Gwyn had gone to such lengths—if she'd threatened a single member of my family, I would've done anything she wanted, no questions asked.

"It's what keeps Gwyn from completely being a monster. She has one limit, one boundary between her and irredeemable depravity—she won't harm her quarry's loved ones," Collith said. I blinked at him. Somehow, he'd guessed my thoughts, even now that our mating bond was gone.

Despite the horrible circumstances we were in, I gave him a searching look, feeling something inside me warm.

In the next moment, Emma entered the kitchen. She drew up short and glanced between us, as if she was worried she'd interrupted something. Collith took another drink of his coffee. I followed suit, averting my gaze. "How was—" Emma started.

Lyari appeared next to the table. "Your Majesty."

Everyone in the room jumped and looked at her. The faerie's expression was tight, but it couldn't be about Gwyn—we'd already argued about that yesterday. It also wasn't like her to cut Emma off, who Lyari had developed an undeniable fondness toward.

"Your presence is required," Lyari said, answering the question in my eyes.

I sighed and pushed away from the table. "I'll get my coat."

A half hour later, I entered the room where today's council meeting would be.

The air smelled like fresh flowers. There was a painting hanging on the wall—a portrait—and a single glance told me instantly whose rooms these were. The artist had managed to capture Chandrelle's remote expression. She sat in a high-backed chair, surrounded by those undoubtedly of her blood-line, but there was no joy or pride in her ageless face. Her posture was perfect. She stared at the artist in a way that, some-how, made it obvious she had all the time in the world, and she would sit there until the painting was finished.

I turned my gaze to Chandrelle herself, who now sat at an enormous dining room table. Her hands were clasped in her lap, and a gold watch glinted on her delicate wrist. Her outfit was more modern than the last time I'd seen her—the elegant gown had been replaced by a pencil skirt and a loose, white blouse. She looked like a CEO or a person who regularly spearheaded elaborate fundraisers. Hell, for all I knew, that was exactly what she did. The fae had been puppet masters for centuries, tugging at strings on every continent. If it wasn't a faerie sitting in the seat of power, there was one behind it, whispering in the fool's ear.

There were several others at the table, every one of them staring at me with their ancient, veiled eyes. By now, I recog-nized all of them.

Fighting my usual sense of insecurity and fear—I was a child, compared to the number of years these creatures had been alive —I strode to the chair at the head of the table, gathered my skirts, and sat. I met Chandrelle's gaze because she was closest to me, and we'd met in her quarters. It seemed safe to assume she was the one who called this meeting.

"You rang?" I asked cheerfully. Out of the corner of my eye, I saw Lyari shift. Probably reaching for her sword in case one of these faeries leaped at me.

Chandrelle's flawless chignon gleamed in the firelight, revealing strands of silver within the brown. "It has come to our attention that Gwyn made you a proposition."

I found Lyari, pinning her with my gaze, and silently asked the question. *Did you tell them?*

She responded with a barely perceptible shake of her head. Seeing it, my rush of betrayal faded. Why was I so surprised? I'd known there were spies in this Court. I'd known there were eyes on me at every moment.

I had just never been so blatantly reminded of it.

Schooling my expression into a bland mask, I met Chandrelle's gaze. Did they know Gwyn was here to hunt me? No, it was impossible. The vultures at the Unseelie Court would already be circling my throne if they knew it would soon be vacant.

"Yes, she did," I said at last. "Gwyn offered to... give me something I want in exchange for Creiddylad."

Micah's voice was mutinous. "You're a fool if you think—"

I whirled on him, and for a wonderful moment, I felt like the person I'd once been. Wild and reckless and stupid. "You know, we all have something to contribute to this conversation, and I think your contribution should be silence," I told him.

Chandrelle stood up, and the entire table went silent. Her fingers formed steeples on the table. She looked at me as if I were the only person in the room, and the intensity of it was unnerving. "I would like to respectfully remind you, Your Majesty, of the vow you made."

It was my first instinct to snap back at her, as I had with Micah, but I reined myself in. With effort, I took two or three slow breaths. "I haven't forgotten, Lady Chandrelle," I said evenly. "Gwyn may have offered a deal, but I didn't say I accepted it."

Another silence fell. Most of the faeries here were good at hiding their emotions, and I couldn't tell if they regarded me with surprise or suspicion. Once again, Chandrelle was the one to speak. "If what you say is true, then we are most fortunate to have such a strong queen. I'm sure there's no need to remind you of what would happen if Gwyn were to regain custody of her lover."

"There would be nothing to stop her from wreaking havoc upon both humans and Fallen alike," another council member chimed in, her honeyed voice at odds with the dark words. "Both worlds would fall into chaos."

I bit my tongue to hold back another cutting response.

Fortunately, the meeting ended shortly after that. Even if there were some who didn't believe that I'd denied Gwyn's offer, nothing short of a truth spell could prove it. I was the picture of detachment as I made my way to the door and the passageway beyond, but with every step, I resisted the urge to haul up my skirts and run. We stopped at Collith's rooms so I could change, and then we were back in the woods. It was all becoming so normal to me, and I couldn't decide if I found the realization disturbing.

Lyari broke her silence when we were halfway home. "You lied to them."

"Not quite," I said without looking at her. It wasn't as cold as it had been the night before, but the tips of my nose and fingers still went numb. I brought my hands up to blow on them. "I told them, 'I didn't say I accepted it,' and that was true. I didn't say those words tonight."

Her tone was full of begrudging admiration. "Well, you bought yourself some time, at least. If the council thought you were going to help Gwyn, they might've attempted to remove you from the throne themselves. Or worse."

I didn't want to know what Lyari considered worse.

Before I could ask her, something hard and wet exploded against my head. I stumbled, my eyes widening with shock, and I whirled. Damon poked his head out from behind a gnarled oak—Lyari and I must've been closer to the house than I thought—and our eyes met. He ducked out of sight too late.

"Oh, you're dead." I launched after him, dripping and shouting. He was already gathering more ammunition, his gloved fingers frantically scraping at the ground. Matthew stood next to him, watching us with wide eyes.

A few minutes later, I swung around to find Lyari, my arm arched back to throw a snowball at her. But she was gone. Then a sound echoed through the air, distracting me. It was fragile, yet hopeful, like something green in spring. I realized what it was and froze.

Matthew was laughing.

It was the first time I'd heard that particular sound. Damon had asked Emma, more than once, if he should make a doctor appointment for his son. Secretly, I'd been worried it indicated a bigger problem than slow development. In spite of what some people thought, children noticed quite a bit—their voices were just quieter than everyone else's. What had Matthew seen while he was being raised by a necromancer? Had he witnessed something since he'd come to live *here*?

But all of that worry had been for nothing. Because here he was, in the snow, laughing as if he'd been doing it his entire life.

Damon carried Matthew back to me, and together, we walked in the direction of the house. When the little boy started squirming, Damon set him back down. The toddler rushed away, wearing so many layers that he was waddling. Damon watched him go, his eyes bright with amusement.

"It suits you," I commented, the sight of him making a flower bloom in my chest.

My brother reluctantly pulled his attention away from Matthew. "What does?"

"Fatherhood."

At this, Damon shot me a look full of gratitude. Before I could say anything else, his gaze shifted to something over my shoulder. "I better go check on Matthew," he said.

He shoved his hands in his pockets and walked away. A moment later, I figured out why—Collith appeared next to me. I could hear the *swish-swish-swish* of Matthew's snow pants as Damon chased him through the trees again. I kept my eyes on them as I said, "Twice in one day. How did I get so lucky?"

Collith made an unamused sound, and he, too, became absorbed in watching Matthew laugh. While the Unseelie King was distracted, I quickly bent over and scraped some snow together, forming another ball in my palm.

"Hey, Collith?" I said. He turned back to me, and he was smiling. It was the first time I had seen that smile since he'd come back from Hell, and for a moment, it felt like I couldn't breathe.

When I kept gawking, his expectant look turned into a frown. "Is something—" he began.

I brought my fist out from behind me and shoved the snowball into his face. Collith sputtered. There was no chance for him to retaliate, because Matthew ran toward us. His face was red with cold, but he was smiling from ear to ear.

"Are you ready to head back?" I asked him in an overly exuberant voice. "Should we go inside and get warm?"

Damon moved to Matthew's other side. If Collith tried to attack, odds were good that he'd get one of them instead. The look he gave me promised that our battle wasn't over. That it had, in fact, only just begun. I gave him a sweet smile in return and turned to listen to my nephew laugh some more.

The four of us started walking, and my hand rested on top of Matthew's small hat the rest of the way home.

CHAPTER THIRTEEN

I fell asleep around midnight.

I fought it. Oh, how I fought it—even now, days after fighting Oliver's shadow, I was wary of the dreamscape. But I'd already missed a night of sleep that week, and despite the cup of coffee I consumed as everyone else went to bed, I drifted off right there on the couch, still surrounded by books I'd had Lyari bring from Collith's library in hopes of finding a trail to Creiddylad. The sounds of the TV faded to nothing.

The next sound I heard was running water, but it definitely wasn't the sea. Had Oliver planned another surprise? I opened my eyes expecting to see meadow and open sky. Instead, I found myself surrounded by a moonlit garden. The air was warm and smelled like roses. The water I'd heard came from a fountain, which trickled nearby. A house loomed overhead, and its bright lights cast squares onto the ground. There was something familiar about it. My brows knitted together as I stared up at one of the windows. It triggered a memory, and I saw myself standing on the other side of the glass.

This was Collith's home. I'd been here once before, in

another dream. Still frowning, I turned around, and the skirt of my filmy dress flared from the movement.

I froze when I saw the house's owner.

He stood in the middle of the cobblestone path, looking heartbreakingly beautiful in a white shirt and a black tie. His brown hair was artfully tousled. In his hazel eyes, I saw the old Collith. The one who played Connect Four, the one who went on coffee dates, the one who danced. I hadn't realized how badly I missed him until this moment.

"But I'm asleep," I blurted, my heart picking up speed, though I wasn't sure why. "We're not mated anymore. You can't... you shouldn't be able to..."

A faint smile curved his lips. The sight of it made me stare at him like some lovesick teenager. "Being King of the Unseelie Court has a few advantages. For instance, I've made connections. Friends. Some of whom can do spells," Collith added.

Now my mouth ran dry as hope was replaced by fear. "You spoke to a witch? Collith, what if this *friend* tells someone where you are? You can't be their king right now, not until you're—"

"She won't betray me. There *are* good people in the world, Fortuna." I opened my mouth, about to argue, but he shook his head. "Can we just let it rest tonight? Please?"

The sound of the trickling fountain floated between us. I looked at him for another moment, searched his weary expression, then started walking down the path. My heels made soft sounds on the stones. "This is a beautiful garden," I remarked. "Did you do all this?"

"I did." Collith fell into step beside me, adjusting his long strides to match mine. I'd never considered myself short, but next to him, it felt that way. "My mother taught me how—it was something we used to do together. But I can't be here as much as I'd like to, so I had to hire a gardener to take care of it while I'm away."

My gaze roamed over the flowers and hedges. It must've

been summertime in this dream, because everything was in bloom. There was a wide variety of colors nestled amongst the soil and leaves. Pink, yellow, red. "How is she?" Collith asked suddenly, making my gaze snap back to him.

"Your mother?" I clarified. He nodded. I stopped walking and turned toward him. I'd been dreading this moment, but he needed to know the truth. I said the words knowing they would bring him pain. "She's dying, Collith. I don't think she has a lot of time left. Maybe we should reconsider trying to sneak you in. We'll disable the cameras and—"

"No." His eyes had gone dark again. "She can't see me like this, Fortuna. I'm not ready."

"But if you wait until you feel ready, it may be too late."

"She can't see me like this," he repeated. The words were cold and clipped, and I tried not to glare at him. The last time Collith had used that voice with me, he'd been sitting on his throne, watching Death Bringer beat with me a cat o' nine tails.

Once again, I fixed my attention on the flowers. I walked farther down the path. Collith's shoes didn't make a sound, and I glanced back to make sure he'd followed.

"This one is my favorite, I think," I decided, pinching a petal between my thumb and forefinger. The flower had a red center and yellow fringes. I knew it wasn't real, in the literal sense, but Collith had created this dream from a memory. At some point, this flower had really existed. I was still holding it as I turned to look at him. "Do you ever think about a life where you don't have to hire someone? A life that lets you tend your own damn garden?"

"Of course I do. But I try not to dwell on it—that's not a life within my reach." He held out his hand, and I knew what he was going to say before the words left his mouth. "Dance with me, Fortuna."

"What is it with you and waltzing?" I asked, shaking my

head. I was smiling as I said it. I reached for his hand without hesitation.

We moved through the steps as though we'd done them a hundred times before. Maybe we had. Dreams were such slippery things—if you didn't hold on tight, they'd slip right from your grasp. Maybe Collith and I had danced together more times than I could count, and I just didn't remember those nights. Following a faint, gentle instinct, I leaned forward and rested my cheek on his chest. His arms tightened, and I had never felt safer.

"Why did you do this?" I asked.

Collith's voice floated down to me. "You haven't been sleeping. You're always there when I have a bad dream, so I thought I'd return the favor."

At this, I pulled away to look at him, and we stopped dancing. Collith met my gaze without flinching. His scar was more pronounced because of the shadows cast by the in-ground lighting. Before I could say anything else, he spun me, then slowly drew me back to him.

Maybe being in a dream made it easier to take chances—I felt a quake of fear at the thought of what I was about to do next, but it was the good kind of fear. I hadn't felt that in a long time. Keeping my eyes on Collith's, I moved even closer. My breasts brushed against his chest. I stared up at him, acutely aware of the places where our bodies touched. He was affected, as well, but it was obvious he was trying to fight it. I caught myself staring at his mouth, and suddenly I wanted to try kissing it again.

A long-silenced drum started to beat between my legs, but instead of excitement, I felt the familiar stirrings of frustration. Even before we'd both been damaged beyond repair, Collith had denied me at every opportunity. "Why won't you fuck me?" I asked bluntly, raising my gaze back to his.

He matched my directness. "Because the first time we have sex, Fortuna, I don't want to fuck you."

"If you say you want to 'make love' to me, I swear to God…" I stepped away and dropped my hands, glaring at him. "Are you serious? That's why you've been holding back?"

"No. Not the only reason." His focus was unwavering, and as the seconds ticked past, I realized what his other reason was. It was like a thorn, piercing into both of us every time we reached for each other. The question I'd refused to answer for weeks. *What happened?*

"So, what, as soon as I open up to you, you'll open your legs for me?" I joked weakly, looking away.

"Something like that." In my peripheral vision, I saw Collith rub the back of his neck. "I've tried to give you time, Fortuna, but you haven't—"

I interrupted him with an incredulous laugh. "Hold on. *You've* been trying to give *me* time?"

"This isn't something you can just ignore. Having sex with me won't make it go away, either."

For once, I didn't have an immediate retort, but I didn't feel the urge to run either. I did find it darkly ironic that we'd spent the past month in hiding because we thought it was what the other person wanted. As the silence wrapped around us, I imagined giving Collith what he'd been asking for these past few weeks. Telling him the truth about the night I drove to that crossroads. Panic fluttered in my stomach. "You don't have a right to my secrets, you know. We're not mated anymore," I said.

"So you keep reminding me," he retorted, raking his hair back. That single lock flopped back down. "And I do have a right."

My eyebrows shot upward. "Oh? You do? Let's hear it, Collith. What could possibly make you think that—"

"Because you did it to save me," he roared.

"Wow. Someone should alert the astronauts, because I'm pretty sure they could see your ego from fucking space." Completely unafraid, despite the depth of fury I'd just glimpsed, I glared at Collith through a sheen of tears. "Did it ever occur to you that I brought you back to save myself? How was I supposed to live with what I'd done? How could I go on like a normal person when I'd *murdered* you?"

The inferno within his eyes dimmed and Collith sighed. "We're back to this? You pretending you don't feel anything for me?"

As quickly as he deflated, so did I. I'd done enough fighting for one lifetime, and I was so tired. "No. No, we're not. But can we just call a truce for right now?"

"Yes, we can call a truce." He sounded as drained as I felt.

I was about to suggest that we go inside when Collith walked toward the fountain. There were four benches around it, and he sat on the one facing the house. Slowly, I sank down beside him. After a moment, the Unseelie King put his arm around my shoulders and I tucked my head in the curve of his neck. It frightened me, a little, how natural the movement felt.

It would've been easy to fall asleep to the sounds of the fountain and warm, perfumed breezes slipping past, but I held onto consciousness. I stared up at the stars as if the constellations would start moving, like the ones in Oliver's world.

Thinking of him hurt. He would be wondering where I was, and here I sat, feeling glimmers of happiness with someone else. "Collith?" I asked at the same moment I found the Big Dipper.

I felt his response float through my bones. "Yes?"

"Will you promise me something?" My throat was a desert. I swallowed and said, "Don't give up on me, okay?"

"Never."

I shivered from the raw emotion in Collith's voice. He didn't pause to think about it, not even for a second. I tilted my head to peer up at his face. For the millionth time, I caught myself admiring those long lashes, the jagged scar, the defined jawline. "Do we still have time? In this dream, I mean?" I asked now, tracing his lips with the tip of my finger.

I was still tracing them as Collith said, "Plenty."

"Good. I'd like to make out with you, if that's okay. Or try to. I can't make any promises, but that's never stopped you before, right?"

His eyes lit with a soft glow. Before I could take another breath, that wicked mouth came down to claim mine. I kissed him back, burying my fingers in his soft curls.

The constellations above us shone on, entirely forgotten.

It was snowing again by the time I got to Bea's.

An entire day had come and gone, and now the sky overhead was black. I parked my van on Main Street, still fighting the temptation to cancel on Ariel, who'd texted me to follow up on her invitation to get drinks. I'd been in such a good mood—and so desperate to avoid the fact I hadn't found Creiddylad—that I had agreed.

As I turned the key, I reminded myself that I couldn't cancel. I'd managed to sneak away from Lyari and Finn, and after tonight, it was a safe bet I wouldn't be able to again. I stared up at the sign for Bea's and drummed my fingers on the steering wheel. It felt like there was a riot happening in my heart. Why did the thought of actually enjoying myself cause so much turmoil?

Because you don't deserve it, a voice whispered.

In another lifetime, I would have a retort ready. I wouldn't allow anything, not even the voice in my own head, to shame me.

Now, though, I picked up my phone and found Ariel's name in my contacts list. It rang once, then her cheery voice filled my ear. "Bitch, you better be calling me from your car," she said.

I kept my eyes on that neon-bright sign and tried to sound normal. "Look, I don't think—"

"That was your first mistake. Tonight isn't about thinking," she informed me. Before I could respond, a song blared through the speaker. I winced and held the phone away from my ear. Even from the street, it was obviously Lynyrd Skynyrd. The human said something else, but I couldn't make out the words. She hung up a moment later.

Guess that settles it. I heaved a sigh, pocketed my phone, and got out of the van.

The night was in a somber mood, not a ray of moonlight anywhere. I tried not to see this as an omen, and I hurried inside to avoid more second thoughts. A burst of warmth and sound hit me—Fridays and Saturdays were always the busiest nights of the week. All the tables and booths were full, every bar stool occupied. Angela rushed past, balancing food-laden trays on her palms. Cyrus was visible through the order window, his bright mane tucked beneath a hairnet. As always, he was bent over the stove, and steam rose toward his concentrated expression. Diablo was here, as well, busing one of the tables. His scrawny arms struggled to hold the tub, which was dangerously full of plates and glasses.

I lingered near the doorway, loosening my scarf. I scanned the room and noted that Phil stood behind the bar. He was middle-aged, married, and had five children at home. When he wasn't here, he was also a bus driver and an employee at the local lumber company. As I removed my coat, he finally noticed me. His beard split into a welcoming smile. "Need a drink, Fortuna?" he called.

The sound of my name made more than one person turn, including Ariel, who was standing next to a booth. At the sight of her, my eyebrows shot upward. She wore a black dress—if it could be called such—that clung to every curve. As she closed the space between us, I let out a low whistle. "Damn, girl. Who knew you had an ass?"

She jiggled it at me, then turned to the burly bartender. Her dark curls bounced with every movement. "Phil, may we get two shots of tequila?"

I opened my mouth to protest, but nothing came out. I watched Phil set the glasses on the bar, thinking of all the reasons why drinking was a bad idea. I was Queen of the Unseelie Court. There was an ancient faerie planning to kill me. Hell, there were probably a hundred faeries planning to kill me. I needed to stay alert and ready.

Once Phil finished pouring, Ariel held her shot between two fingers and raised it into the air, her red nails gleaming. I didn't move. As if she knew what I was thinking, the girl gave me a look. "Did you know I used to be a psych major?" she asked, nodding at the shot still on the bar.

I sighed and picked it up. "No, but I have a feeling it's about to become relevant."

Ariel tossed her shot back and set the glass back down. She signaled to Phil that she wanted another. "Before I dropped out, I learned that stress can kill brain cells and even reduce the size of your mind. Then there's chronic stress, which can have a shrinking effect on the prefrontal cortex. Which is bad."

"What's your point, exactly? That if I don't let loose tonight, my brain is going to shrivel and die?" I asked dryly.

Ariel shrugged her slender shoulders. "You said it, not me."

I opened my mouth to respond, but Angela rushed up to the bar. Her frizzy hair was secured at the top of her head with a pen. "Phil, can I get a gin and tonic?" she asked, sounding harassed.

"Hey, Angela," I said as the bartender turned away.

The human barely spared me a glance. "Hey. Do you still work here? You're, like, never on the schedule."

"Yes, Angela, I still work here. How are the kids?"

Phil stuck a straw in the gin and tonic. "There you go, darlin'."

With a huff of relief, Angela grabbed the drink, set it on a tray, and rushed away. I watched her head for one of the far booths. Sadly, that was one of the most pleasant interactions I'd ever had with her.

Ariel rolled her eyes at me and jiggled a shot pointedly. I stared at the liquid sloshing within the glass, then realized I was still holding mine. She did have a point—I couldn't remember the last time I'd enjoyed a night out. Was I really going to live the rest of my life like that? Heaving a defeated sigh, I clinked it against hers.

"Well, I don't want my brain to shrink. Cheers." I poured the alcohol down my throat, and the burning sensation was like an old friend. I raised my eyebrows at Ariel. "Happy?"

"Very," she said primly. "And I'll be even happier if you do this one, too."

Phil set more shots in front of us. I stared down at them, and it felt like I was two people. Like the halves that formed me were fighting each other in hand-to-hand combat. For the past month, I had just been existing. Surviving. There was a constant ache in my chest I didn't acknowledge or talk about, because everyone around me had aches of their own. Why would I burden them with more pain, more worry? Especially when I'd brought it on myself, anyway?

I poured the alcohol into my mouth. Before it was even down my throat, Ariel asked Phil for yet another round, and I stopped resisting. Already I felt warmer, looser.

We did two more shots together, or maybe it was three. I lost track of time after that. Ariel and I ended up on the dance floor —a generous term for it, since it was just an open space that the regulars created every Friday and Saturday night—and colorful lights flashed over us as we moved. Music crackled from the old speakers. More and more people came through the door, filled the booths and tables, danced around us. Despite her size, Ariel was surprisingly efficient at keeping my ardent admirers at a distance. For the first time in a long time, I was able to enjoy myself unimpeded by unwanted touches or passionate declarations. The alcohol also softened my abilities, making it bearable every time Ariel's skin brushed against mine.

Why did I ever stop drinking?

As the night went on and the shots kept coming, I forgot to be careful. Someone should listen to the words I had to share, words that had been momentarily misplaced. Someone should hear about my secret pains and struggles. Maybe if I gave the burden to someone else, my shoulders would not feel so heavy all the time.

I leaned closer to Ariel, trying to ignore how the world tilted. Before I could say anything, a hiccup popped out of her, and she laughed. I laughed, too. Then we were both standing there, just laughing. The current song wasn't as loud as the last one, so I didn't have to shout as I asked, "Want to know something?"

"Always," she managed.

I held her arm for balance. Then I said, still speaking between giggles, "I *hate* being the goddamn queen."

The girl laughed some more, shaking her head. "What do you—"

Someone grabbed my wrist. My senses were so dulled that I didn't react right away. When the hand tightened and pulled me away, though, I started to think more clearly. I heard Ariel call my name just as I wrenched free. "Touch me again and I'll fry your brain," I snarled, raising my gaze.

It was Finn.

Something in his expression got through the tequila-induced haze over my mind. "Are you okay?" Ariel demanded, elbowing past the pastor's drunk daughter.

I mustered the most convincing smile I could. "Sorry, yeah, we're fine. This is my roommate, Finn. Finn, this is my co-worker Ariel."

Ariel tipped her head and appraised him. Her eyes were bright with interest. The song ended and a new one started, this one with more bass. The floor trembled beneath our feet. "I'll be right back!" I shouted to Ariel. She waggled her fingers—more at Finn than me—and started dancing with a group of drunk college girls.

I met Finn's gaze and pointed toward the back door. He nodded and turned, weaving through the crowd like a wolf running through the forest. I stayed close, taking advantage of the openings Finn had created. It was the first time I'd walked through Bea's on a busy night without learning a dozen people's fears along the way.

He stopped when he reached Cyrus's order window. It was quieter in this spot, as if Cyrus had literally created his own world back here. I faced Finn, and with fewer distractions around us, I finally noticed the urgency burning in his dark eyes. It was also in his voice as he asked, "Did you get my text?"

"I haven't checked my phone for a couple of hours," I said, reaching for it now. The screen brightened and revealed several unread messages. *Shit.* "What's going on?"

Finn answered at the same moment I read it in his text. "I found Ian O'Connell's body in the woods. He was murdered."

The werewolf paused, probably to give me a chance to process it. For a moment, my mind was stalled on the fact that Ian O'Connell was dead. Murdered. I would never see him again. I didn't know what to say, how to react, because I knew it was wrong to be relieved. As a result, I had no idea how I felt. "Did you leave him out there? Does anyone else know?" I asked finally, looking back up at Finn.

His expression was fathomless, but he spoke slowly. "There was another scent on him... one that I recognized."

"You think someone we know killed Ian." My eyes flicked between his. "Whose scent was it, Finn?"

"It was Laurelis," he said after another pause. There was a shadow in his voice that I didn't understand. Worry, maybe. He thought I was going to break, I realized. From which part, though? The revelation that a human I hated was dead? Or that someone I cared about—no matter how hard I tried not to—had done something so terrible?

"Did someone say my name?"

The Seelie King materialized by the door to Bea's office. Finn moved quickly, pressing his back against my chest. "He's not going to hurt me," I said softly, knowing the werewolf's sharp ears would hear it. The music was still making the floor and walls pound.

Laurie observed our interaction with an impatient scowl. "I left a state dinner for this," he informed us. Based on his outfit, I believed him. I'd never seen him in evening tailcoats before.

"May I speak with you? Privately?" I asked, laying a reassuring hand on Finn's arm when he growled.

State dinner or not, Laurie could never resist a mystery. His bright gaze dropped to my hand, and he quirked a brow. "Lead the way."

I felt both Cyrus and Finn watching us. I walked past Laurie and pushed the back door open. A burst of cold air blew past, mussing my hair. Laurie stepped outside, went down the steps, and turned as the door slammed shut. His lip was curled with disgust. "I understand that you have needs, Fortuna, but I refuse to do this on a pile of garbage. Let me take you to Italy for the rest of the evening. We'll drink wine and fuck in the best hotel suite money can buy."

As he spoke, I searched his face, only half-listening to his words. There was no proof of it on his person. No blood on his hands, no smell of death. But deep in my gut, I knew the truth. Suddenly I had never felt more sober.

"Did you kill Ian O'Connell?" I asked.

Surprise flickered in Laurie's gaze—he probably hadn't expected Ian's body to be found, or at least not so soon. He glanced at the door behind us and I could practically hear him putting it together. *The werewolf found it.* After a moment, he refocused on me with an expression I recognized. It was the same one he wore every time I confronted him or challenged him. Bored. Superior. Fae.

"Yes, I did," he said airily. "Oh, don't look so surprised, darling. I've always been entirely capable of murder—I'm just not interested in the cleanup. That part always gets me in trouble. I knew I should've buried him…"

I was going to throw up. My stomach flipped over and a bitter taste filled my mouth. Desperate to avoid the humiliation of vomiting in front of a faerie, I looked down at my shoes. I was standing on a flattened piece of toast. The sight of it almost made me throw up anyway. I forced myself to take some deep breaths. *One. Two. Three. Four. Five.* The nausea subsided enough that I was able to look up at Laurie again, and even though I knew better, I hoped he could give me a good reason for what he'd done.

"Why? Why would you do that?" I asked.

"He frightened you," the Seelie King said, as if it were that simple. He even accompanied the words with a shrug. "And from what I've heard around this grimy little town, he wasn't well-loved, anyhow."

I stared at him, and my mind latched onto a question that didn't really matter in the grand scheme of things. How did Laurie know Ian had frightened me? My frown faded when I remembered. We'd been standing on the street. Ian drove by and acknowledged me, and Laurie was there to see my reaction to it.

My fault. This was my fault. I swung away and resisted the urge to hit a brick wall. The smell coming from the dumpster made my nostrils sting. I turned back around and glared at the faerie through a sheen of tears. "*Fuck.* You can't just kill people, Laurie!"

"I think you've forgotten who and what I am." His voice was level, but his eyes gleamed in a way that made my blood run cold. "I don't abide by human laws, little Nightmare. I am not governed by human guilt."

I went down the rest of the steps and faced him at the bottom. "Well, you should act like you care for five minutes. Seriously, new experiences are good for people. How am I supposed to look Bella in the eye next time I see her?"

Laurie still looked bored. "Who's Bella?"

"His wife! No, excuse me, his *widow*." I whirled away yet again, struggling to control the anger rising in me like lava. My eyes burned, and I didn't need a mirror to know they were shining a bright, unnatural red. No more tears, because now I was *pissed*. I took three steps, getting control of myself, then faced the silver-haired king again. When he didn't react, I knew I'd succeeded in changing my eyes back. "Laurie, you've made me responsible for another human's death. He was a shitty human, yes, but I didn't need his murder on my conscience. You don't, either, whatever you may say. I refuse to believe you don't feel guilt—that would make you a sociopath. And my taste in friends just can't be that terrible."

"Can we talk about this later?" Laurie sighed. When I continued glaring at him, his lovely mouth turned into a pout. "Let's go for drinks. I'll take you to this café I love in Croatia."

I gritted my teeth and shoved past him. "I have to go back inside. My friend is probably looking for me."

That was when I saw a figure standing at the top of the steps.

My heart lurched—I hadn't even heard the door open—but I let out a relieved breath when I saw it was Dracula. His eyes glowed like those of a nocturnal animal, and the effect was unnerving.

"Are you here for a beer or to go another round?" I managed, knowing the vampire could hear how badly he'd frightened me.

There was a long pause. Dracula didn't blink or speak, and suddenly I felt like a mouse beneath an airborne bat. Small, exposed, vulnerable. Laurie stepped closer to me, so close that his chest brushed against my back, and something stopped me from instantly moving away. Probably the fact that I'd barely used my abilities since I killed Collith, and even now the thought of using them was terrifying. I was no longer a force to be reckoned with… which meant I needed the help of creatures like Laurie.

"Neither," Dracula said finally. He shifted into the light, and that eerie glow in his eyes faded. He gave me a faint, enigmatic smile. His leather jacket gleamed. "I came to speak with you, Queen Fortuna."

Still wary, I was slow to respond. Laurie subtly nudged me from behind. "Talk to me about what?" I asked, and somehow my voice sounded casual. Normal.

Dracula opened his mouth to respond, but something landed between us with a jarring *thud*.

I saw Dracula reel back as I lost my own balance. I hit the side of the building, but not hard enough to hurt, and I recovered quickly. Out of the corner of my eye, I saw Laurie moving to my side—most of my focus was on the creature. At first, all I saw was a mass of white feathers. My gaze dropped lower, though, and I caught a glimpse of a massive paw.

"What the actual fuck?" I whispered.

At the sound of my voice, the creature swung around, and the wings snapped out of the way. To my horror, I realized I was gaping at multiple heads. I saw a man, a lion, a cherub, and an eagle. All of its milky, malevolent eyes were fixed on me.

"Fortuna, get—" Laurie started, his voice low and urgent, but the creature launched at us in a burst of preternatural speed. In that instant, my mind went blank. I knew we were about to die.

Death never came, though. Instead there was a flash of silver —Dracula's cane had turned into a sword—and a blur of darkness. A bellow of pain filled my ears. Laurie pushed me against the brick wall and used his body as a shield. I peered over his shoulder, frozen and wide-eyed.

The streetlight shone down on the scene as if it was a stage. Like a warrior from some ancient legend, Dracula wielded a bright sword. His rings glittered as he swung. He was the best fighter I had ever seen. Every movement was certain and true, then it blended into the next, making it seem like a deadly dance. The creature—whatever it was—was only saved by its speed, and it evaded every swipe of Dracula's blade.

I was still staring in open admiration when the second creature landed.

Moving faster than my eyes could track, Laurie bent and straightened, holding something in his hand. It looked like a compact umbrella. I heard a *click*, then another sword was gleaming in the sickly tint of the streetlight—the black part I'd mistaken for an umbrella was its hilt. *Okay, I need one of those,* I thought just as screams tore through the night. When I realized it was coming from the bar, panic exploded in my chest, and I ran for the door. *Cyrus. Ariel. Finn.* Fuck Angela, though. They could have her.

"Fortuna!" a familiar voice shouted. I turned in time to see the Seelie King nearly slice one of those pearly wings off. The eagle shrieked. The creature reared back, the lion's head baring its teeth in a snarl. Laurie put his weight on one leg and swung the other, landing a merciless kick to its chest. The creature hit the opposite wall so hard I heard bones crunch, and it stayed down for a few seconds. Despite its obvious outrage, the wound on its wing was already knitting together.

Laurie twirled the handle of his sword, sending it through the air in a graceful arc, and faced me. "You—"

"There are more of those things inside," I told him, wrenching at the handle.

He swore, but that was the only response he was able to give, because the creature was getting back up and I was darting inside.

The bar was chaos. I paused for a beat, scanning the room for the humans I loved, and that single glance told me there were at least four of those creatures here. Glamour shimmered over them, but apparently it was a bit harder to fool the Unseelie Queen. All I saw was the grotesque, patchwork monster. Whatever everyone else saw still brought fear to their eyes, though. Ariel seemed to be holding her own, surprisingly enough—she had a frying pan in each hand—but I couldn't find Cyrus or Finn. Angela was huddled in a corner booth, clutching a steak knife. She was also screaming hysterically, over and over again, and it drew one of the creatures right to her.

For a moment or two, I considered letting Angela get eaten.

She must've managed to cut the creature's snout, because it jerked back with a cacophony of sounds. My instincts finally surged forward, and I did my own version of Laurie's kick from the alley. As the creature stumbled back and fell over a table, I shoved myself into the space next to Angela. She shrieked and brandished the knife at my face. I barely managed to dodge it in time, but the abrupt movement sent me tipping back into the open. The creature I'd sent tumbling recovered, its heads growling, shrieking, or hissing, and came at me again.

I had no idea if it could be killed, but at least I knew it would bleed.

With a small and vicious smile, I picked up a steak knife from the closest table. The creature froze, but it wasn't because of the blade in my hand—the head shaped like a man had finally looked at me. This thing had probably never met a Nightmare before. It grinned back, and there was a dark promise in the curve of those thin lips. "I pick you," I crooned.

The man head was still leering, its instincts slowed by my influence, when I burst forward and put my knife through one of those white eyes.

While it was screaming in pain, I picked up another knife, jammed it into the creature's gut—at least, where I thought its gut was—and used all my strength to pull the blade upward. Its flesh was tougher than it looked, though, and I lost hold of the hilt when the creature recoiled. Taking advantage of its retreat, I cast another glance around the room. Cyrus was beside Ariel now, holding a shotgun, but there was still no sign of Finn.

Angela was sobbing now. As I rushed toward her hiding place again, she repeated her attempt to stab me. "How do you expect them to take you seriously if you can't even hold a weapon correctly?" I hissed. "Your grip is all wrong on that. Oh, for Christ's sake, just give it to me."

"It won't do any good, anyway! These people are *crazy*," she wailed.

People? I thought. Right, the creatures were wearing a glamour. Telling myself to ask Angela what she'd seen later, I crawled back under the table, grabbed the knife from her, and lodged myself so that she was protected by my body. At the same instant, so quickly that I had no chance to block it, a hairy arm shot into the space and yanked me right back out. The creature tossed me like I was a rag doll—it was the one I thought I'd gutted, but the hole in its body was already knitting itself shut— and I slammed into the opposite wall with such force that I went through it.

Agony tore through me. I nearly succumbed to the darkness then and there. I fought it, though—my friends needed me to stay conscious. As the haze of pain ebbed and flowed, I realized the creatures were filling the air with their rage. I lifted my head and saw that they'd descended upon the one that threw me. Body parts started landing on the floor, and the beast bellowed and screamed in equal parts as they ripped it apart.

They're killing it, I thought dimly. But why? Were these things so monstrous they just randomly turned on each other?

No... they'd only reacted when I got hurt. It seemed like a safe bet these things were here for me, and whoever had sent them apparently wanted me alive. A new idea formed in my head. "Hey!" I shouted, climbing out of the wall. Colorful spots filled my vision and I went still.

My eyesight cleared in time to see every head in the bar swivel toward me. I was still holding a knife—I probably had Dad's training to thank for that. Once I knew I had the creatures' attention, I placed its edge against my stomach. I chose my next words carefully, because there were people here who had no idea what I was or that a supernatural world existed.

"Get the fuck out of this bar, or I swear to God I'll gut myself," I called. Music was still playing from the speakers, and I didn't know if these creatures had good hearing. "And then you'll have my death to atone for. Is that what you want?"

It seemed my theory was correct—most of the creatures didn't look away from the knife.

Some humans saw their chance and slipped away. One of them was Phil's daughter, who must've been back in Bea's office while he was bartending. She always sat at the desk and worked on homework. A creature noticed Amy crawling past, and maybe it had seen my fear for her, because it seized the girl by her ankle and hauled her up. The twelve-year-old screamed and swung her fist at the lion's head.

Without letting myself think about it, I flicked my hand, and within seconds blood seeped through my shirt. Someone cried out in horror. The creatures definitely had a heightened sense of smell, because every single one of them was already surging forward. The one holding Amy dropped her in its rush to reach me. I saw her run out the door, and relief ballooned in my chest before I turned my attention back to the horde of monsters.

"Get back. *Get back,*" I shouted, moving as if I was going to cut myself again. The creatures hissed and yowled, and they all clustered at the other end of the room like frightened sheep. Their pale eyes glared at the knife. I maneuvered around overturned chairs and fallen tables, getting them into a corner. Behind me, I heard shoes squeaking on the floor and the door banging open. Good—the rest of the humans were fleeing.

I stayed where I was and held off the winged monsters. Once everyone else was safe, I'd figure out how to end this standoff. Despite the grating music, a silence draped over the room, and the entire scene was like something from a horror novel. Then, slowly, one of the creatures drew closer to me, making a clicking sound that somehow emanated defiance. It was bigger than the others, I noted as it drew to its full height. It didn't attack or try to take me, and all at once, I realized what it was doing.

This thing was calling my bluff.

It couldn't talk, apparently, but I understood it perfectly. *Fuck.* My mind raced. Maybe I could give myself another shallow cut to scare them off. But my hand was so unsteady...

The thought cut short when the monster exploded.

Gore splattered all over me. I stood there, blinking, and watched what remained of the thing's body topple over. I turned my head to the side, wary of putting my back on them. Cyrus stood by the windows, and he was holding up his shotgun. His chin trembled but his eyes blazed with an inner fire I hadn't seen before. We stared at each other.

"Cyrus," I said as a piece of the creature's flesh fell off my chin, "were those bullets dipped in holy water?"

His expression was, as always, impossible to define. "Yes."

It occurred to me that I might be in shock, because I let my mind consider this new piece of information, even with milky-eyed monsters standing across the room. Cyrus had known what Nuvian was. He knew how to kill the supernatural. Was one of my closest friends... a Fallen hunter?

Someone started screaming outside, reminding me this really wasn't the time to think about it. I glanced at the shotgun he was still holding and remarked, "Please tell me you've got more rounds in that thing."

He shook his head. Before I could do a thing, Ariel strode past me. I saw her arms move—she was throwing something. Then she was running back at us, yanking at our arms, and the room detonated.

We spilled out into the back alley with the creatures' screams lingering in our ears. The door bounced off the railing and slammed shut with a thunderous sound. I was surprised to see that most of the people who'd fled were still here, huddling together, their expressions rife with fear and confusion. There was no sign of Laurie, Dracula, or the two creatures they'd been battling.

But I did see Finn. He was shirtless and kneeling on the ground next to Amy. He nodded at me when our eyes met. His hands were holding his T-shirt against the girl's wounds. I nodded back, looking from him to Amy. I wondered if she was the same age his daughter would've been.

Someone said Cyrus's name, and he stopped, but Ariel gestured for me to follow her. There was a ringing in my ears as I obeyed. With every step, the cold sank deeper into my bones, and I remembered that I'd left a coat inside the bar. It would definitely need to be dry cleaned after tonight.

"What was that thing you threw?" I asked once we reached the street. I suspected the explosion was responsible for why I felt so strange.

In spite of the horrors we'd just witnessed, Ariel's response was cheerful. "Smoke grenade with a pull ring igniter. I've used them in training, but never in the field! Aren't they fun?"

I glanced at her while she spoke, and then I did a double-take. I stopped walking and stared at her ears. They were pointed, exactly like a faerie or a goblin. But that wasn't the only change—my gaze moved to Ariel's face and everything inside me slowed. Her dark skin was too flawless, too smooth, and there was a sharpness to her features I saw at the Unseelie Court every day. The realization hit me like a freight train.

Ariel was a faerie.

All this time, she'd been wearing a glamour around me. It must've been a talent of hers, because it was nearly impossible to make magic undetectable. If she hadn't been forced to fight those monsters tonight, I never would have suspected the truth. I shook my head, knowing I looked as bewildered as I felt. "Ariel, how—"

"It's Aerilaya, actually," she corrected with a brilliant smile. I should've known what she was the moment I first saw those teeth. People with perfect teeth couldn't be trusted.

Shock. You're in shock, Fortuna.

"My van is parked on the street," I said distantly, pulling the keys out of my back pocket. I pointed the fob, and the headlights flashed. I rubbed my bare arms and started walking again. "We need to talk."

Ariel didn't argue, and we approached the van without another word between us. Police sirens wailed in the distance. We got in at the same time, and the sounds outside became muffled. I stared through the windshield and gathered some coherent thoughts together. There was an instant of charged silence. Then I angled my body toward her and blurted, "Why the *hell*—"

"I was sent here to protect you," Ariel said firmly. "His Majesty worried for your safety after you gained so much attention at the black market."

The black market? That was so long ago. The timing of it made sense, though—Ariel had started working at Bea's just after I met Collith. I knew I should probably be furious with her. But there was an openness to this faerie that made me want to reach toward her, like a door that needed the slightest tug to reveal everything on the other side.

"So you've been following Collith's orders from the beginning?" I asked, turning in my seat again. I watched a swarm of police surround Bea's.

"Correct. He placed me in the bar to watch over you. Romantic, isn't it?"

It felt like my head was swimming. I wasn't sure whether to be livid with Collith or grateful to him. Ariel had probably saved everyone tonight, and if he hadn't sent her here, it could've ended a lot differently. I didn't want to think about it, or picture it, but I held onto the steering wheel as though we were spinning out of control. My mind filled with the image of that milky-eyed creature grinning at me.

"What were those things?" I asked, keeping my gaze on the scene unfolding up the street.

"Cherubim," Ariel answered promptly, her rosebud mouth turning down into a frown. "They must've fallen with the rest of us after the Battle of Red Pearls. I didn't know they existed, but there you go."

"Someone sent them," I said, remembering the creatures' strong reaction when I'd threatened to harm myself. "Probably the same one who set Gwyn on me. Or, hey, maybe it's a brand-new enemy! I tend to make them pretty easily. It means that, no matter where I go, I'm putting people in danger."

As Ariel studied me, probably uncertain what to say, Lyari's warning chose that moment to reverberate through my mind. *Soon, Your Majesty, you will have to choose.*

A heavy silence fell. The humans had started blocking the sidewalk with yellow tape that said POLICE LINE DO NOT CROSS on it. They weren't rolling any body bags out, and that seemed like a good sign. I looked for Bea, who must've arrived by now, but I didn't spot her amongst the police uniforms or witnesses. She was probably in the alley—she usually parked back there.

"Are you okay, Your Majesty?" Ariel asked.

"Yeah. I'm fine." I forced my expression into a mask of neutrality and glanced at her sidelong. "Don't *you* start that now —just call me Fortuna. Please."

The faerie laughed. There was something beguiling about the sound, a hidden quality that hinted at a world of magic. Now that I knew the truth about her, I was embarrassed I hadn't seen it.

Something else occurred to me as we sat there. *No wonder Lyari didn't try to tag along tonight... or any time I'm at the bar,* I thought with a touch of bitterness. No doubt my trusty sidekick knew exactly who Ariel was and why she was in Granby. We would definitely be having a talk later—I didn't like my Right Hand keeping secrets from me.

"...to Court," Ariel was saying. "I need to give Nuvian a full report."

Oh. She wanted to leave. It was so strange hearing Nuvian's name come out of her mouth. Feeling disconnected from everything, I nodded and unlocked the doors. "I guess I'll see you soon."

"You sure will!" the faerie tossed over her shoulder as she got out. Cold air darted past, rushing at me, and I remembered that I had a hoodie in the backseat. While I pulled it on, Ariel jogged across the street, probably heading for the grocery store parking lot—that's where everyone parked when the street was full. I watched her black curls flutter in a wintry breeze. She wasn't powerful enough to sift, then. Collith must have chosen her for the glamouring, which meant he'd valued secrecy over strength.

If he'd kept something like this from me, what else could he be hiding?

Ariel was out of sight now, and red and blue lights continued to flash over the street. I knew I should stay and give a statement, but I was tired. So incredibly tired. No one had died tonight and none of my loved ones were hurt. I still hadn't spotted Laurie, but he'd probably rushed back to his state dinner once he saw that I had made it out. Would it be so wrong to find Finn and just... go home?

I was about to start the van when I spotted him.

Dracula stood beneath a nearby streetlight. His still figure was out of place, compared to the activity farther down the sidewalk.

It was obvious he wanted to speak with me. It was the reason he'd been at Bea's in the first place. Most likely, the vampire would just keep showing up until he got what he wanted—he didn't exactly have any shortage of time. I stepped out of the van, and when I pushed the door shut, it felt like the night swallowed the sound it made. I shoved my hands in the pockets of the hoodie and walked over the icy pavement.

He stared up at the moon. Ironic that it had decided, after so much terror and bloodshed, to finally show its serene face. Standing there, the sky's luminescent glow washing over his dark skin, Dracula had never looked more otherworldly. He must've been more powerful at nighttime, because his power brushed against me like an ocean wave. It was so vast, so cold, that I wasn't certain who would win if we were to truly fight. An instinctive shiver of trepidation went down my spine.

"Did the dragon survive?" Dracula asked, startling me from my reverie.

I frowned. "What do you mean?"

He looked at me, and while the rest of him seemed entirely supernatural, those strange-colored eyes shone with humanity. There was so much in his head I hadn't been able to explore. I wondered what ghosts haunted this creature, what memories came for him during those vulnerable moments we all experienced, no matter how fast we ran. And he'd had centuries to make mistakes, to fall in love, to forge alliances and create enemies. I couldn't imagine what I'd manage to do in that time. Probably bring about the end of the world, somehow.

"The dragon," Dracula insisted. There was nothing in his velvety voice that hinted at the sorrow I could see in his gaze. "From the bar where you work. I noticed him while I was looking for you. Did he survive the attack? It would be most unfortunate if he met his end. His kind is on the verge of extinction, after all."

"I have no idea what you're talking about," I said. A strand of hair blew across my mouth, and I pulled it away with impatient fingers. There were still sounds drifting down the street. I kept my eyes on Dracula. I had a feeling—it was the same one I'd had when I saw my mother's body slumped against the wall, and again when I stood at that crossroads to meet a demon—that everything was about to change. A sort of hollow sensation in my middle.

"You truly don't know." The vampire sounded faintly amused now. "The fry cook, my lady. He is a dragon."

CHAPTER FOURTEEN

$\mathcal{M}$y knee bounced restlessly as I waited.

It felt wrong sitting in a therapist's office when the world was falling apart just outside it. Not only had a man been murdered yesterday, which no one knew about except me, Finn, and the faerie who'd done the killing, but now the cherubim were hunting me. In addition to the ones that already had been.

I'd been planning to cancel this appointment, but Collith must've finally noticed the magnetic calendar on the fridge, because he'd made a show of finding my car keys and putting them on the table in front of me. "Better get going, or you'll be late," was all he said.

I thought about bringing up Ariel, and the fact that he'd secretly planted her in the bar and in my life. But after the dream we'd shared, there was a renewed sense of connection between us. I was scared an argument would break it again, so I said nothing.

It had been a strange morning. Instead of working a breakfast shift, I slept in—Oliver was still lying low after the incident with his shadow, so we'd passed the time with him painting and me reading—and I joined my family in the kitchen for a late breakfast. The bar was effectively closed until Bea could do repairs, a fact which kept making me feel random pangs of guilt. I clung to the knowledge that her insurance should cover the costs. According to a text I'd gotten from Phil, the police had concluded it was a robbery gone wrong. Multiple witnesses had described the rough-looking men who'd come inside, waving guns and shouting over the music.

So far, no one had questioned me about my bizarre display with the steak knife.

I'd tried not to stare at Cyrus as we ate. He looked the same, despite last night's chaos and the new information I'd learned from Dracula. What had the vampire seen at a single glance that I hadn't after years of friendship? What characteristic or feature gave away Cyrus's true nature? He ate a bowl of oatmeal with his usual concentration, and it seemed impossible Cyrus Lavender was anything more than human.

Finn never came back to the house. I sent him a text, but I already knew what had sent him deep into the woods, trying to survive his pain with the strength of a wolf. Saving Phil's daughter had affected him like seeing Ian O'Connell had affected me.

Ian O'Connell, who was dead. The realization kept fading and returning in bright, startling bursts. Ian O'Connell was dead.

Now I sat in Consuelo Thompson's office, my mind writhing with images of the cherubim and the Wild Hunt. I was on the verge of leaving when the door opened. The human filled the doorway and greeted me with a warm smile. "Come on in, Fortuna."

I held onto the strap of my purse with an unnecessarily tight grip and followed her into the other room. Consuelo closed the door behind me. Perfume followed in her wake as she moved to sit in her cream-colored chair. Once she was settled, she picked up her notepad and crossed her legs, revealing that she had better calves than me. "How are you?" she asked.

I stared down at my clasped hands and shrugged. "I've had better days, I guess."

"What made this one difficult?"

"Nothing." It was the truth. I'd spent most of the day studying Enochian on the couch.

We went back and forth like that for a while. Consuelo asked a question that sounded simple, and I answered it as briefly as I could. Then she asked, her tone polite as ever, "Have you masturbated yet?"

At this, I went still. I'd never talked about my sex life so freely with someone before—it was one thing to hear people's conversations in a bar, but it was another thing entirely to expose my own experiences. "Does that matter?" I asked after a noticeable pause.

Consuelo didn't repeat the question. Instead, she just sat there and continued waiting for me to answer. I glanced at the door, wishing a gust of wind would blow it open and suck me right back out of the room.

The human gave it another twenty seconds or so before relenting. "It can be a healing practice after the trauma you've been through. Realizing you're capable of sexual satisfaction is an incredible, powerful feeling," she told me. "But sometimes it takes a while to feel wholly reunited with your body. You're allowed to take all the time you need. Sexual exploration is a journey, not a destination."

"You should put that on a T-shirt," I muttered.

Consuelo smiled again and leaned forward. "You are capable of loving again, Fortuna. Someday you'll want to give yourself to someone completely. If it's your instinct to hold back right now, that's all right. You are allowed to be fearful... but you are also allowed to trust again. Your healing process is your own. Regardless of how you get there, know that as long as you are taking care of yourself, nobody has any right to tell you differently."

"What makes you so sure I'm capable of healing?" I asked. "Most of the time, I can't even touch someone without thinking about it."

"Because you're sitting on that couch right now, which tells me you're a strong person. You're going to have good days and bad days. You're going to have good sex and bad sex. But you're still alive. Remember that, Fortuna. Write it down in that journal." She glanced at the clock hanging over the door. "It looks like we're done for today. Same time next week?"

This question startled me, too. When had I stopped keeping track of the seconds and minutes I spent here? Recovering, I nodded my agreement, picked up my bag, and followed her to the outer door. As I passed, my arm almost brushed her shoulder. It wouldn't have mattered—I was wearing a coat—but I jerked out of the way instinctively. I saw Consuelo take note of my panic.

We exchanged some more polite words, then I left, reemerging into the cold. I walked to my van and rummaged for the keys as I went.

"I must confess to some disappointment," a familiar voice said. "You didn't even send a text to make sure I was all right. And here I thought we were friends."

Laurie was leaning against the door. I wasn't surprised—part of me had been expecting him. It was as though he could sense whenever I was alone. Or maybe just lonely. These days, it was impossible to tell between the two. "I didn't need to make sure you were all right," I replied without looking at him. "You're like a cockroach, and cockroaches are hard to kill."

There was a familiar jangling sound, and I pulled the ring of keys out with a flourish. Still keeping my gaze averted from his face, I pointed the key fob and opened the door. "So, what, you hate me now?" Laurie demanded, stepping aside.

"Oh, I never said I hated you," I countered, sliding onto the driver's seat. "If you were on fire, I'd get out the marshmallows, but there's a difference between that and hate. Well, no, maybe not."

As I reached for the door handle, I waited for his snappy comeback. It didn't come. When I glanced toward him, I instantly saw why—Laurie was gone. But there was someone else coming toward me, his elbows swinging casually, sunglasses flashing in the sunlight. He moved down the sidewalk as if the concrete was an autowalk, and he held a coffee cup in each hand. "How are you people finding me? Do you have a tracking device on my van?" I demanded.

Dracula stopped when he was so close that I could touch him. My words made the corners of his mouth tilt upward. "Actually, that's exactly how I found you. Will you take a walk with me, Your Majesty? I won't take up too much of your time."

Did he just admit to putting a tracking device on my van? Well, *that* was definitely something I was going to find and remove later. "Why?" I asked, unable to hide my annoyance.

"I have a proposition for you." He held out one of the coffee cups.

A sigh filled my chest, but I didn't let it out as I accepted the beverage.

I didn't expect the vampire to come so soon, but I only had myself to blame. Last night, while we were standing beneath that streetlight, I'd felt overwhelmed and exhausted by his revelation. *Can we do this tomorrow? I'm tired*, I had said to the immortal. He courteously agreed.

It was strange to see Dracula in the daylight now. Looking at him, it seemed obvious he wasn't human. There was something off about his movements—like the fae, he was too graceful. I got out of the van and locked the doors again. I joined Dracula on the sidewalk and took a sip from the coffee cup. The taste of espresso and milk filled my mouth.

We'd only taken a few steps when he asked, "Did you know *dracula* is Enochian for 'night'?"

That actually *was* interesting. "No, I didn't," I admitted. I took another sip.

The vampire's face turned toward me. "This is why so many mistake it for a name, rather than what it truly is."

My eyebrows rose as I understood his meaning. I stopped and stared up at where his eyes should be. My own reflection stared back. There was only one other person on the street, and she was a block away, so I didn't worry about us being overheard as I said, "It's a title?"

"As you discovered during our, shall we say, *spirited* training session, the name given to me at birth was Bako Okafor. I lead a faction of elite fighters... and I do mean fighters, Queen Fortuna. Each of them has survived the stuff of nightmares. But they don't turn to the darkness, because their pain and sorrow are given a purpose. A direction. Not to mention an extremely generous salary."

Purpose. That word caught my notice. It was the same one I'd seen in his head. "What kind of purpose?" I asked, trying to sound casual. My grip tightened on the coffee cup.

"To keep the two worlds separate," he said without hesitation. "Humanity on one side, Fallen on the other. We guard the night, and it is long."

His voice shifted during this last part, and it sounded like something he'd said a thousand times before. Like a creed. All at once, I understood the fear I'd found in the vampire's mind. While I'd been stealing from his library, I learned that his entire existence centered around one thing, and he dreaded failing at that thing. The fact that it wasn't dark or nefarious was almost as surprising as the truth behind Dracula's legend. "So, wait, are you... offering me a job?" I asked.

"Indeed I am, my lady. I was most impressed by your display at the restaurant."

"I don't know if you've heard, but I'm Queen of the Unseelie Court. It's kind of a full-time job," I told him. My mind was racing again, not to consider his offer, but to evaluate how this new information could be used. If Dracula's purpose was to keep the existence of Fallen under wraps, maybe he really was an ally.

His face showed no disappointment. Instead, he took a sip of coffee and said, "Take some time to consider my proposal. I will contact you soon."

"Wait, what does 'soon' mean?" I called, but Dracula was already moving on.

Down at the corner, he walked past an old woman and her dog. I watched, frowning, as both human and canine gave Dracula a wide berth. The woman's expression didn't change, and there was no fear in the air. She seemed unaware that she'd done it. But as the two parties went on their way, neither looking back, I realized why.

Despite his beauty, despite his apparent youth, humans and animals shied away from Dracula. As if something living couldn't bear being so close to death. It struck me as terribly… lonely. Once, the prospect wouldn't have seemed so gray. But now I had known love. I had been reminded of what it was like to have a family. Every night I fell asleep surrounded by pack, and woke up to their sounds. I couldn't go back to the quiet.

It was why I would rather be in Hell than turn to vampirism to save myself, should Gwyn successfully complete her hunt.

At least in Hell, I'd have company.

***

Fortuna.

The whisper was so intense it seemed as if it were right in my ear. I jerked upright, the conversation I'd been having with Oliver fading as I heard it again. *Fortuna.*

Silence coated the house like a fine mist. Following a faint instinct, I got out of bed and crept to the window. It was covered in a layer of frost, which I scratched at to see the yard. Shavings lodged under my nails and fell to the floor.

It was one of those nights so dark that it seemed as though an enormous creature had swallowed the world whole. Gwyn stood in the snow, legs apart, boots planted. *A battle stance*, I thought with a rush of fear. Slowly I pulled back from the glass, and the blinds fell back into place. The frost was creeping back, obscuring the tiny opening I had made.

I walked soundlessly to the front door—I didn't go in search of Finn, because if he wasn't in an exhausted sleep from changing back, he was out in the woods. Once again, I put on the first pair of shoes I could reach, along with a random coat I took off a hook. I stepped into the cold and felt it down to my bones. For a moment or two, I wavered on the porch, wondering if I should run back for my weapons. But what use was bullets or blades against a creature that couldn't be killed?

"I grow impatient, Fortuna Sworn," Gwyn called.

Worried she would wake the others, I hurried down the steps. Frost glittered on the gravel, making the night seem whimsical and childlike. But as I drew closer to Gwyn, and saw her grip on the sword gleaming at her hip, I knew it was anything but. She hadn't been holding it like that during our last conversation—touching her sword was a warning. A promise.

Suddenly a terrible thought occurred to me, and I slowed. What if Collith had been wrong, and Gwyn didn't stop at my death? What if she planned to slaughter the others, too?

Without thinking, I glanced back at the house, anxious for my family's safety. The faerie followed my gaze. I was still several yards away, but she pulled her weapon from its leather sheath and held it aloft, admiring a gleam of moonlight along its deadly edge. The flared blade seemed to emanate an eagerness that sent another whisper of fear through me. "It was a gift from Arthur," she commented finally.

There was something in her tone that made my eyebrows go up. I pulled my coat tighter around me, trying to ward off anxiety and cold. "Are you talking about King Arthur?" I asked lightly. "My mom read those stories to me when I was a child. Great pieces of fiction."

Gwyn lowered the blade and fixed her eyes on me. "And who are we? Gwyn of the Wild Hunt and Queen of the Unseelie Court. I suppose we are just stories, as well?"

I mustered a faint, bitter smile. "No. We are tragedies."

My words brought an odd light to her eyes, like I'd surprised or amused her. Tilting her head, Gwyn slid her sword back into the sheath and searched my face. I knew I was looking back at her with a wary expression, which was probably like bleeding in shark-infested waters, but I couldn't suppress how terrifying I found her.

"You're frightened, but not nearly as frightened as you should be. Do you hope to find another means of survival?" the faerie asked suddenly. "There is no quarry that can hide from me, no prey that can outrun me. You *will* die by my hand, Fortuna Sworn. All that's within your control is when."

There was no pity in Gwyn's voice, no regret in her face, and she was so fae that it sent a quake of panic through me. There was *nothing* mortal about this creature. Even Jassin had seemed more human.

"Maybe I'm just confident in my ability to find Creiddylad," I said. My voice was uneven.

She closed the distance between us, moving swiftly and silently. I felt like a gazelle before a lion, too afraid to move. It was only when her fingers brushed the edge of my jaw that I recoiled... or tried to, anyway. There was nothing natural about the instant change in me, and I realized too late that Gwyn must possess an ability the history books didn't know about. Lust crept through my mind like fog. When she kissed me, it felt like pressing my finger upon a knife's edge, dreading the consequences, but alive with adrenaline.

Then the fog began to retreat.

I had the power of an entire Court at my back. Just as Collith couldn't be affected by a Nightmare's influence, so I couldn't be overtaken by Gwyn's. Feeling clear-headed again, I tilted my head to give her better access as she kissed her way up my neck. She probably felt the vibrations of my voice as I murmured, "You know, for all your prowess and power, there's one thing you don't have."

Her voice was thick with passion, and her accent was stronger as she said, "Mmmm? What's that?"

"Consent," I whispered.

Moving faster than I ever had in my life, I rammed the heel of my hand into her nose. Gwyn's head snapped back, and an explosion of blood—*blue as a berry*, as Laurie had so eloquently said once—splattered down her chin.

I was already backing away. I didn't run, but it took all the self-control I had. Gwyn grinned at me, her mouth stretching too wide. Blood smeared her teeth. "Oh, you're going to be fun," she purred. "I can tell."

Before I could respond, her gaze flicked to something behind me. Surprise flashed across her face. I turned slightly, wary of putting my back to the huntress. My stomach fluttered when I saw Collith, sitting on the porch steps. He wasn't looking in our direction—his eyes were staring upward, toward the smattering of stars—but there was something about the lines of his body that made me think he was very, very aware of us.

"I'd heard rumors that you murdered your mate in cold blood," Gwyn commented, swiping at the blood still spouting from her nostrils. "I think I'm disappointed. Rest well, Your Majesty. You're going to need it for my next visit."

With that ominous statement, she turned her back on me and returned to the Hunt.

The thunder of their departure followed me all the way to the house. Without a word, I sat beside Collith. The two of us gazed up at the moon, speaking in the language of silence and souls. Then our eyes caught, and neither of us looked away.

"You smell so good. It makes me want to run my tongue up the side of your neck," I said abruptly.

Collith's brows drew together. His expression probably matched mine. "Fortuna, did—"

Blood had already rushed to my face. "No, I didn't mean to say that. What's happening to me?"

"Gwyn must've slipped you a truth spell in her kiss," Collith said flatly. "She does love her witches. That sort of spell is supposed to be drawn out and painful, but somehow she's made it into a painless trick—a trick so old, in fact, that it's become part of our nursery rhymes. It sounds a little odd in English, but the words translate to something like, 'The hunter is old and cunning. Careful not to kiss or taste, for she will take your life and secrets.'"

He paused. I watched his expression shift as we both realized what this meant. With Gwyn's spell still on my tongue, I had to tell the truth about everything. I'd have no choice.

Dread felt like a fingernail scraping the lining of my stomach. Though there was no longer a bond between us, I knew Collith was thinking about the question, because it was what I was thinking about. The question he asked nearly every night, after every nightmare, and never got an answer to. *What happened?*

I waited for him to ask.

But he didn't. In the end, Collith just looked up at the sky again, and gratitude swelled in my throat. I knew I didn't owe him an explanation, but I wanted to give one regardless. "I can't talk about it. It's not that I don't trust you. I just... can't."

Collith's face lowered again. He stared at me for a moment. Then, moving slowly, he reached up and brushed my cheek with the back of his knuckles. Electricity crackled between us. I put my hand over his without thinking, and an image blinded me like a strobe light. I caught a glimpse of my own face.

Certain that I'd imagined it, or it was just the heat of the moment, I grabbed his head. Collith blinked at me, his eyes once again bright with bewilderment. "What are you doing?"

It was his fear that let me in. Not fear of me, exactly, but of how I would react to the heat between us.

Now that I was putting some effort behind it, a memory filled my head. I saw my own face again. In this strange playback, I wasn't looking at Collith—my eyes were fixed upward, tracking the progress of a hawk. We were surrounded by trees and sky, and suddenly I recognized it. We were on our way to Astrid's pack.

As we hiked, Collith's gaze strayed to me again and again. How could I have been so oblivious to it? How could I not have felt the gentle pressure of his eyes, caressing my face, my body, my mouth?

Before I could withdraw from the memory, Collith's thoughts whispered through me. No, not thoughts, exactly— they were emotions and sensations. That day, while the Unseelie King watched me, he compared me to moonlight and fire, everything bright and burning. He admired my fearlessness, my determination, my endurance. There was no other name for the feeling inside of him. In that moment, I knew.

It was love. Collith *loved* me.

Somehow, he'd kept it hidden all this time—our relationship was more than some faerie game to him. He wasn't using me or plotting against me. All this time, I'd resisted him, thinking he was like all the others, when in fact Collith Sylvyre was unlike anyone I had ever met before.

Tears were streaming down my face. "Why didn't you tell me, you idiot?" I whispered.

He didn't answer; maybe he couldn't. Feeling braver than I had in a long time, I reached down and folded my fingers through Collith's, then pulled him to his feet. The porch groaned under our feet. A second later, we were inside. I let go of him to take off my boots and coat. When I turned back, it looked like the faerie king hadn't moved. I took his hand again and walked toward my bedroom.

I closed the door gently, still wary of waking Finn. The darkness pressed in on all sides. I faced Collith and, after flattening my hand on his chest, guided him toward the bed. The backs of his legs hit the mattress. He sat down carefully, as if he thought I was going to change my mind any second.

I wasn't. Not this time. "Do you want me?" I asked, meeting his gaze across so much pain and so many shadows.

Collith was breathing hard now, as though he'd just run for miles and miles. He responded to my question by gripping my waist and, slowly, guiding me down until I was on his lap. The new wetness between my legs made me shiver. His head dipped and he sucked my neck while his hand traveled lower. I gasped against him, my chest heaving. I fumbled for his zipper, feeling so inexperienced. It was all so new. The desire to want more with someone and knowing that I might be able to have it. Finally.

But then, with a pained sound, Collith turned his head away, effectively ending our frantic kiss. I reached for him instantly and he resisted turning back. "Good night," he said.

Before I could argue, he lifted me off him and stood up. His expression was a combination of frustration and disappointment. Seeing that, I realized why Collith kept refusing me—he thought I was doing this out of guilt or pity.

He couldn't have been more wrong.

I perched on the edge of the bed and stared up at him, letting everything pour from my eyes. I didn't care if Collith saw how much of a hold he had on me, how much he consumed. The stark truth shone, an inner sun that burned any fear or embarrassment away. If he wanted it, Collith could have my heart, my very soul if I had one.

He didn't move. Maybe he still didn't believe me.

I took his hand and guided it under my waistband. When he reached my lower stomach, I let go and leaned back on my elbows. Our eyes met in a slow simmer. Then, slowly, Collith's hand went lower. His fingertips brushed my wet clitoris and I gasped. Collith glanced at me sharply, his expression assessing. But it was pleasure, not fear, that pulled the sound from me. When he recognized that, Collith moved the ball of his thumb in slow circles.

He needed no convincing after that.

Pulling his hand away, he took off his shirt at the same time I reached for his pants.

I'd seen Collith's penis before, but I was struck anew by the perfection of it. The shaft was long and thick, and I trailed my fingers along the soft skin. My faerie king made a sound as though I were tormenting him, and I tipped my head back to give him a wicked grin.

In response, he reached down and pulled a wallet out of his discarded jeans. I watched as Collith opened it and produced a condom. I wanted to make a joke about the fact he'd been carrying it around in his wallet, but nothing else about the moment felt funny. He ripped the wrapper open with his teeth. In a swift movement, Collith slid the condom onto his hard cock, and the muscles in his stomach shifted as he settled beside me.

I tensed, expecting him to tug down my pajama bottoms and enter me right away, but apparently Collith was in no hurry. His hand curved around my hip and he kissed me again, the movements of his tongue skilled and thorough.

Collith only began to undress me when I was so consumed by him that I'd forgotten to be nervous. Every time he removed an article of my clothing, he made sure to lick and explore every part of exposed skin. Within a minute, I was impatient and ready for him again. I reached down and stroked his length, hoping to wear down his resolve. "Don't make me beg," I whispered.

Collith's eyes flashed. After another kiss that left me breathless, he moved so that I was on my back and he was perfectly aligned with my opening. "You need to relax, sweetheart," he said, hovering above me.

At first, I didn't know what Collith meant, then I realized every inch of my body was stiff as a board. I let out a breath. Once the tension had left me, Collith finally pushed inside, easing himself deeper little by little. It was tight and strange, but not painful. Nothing like the experience I'd prepared myself for.

After he'd withdrawn, Collith waited for me to open my eyes —I hadn't even realized they were closed. I met his gaze and nodded to let him know I was okay. He entered me again, dropping feathery kisses anywhere he could reach. When his teeth lightly closed around my nipple, I made a sound of surprised pleasure, and Collith started moving faster.

His strokes were just like him—deliberate and powerful. My fingers dug into Collith's back and I clamped my legs harder around his waist. He drove himself even deeper. Harder.

I started rising to meet his thrusts. *This is my choice. This is my first time*, I thought. It felt as though I'd been trapped inside a glass encasing for weeks, and with every movement we made, a new crack went through it. Soon it was on the verge of shattering completely.

Only once did I freeze in remembrance. Only once did I tremble with terror. When Collith realized what was happening, he paused to murmur reassurances. He cupped my cheek and his eyes looked into mine. I was coming to know his face even better than my own, and as I stared up at him, nothing else stood a chance of stealing my attention away. I wrapped my fingers around his and slowly nodded. *Keep going. Don't stop.* Collith bent down and kissed me, long and deep, and began to thrust again. It was a delicious build-up returning to our previous urgent rhythm.

After that, I didn't—couldn't—think about anything except how good this felt, how good *I* felt, and how freeing it was to want this. To want him. I thought of nothing else but Collith. At one point I felt him shift, and then his fingers found my clitoris again. I groaned and held him tighter, moving my hips more frantically.

"Fuck," Collith said through his teeth. He didn't last long after that—a few seconds later, he came in long, trembling runs.

Seeing him finish, along with the skilled touch of his fingers, sent me over the edge, as well. Heat and light washed through me, and I heard myself release a breathy moan.

Collith kissed my shoulder and murmured something about the bathroom. My euphoria had quickly faded into drowsiness. Nodding, I curled onto my side, eyelids fluttering, and tried to think of a reason I shouldn't fall asleep.

I must've drifted off, because it felt like only a moment had passed when I heard the door hinges whine again.

"Fortuna? Are you awake?" Collith asked, spooning against my back. "There's something I want to tell you."

There was something in his voice that unsettled me. Without knowing why, I kept my eyes closed and my breathing even. After a moment, Collith nestled closer and put his head down. It only took him a few minutes to fall asleep.

Once I was certain the Unseelie King was unconscious, I opened my eyes and stared into the darkness, frightened by the sensations happening inside me. It was too late to stop it, I knew. The time for pretending was long behind us.

Suddenly I heard Mercy's voice, the words low with warning. A memory. *Anyone who loves you will pay a price. It will cost you, as well.*

I squeezed my eyes shut and pressed back against Collith, banishing the witch from my mind. No more prices. No more costs. Collith and I were different.

But the air felt thick with my own doubt.

CHAPTER FIFTEEN

*N*ow that the afterglow of sex had faded, and my thoughts were back to torment me, I remembered what waited on the other side of sleep.

I began to fight the darkness, rather than succumb to it.

Exhaustion seemed like a small price to pay to avoid seeing Oliver. Or rather, Oliver seeing me. Because I was afraid he'd take one look at my face and know what I'd done with Collith. Happiness was as powerful as sorrow—you could sense it on other people as if it were a visible thing. As if it had a stench.

I would get up, I decided, and make a cup of coffee. Pass the next few hours trying to think of a way to beat Gwyn. I opened my eyes reluctantly and, once my vision adjusted, let out a low curse.

I was in the dreamscape.

The sky was red. Not pink, not orange, but a firetruck red. Unnatural. Everything else looked normal enough. Still, I moved forward cautiously, my eyes darting in every direction. I was wearing boots, jeans, and a wool sweater. A lonesome breeze blew past, heading for the cottage. The door was tightly closed, and I looked to the sea. There Oliver sat, a black silhouette against a bloody backdrop. The shadow he cast against the ground had no wings, reassuring me that it was really him. I started toward my best friend, a path I'd trekked so many times that the ground was packed earth instead of tall grass.

"Ollie? Are you okay? The sky is a little—" I cut short when I drew alongside him and saw his expression. Shame dug a hole in my chest, leaving a dark ache. This was it. This was the conversation we'd both been putting off for so long. I'd been so busy unraveling these past few weeks, I hadn't seen it happening to Oliver. Now there was nothing left but two piles of thread. Swallowing, I lowered myself to the ground.

Oliver's legs dangled off the edge. I didn't worry about him falling—as children, we'd grasped hands and leaped together. All that awaited at the bottom was warm water. This was Oliver's world and he controlled what happened in it. *But he can't control what happens outside*, that inner voice reminded me. As though I needed a reminder. If he'd had any power beyond these boundaries, Oliver would've left his prison a long time ago. He would've been free to have a life of his choosing, instead of mine.

I opened my mouth to speak. At the same time Oliver said, "I can't do this anymore."

"What do you mean?" I asked. I wasn't sure why, because I already knew the answer. Maybe I just needed to hear him say it out loud.

As silence hovered between us, snow started drifting down from the red sky. It should've been impossible—there were still no clouds overhead. The small flakes looked eerie against the horizon. They settled into Oliver's hair and on his shoulders. "I mean that… I think you're bad for me," he answered finally, keeping his blue eyes on the sea. "Or maybe we're bad for each other. Either way, I'm done. Being your second choice. Waiting around."

Looking at him hurt. With jerky movements, I pulled a

handful of grass out of the soil and threw it over the cliff. "You're *not* my second choice, Ollie. That's not why I didn't choose you."

"Did you fuck him?" he asked flatly.

The directness of it made me flinch. Now it was his turn to wait for an answer. But Oliver had spent his entire existence waiting, and I didn't want to make him do it anymore.

Knowing this didn't make the words any easier to say. I bit my lip and tried to turn my heart to stone through sheer force of will. "Ollie, I..."

That was all the answer he needed.

He pulled his legs back and stood up. I looked up at him, blinking rapidly. Oliver stared at the ground as he said, "I felt it, Fortuna. Every second. Your emotions were so powerful that I was forced to endure them along with you. Your joy. Your desire. Your love."

He said the last word in a whisper, and his eyes were bright with torment. The realization that Oliver had seen those intimate moments with Collith sent a rush of heat to my cheeks. I turned toward the skyline, unable to face him anymore. It was still snowing. I buried my fingers into the earth, needing something to hold onto, and wished I could see the sun one more time. We'd spent so many years in this place, bathed in golden light, wild things that couldn't be touched or tamed. When had it started to change? When did we lose our innocence?

But we couldn't have gone on like that forever, no matter how badly I missed it now. Every dream ended, and eventually, you woke up. If you spent your life living in a fantasy world, there would be no time for the real one.

"Please," I said, knowing even as I said it, there was no point. I couldn't undo my night with Collith, and I didn't want to. But that didn't mean I was ready to lose my best friend. "Please don't do this."

Oliver didn't move. Not yet. I saw him in my peripheral

vision, his golden hair tousled from the wind. The temperature noticeably decreased. The sky kept bleeding snow. "At least my shadow will die with me. You don't need to be afraid anymore," he said.

"But I *am* afraid. I'm afraid of a life without you in it, Ollie. You're my best friend." Without thinking, I started to reach for him. Oliver moved to avoid my hand. I swallowed again, dropping it back to my lap. A fresh wave of loss crashed over me as I pictured it. No more laughter. No more ever-changing landscapes. No more relief from the bad things that happened while I was awake. Oliver didn't say anything, and I stood up to face him. "You said you'd go into the afterlife with me. You said your greatest fear was—"

"Everything I said was just what you wanted to hear, Fortuna. After all, I'm an extension of you, right? A figment of your imagination." Oliver shoved his hands in his pockets and studied me. I looked back at him, unnerved by the detachment in his voice. The cold was so intense that I wondered if his eyelashes had frozen or my lips were turning white. For a moment, neither of us spoke.

When the silence lingered and Oliver didn't leave, I felt my traitorous heart lift, thinking that he might have changed his mind. That he'd pictured his life without me, too, and it was unbearable.

Instead, he walked away. Even as I watched him do it, I couldn't believe he was. With every step my best friend took, he faded, until he looked like a spirit in the moors.

Then he was nothing more than a memory.

Upon waking, I saw that Collith's side of the bed was empty.

Something caught my eye on his pillow, though. Thoughts of Oliver faded as I lifted my head, frowning, and confirmed there was an envelope resting on the white linen. I reached for it, noting my name written in elegant script on the back. Unease rippled through me as I ran my thumb beneath the wax seal—I knew Collith's handwriting and this wasn't it.

Inside was a single piece of paper. In the same loopy hand, someone had written a single line across its center. *My patience wears thin. Consider this motivation.*

The truth settled into my skin with the gentleness of a thousand needles.

Gwyn had Collith.

Suddenly I thought of the last words she'd said to me. *Rest well, Your Majesty. You're going to need it for my next visit.*

She'd seen how I reacted last night, when I turned and spotted Collith on the porch. It must have been painfully obvious that I felt something for the Unseelie King, and like a typical faerie, she'd used my weakness for her own gain.

As my mind struggled to accept this new reality, I felt sick. What if she was hurting him? What if she'd already killed him? How long had she been in here, watching us, standing over us while we slept naked and vulnerable?

Creiddylad. I had to find Creiddylad. I rushed out of bed and nearly tripped in my rush to the dresser. There were clothes all over the floor, but everything was mine—at least Gwyn allowed Collith to get dressed before she took him. I yanked at a drawer with such force it completely came out and hit the floor. I picked out a random shirt and pulled it on, then reached for another drawer in search of pants. "Laurie!" I barked.

He materialized instantly, and as I turned, I caught his silver eyes lingering on my bare legs. "And here I thought you despised me," he commented.

"Gwyn took Collith," I said bluntly, ignoring this. I shimmied into some pants and dove for the nightstand. I chose some weapons that would work with my clothes. When I faced Laurie, he was holding Gwyn's letter. He must've read it, because he looked out the window with the stillness of someone deep in thought. I couldn't sense any fear—he'd always been guarded against my abilities.

"I'm going to see Viessa," I told him as I found hiding places for the Glock and a couple of pocketknives.

Laurie frowned at the mention of her name. "Why?"

"Because she knows things."

"*I* know things," he protested.

"Great. Can you tell me where to find Creiddylad?" I demanded. I waited, but after a moment, Laurie turned his face back to the window. "That's what I thought."

I hurried into the hallway. There was still no Finn, and I made a mental note to talk to him once we had the chance—it worried me how much he'd been wearing his wolfskin. If he went too long without changing, he might lose the ability altogether.

But I couldn't think about that right now. Right now, Gwyn had Collith, and my search for Creiddylad had become even more urgent. I rushed to the front door. By a stroke of luck, there was no one in the kitchen or living room. No one that I needed to lie or make excuses to. I yanked on a pair of thick boots, lined with faux fur on the inside, and my coat. After brief contemplation, I switched the Glock to a pocket where it would be easier to grab, and the knives in other various places. Then I pulled the door open and hurried out.

Laurie didn't ask if he could accompany me—he just reappeared at my side the moment I reached the tree line. I started in the direction of the Unseelie Court, the force of my anxiety making it difficult to breathe.

"There's something about nature I just love," Laurie mused suddenly, looking around as though we were at Disneyland.

"Despite what it did to you?" I muttered. He was probably just trying to distract me, I knew, but I refused to pretend everything between us was fine. My cell phone rang, and I pulled it out to look at the screen. It was a number I didn't recognize. "Hello?"

"Have you given thought to my offer?" Dracula asked, undeterred by my curt tone.

Dracula was calling me on my cell phone. I paused to let the thought resonate. How the hell had he gotten this number? Less than a second later, I answered my own question. *Adam gave it to him, of course.* My terror for Collith was making me slow, which was the opposite of what I needed to be to get us all out of this. Realizing that I'd stopped, I started walking again.

Dracula was quiet on the other end, and in a rush, I remembered that he'd asked a question. "I thought I already gave you an answer," I said cautiously, feeling Laurie's eyes on me.

"Where are you, Your Majesty? You sound out of breath."

I couldn't tell a vampire who was obsessed with keeping Fallenkind a secret that I was planning on unleashing a powerful, vengeful faerie into the world. "Just going for one of my morning runs! Listen, I'll call you later, okay?"

I hung up before he could respond. Laurie didn't get to ask any questions, either—as I tucked my phone away, I actually did break into a run.

It was hard to sprint through snow, but I didn't slow down or take any breaks. All I wanted was to see that jagged hole in the earth rising up in front of me, and the irony of this wasn't lost on me. Laurie ran at my side. He was wearing jeans and a peacoat, yet somehow he made it look effortless. We put miles behind us as if it were a marathon.

Sooner than I thought it would, the entrance appeared through the trees. Someone must have sent word we were coming, because Nuvian emerged from the mouth of the tunnel just as Laurie and I arrived. He was already frowning. "What are you doing—"

"I'm here to see Viessa," I cut in. There was no time for his bullshit, and I was still struggling to breathe. "Please take me to her."

Nuvian wasn't a complete fool; he didn't utter a single word of reproach or disdain. Maybe there was something in my voice that frightened him. He turned around without looking at Laurie, and I assumed this meant the Seelie King was hiding himself from sight—probably for the best. We both followed Nuvian into the darkness. The silence was so thick that it felt malignant. I told myself it was all in my head, but not even Laurie had anything to say during our descent. An eternity later, after a dozen twists and turns, we reached a flight of familiar narrow stairs. Nuvian held a torch up and continued to lead the way.

The dungeons smelled worse than before, if that was possible.

Every line of my body was tense as we went down. I understood why there was no light for this part, since the path was too narrow to put anything on the walls, but knowing didn't make it easier to accept. Once I reached the bottom of the steps, I could see more of our surroundings and my breathing slowed. Torchlight danced along the uneven walls. Nuvian was on the move again, plunging even deeper into the depths of this place. I was still rigid as I followed the faerie to Viessa's cell. I couldn't hear Laurie behind me, but miraculously enough, I could smell him. His pleasant scent was a welcome reprieve from the wealth of horrible odors around us.

Nuvian finally stopped, and I stood in front of the cell he'd selected.

"I'd like some privacy," I said without looking at him. The faerie must've expected it, or was still unnerved by me. Without a sound or an argument, he stepped around me and walked away. I strained to see any movement within the cell as Nuvian's footsteps echoed, then faded. "Viessa?"

The assassin's voice floated from the back wall, where the

shadows had taken over so completely that no light would ever break through again. "You have ignored my summons, Queen Fortuna."

"I've been busy." I paused, casting an involuntary glance toward Laurie in hopes of guidance, but he'd completely hidden himself. Or maybe the smell had just gotten to him. I returned my gaze to Viessa and reminded myself that I didn't need a faerie king next to me. "I'm here now."

She scoffed, but the sound was weak. "You're not here to repay your debt to me."

I should've known she would spot a lie. Viessa was smart—smarter than Collith, Laurie, or any of the Guardians gave her credit for—and she wouldn't have survived down here so long without knowing friend from foe. The problem was, I still wasn't sure which one I was to her.

"I'm looking for Creiddylad," I admitted after a long pause. I opted not to tell her that finding Creiddylad would save the king Viessa had once tried to kill.

"And if I tell you what I know, what then? You don't honor your word. I have nothing to gain from this conversation."

"This is not a time for bargains," I hissed, gripping the bars tightly. It felt like I was coming down from a bad trip—my veins were jittery and I wanted to run from this place. But the next step after Viessa was going to the council members, and if they wouldn't willingly tell me what I needed to know, I would have to force it out of them. I worried my soul wouldn't survive that.

The thought had a strangely calming effect on me, and I felt my face harden. I raised my gaze to the spot I thought Viessa was standing. "This is an order from your fucking queen. You want to know what you have to gain? Your *life*. Because I need to find Creiddylad and I'll do whatever it takes."

Silence fell. I could feel Viessa looking at me. Reassessing. I stood there, in dark and firelight, and allowed my power to saturate the air itself. Moans and cries echoed up and down the corridor.

"All I know is that one of the original council members hid her," Viessa said. There was no flavor on my tongue, but I knew she was afraid. "This member gave the location to one other. It was a safeguard, you see. Two secret keepers. Two bloodlines. Should one of them perish, Creiddylad's location would not be lost. Who can say whether that secret survived, though?"

Shit. This meant that I really did need to speak with the council members—they were literally the only ones in the world who knew where Gwyn's lover was. While the notion of hurting Micah didn't cause me much discomfort, I tried to imagine doing the same to Chandrelle or the others. Most of them hadn't personally done anything to me or my family. "And you don't know which bloodlines? You've never heard a rumor or a whisper of the name?" I pressed, wincing at the edge of desperation in my voice.

The assassin finally shifted into the light. I couldn't see her face, but the flames flickered over her half-starved body, still covered in the rags she'd been wearing last time we spoke. Viessa lifted one shoulder in a graceful shrug. "Even my knowledge has its limits. From this point forward, you're on your own, Queen Fortuna."

I believed her—there was a coldness in her voice that had nothing to do with ice or magic. Footsteps sounded again and, seconds later, Nuvian reappeared. He stopped beside a torch and his braids gleamed. "Are you finished here, Your Majesty?"

"For now." I didn't thank Viessa, but I made sure to say the next part in front of her. "Get this prisoner a change of clothes, please. Warm and clean ones. She will also receive some blankets and a hot meal. If I find out my orders weren't followed, I'll send the Guardians responsible into Death Bringer's chambers. I'm sure he'd enjoy that."

Nuvian bent in a sorry excuse for a bow, and I started walking toward the stairs.

"Wait." Viessa's voice rang into the stillness. Against my better judgment, I looked at her again. She had her face pressed against the bars, and the effect was eerie. Like a wraith from a dark fairy tale. Frost clung to her red hair. "Twice now I have helped you. Twice you have walked away without paying a price. There will not be a third. And I *will* collect my boon very soon."

A response didn't seem necessary, so I kept walking. The promise followed me down the row of cells and back up the stairs. Nuvian stayed in the dungeons, and there was still no sign of Laurie. I emerged into the tunnel alone.

I saw Lyari instantly, who seemed to be pacing. She whirled when she heard my shoes crunch over the dirt. "Why would you speak with Viessa again?" the Guardian demanded without preamble. "No good can come of it. You should stay away from—"

I grabbed her arm and pulled her closer. I expected Lyari to fight my hold, but apparently she trusted me more than I realized. Putting my lips next to her ear, I spoke so quietly that no one except a faerie or a werewolf would be able to hear. "Gwyn took Collith. She thought it would motivate me to find Creiddylad faster."

I moved away and saw that something in Lyari's eyes had changed. It was the same focus that brought me here, willing to do anything to get Collith back. "My current plan is to... speak with every council member," I told her, putting heavy emphasis on the word *speak*.

Lyari didn't respond right away. There was a line between her eyebrows, and she stared at the wall behind me with a concentrated expression. Something kept me from asking her what was wrong—it felt like I would be interrupting, somehow.

A few seconds later, Lyari raised her gaze, looking as if she'd made a decision that caused her physical pain.

"I think I have another way," she said finally. At my questioning look, Lyari seemed to swallow a sigh. "Follow me, Your Majesty."

"Where are we going?" I asked, hurrying after her.

But of course, she didn't answer. I followed the tall faerie through passageways I'd never seen before. It felt like we were going west, but there was no way of knowing underground. Not without a damn compass. We passed doors with brand-new carvings—new to me, at least—and the earth itself gradually changed. The dry dirt became clay, and it was obvious more care had gone into these tunnels. The paths were even and the ceiling was high, lessening the effect of being so far beneath the earth's surface.

At long last, Lyari halted in front of a door that was covered in carvings of swords. It seemed fitting for my fierce Right Hand. "Will you wait here for a moment?" she asked, oblivious to my thoughts.

I nodded. Lyari slipped behind the door, and suddenly I found myself surrounded by quiet. Quiet wasn't good, because now I could hear the anxious voices at the back of my head, saying Collith's name over and over. I reached for my phone. It was useless down here, but it was still a distraction.

As I scrolled through my photo albums, which were essentially made up of Matthew's face, I realized I had no pictures of us together. Me and Collith.

What if Gwyn had killed him? There wouldn't be a single image to remember him by. Not a scrap of nostalgia to comfort me when the grief became too much.

Good thing Collith isn't dying, then. I shoved the phone back into my pocket and stared at the sword carvings, memorizing the faded edges and intricate detail. Moments later, an appealing scent greeted my senses, and it was becoming as familiar as anyone in my family's. "Where have you been?" I asked in a monotone, hiding how much this disturbed me.

Laurie leaned one shoulder against the wall. His hair looked like copper in the flickering light. "Elsewhere."

I gave him a humorless smile. "You were calling in some favors, weren't you? You're trying to find Creiddylad, because you want to save Collith just as badly as I do."

Laurie started to respond, and Lyari chose that moment to open the door. Her eyes flicked to the Seelie King. The vulnerability I'd seen earlier was gone, and she wore her best Guardian face now—however she felt about me running around the Unseelie Court with the Seelie King, it was well-hidden. Without a word, Lyari put her back against the door, holding it for us. I walked over the threshold and into a set of connected rooms.

Like Chandrelle's, the space was unexpectedly lovely. Unlike Chandrelle's, there was a distinctly Moroccan feel to this one. The rugs were bold print, every pillow a bright pattern, and the floor itself was black and cream tile. Several poufs hung on the walls and pendant lamps cast a glow over everything.

"I present my father, Paynore," Lyari said, drawing my attention back to her. Another faerie was already moving forward, giving me a gap-toothed smile that was shocking to see within the Unseelie Court. His left hand held a martini glass, and there was barely a ripple across the alcohol's surface as he approached.

I wasn't sure what I'd been expecting when it came to meeting Lyari's father, but this certainly wasn't it. The faerie's belly was round and extended, his waist-length hair almost the same color as Laurie's. Where the Seelie King's lashes were dark, though, Paynore's matched his startling hair. He wore sandals on his pale feet, and there were bells on the straps, jangling with every step. He was also wearing a red kimono, which flowed behind him like a dramatic gown.

Lyari must have inherited her mother's physical traits, because my Right Hand looked nothing like her father.

I was so distracted by Paynore's appearance that, when he took my hand to pump it up and down, I twitched in surprise. His palm was dry and warm, but I grimaced as though it were the opposite. I steeled myself for the inevitable tsunami of terror.

The tsunami never came.

Despite this male's amiable demeanor, his mind was a fortress. Touching him only elicited what used to be the normal effects for a Nightmare—a taste in my mouth and a smattering of small, simple fears. Paynore was scared of deep water and outer space. The flavors were an oddly pleasant combination of apple and cigar smoke.

"It is truly a pleasure to meet you, Queen Fortuna," Paynore said. If he noticed my grimace, he pretended not to. "Truly a pleasure!"

Strangely enough, I believed him. I glanced at Lyari, uncertain what to say, and she finally revealed the reason she'd brought me here. "I thought my father might know where Creiddylad is."

"It's been a long time since I've heard that name... but as I've just informed Lyari, I'm afraid I can't help you, Your Majesty. I was not one of the members entrusted with that secret." Paynore's regret seemed genuine. I swallowed my disappointment, trying to harden myself to the reality that I had to interview the council members, one by one. Then Paynore added, "There is someone else you could ask, though."

Hope stirred. "Who?"

But Paynore looked at Lyari instead of answering. When I glanced over at her, the Guardian's expression was unhappy. No, resigned. I raised my eyebrows. "Am I missing something?"

Lyari faced me, her expression smoothing again. "He's talking about my mother."

"Your mother?" I echoed, my brows rising higher.

One corner of her mouth tipped upward, but it wasn't a smile. "You thought she was dead? If only that were true—at least then we'd have a grave to mourn. There may not be much left of her, but she's still very much alive."

On that cheerful note, Lyari gripped the hilt of her sword and walked toward a doorway to our right. She didn't say whether we were supposed to follow, but I did, driven by desperation and maybe a bit of curiosity. Laurie sifted and reappeared at my side. At that moment, it struck me how quiet he'd been through all this.

Paynore stayed where he was, and I saw him take a sip of his martini before we moved out of sight.

I faced forward and immediately noticed the metal door. It was embedded in the farthest wall of the farthest room—it looked like the sort of door you'd find on a vault or a safe room. When we reached it, Lyari didn't waste time on dramatics or warnings. She wrapped her hands around the wheel and used her considerable strength to turn it. Rods around the edge of the door retracted, and Lyari pulled it open.

This time, I waited for her to enter first. The doorway wasn't quite high enough for her, and Lyari bent her head as she went inside. I heard the heels of her boots on a hard floor, the low murmur of her voice. Whatever reservations I had were overpowered by the realization that, just a few feet away, there was someone who might be able to help me get Collith back.

A strange smell assaulted my nose as I started after Lyari. It was like a garbage bag that had been left to rot. Worried I'd offend someone, I schooled my features into a disinterested mask.

Laurie had no such qualms—once he was close enough to pick up that smell, he pulled back. His nose wrinkled. "You know what? I'll wait out here. Stand guard and all that," he said casually.

I rolled my eyes at him and stepped through the doorway.

The instant I was over the threshold, someone closed the door behind me. The sound echoed as if we were in a cathedral. Slowly, I took in the enormous space. It was a circle made of stones and mortar. The floor was stone, too. The walls were bare and there was only a bed, a bucket, and a stack of books. Wondering about the echo, I looked up. The Paynore rooms were closer to the surface than I'd thought—high above, two or three stories, there was a circular window.

And across from us, squatting against the wall, was Lyari's mother.

I'd studied the bloodline trees; I knew her name was Kindreth and that she was one of the original angels to fall from Heaven. I didn't see Lyari's resemblance to her, either. Her hair was dark and long, the ends feathery, as if it hadn't been cut in years. What I could see of her face was the color of chalk. Her mouth was a wide, thin slash. She wore a nightgown that looked freshly-washed and ironed, with a scooped neckline and a lacy hem.

The Ring, I realized suddenly. *She looks like that girl from The Ring.*

I was so unnerved that I almost missed it when Lyari said, "There's someone here to see you, Mama. Our new queen. Isn't that exciting? Be respectful, please."

I'd never heard Lyari use that voice before. If I didn't glance at her just as she finished speaking, I wouldn't have believed it. She sounded young and timid. With effort, I turned back to Kindreth and opened my mouth to greet her.

She launched herself at me.

It was so unexpected that I didn't have a chance to defend myself. In the next moment, I hit the wall. The faerie's foul breath assaulted every sense as she buried her splintered nails into the hair at the back of my skull. Her forehead—it was hot, I noted with faint revulsion—pressed against mine. I couldn't move, though I could picture the exact Krav Maga technique that would free me.

"See how we sinned," Kindreth hissed. Spittle landed on my cheek. "Oh, see what wicked things we did. How far we fell. Down, down, down…"

From a distance, I could hear Lyari shouting. I couldn't see her, couldn't answer, couldn't do anything besides look around with horror. Death was everywhere. Swords clashed and agonized cries filled the air. I stood in the center of chaos, horrified as I watched my comrades and loved ones die. No, not my loved ones—Kindreth's. This was her memory. Her biggest regret. The golden street beneath my feet was slick with blood. Bodies slumped against the pearl-crusted gates. *A mistake*, I thought. *I've made such a terrible mistake…*

Kindreth's nails pulled out of my skin, and my vision cleared.

Laurie stood between me and the faerie now—he must've sifted into the room—while Lyari held her mother's arms back. The two of them were across the space, where Kindreth had been when we first entered. "I need to know where you hid Creiddylad," I rasped, holding the back of my head to staunch the bleeding. There was no time to be affected by what I'd just seen. Only Collith mattered.

"Creiddylad?" Kindreth echoed, her voice high now, like a child's. She stopped yanking at Lyari's hold, and a moment later, her skeletal frame slumped. Lyari's fingers loosened cautiously. Kindreth didn't attack again—she dropped to her knees and started rocking. With every movement her temple beat against the wall. It didn't look hard enough to cause any real damage, so neither of us tried to stop her. "How will we know if the spell worked?"

She said it so quietly that I almost missed it. I didn't dare step closer, but I leaned toward her in my eagerness. "What spell, Kindreth?"

Impatience flitted across her haggard face. "The spell you had placed on the door, you little fool!"

Lyari tensed, ready to move at the first hint of violence, but Kindreth just kept rocking. It felt like her words were branded on my mind. *The door.* Even finding this small piece of the puzzle gave me hope. It made sense the council members who hid Creiddylad had also made it difficult to remove her, in the event she was found. I tried not to think about what we would've done, if we'd gone through all the trouble of leading Gwyn to her lover only to discover she was guarded by ancient magic.

"Will you remind me what kind of spell it was?" I asked, holding back a wince when I pressed down too hard on the holes in my head. "I've forgotten."

"Sacrifice, sacrifice, sacrifice," Kindreth started to chant. Her temple hit the wall. *Thud. Thud. Thud.*

"Are you saying a sacrifice will open the door? Or that you made one to complete the spell?"

Kindreth started to laugh. There was a jagged edge to the sound that affected all of us; I could see it in the way Lyari shifted and Laurie stepped in front of me. "How could you forget, Naevys?" the mad faerie asked between her gasps and giggles. "Has your mind gone to rot? It was *your* blood we used to complete the witch's spell! You insisted no one but the Unseelie Queen would be able to set the human free. You felt responsible for all the death your precious huntress had caused."

Okay, that was actually helpful, I thought dimly. If what Kindreth said had any reliability—which was doubtful, as much as I hated to admit it—then we now knew what it would take to free Creiddylad. The blood of the Unseelie Queen. The blood that ran through my own veins.

I was the key.

"Are you toying with me?" Kindreth asked suddenly. When I looked at her, she was looking back, but there was still a glassiness to her eyes I found frightening. "Are you pretending to be a simpleton to find out where the tomb is? It won't work. It won't work! I won't let you find her!"

She tried to throw herself at me again, but this time Lyari was ready. The steel-eyed Guardian restrained her mother, holding onto her with an unrelenting grip. Kneeling there, her arms bent at unnatural angles, Kindreth looked like a featherless bird that had fallen out of the nest. The sounds she made, though, were anything but innocent or hopeful. Goosebumps raced over my skin at the same moment the door opened behind us.

I glanced back and saw a woman standing there. Kindreth's caretaker, probably—between the fresh nightgown and her clean hair, someone was looking after her. Laurie took a cautious step forward and touched my arm. His fingers caused nothing more than a moment of pleasant warmth. "We should go, Fortuna," he said.

I stared at Kindreth, wracking my mind for the right combination of words or the right question… but some broken things couldn't be fixed. I'd already spent so much of my life trying.

But what about Lyari? I glanced at my Right Hand, reluctant to leave without her. "I'll be right behind you," she said shortly.

"Better be," I said back. As I turned, I caught Laurie's gaze lingering on my shoulder. I followed it and saw bloodstains on my shirt. His concern made me bristle; I didn't like how it made me feel. He was still a murderer, I reminded myself. My voice was curt as I told him, "I'll be fine. I've had worse."

Whatever I'd seen in his eyes disappeared. Laurie nodded, and together, we left that place of pain.

The mad faerie's laughter followed us through the door.

CHAPTER SIXTEEN

*P*aynore was still nursing his martini when we walked back into the room. Or, when *I* walked back into the room, I noted with faint annoyance.

Laurie had disappeared again.

As promised, Lyari caught up a few seconds later, saving me from making small talk with her father. Paynore reiterated what a pleasure it had been to make my acquaintance, and after murmuring the correct words back, Lyari and I left the Paynore chambers.

The moment we were in the passageway, I took one look at her face and started walking. I walked as if we had somewhere to be, or something was on the line. But something *was* on the line—a piece of Lyari's soul. I recognized the darkness in her eyes because I had seen it in my own.

We didn't exchange a single word, not even when we stepped into the open. After being in Kindreth's prison, the air itself poisoned with grief and insanity, it felt like darkness should've claimed the rest of the world. But it was daytime— bright, normal daytime. Lyari took a breath, as though she'd been suffocating beneath the ground, and only now amongst the pines could she breathe again.

I gave her a few seconds, then I moved forward again. I waited until we were past the small clearing and within the cover of dead trees. "Let it out," I commanded.

Lyari didn't argue. She swung away, her shoulders hunched, and she took a few steps in a random direction. The faerie faltered when she realized she had nowhere to go. I understood that urge better than anyone. To outrun the relentless, limitless thoughts of whatever it was you were trying to forget. I could only see the back of Lyari's head as she was swarmed by them. Her hands clenched and unclenched at her sides.

Then, finally, a sound slipped out of her—the smallest of sobs. I saw her arm move, and I knew she was probably pressing it against her mouth to keep the rest at bay. Watching the faerie's slender body shake, I remembered her words from the revel. Now I understood them. *Do you think you're the only creature to know real pain? Why should you get the luxury of falling apart, while the rest of us pick up the pieces and press on?*

Lyari stayed like that for a while.

I pretended to be absorbed by the sky as I waited. There wasn't much to see; it was probably going to snow soon. The sound of footsteps drew my gaze back down.

"And that, Your Majesty, is my lovely mother," Lyari said. There was a note of finality in her voice, as if we'd reached the end of a story. "She is what they speak of when bloodline Paynore comes up in conversation. She is what they see when they look at me. You asked, once, why I hide my power? I don't. They just don't care that I have it. Because of where I come from."

Her expression created an ache in my chest. From experience, I knew there was nothing I could say that would change her mind... but that never stopped me from trying. "Lyari, you're nothing like her, and you never will be. Whoever believes that is a fucking moron," I said firmly.

"The same blood runs through my veins," Lyari countered. Her voice lowered to a whisper. "The same weakness."

Before I could keep arguing, she gripped the hilt of her sword and charged into the woods. It certainly was an effective way to end a conversation, I thought. Then I sighed and went after her. "We should go back down, Lyari," I called. "I need to start interrogating the council members."

Kindreth was a dead end, but even if she had been one of the members entrusted with Creiddylad's location, there was at least one other person who possessed that information. The trick would be to conduct the interviews quietly, without them alerting each other about what I was doing. I couldn't have any of them going into hiding...

Lyari didn't slow or look back. "If you do that, their bloodlines will turn on you," she said flatly.

"Do you have another idea? Gwyn has Collith. Every second he's with her, she could be—"

"My father has granted you temporary use of Kindreth's journals. She was meticulous about documenting her history—our history—until she couldn't anymore. They were delivered to the house while we were speaking with her. We should exhaust every other resource before you start torturing our people."

"Fine," I said, swallowing. "I'll spend the day going through them. If I don't find anything by tomorrow morning, I'm still looking for the council members."

Lyari didn't reply, but she did quicken her pace. I was too tightly wound to attempt a normal conversation, so I trudged along behind her.

It wasn't often we made this journey in the daytime. We traversed over ice and snow, and every few yards, there was movement in the naked forest. A fat squirrel, hopping across the ground in search of food. A lone bird, calling from the treetops as if there was a flock nearby.

"Your Majesty," Lyari said suddenly.

Her tone made my head snap up, and when I saw who stood in our path, I tried not to sigh again. *Son of a bitch.* "I thought you left."

Laurie stood legs apart, hands clasped behind his back. He looked like he'd been waiting for us, but knowing him, this was probably for dramatic effect. His new outfit certainly did that on its own—there was a bearskin draped over his shoulders, and what I could see underneath was made of black leather. Had he seriously left us to *change*?

"I'd like to speak with the queen alone, Guardian," Laurie told Lyari, pretending not to notice my stare. "I will accompany her from here."

"No, he won't," I said coolly. "Don't listen to him. Let's go."

Laurie's eyebrows drew together, creating an expression of contrition. Too bad it didn't match his words. "You should know that I'm not above blackmail," he informed me. "If I have to make your brother think he's transformed into a goat to get your attention, I will."

"You wouldn't." Fury flitted like embers through my stomach. I was about to respond with an insult, but I realized that was exactly what Laurie wanted. What he was hoping for. I decided to try Lyari's method for ending a conversation.

When I started walking toward him, though, Laurie dropped the act. The corners of his mouth tilted up and his eyes gleamed like metal. "Try me, Firecracker."

"I hate you," I hissed as I shouldered past him. However slender he appeared, Laurie was surprisingly steadfast, and he hardly moved. *Damn it, he smells good.* I scowled and quickened my pace, noting that Lyari was no longer behind us. After the morning she'd had, I could hardly blame her.

"It's true what they say, about the line between love and

hate," the Seelie King mused, following me. "It's thinner than my aunt Gaylia. So, essentially, you're saying you love me."

For once, he'd frustrated me to the point of speechlessness. I kept walking, eager to get home so I could continue the search for Creiddylad. Laurie was the least of my problems. The thought inevitably turned my mind to the encounter with Kindreth—if her journals were anything like the writer, they wouldn't help us. With every hour that passed, Collith could be losing body parts or sanity.

"I should've just stayed in my quiet little life," I muttered, talking more to myself than Laurie. "None of this would be happening if I'd just found another way to save Damon."

He responded anyway, of course. His breath sent clouds through the air as he said, "The meek don't inherit the earth, baby. That's just what the bold told 'em, so they'd get out of the way."

I could see the barn now, and I walked faster again. The weathervane rose up against the horizon. "What makes you think I care about inheriting anything?" I asked over my shoulder.

"Right. Sorry. I broke character for a second—I forgot that we're both heartless monsters who don't give a fuck about the world."

Would Kindreth's journals be on the porch? Urgency pounded through my veins like blood. I stopped caring what Laurie thought and broke into a run. I left marks in the snow all the way to the porch, and clumps of it fell off my boots as I went up the steps.

As promised, there was an enormous chest waiting for me. Leather straps secured the lid down, and the wood was warped and faded by time. I could tell from one look that it was too heavy to move on my own. I glanced back at the Seelie King, who'd sifted to my side. His eyes alighted on the chest with bright curiosity.

"It's full of Kindreth's journals," I told him, knowing he was worried about Collith, even if he refused to show it. "Lyari thought I might find something in them."

"Do you need assistance bringing this horrendous trunk inside?"

"No," I said quickly. I knew it wasn't logical—honestly, I could use his help reading the journals, too—but Laurie had gotten under my skin. He made me feel things that were dangerous and futile. Without another word, I went inside and closed the door. I formed a plan as I turned the locks and kicked off my boots. Finn was probably here; the two of us would have no problem moving the chest.

I turned around and yelped at the sight of Laurie standing in the hallway. "What the hell are you doing?" I demanded, darting a glance toward the kitchen. I saw Damon poke his head past the doorway, a question in his eyes.

"She's fine, Nightmare," Laurie said to him. Completely ignoring me, he went into the living room and reappeared moments later carrying a cardboard box. He set it gently on the floor and lifted something out. "I realize the timing isn't ideal, but I set the wheel in motion before Gwyn took Collith."

Whatever he held was... moving. Shock vibrated through me when I saw that it was a kitten, tiny and gray and clearly terrified. Laurie released it, and the little thing walked across the floor as if it wasn't used to its own legs yet, mewling the entire time.

I instantly got down on my knees. The kitten veered for the safety of the sofa table, and I caught it, reveling in its soft fur and the feel of its heartbeat against my palms. I held the kitten against me, crooning to it. "Oh, it's okay, it's okay. No one is going to hurt you. Yes, you're so cute, aren't you?"

"She doesn't have a name yet," Laurie said, watching us with a satisfied expression.

Damn it. I'd fallen right into his trap. Feeling uncomfortably hot now, I leaned away from the kitten to peel off my coat. "Look, I know you're trying to do something nice, but I can't keep her. This is Cyrus's house and—"

"I already spoke to the human that smells like grease," Laurie interjected. "He's the one who set up a litter box. It's in a place he called 'the mudroom.' Humans are truly revolting sometimes."

This made me pause. Cyrus was okay with it? And he'd set up a litter box already?

"I've never had a pet before," I murmured, touching the tip of the kitten's ear. She peered up at me with big blue eyes and cried again. I knew just how she felt, being forced into a new world where nothing was familiar and everything was frightening. Feeling as though nothing would ever be all right again. But it would. For this kitten, at least—I'd make sure of it.

"Where did you get her?" I asked, setting the tiny animal back on her feet. Laurie cleared his throat and mumbled something. I frowned and shook my head. "What?"

"It's from a shelter I own in Santa Monica, okay?" he said sharply.

I was silent for a moment, wondering if I'd heard him right. "You... you own an animal shelter?"

"Yes, but don't tell anyone, damn it. I have a reputation to maintain."

I looked from Laurie to the kitten. I'd thought it was just a tactic to get me talking to him again, but now I wasn't certain. He looked so discomfited, so defensive at my discovering something new about him. "What is this, Laurie?" I asked.

"Emma told me about the fox you saved. You're happier when that fucking werewolf is around. So I thought... cat." His color was high, his eyes snapping silver fire.

That was when I understood. The kitten was an apology, or as close to one that I was going to get—it didn't seem like something he did very often. I studied the lines of tension around

Laurie's mouth, wondering if it was all an act. But what would be the purpose? What did he stand to gain from my forgiveness?

"You really didn't have to do this," I said eventually. It felt like the safest response.

"I wanted to." I felt Laurie watching me again. Trying to hide my confusion, I looked up at him. His shoulder-length silver hair had fallen into his face, and my fingers twitched with the urge to push it back. Laurie's eyes said he knew exactly what I was thinking; he always knew. "So what are you going to name her?"

The question made my stomach clench. Regardless of how conflicted I felt about him, I couldn't have a casual conversation with Laurie and pretend that Ian O'Connell wasn't dead. I glanced toward the kitchen. I could hear Damon and Matthew clearly, which meant they could probably hear me. Us. Pursing my lips, I brought the kitten to the laundry room, then came back out and made a gesture at Laurie. *Follow me.* He meandered to the front door while I put my coat and boots back on.

There was a spot, on the other side of the garage, that wasn't within view of the driveway or the house. I led Laurie there and faced him, crossing my arms. "You can't just give me a cat and I'll suddenly be okay with the fact you murdered a human being, Laurie," I said.

"I know."

The response made me blink. I'd expected more quips, more games, but Laurie wasn't smiling and there was no twinkle in his eye. Silence floated between us. I didn't know what to say now that he'd changed our dynamic and actually agreed with me on something. "Great," I said lamely. "Glad we got that established. I'll see you around, I guess."

Laurie didn't move. A line deepened between his brows, as though something had occurred to him. Something he didn't like. Then his eyes cleared and he said, "One of my favorite witches stopped by your home earlier. A spell has been put into place. The spell you asked for when Gwyn first arrived?"

I must've been giving him a confused look. Laurie pulled something out of his pocket. He wasn't wearing gloves, but his long fingers weren't red or bothered by the cold. "The ingredients for a protection spell of this magnitude takes time to assemble, thus the delay. But Betty has done most of the groundwork. These are the words needed to activate the spell—just read the writing out loud and think of the one you want to keep out. Once you do, there's no telling how long it will last. She mentioned that the spell faded after a few hours, on one occasion, and lingered for three weeks on another. Magic isn't an exact science, as you know."

"Your favorite witch's name is Betty?" I asked, biting my lip. Laurie glowered at me. I took the piece of paper, being careful not to touch his fingers, and glanced at the Enochian words scrawled across it. "I... I appreciate that you did this."

I expected him to mention debts or favors, as he had the last time he helped me. But once again, Laurie displayed uncharacteristic restraint. "I feel as though I should reiterate that a spell won't keep Gwyn out," was all he said.

I raised one eyebrow at him and held up the paper. "Then why did you get it?"

"Because you asked me to." I waited for him to say more. Laurie just stood in the snow, his silver gaze lingering on mine, no trace of teasing within those wintry depths.

"I'm going to tell you something," I said abruptly. I wasn't sure who was more surprised by this—me or Laurie. I couldn't seem to stop, though. "Something I haven't told anyone, not in so many words, and I need to. God, I really need to. I don't know why it's right now or why it's you. It just is."

When it was clear I'd reached the end of my rambling, Laurie cocked his head a bit. The gesture reminded me of Collith, which led to thoughts of their shared history and how untrustworthy this faerie truly was. But I'd said too much to stop talking now.

Knowing what came next, I dropped my gaze. I didn't want to see the exact moment Laurie's opinion of me changed forever.

"I let a demon fuck me to bring Collith back from the dead," I said.

Once I'd spoken the truth out loud, I wasn't sure what I expected to feel. A sense of relief, maybe. All I experienced was another surge of fear. I waited for Laurie's reaction, and it felt like my insides were made of feathers, fluttering everywhere. Amusement, disgust, boredom—I could see him exhibiting any of the three. Or all of them at the same time. Laurie was nothing if not versatile.

Instead, the King of the Seelie Court stepped forward and kissed my forehead. "You are beautiful, Fortuna Sworn," his voice said in my ear.

I moved back, not to get away from him, but in response to the emotions he'd just set loose in my body. Now that I had acknowledged one secret, all the rest were clamoring to be freed.

"Kindreth said a sacrifice made by an Unseelie Queen would break the spell on the tomb," I told Laurie, meeting his gaze again. I took a shuddering breath. "I don't think I would survive giving anything else up or spilling more blood. But I owe it to Collith. After what I did…"

To my embarrassment, I felt my chin wobble. Laurie didn't ask for permission—he just cupped the back of my neck and pulled me to him. For a minute, I was stiff against him, thinking that I should push him away. But I didn't. I had sixty seconds, sixty opportunities to make the right choice, and I let every one of them pass me by.

Then the tears came.

It was in Laurie's arms that I cried again. But this time, I cried how I'd been wanting to since driving away from that crossroads, feeling as if a part of me had died and I was leaving it at the base of the tree.

And the Seelie King, a faerie of bright-eyed whimsicality and a terrifying lack of morals, didn't say a word. I sobbed against his chest, dampening what was undoubtedly an expensive shirt, and he wrapped his arms around me. As always, he smelled like sunshine and spring and everything good in the world. I felt Laurie's chin rest against my temple. He didn't make a joke or remark on the fact my breasts were pressed up against him. He just… held me.

"Damn it," I whispered after a few minutes had passed.

His voice traveled through my body. "What?"

I let out another ragged breath. "I can't stay mad at you. How do you do it?"

"I'm magic," he whispered back. Then, as if we were stuck in a time loop, Laurie pulled me into him again. Once again, I didn't put the distance between us I should've.

More time went by. Snow began to fall from the sky, and the tip of my nose was numb. I knew I needed to get through Kindreth's journals. But as the seconds turned into minutes, I didn't leave the circle of Laurie's arms.

Not yet.

Laurie and I read Kindreth's journals for the rest of the day.

We stayed in the living room. Laurie sat next to the fireplace, his back supported by the base of the couch, and I was on the loveseat.

My new pet grew bolder by the hour. Soon she was darting across the room and batting at our feet. Both Emma and Matthew squealed upon meeting her. Finn, who made an appearance in the early afternoon, was decidedly less excited.

He was in his wolf form, and instead of finding him terrifying, the kitten was fascinated. She pawed his face and slept against his stomach in equal turns. Finn ignored her, and his breathing was loud and even, the sound of someone in a deep sleep.

Once she'd finished doting over the kitten, I saw Emma take note of the chest and the journals—they were impossible to miss, spread out in the busiest part of the house as they were.

Holding the corner of a page between my thumb and index finger, I told her the truth about why I had them and why Laurie was here. Emma hid her fear better than most, but I could sense it. "I thought he was in the barn," was all she said. A frown hovered around her mouth.

After that the old woman continually brought us meals, snacks, mugs of hot coffee, and glasses of water, contributing the only way she knew how.

Throughout the evening, a fire crackled in the grate, which Laurie fed a log to every time it burned low. Stacks of journals started to appear around us, organized by those we'd read and those we hadn't.

The books themselves were bound in various materials— leather, fabric, snakeskin—and the paper smelled different in each one. Some were as thick as a thesaurus while others contained only a few months' worth of entries. Kindreth's mental decline was evident in her handwriting as I moved through the years with her. She'd written everything in Enochian, of course, and my progress was slower than Laurie's because of my fumbling translations.

I also kept a notebook on the cushion next to me, tracking any information that might be of use—and not just information pertaining to Gwyn. Kindreth had documented everything during her long life at the Unseelie Court, and even the time before that, when the fae had yet to divide into two courts. She envied the exorbitant wealth of the bloodline Ettrian—they'd invested in the petroleum industry during the 1900s—and blamed the Cralynns for The Great Depression. She resented the Tralees for their constant inbreeding, as she called it, and suspected the involvement of the Sarwraeks in the evolution of infamous serial killers like Ted Bundy, Charles Manson, and Jeffrey Dahmer.

Lyari shimmered into view during dinnertime. Matthew, Damon, and Emma were in the kitchen, dishes clinking and soft sounds emanating from the doorway. Laurie was with them; he'd been intrigued by the smells and left his spot to investigate.

"Anything?" Lyari asked, taking in the messy room. The stacks had gotten more spread out and haphazard as the day went on. There were several coffee rings on the table, along with plates of half-eaten food. The kitten, who was now a drowsy ball on the rug, had entertained herself for several hours unraveling a string dangling off the hem of my shirt.

My lips pursed as I shook my head. "Nothing relevant to Creiddylad, but Kindreth did write about Gwyn when the Wild Hunt was formed. Oh, since you're here, will you translate something? I don't recognize the words and I can't find them in the Enochian Dictionary."

I found the journal and held it up for her, pressing my finger beneath the passage I'd struggled with for nearly a half hour. Lyari's braid fell over her shoulder as she leaned closer. I watched her eyes scan the words. "This part? Right here?" she clarified. I nodded. Her breath puffed against my cheek. "'No weapon of man can harm her.'"

The wording piqued my interest—faeries were rarely specific unless they were being sneaky about something. I reread the sentence with a thoughtful frown. "No weapon of man... but what about a weapon of angels?" I wondered aloud.

Lyari straightened. "Or the weapon of a Nightmare."

I knew instantly what she was suggesting; it wasn't exactly subtle. I began to consider the possibility... but then I remembered the line of blood that came out of Collith's nose. The light in his eyes fading. I relived the moment I had realized what I'd done, standing in that smoke-filled yard, surrounded by rage, magic, and pain. "I've been in her head," I said finally. "Gwyn isn't afraid of anything. I could try to create one, sort of... plant it there like a seed, but she's ancient. Chances are her mind is too strong for that."

Lyari thought about this for a moment. Firelight flickered over her face, making the hollows of her cheeks look darker. "Did you wield the full strength of the Unseelie Court during your search?"

"No," I admitted, holding the journal tighter. "Look, even if Gwyn had fears, I don't think I could do it again. Use my ability to murder someone, I mean."

"How strange. You were willing to torture innocents a few hours ago."

Her tone made me glare. "Torture. Not kill. I wasn't exactly crazy about the idea, either."

She glanced at the stacks of journals. "Well, let's hope there's something within the volumes you haven't read yet."

The faerie didn't offer to help, and there was tension in the way she stood. I thought about our morning and the glimpses of vulnerability she'd shown, both below the ground and on the surface. "How is your mother?" I asked, unable to hide a hesitant note in the question.

Lyari touched her sword. In that moment, I recognized it as a tell—she was an expert at keeping reactions and emotions from her face, but she still felt them. Gripping her weapon gave my Right Hand a sense of strength and control. I was embarrassed it had taken me this long to figure it out.

"...been with her most of the day," Lyari was saying, pulling my attention back to her. "She hasn't been this agitated in a decade."

We both knew the only variation in Kindreth's routine was my conversation with her, however brief it had been. I met

Lyari's gaze and hoped she heard the sincerity in my voice. "I'm sorry."

She acknowledged this with a slight shake of her head, as if to say, *Not your fault.* "I'd better get back. Mother's nurse isn't strong enough to restrain her during the... episodes."

Where is Paynore during all this? I almost asked, then bit my tongue to hold the words at bay. I didn't know enough about her family to pass judgment. It didn't matter, anyway—Lyari had vanished without bothering to say goodbye.

"Emma made us something called a casserole," Laurie announced, striding back into the room. He held two plates in his hands, and steam rose from the mass of cheese and potatoes. My stomach was already rumbling. Finn and the kitten both perked up, as well.

"Change into your other shape, and maybe I'll share," I told the werewolf. He exhaled through his nose and laid his head back down, his eyes sliding shut. I tried to hide my worry by shrugging. "Suit yourself."

We ate and continued making our way through the journals. Outside, the sky darkened to black. Music and smells drifted from the kitchen as Emma made banana bread. Despite the circumstances, and how poignantly I felt Collith's absence, there was something... cozy about the scene. More than once, I caught myself staring at Laurie as he read, remembering a comment Collith once made about the Seelie King. *Whatever he told you, Laurelis is not just here to torment me. He cares about you.*

I pulled my eyes away, perturbed by Laurie's beauty and the realization that I could stare at him all night, if we weren't so focused on our task.

More time crawled by. I hadn't let myself look at the time all day, but I knew it was late, because my eyelids began to feel weighted. Kindreth's handwriting blurred in front of me.

You're falling asleep, I realized distantly. *Open your eyes and keep reading.*

But the fire was too warm, the room too gently lit, and the kitten had started purring. The sound lulled me into that halfway place between awake and dreaming, and when I didn't fight it, my mind moved deeper into the darkness.

When my eyes snapped open, I saw that Oliver had been true to his word—he was gone, along with our dreamscape.

The eternal sunshine and endless hills were replaced by night. But this was not the night I had once loved so dearly. Menace clung to the air, and the black, hulking trees that surrounded me on all sides watched with eyeless faces. It felt like they were waiting for something.

Suddenly I was nothing more than a child, lost in the dark, vulnerable to every monster or hungry thing that lived in this joyless place. And even though I knew it went against every rule of survival or intelligence, I ran.

I hadn't gotten more than a few steps into my panicked flight when I started seeing them.

They looked out at me from behind trees or through the scraggly underbrush—every bad memory or past nightmare come to life. There was the person I'd killed in place of Damon, still tied to a chair even as blood flowed out of the wound in his chest. His sounds of agony were muffled by the bag over his head. Next I spotted one of the goblins who had plucked me off the mountain and tried to sell me in the black market. He grinned with broken, yellow teeth and reached a single hand into my path. I recoiled, screaming, and bolted in the opposite direction. Leaves clung to my pajama pants and dirt caked my palms. I rushed past the siren, who stood between two trees, holding her naked body and shivering. Her face was blue and misshapen, like a corpse that had been submerged in water too long.

Like every bimbo in a horror movie, I didn't see the root until it was too late. It stretched across the ground like an emaciated arm, and my foot slammed into it. There was a burst of pain before I went flying, and I landed so hard that I couldn't breathe.

In the ensuing silence, footsteps sounded from behind. I still couldn't move, so running was no longer an option. I found the strength to roll over, but that was all I could manage. I arched my head back with the slow, horrified resignation of someone about to die, wondering which one of my nightmares had come to take its vengeance.

Ayduin glared down at me.

The front of his shirt was drenched with blood. Faeries bled blue, but his looked black in the darkness. He moved faster than my eyes could track, reaching down and gripping my throat. Slowly, he lifted me into the air. I dangled there and grappled at his hand. A hoarse gagging sound left me. My vision dimmed.

Just as my head started feeling like a balloon—full of helium, floating away—Ayduin let go. I crashed back to the ground at the same moment my airways opened up again. I gasped, touching my throat, but Ayduin's hand was gone. *He* was gone.

When I sat up, wheezing, I instantly saw why. I didn't have a chance to run this time.

The zombies piled on me like ants. I felt their fingers scraping at my stomach and throat, trying to open me up, and all I could do was scream. I knew, in an instant of terrible clarity, that they were about to eat me alive. Hitting and kicking did nothing; there were only more zombies to take the place of the ones I managed to fight off. Within seconds, I felt dull teeth clamp down onto my shoulder. Another set of teeth tore into my calf. Agony blazed through me.

Before I could scream again, the horde of zombies vanished.

They didn't lose interest or lumber away—they just stopped existing. For a few seconds, I stayed on my back, shaking and panting. There was a low-pitched ringing sound in my ears. Part of me wanted to stay there, frozen like a child beneath a blanket, but the other part was more afraid of what I couldn't see. I sat up and, after a beat of shock, took in my new surroundings with wide eyes.

I was still in the forest, but it wasn't sinister anymore. The trees were shrouded in mist and the leaves were vibrantly green, as if it were the middle of summer. Blue flowers swayed in a warm breeze, and they were so numerous the forest floor wasn't even visible. Crickets, cicadas, and frogs crooned to stars overhead.

Everything inside me was tense, as though sitting up had sent some kind of signal, but nothing happened or appeared. After another moment, I stood. My toes curled through the damp earth. There was a sting of pain as one of them scraped against a rock. Where was I? Why did it feel so real?

My gaze latched onto a figure standing in the trees.

I should've been terrified, but the moment I spotted him, it felt like my heart was gripped by need. The need to speak with him, know him, see what color his eyes were. A branch stretched across the path, hiding his face, but I could see bright, golden hair gleaming in moonlight. It wasn't as pale as Laurie's, or dark as Oliver's—it was the same shade of gold as the gleaming streets in Kindreth's memories. As I watched, he stepped back, deeper into the foliage, and disappeared from sight.

Another dream, I thought. *This is another dream.*

Maybe that was why I followed him.

It wasn't Oliver, I knew, but there was still part of me that hoped. The man led me through the woods for a mile, at least. Every time I thought I'd lost sight of him, he reappeared long enough to catch my notice, then he was gone again.

I only stopped when I saw the sign.

It rose out of the flowers on a wooden post. I couldn't read it. The letters weren't English, or Enochian, or anything else I would've understood. But one word stood out, both in size and color, and my gaze was drawn to it. *"Hallerbos,"* I murmured.

Something rustled nearby. I jerked toward it, forgetting about the sign. I caught another glimpse of that hair, lovely as a lion's mane, just before the figure disappeared from sight again.

I didn't catch sight of him again, but I could hear him, almost as if the man were purposely stepping on every stick. I didn't know why I felt such an urgent desire to catch up, to hear his voice, but there was no time to question it. I ran through the trees, shoving branches and leaves out of my way. I wanted to call out, but there was something strange about this dream—while I could form the words in my head, they wouldn't come out of my mouth. As if the pathway between the two didn't exist, and this was a world of only thoughts, trees, and impulse.

Suddenly I could hear water. It wasn't a river, I decided as I kept moving forward. The sound of it was too gentle, too faint. Most likely it was a creek or a small trickle feeding into a pond. I didn't think much of it, and then I forgot about it completely when I realized I'd lost track of the golden-haired figure.

A rock wall rose up. There was a deer at its base, standing directly in front of me. Its round black eyes met mine for an instant before it moved out of sight. The instant it moved, I spotted a narrow gap in the rock the deer's body had been blocking. It was probably just a shallow cave, but something within that darkness called to me like a siren's song. I stared at it, willing myself to turn around and walk away. This was a dream, and Oliver was no longer here to keep the bad things away.

But when I tried to do exactly that, it felt like unseen hands pushed my feet into the ground, forcing me to stay. Panic flashed, then dimmed as my mind melted down into a single thought—I had to go inside. I had to see what was in there. It was important.

The urge became so strong that I burst into movement, hurrying toward that dark opening. The sound of rushing water got louder. I stepped into a place that felt like the set of a movie.

A movie about magic or wild things. The walls glistened with water and moss grew everywhere. Like the Unseelie Court, torches burned and lit the way. That wasn't the only similarity they shared, but I struggled to define the other one. *Unnatural*, I thought finally, creeping down the jagged path. That was the word my mind kept reaching for. It felt like there were a hundred spiders crawling over my skin, like the air was bloated and sentient. Everything about this place was unnatural.

There was a chamber up ahead. I stepped out of the tunnel, which was shorter than it had seemed, and stared. There was nothing else in the room save a stone slab... and the woman lying on it. That was the moment I realized this wasn't a cave.

It was a tomb.

My heartbeat felt like the violent vibrations of a gong. Still propelled by an inexplicable urgency, I walked toward her. The closer I got, the more I fought it. I wasn't sure why, but every instinct I had was shrieking. *You don't want to wake her up. You don't want to see those eyes open.*

And then I was there, at her side, despite how much I didn't want to be. She was one of the most beautiful people I'd ever encountered. With skin luminescent as a pearl, perfectly arched brows, and full lips, a flame of wild hair to set it all ablaze, it was no wonder someone as ancient as Gwyn hadn't managed to forget about her. For this was, indeed, Creiddylad. I knew it with all of my being, as though someone had whispered the name in my ear.

Without warning, her eyes snapped open and stared into mine. They were black as a starless sky. I would've reared back and screamed, but I had no control over my body.

"Wake up," she whispered. Then, as I watched, her face began to rot.

This time I was able to scream. I was still screaming when I lurched upright in bed.

It took a few seconds to realize that my surroundings had

changed again. The tomb was gone, replaced by Cyrus's house. I wasn't standing next to a stone slab, but sitting on a mattress. My eyes darted around, prepared to see more horrors hiding in the shadows. That's when I spotted a paycheck stub resting on the nightstand and realized I could read the words.

This was reality, which meant the cave and the rotting woman hadn't been. *Just a dream. It was just a dream.* It made sense I was having nightmares now—Oliver was gone, and without him standing guard, everything from the past had emerged, like monsters out of a dark closet.

As my mind struggled to adapt, I finally realized there was another person in the room. I gasped and pressed my spine into the corner. Laurie sat in a chair near the door, his legs elegantly crossed, his tapered fingers holding a book upright. His gaze met mine, and I realized that he must've carried me to bed—I'd fallen asleep on the couch, with one of the journals on my chest.

Laurie waited for me to say something, holding the edge of a page between his fingers. His expression was fathomless. I stared at him again, but this time, my mind was elsewhere. I thought about the dream. I saw the sign I hadn't been able to read. I heard that woman's voice slithering over my skin.

In a rush of certainty, I met Laurie's gaze.

"I know where Creiddylad is," I said.

CHAPTER SEVENTEEN

We sat at the kitchen table while we waited.

It was that time of morning no one liked to be awake, unless they were an insomniac or ninety years old. Or a kitten, because mine—still unnamed—had been darting around the room like a ping pong ball. Beyond the window over the sink, there was no hint of sunrise. Only deep, endless dark. Summer's soothing song of crickets and cicadas had been replaced by the austere silence of winter. Collith's absence still felt like a soundless scream.

Every time I heard it, I reminded myself that it was going to be all right… because it would. I had a plan.

The idea had come to me as I told Laurie about my dream. I'd described the tomb, the magic I'd felt, Creiddylad's body on that stone slab. And then, as if I had been weaving a string with every scene I talked about, I finished and saw the pattern. It was so simple.

Now Laurie, Finn, and I sat in a small kitchen and waited for Lyari to arrive. I'd tried summoning her without results. I knew she would come as soon as she read my text, but that could be hours. I was on the verge of suggesting we reconvene in the morning when Laurie raised his gaze and looked at Finn.

"You know, I've always been curious about something," he said. "When it comes to doggy style—"

A figure appeared in the doorway, and each of us turned to see who it was. "Lyari, thank God," I blurted, rising from my seat.

She assessed the room in a single glance. She was in full armor, of course, always ready for a fight or a challenge. "What is this?"

I sank back down and took a breath. It mattered to me, what Lyari thought, and that was more unnerving than what I was about to say. "I think I know a way to save my life and get rid of Gwyn for good. Without spilling a single drop of blood," I added.

Her eyes widened. "No. Anything you do will just aggravate her, Your Majesty."

"If we don't do anything, I'm dead," I reminded her. "Please sit down and hear me out."

But the beautiful faerie took a step back. Her nostrils were flared and the scent of her fear bloomed in the air. *Lilacs*, I thought. "I will not play a part in this. You already know how to survive," she snarled.

I could feel Laurie and Finn looking at me now. Finn didn't pry, of course, but Laurie had no such qualms. "What does she mean?" he asked.

My jaw worked. *Thanks, Lyari.* She just stared back at me, unrepentant. I looked across the table at Laurie, and his eyes were bright with curiosity. I resisted the urge to groan. If I avoided the question now, he would pester or manipulate me until I wanted to scream. "Lyari thinks that if I channel the power of the Unseelie Court, I may have enough to kill Gwyn… as a Nightmare," I told him. "She already knows that isn't an option, though."

"Part of the spell upon Gwyn translates to 'no weapon of man can harm her.' It says nothing about the power of the Fallen," Lyari put in. "Our kind has always been too afraid of her to try."

There was a pause. I steeled myself for the question I knew was coming—it was inevitable. *Why isn't Lyari's idea an option?* But Laurie didn't ask me why. He leaned back in his chair and refocused on Lyari. "It's an intriguing theory," was all he said.

Finn, looking weary from his recent shift, kicked an empty chair toward her. Lyari didn't move. The werewolf's eyes brightened, and in response, Lyari casually rested her hand on the hilt of her sword. The air seemed to thicken.

"I know the truth about Ariel," I growled at her. "Which means I know you kept it secret from me. If you sit down and listen, I'll consider us even."

Her chin rose. "I was following the orders of my king."

"You swore fealty to me, too," I said. My voice emerged softer than I intended, and something in Lyari's eyes flickered when she heard it. The faerie sat down, but she made sure we knew how unhappy she was about it—her spine was stiff and her eyes spat dark fire.

"We've already ruled out killing Gwyn. But are there any legends or lore that say she can't be caught?" I asked. Silence met my words. Laurie's expression became speculative. I leaned forward, feeling more confident now. "Here's the plan. I tell Gwyn the spell can be undone with the blood of the Unseelie Queen—that's how we'll guarantee our presence at the tomb. While it's being opened, Gwyn will be distracted. Using the same spell that trapped her lover, I think we could seal her inside. Forever."

"When do we want to do this?" Laurie asked.

That's when I knew he was going to help me. "Tomorrow night," I said, meeting his gaze. "I want Collith out of her clutches as soon as possible."

"Your plan has one flaw," Lyari muttered. We all looked at her. "There isn't a single witch alive who will risk pissing off Gwyn. Not to mention one who's powerful enough to work such an enormous spell."

I entertained the idea of asking the Tongue to do it, but even now, I didn't fully trust him. What if he went to the council after I revealed our plan?

Who else did I know that was capable of working complex spells? In a flash of memory, I saw that arrogant, blue-haired faerie from the revel twisting into a tree. My mind drifted down the hall, toward my room, and into the nightstand drawer where a business card lay tucked in shadow. *I don't like bullies.* "I might know one, actually," I said slowly.

"Do you know how to contact her?" Lyari asked. Apparently she'd thought of Mercy, too. I nodded. The faerie sighed and leaned forward, her perfect mouth tight with resignation. "If we're really going to do this, then we need to cover our tracks."

"I've already considered that, actually," Laurie said, startling me. Lyari gestured for him to continue, as if they were equals instead of a king and a guard.

Laurie elaborated on his idea, and for a few minutes, I watched my friends work together to perfect the plan that would save my life and free Collith. If someone had told me a few weeks ago that I'd be calling these people my friends, and that they would show me more friendship and devotion in one month than I had experienced in one lifetime, I would've laughed in their face.

I focused on Laurie again, knowing that every word was vital and I couldn't miss a single detail. This would work, I told myself when the fear crept in, hoping no one at the table could see it on my face.

It had to.

Laurie and I used the doorway at the Unseelie Court.

He hid us from view as we entered, walked partway down the tunnel, then turned around again. We didn't hesitate or attempt conversation. The tension in my veins felt like a drug, a ride that I wasn't capable of stopping. I was jittery with worry. As we passed through the opening a second time, exiting the Court now, I closed my eyes and pictured that vibrant wood. It wasn't difficult—my dream was all I'd been able to think about.

Last night, after an internet search, we'd learned that Hallerbos was in Belgium. It was called The Blue Forest because of the bluebells that appeared every spring, just as they had in my dream. Millions of them, spreading over the forest floor like carpet.

But when I opened my eyes, reality was nothing like the place I'd seen or the pictures we found online.

The cold had driven away every flower and color, leaving Hallerbos ordinary and tired-looking. It was also dark. This was how it should've appeared in my nightmare, I thought. Nothing about this forest felt like a fairy tale.

"How do we know we're in the right place?" I asked, instinctively keeping my voice low. We started walking, but I had no idea which direction would take us to the cave I'd seen. Would Gwyn already be waiting there? Had the text I sent this morning—whose number Lyari had procured from one of the council members—given her sufficient time to cross an ocean? She hadn't responded, so I had no way of knowing if she'd even gotten it.

I couldn't be sure, but I thought I saw Laurie shrug. "If we don't, I suppose we'll wander around for a while and eventually be hunted down by a very pissed off Gwyn," he said, sounding entirely unconcerned. "She knows she can't enter the tomb without you, correct?"

"If she got my text, then yes."

The Seelie King walked ahead of me, making our dark hike

look effortless, despite the illogical clothing he'd chosen for tonight. He wore knee-high boots, pants so tight they left little to the imagination, and a long coat trimmed in fur. An ornate sword dangled at his narrow hip and rings gleamed on his fingers. His angelic hair had that freshly-washed bounce to it. He looked more prepared to strut down a runway than ensnare an ancient faerie.

"Do I meet with my queen's approval?" Laurie asked with a knowing glint in his eye. He'd paused and looked back at me.

"Your presentation is fine, but we'll have to put a bag over that personality," I said as I brushed past him. My cheeks felt hot.

The farther we ventured, the more hostile the night seemed. The moonlight was stark and harsh, every sound muffled and wary. Plumes of air left my mouth with every exhale. Thankfully, the steep terrain held most of my focus—Nightmares healed more quickly than humans, but we could still die from a broken neck. In the meantime, Laurie had fallen silent. It was so uncharacteristic of the Seelie King that I almost wished he would resort to his usual teasing and taunting.

It felt strange, walking through night-darkened woods without Finn or Lyari. My werewolf had remained at the house —in the extremely possible event that the spell didn't go as planned, and Gwyn *did* go after my family in retaliation, he'd be there to defend them until his dying breath. He hadn't been entirely happy about it, but he didn't argue when I made my request.

"Protect them, Finn. They're our pack," I'd said to him. Those were the magic words, and my werewolf's eyes darkened with resignation.

Lyari and Ariel were elsewhere—that part was Laurie's idea. They'd make sure to be spotted in the Unseelie Court while Ariel wore a gown and cloak from my wardrobe, the hood drawn over her dark hair. She was shorter than me, but heels easily fixed that. Rumors would circulate, as they always did, for every spy and council member to hear. No one would interfere with our plan tonight, and I wouldn't be dethroned for eternally imprisoning Gwyn. In the Court's eyes, it would probably be equivalent to killing her. If anyone ever found her, that was.

My thoughts cut short when something moved nearby. I nearly shrieked, only to see that it was just an owl. It flapped away into the night sky. Behind me, I heard Laurie snicker. "Shut up," I mumbled, hunching my shoulders.

We continued on through the unfamiliar forest, and with every step my anxiety increased. *Where is Mercy?* I didn't voice the question aloud, for fear of someone overhearing, but my gaze darted toward every movement. A branch swaying in the wind, a dead leaf flitting over the snow.

Without a witch, the entire plan fell apart.

Last night, she'd responded to my text within minutes. *When and where?* was all she said. As if the thought of pissing off an ancient, all-powerful faerie didn't daunt her in the least.

When I'd told her the cave was in Belgium, an entire ocean away, she still didn't hesitate. Apparently witches had more tricks up their sleeves than I ever realized.

I'll find you, she said. *These are the ingredients I will need for a sealing spell of that magnitude. Make sure to arrive shortly before the Witching Hour.*

Most of the ingredients had been painless to obtain. Mint, sage, and ginger, for instance. Others had been more challenging and required a drive to Denver, like the mercury and the moss. All of it was in a backpack resting against my spine. I tried to comfort myself with the reminder that it wasn't time yet. But there was a reason a Nightmare's power was so potent —fear had a way of sneaking in. Creeping past any defenses. I walked through the dark and found myself worrying again. If our witch didn't show, Gwyn would collect her lover and continue to terrorize the world, which included killing me at some point. Probably sooner rather than later.

Finally succumbing to the agitation racing through my veins, I took my phone out. The screen brightened. No texts or missed calls. It was 2:52 a.m.

"I think we've arrived," Laurie murmured. I raised my gaze and immediately saw the torches, two burnt lights shining weakly through the sleeping trees. I could feel Laurie looking at me—no doubt he could hear my traitorous heart, accelerating at the thought of seeing Collith—and I hurried forward. But with every step closer to the cave, my throat crowded with fear. What if Mercy had gone to the cave instead of finding us? What if Gwyn found her? There were so many ways this plan could go wrong.

Just as I was about to step through the trees, Laurie caught hold of my hand. I stopped and looked back at him, heart in my throat. "What is it? Do you hear something?"

"When this is all over, remember that it was me. It was me who saved you, and not him," the faerie said quietly, firelight moving on his cheek.

There was something in his eyes I couldn't name. Not obsession or desperation, like so many under a Nightmare's influence. It almost looked like... pain. But I was too impatient to ask what Laurie meant. I shot him a bewildered frown and turned around, rushing into the open.

Gwyn and Collith stood between the torches.

The sight of him stole the breath from my lungs. At a single glance, he looked whole and unharmed, but a glance was all I had time for—completely ignoring Gwyn, I broke into a run and flung my arms around Collith's neck. He responded instantly, holding me against his hard chest. He ran a hand over my hair, as if attempting to soothe me, and it made the thunder inside me rumble louder. Even though he'd been gone for days, he still smelled like himself.

"What are you doing here?" Collith growled. I pulled back and saw his eyes glinting with that new cruelty he'd brought back from Hell. He was looking at something behind me, and I didn't need to turn my head to know what. I took the opportunity to scan Collith's body more critically, searching for signs of torture, but he truly did seem uninjured. Slightly reassured, I peeled my attention away from him and looked back at Laurie.

The Seelie King stood there, grinning, and had his hands shoved in his pockets. He rocked on his heels and remarked, "Well, anything involving Fortuna is bound to be entertaining."

I gave him a look to show that I was unimpressed. *Really? You're not going to tell Collith that you've been helping me?*

Laurie opened his mouth to say something else—probably a witty comment that would infuriate everyone and only add to the tension in the air—but Collith beat him to it. "Laurelis shouldn't be here when the door is opened, huntress," he told Gwyn, his voice full of warning. "He's a liar and a thief who would con his own mother."

She chuckled. "Are those supposed to be flaws?"

"Actually, those are his virtues," Collith countered, a muscle twitching in his jaw.

Gwyn threw back her head and laughed. I flinched at the sound, wary of alerting other creatures to our presence. After a moment, I realized that Gwyn didn't care whether something heard her, even out here. She couldn't be killed and she didn't care about anyone besides Creiddylad, who had been safely tucked inside a tomb for the past century or two. How freeing it must be to be utterly invincible. To have no weaknesses.

Envy curled around my heart like a vine.

We had to stall for time. If we opened the tomb now, and Gwyn took Creiddylad, there was nothing stopping her from walking out and disappearing into the night forever. Or until she decided to come back and kill me. I glanced at Laurie, hoping he would understand the message I conveyed with my eyes.

The Seelie King refocused on Collith and raised his silver brows. "Truth be told, I'm not entirely certain I want to free you from dear Gwyn's clutches. Fortuna and I spent the night together and I'd like to repeat the experience."

I glared at him now. That definitely *wasn't* the distraction I'd been hoping for.

Collith reacted just as Laurie knew he would—his lips curled into a snarl. As swiftly as it had come, the mirth in Gwyn's countenance vanished. She put her arm across Collith's chest, preventing him from surging forward. "While I find you both entertaining, I've never cared for dick measuring contests. They're tiresome. I'll tell you right now, it doesn't matter whether yours is an inch longer if you don't know how to properly use it. As the humans say, shall we get this party started?"

Maybe I could stall once we were inside, then. I gave Gwyn a hard stare, knowing even as I did that she could end me with a single blow. "Don't forget about our bargain."

Her eyes glittered. "Little chance of that, Your Majesty. I have a long memory."

Mercy, where are you? Trying to think of another distraction, I started toward that yawning darkness. Fingers bit into my shoulders, so tight that white-hot pain shuddered through my muscles. I wrenched free and spun around. When I saw that it was Laurie, I frowned. "What are you—"

"Step back, Fortuna," he said. If I hadn't been looking at him, watching his mouth form the words, I wouldn't have believed it was his voice. It sounded like a stranger's, and as it echoed through my head, I realized why. That ever-constant layer of mischief was gone, as if someone had torn it away. Without it, Laurie wasn't... Laurie.

When I didn't move, he cupped my elbow in his warm palm and forcibly shifted me toward Collith.

"What are you doing?" I demanded finally, yanking away once again. Internal alarms blared and shrieked. I kept my eyes on Laurie, noting how he wouldn't meet my gaze. It was one of the few times I'd looked at him and he wasn't already staring back.

"Because I'm going to open the door," he said.

I frowned and shook my head. "But you heard what Kindreth said. It requires—"

"I know what it requires, Fortuna."

And that was one of the few times he'd used my name. Conscious of Gwyn and Collith watching us, I swallowed whatever arguments I'd been about to use. I stepped closer and tilted my head back. Standing directly in a moonbeam, Laurie's eyes were brighter than they'd ever been, looking more like water than metal. His pale hair had a wave to it I'd never noticed before. "I can't ask you to do this," I said quietly, wishing we were alone.

"Good thing you're not asking me, then." I was still staring when Laurie added, "I only ask for one thing in return."

He waited for my response, and it hit me—I wasn't going to stop him. The realization sent shame through my veins like fast-acting poison. All my life, I'd been trying to be the protector and fighter Mom and Dad had taught me to be. I paid the price, again and again, driven onward only by my survival instincts and outright stubbornness.

But tonight I was letting someone else pay it, because I didn't have the strength to. Not anymore. I raised my face toward Laurie's, feeling as though I were being ripped apart from the inside. "What?"

He grinned, but it was a shadow of the real thing. "A kiss," he answered.

Pain bloomed in my chest like some dark flower. I let all the disappointment I felt show in my eyes. "I trusted," I growled. "I *told* you about that night at the crossroads. And still you're willing to destroy our friendship, just for one unwilling kiss?"

"Would it really be so unwilling?" Laurie murmured. "Tell me it is, and I'll never darken your doorway again."

I opened my mouth to do exactly that... and the words stuck in my throat. *Son of a bitch.* He had me, and we both knew it. Laurie was a faerie, so he would sense a lie. Unless you were a psychopath, your body always reacted in some way. A drop of sweat, a leap in the pulse. There was no point denying it. Yes, I was attracted to Laurie, and there were other things about him I was drawn to. His humor. His intelligence. How I never knew what he was going to do next.

I swallowed and looked up at him again, tempted to punch the faerie in his stomach. "Sometimes I genuinely do hate you."

"I know," he said. From the sympathy in his voice, he really did. But there was no hint of that sympathy in his eyes as they dropped to my mouth. I looked at his, too, and something deep inside me fluttered.

Collith. He was here. Watching us. Hearing every word. Flushing, I turned around and forced myself to meet his gaze. He must've seen the truth in my eyes—that I was going to kiss the King of the Seelie Court—because his countenance darkened. He looked down, his lovely face losing all expression, like wiping a pane of glass with cloth. I glanced at Gwyn, thinking she'd be observing our little drama with her usual amused smile. But her head was tilted and she stared at Laurie with something akin to... interest.

It was the same way she looked at me sometimes. She'd seen something in the Seelie King that she hadn't expected. And she was wondering if there was a way she could use it. All the more reason to make sure we trapped Gwyn of the Wild Hunt forever.

This train of thought came to a screeching halt as Laurie drew closer. Any remnants of playfulness had left his silver eyes, and his alluring scent surrounded me now. *Let's get this over with.* Hoping to gain the upper hand, I closed the gap between us and kissed him like we'd done it a thousand times before. But I didn't count on Laurie's almost-instant recovery—his mouth slanted to mine, and he responded with skill, knowing exactly when to tease, to brush, to be more assertive. The hand on my neck tightened, and when I started to press closer, I remembered myself and jerked back.

Our eyes met for a shocked, breathless instant... and then Laurie was kissing me again. His tongue flicked at my lips, a silent request for entrance. After a moment of breathless hesitation, I answered it by opening my mouth to his.

He responded by pulling me fully against him. I immediately sensed that, despite our audience, the king didn't plan to hold back. He knew this would be our first and last kiss, and apparently, he didn't intend to waste it.

Though his hands didn't wander to dangerous places—one tangled in my hair while the other lay flat against the small of my back—Laurie devoured me. There was no other word for it. He tasted sweet, somehow, but I couldn't think straight enough to put a name to the flavor. Despite my vow to be unaffected, to resist the charming Seelie King, I kissed him back with a desperation I never could have anticipated. I knew I'd agonize over it later, but for now, I allowed myself to forget everything else but him.

At last, though, I found the willpower to put my hand against his chest and give it a light push. Laurie stepped back instantly. My heart rivaled a herd of wild horses, thundering across plains and racing the wind. I stared at him. His mouth was swollen, his hair mussed, and his eyes had never been so bright. They shone like stars.

"There," he whispered, smiling faintly. "That's what I wanted."

"Yes, you got your kiss. Good for you," I managed, wishing the ground would open up and swallow me.

Laurie's eyes never left mine as he shook his head. "No. I wanted you to admit that you feel something for me."

"I didn't say a thing," I retorted. There was a tremor in my voice I hoped he wouldn't notice.

He flashed a grin. "You said plenty, Your Majesty."

"Fuck you."

"Just name the time and place, Firecracker."

My hands became fists, and once again, I imagined what it would be like to punch him. I swung away, suddenly eager to get this night over with. Gwyn was leaning against a tree, her arms crossed, a smirk hovering around her red lips. Heat crawled up my neck, but I ignored her and looked for Collith. There was no sign of him.

When I looked back at Laurie, his focus was on the tomb. "'I know not all that may be coming, but be it what it will, I'll go to it laughing,'" he murmured.

It took me a moment to place the quote. Of course he had read *Moby Dick*; it was so typical of Laurie to reveal another layer, another depth within himself, just when I wanted to hit him most. I opened my mouth to say something I'd probably regret, and then something else occurred to me.

"Wait, how do you know what book I'm reading?" I hissed, glaring even harder. "Goddamn it, Laurie, did you snoop while you were in my—"

I cut short with a gasp of pain. I glanced down, stunned at the sight of blood running down my arm. The panic slowed when I saw it was just a shallow cut, slightly above my elbow. I lifted my head to shout at Laurie, but he was already walking away, a dagger in his hand. The tip of it glistened with my blood —exactly what he'd need to undo the spell. A moment later, the darkness swallowed him whole.

I stood there, straining to hear something, anything, but the air held only silence.

Gwyn was talking now, but my phone chimed into the stillness. God had to exist, because it seemed impossible I'd gotten a signal out here. Collith reappeared at the same moment I pulled my phone out. A text from Mercy. I stopped breathing as I unlocked the screen to read it. *Received word on Savannah's whereabouts. Won't be able to help you take down the ancient bitch. My apologies.*

I felt like I was about to vomit.

I raised my gaze and stared into the cave. Whatever Laurie had sacrificed, he'd done it for nothing. More time for me to say goodbye, maybe, since technically I'd upheld my end of the bargain with Gwyn, but that wouldn't be worth his loss. I could feel Collith's eyes on me as I stood there and swallowed a scream of frustration.

When Laurie emerged seconds later, he looked pale and shaken. Trying to hide my frantic worry, I examined every part of him, just as I had for Collith minutes ago. I didn't know what I was searching for, exactly—a wound, a missing limb, a spot of blood—but I could see pain in his eyes and knew it had to originate from somewhere. "The spell is broken," was all the Seelie King said as he came toward me in strangely slow strides.

Without a word, Gwyn sifted.

You're welcome, I thought darkly. Under normal circumstances, I would've said it out loud. But Laurie's bleak eyes created a lump of guilt in my throat, making it impossible to say anything. I knew this was the part where I showed him the text on my phone. My hand wouldn't move, though. Collith appeared next to me a second later. I glanced at him, expecting that he'd be looking back. Instead, he was staring at Laurie, wearing an expression I'd never seen on his face before.

Before any of us could speak, a cry rent through the stillness. It was coming from the tomb. I bolted, knowing Collith and

Laurie would be right behind me. I plunged into the darkness without a second thought.

To my surprise, there were torches burning on the walls—they must've been spelled by the same witches who put Creiddylad here. I pulled my gaze from those dancing flames, curious about this place in spite of myself. Like the rest of the forest, it was vastly different from what I'd seen in my dream. Besides the lack of growing things and rich scents, the tomb was larger than it looked from the outside. I couldn't see the creek, but now that I was closer I could hear trickling water again—in these temperatures, it should've been frozen. Maybe the magic had something to do with that, too. The walls on either side were covered in dead vines. The earth beneath my feet was dry and crunched with every step. This place *felt* forgotten, like a corner of the world that had been suspended in time, unnoticed and forlorn.

It was toward the back of the cave, partially hidden in shadow, that Gwyn knelt beside her cursed lover.

"What happened? Why did you scream?" I demanded as I reached them, my voice instinctively hushed. There was something about the air in here—it felt like I'd stepped into a cemetery. As if the ground itself was full of sorrow and death.

Gwyn didn't answer or spare me a glance. Her entire being was focused on the woman she was lifting from a stone slab. A modern Sleeping Beauty. I glanced behind me, expecting to see Collith and Laurie. Instead, they stood at the entrance to the tomb. Collith was frowning and Laurie's mouth moved, as though he were saying something, but no sound emerged.

"What the hell is this?" I muttered. "Gwyn?"

When I turned back, she still didn't acknowledge me. Something in her face stopped me from voicing the question again, and I couldn't help but stare at Creiddylad now. She bore no resemblance to the beautiful person in my dream. Her skin looked like it was made of paper-mâché. The gown she wore may have been colorful once, but time and decay had reduced it to bits of gray lace. I could see every part of the body beneath it, and the sight made my stomach churn. Creiddylad was more skeleton than human. The only thing that had kept her alive—if she *was* alive—was the cruel spell placed on her.

As I watched, Gwyn cupped the back of Creiddylad's near-bald head and murmured in a language I couldn't place. Her voice was more tender than I'd ever heard it. Startling me, Creiddylad looked up at the huntress with pale, overly large eyes. Her features were so gray and haggard it was impossible to decipher whether she recognized the one holding her. Was she about to say something? I hardly dared to breathe.

Then, in a movement so swift my eyes couldn't track it, Gwyn plunged her hand into Creiddylad's chest and yanked out her heart.

I thought I made a sound—a gasp or a croak—but I couldn't be sure. Gwyn lowered the corpse back to the stone slab, still holding Creiddylad as though she were made of glass.

"You killed her," I said dumbly, staring at the faerie's hand. It should've been dripping. The heart she held should've been large, red, and bloody. But the thing clutched between her fingers was shriveled and gray. More like a clump of dust than the organ that caused so much agony and euphoria.

"I set her free," Gwyn countered. However cool she seemed, I saw pain in her eyes, an ancient sadness that had been unearthed along with her lover. She put the heart inside her pocket and stood. "And now no one will ever control me again."

I looked back at Laurie and Collith, wondering what was keeping them outside. Kindreth had told us how to break the spell... but she'd never said the effect would be permanent. What if Gwyn and I were trapped in here forever? A hysterical laugh lodged in my throat. Now *that* would be irony.

"They can't help you," the huntress told me, bringing my attention back to her. "One of my hunters is a witch. I had her work a spell to give us some privacy, since I didn't want to be interrupted by your pretty kings. Alas, it will only last a few minutes. We'd best get started, yes?"

Her voice was too calm, too casual. It sent goosebumps racing over my skin, and suddenly I understood Jassin's fascination with her—Gwyn was the furthest thing from human I'd ever met. My gaze flicked to Creiddylad's emaciated body and back to the faerie's cold expression.

"Don't look at me like that, Your Majesty. Someday you will know what it is to choose between love and power. Someday you will be just like me."

"I will *never* be like you," I snapped, itching to reach for the Glock.

The faerie tilted her head and studied me. Then she grasped the hilt of her sword, and a ringing sound cut through the stillness. "You're right," she said, admiring the long blade. It flashed in the firelight. "You won't live long enough to see that day."

"Naevys told me there was still some good in you," I blurted, holding out one hand, as if that could stop her. My heart beat so hard it actually hurt. I tried to gather my power, to channel the Unseelie Court, but I only felt fear. "It was the last thing she said before she died. I don't think Naevys would've wasted those words on a lie."

"You keep surprising me," Gwyn remarked. She was staring again, and I stared back, wondering if I should say something else. Say anything that would make her reluctant to cut off my head.

Then Gwyn moved in a blur again. Before I could blink, she had her hand in my hair. I crashed to the ground, crying out at the pain that flared through my shoulder, but she was already on the move. She must've discarded her sword, because it wasn't in her other hand as she dragged me deeper into the cave. *She's taking me to the water,* I realized. Was she going to... drown me?

Knowing it would be pointless to claw at her hand, or resort to my abilities as a Nightmare, I used the faerie's distraction to get my Glock... but it was gone. I wrenched around, searching for it in the dirt, but Gwyn's fingers sank deeper into my scalp. I screamed and fumbled blindly for the knife in my boot. *There.* I pulled it out, flicked it open, and jammed the entire blade into Gwyn's calf.

She laughed. Then, with a strength I hadn't known she possessed, Gwyn pushed me beneath the freezing water and held me there. I forgot everything I'd learned as a fighter, as a Nightmare, and let the fear take over. I clawed at her wrists, screaming, and immediately choked on the rush of water.

It didn't take long after that.

There were a lot of theories about what happened when someone died.

I'd been high a few times in my life, and death was fairly similar to that sensation. A feeling of... dreaming. Uncertainty toward what was real, not physically, but of concepts themselves. Time, exhilaration, peace.

Despite the theories I'd heard, I didn't think about all the things I should've done or what I wished I had done differently. I did think of the people I loved, but their images were faint, surrounded by wisps of contentedness. They were safe. They would be okay.

With a faint smile, I closed my eyes, and I felt my fingers loosen from Gwyn's wrists. At last, I could rest.

And then I died.

CHAPTER EIGHTEEN

ot once, in my entire life, had I been tormented by questions about what came after death. Being Fallen meant knowing what, exactly, awaited you on the other side. We were living proof of Heaven and Hell.

There was also no question of which one I deserved.

When I opened my eyes again, I fully expected to be facing a demon or a wall of flames. Instead, I was lying in a cave. At least, I thought it was a cave. The walls and ceiling were made of jagged rock. Suddenly I was having trouble remembering why I was upset. What had I been thinking about a few seconds ago? Why was I here?

"...don't bring her back, I will remove every inch of your skin and force you to eat it," a silky voice said.

"Calm yourself, pretty prince." This was from a person hovering above me. I looked up at her and couldn't recall ever seeing that face before. "It is prince, isn't it? Now that you're no longer a king? 'Twas my plan all along to revive Fortuna. Why else would I *drown* her?"

"Don't act like you care about her," a new voice snarled.

I turned my head, startled at the sight of a third individual standing in the cave. It was another man. He was… beautiful, I admitted, even with the jagged scar darkening one side of his face. He had a strong jaw and a straight nose. His slightly too-long hair gleamed in the firelight. His full lips were turned downward, and I caught myself wondering what his smile would look like.

Someone else was speaking now. Since turning my head didn't hurt, I felt brave enough to sit up. This led me to notice there was something on the ground beneath me. I squinted, struggling to see in the dimness, and it took another second to realize I was looking at an arm. Farther down, I saw the curve of a hip and then a leg.

I was sitting on someone.

Shrieking, I scrambled to my feet. My cheeks were on fire and I stammered, trying to get out an apology. But my gaze fell on the woman's face and I went still. She looked so familiar. She looked… dead.

There was a woman sitting at her side who looked very much alive. She was the one I'd been looking up at, I remembered. She had a long braid down her back and every part of her was hard with muscle. The silver-haired man was talking to her again. His voice seemed unkind, but the woman just chuckled.

She was doing something strange to the person on the ground—her hands came down hard and fast, again and again. The dark-haired man started pacing. I could see their fear, sense their urgency, but none of it touched me. I turned to examine the rest of the cave, hopeful to find some clue to my identity and how I came to be here.

At that moment, a figure appeared at the far end of the tomb. A man, I guessed from his outline, and though I couldn't see his face there was something vaguely familiar about him, too. "Hello?" I called, breaking into a run. "Who are you?"

"Fortuna!" one of the men shouted from behind. There was something in his voice—a true note of terror—that made me hesitate. I slowed and looked over my shoulder. He wasn't even looking this way; he was looking at that prone form next to the water. I didn't want to think about her. I turned back to the forest, but the sound of the woman's voice stopped me again.

"She doesn't want to come back. I'm an expert at taking lives, and she should've been able to reclaim hers by now. I didn't hold her down long."

"Shut up," the dark-haired man said through his perfect teeth. He'd taken over the strange chest motions now. The silver-haired man struck at the wall with his bare fist. Bits of stone went flying, and I drew back, wide-eyed and baffled at this display of strength. The man turned back, two spots of color on his cheeks, jaw clenched. My gaze dropped to his fist, expecting to see torn flesh or broken bones. To my astonishment, the wounds on his knuckles were knitting together. Healing.

"No wonder she resisted my advances," the woman remarked, undaunted by the violence. "I see her heart is quite full already... with the two of you."

The silver-haired man was breathing hard. He ignored the woman's commentary, and his bright eyes finally went to the one still doing chest compressions. "Collith. She's gone," he said. His voice was hollow.

It was that name—hearing it out loud did something to me. *Collith.* I swayed on my feet, and if the man said anything else, I didn't hear it. Dizzy, I was so dizzy. I looked at the dark-haired man and finally noticed his pointed ears. *Faerie*, I thought.

Images accosted me, one after the other, full of color and sound and faces. It felt like I was traveling through time, soaring down a tunnel of moments. Collith was in so many of them. His voice had become part of the material I was formed of. I saw our beginning, a morning of mist and cold—I was hunched in a cage and Collith stood in front of me, shining with immortality.

How refreshing. A slave with spirit left in her.

I'm not a slave.

I remembered everything now. Comprehension slammed into me with such force I had to sit down. That was my body on the ground, I realized with slow horror. Gwyn had drowned me in that dirty creek, and Collith was trying to push air back into my lungs. But I watched him put his mouth over mine, and I felt nothing. It wasn't working.

After everything we'd been through, this couldn't be how we left things. Our story couldn't end in a cold, dusty cave. Anguish expanded in my chest as I crawled over to Collith. He didn't look up or stop. His breath was fragmented, as if he was on the verge of breaking.

"Collith." I put my hands over his. "Collith, I'm so—"

Suddenly I was on my back again, staring up at an earthen ceiling. Collith must've seen my eyes open, because he'd stopped doing CPR. There was an instant of hushed, shocked silence.

Then I shot upright and vomited water onto the frozen dirt.

A hand held my hair back and comforting words filled my ear. Once I was done, I turned to see who it was, even though I already knew.

"Collith?" I whispered, hardly daring to believe this was real. That we were both alive.

Silently, he pulled me to him. His fingers were gentle, but I felt the tension in his body as I rested against it. Collith bent to bury his face in my neck. He still didn't make a sound. We sat there, holding each other, and I gradually became aware of our surroundings again. Gwyn had vanished, along with Creiddylad's body. As I searched the tomb, my gaze met Laurie's.

I felt a flicker of surprise; I would've bet money that he'd disappear the instant we were all safe. He was still too pale, and

I remembered the sacrifice he'd made to open the tomb. *Thank you*, I mouthed. The words felt inadequate. Laurie gave me a faint smile in return, but there was none of his usual vibrancy. It was then I remembered what Gwyn had said, when I'd been a spectator to my own death. *It is prince, isn't it? Now that you're no longer a king?*

The taunt went around and around.

Had Laurie… given up his throne for me?

My mind tried to reject it. Rationalize it. Deny it. But no matter how hard I fought the truth, it came back. The King of the Seelie Court, a creature capable of murder and cruelty, had made the ultimate sacrifice so I wouldn't have to.

Reluctantly, I pulled away from Collith. When our gazes met, I darted a glance toward Laurie, hoping he would understand what I was about to do. What I needed to do. Collith said nothing, but the rage had gone from his eyes. He stood and helped me up.

Without a word, I crossed the space and wrapped my arms around Laurie. I made my grip tight, because I knew he was falling apart. However old Laurie truly was, no amount of years could prepare someone for loss. No matter what kind.

He didn't hug me back, but he didn't move, either. His chin rested on top of my head, the barest of touches. Why, then, did it feel as intimate as the kiss we'd just shared? I squeezed my eyes shut against the thought. For a tilting, disoriented instant, it felt like we were back in the snow, embracing in the shadow of the garage.

Then I remembered the embrace with Collith, next to the barn. It was strange, how our stories kept coming together, mirroring. Two souls. Two embraces. Two such wildly different feelings when I was with them. My chest hurt, like I was being pulled in opposite directions.

Laurie was the one to step back.

"I need to return to my Court," he said. He didn't meet my eyes as he spoke. "They would've felt the bond break."

At least some things hadn't changed—he didn't let me have the final word. Laurie sifted, leaving me in the tomb with Collith.

The Unseelie King was still standing next to the water. I turned toward him, uncertain what to say. But Collith just walked over to me. "Let's leave this place," he said.

His expression was impossible to read. I nodded, and he moved toward the door. I finally retrieved my Glock from the ground, then followed Collith eagerly, more than ready to get away from the creek, the stone slab, and everything that had happened here tonight.

The return journey was hazy.

Later, I would remember walking through the forest, looking up at the dead branches stretching overhead. I would remember the entrance to the Unseelie Court, looming up ahead like a hungry mouth. I would remember seeing Finn's enormous silhouette on the porch. His anxiety rode on the wind, palpable as a gust of leaves. Every light in the house was on, streaming through the windows and lighting the way for our final steps. *Home.* I started to cross the yard, and my eyes stung with tears of profound relief.

"Good evening, Your Majesty."

For once, I was too weary to be startled. I turned around and mustered an empty smile for the vampire standing there. Apparently I was too tired to be polite, as well. "What are you doing here?"

The front door opened. Emma came outside, a welcoming smile brightening her face. Collith and I exchanged a glance, and he moved quickly to intercept her. Cyrus stepped on the porch, too, wearing his usual stoic expression.

The sounds of their reunion filled the air as Dracula and I stared at each other. Finn was watching us, though, his lip curling into a snarl. I was faintly surprised to see he was still wearing his human shape.

"We keep the balance, Queen Fortuna," the vampire said, finally answering my question.

There was a shade of expectancy in his voice, as if he'd given me a riddle and now I was supposed to solve it. It was my first instinct to walk away—I'd died tonight, and I wanted to spend the rest of the evening with my family. But then I couldn't help thinking about Dracula's timing. I also thought about his little Fight Club's purpose. *Keep the two worlds separate. Humanity on one side, Fallen on the other.*

"That's why you came to Granby. You knew Gwyn wanted to release Creiddylad," I said slowly. Dracula just gave me a serene smile, and I scowled back. "If you were supposed to stop her, you're a little fucking late."

"We arrived exactly when we needed to—we watched Gwyn remove Creiddylad's heart. It became clear that, if she'd intended to wreak havoc on the world, she would have done it by now. Clearly she didn't care about the fate of her lover. We are soldiers, Your Majesty, which means we choose our battles carefully. This one did not require our intervention."

My mouth almost dropped open as he offered his explanation. When I could speak again, my voice shook with rage. "Oh, great, so you were also there when she drowned me? Thanks for the help."

"You would not have died, Queen Fortuna. Well," Dracula amended as I stormed past him, "not entirely. I do so hate to see talent go to waste, so I made certain we would have this conversation, regardless of tonight's outcome. Vampire blood, when consumed, will linger in the body for two weeks."

I froze, staring at the house without seeing it. My mind rolled the words around like a Rubik's Cube. *Waste. Vampire blood. Consumed.*

"The coffee," I breathed as it clicked into place. I faced the vampire again, and I felt cold. Colder than I'd ever felt before. "You put vampire blood in that coffee you brought after my therapy session. You would've made me into one without my consent? Without giving me a choice?"

Dracula stood with his arms tucked behind his back, unruffled as ever. "Oh, there would have been a choice. We always have a choice."

"Fortuna?"

The voice came from the porch. I turned around and saw that everyone was watching us. Cyrus was as imperturbable as ever, but Emma and Damon both wore expressions of wariness. Finn seemed moments away from leaping over the porch railing and charging through the snow. As for the Unseelie King, his eyes were bright. Not with fear, I thought, but a cold readiness. The set of his jaw and the lines around of his mouth spoke volumes—he wasn't going to watch me die again.

I wasn't sure which one of them had said my name, but it didn't matter. After what I'd been through, I needed to be with them. But as I turned back to Dracula, I realized this might be the last time I laid eyes on the infamous vampire—there was still something I wanted from him. I didn't know enough about my own abilities, and Dracula had access to the past. To countless Fallen with long memories and even more connections. "Are you leaving town now?" I asked. The words were clipped.

The vampire's eyes continued to roam my face, and I got the sense that he hadn't looked away, not even when I'd been looking at my family. "Not yet," he answered. "The huntress is still lingering in this area, and we won't depart until she does. Call it a precaution, I suppose."

"Maybe I'll see you at Adam's, then." I didn't know what else to say, because what I *wanted* to say would be much worse. Dracula wasn't an enemy, but he wasn't a friend, either. Of that I was certain.

The vampire smiled again. "Oh, I can guarantee we shall see each other again, Your Majesty."

I couldn't decide if the words were friendly or ominous, but the conversation seemed over. As I started to turn away, I felt a rush of air. I glanced at the place Dracula had been standing, and it didn't surprise me in the least that it was empty.

At last, I crossed the yard. My family was still waiting for me, gathered in a cluster at the top of the stairs. Emma's hair glowed like a beacon in the porch light. She held out her hand and Damon shifted to make room for me.

I stepped into the circle of their arms, smiling.

Lyari and Ariel arrived a few minutes after everyone went inside.

There were six of us in the kitchen. The air was full of laughter, ice clinking in glasses, and murmured conversation. We were all conscious of Matthew sleeping in another room. Every once in a while, the baby monitor on the table lit up with soft sounds.

My Right Hand came through the door without knocking, and her eyes immediately scanned the room, searching for me. She wore her Guardian uniform, along with a glassy sword at her hip, and her pointed ears weren't disguised in glamour. If anyone had thought she was human before, the jig was definitely up.

"Lyari! Would you like a cocktail?" Emma exclaimed. Her attention went to Ariel and she gave the faerie a welcoming smile. "Hello! I don't think we've met before, have we?"

Bubbly as ever, despite the reasons bringing us together tonight, Ariel danced forward to introduce herself. Lyari stayed where she was, and I gave her a weary smile. The faerie's gaze sharpened, as if she could see something in my face that no one else had. "Sit down and have a drink with us," I said, gesturing at the empty chairs.

But Lyari didn't move from the doorway. Her body practically thrummed with tension. "I should let Nuvian and the Tongue know you're alive," she answered, keeping her voice low. The others were occupied with Ariel, though.

Let them know I'm alive? I thought, nonplussed. Then it hit me —the entire Unseelie Court would've felt the bond breaking the moment my heart stopped beating. In all the chaos, I'd forgotten. If they thought both the king and queen were dead, what was to stop the power-hungry courtiers from taking our thrones?

"Do you need me to come?" I asked, hoping no reluctance showed in my expression or my voice. It had been a long, long night—amongst everything else that happened, I had died and come back to life. I wasn't sure I possessed the strength to fight another battle.

Collith, who'd been silently listening to our exchange, was stiff and silent beside me. I glanced at him but I couldn't tell what he was thinking.

Lyari shook her head. "If that changes, I know how to reach you. I'm… glad you're alive."

Coming from her, the words may as well have been an embrace. I smiled again, more genuinely this time. "Thanks. Me, too."

While she made a show of leaving through the front door—it occurred to me that everyone here knew what she was, especially after arriving in all her fae glory, and there was no more need for pretense—I took another sip of my drink. Ariel had settled into one of the chairs, her laughter chiming through the room like a bell. Someone had already made her a cocktail, and once she saw my conversation with Lyari had ended, the faerie raised her glass into the air. "To beating the bad guys, and living to fight another day," she declared.

There was only one person who wouldn't understand her toast, but as usual, Cyrus didn't ask any questions. That was why he'd been so adamant about not acknowledging us, I realized as I watched him. That was why I'd never guessed he was anything more than human. Cyrus ignored the part of himself that was Fallen. He did his best to pretend it didn't exist. And if a dragon didn't exist, how could a Nightmare? Or a werewolf? Or a faerie?

I pulled my gaze away from Cyrus and listened to Emma talk about how to evaluate marijuana quality. Ariel got up to make everyone another round of cocktails. Before I knew it, an hour had gone by. Gradually, like driftwood being carried along by a river, our small gathering drifted away piece by piece.

"I think those cocktails snuck up on me," Emma said eventually, using the table as leverage to push herself up. The movement seemed slower than usual.

I tried to hide my worry. Collith started to rise, too. "Are you okay? Do you need—"

"Sit down and finish your drinks. Alcohol should never be wasted." Emma gave Collith a look I couldn't decipher. The floor creaked as she walked away. "Good night, you two."

Collith and I both watched her leave. Once the sound of her footsteps faded, silence settled between us. Strangely enough, it was… uncomfortable. Uncertain. I stared down into my glass and remembered our last night together, before Gwyn stole Collith away. In spite of everything we'd been through tonight, I still wanted him. Apprehension fluttered in my stomach and I raised my gaze. "Do you—"

"Good night," Collith said. He wouldn't look at me. He got up from the table, holding his empty glass, and crossed the room to put it in the dishwasher. The sound of rattling plates made me jump.

"Good night," I said to his back, frowning. Moments later, I heard the bathroom door close. A pipe in the wall groaned, a telltale sign that Collith had turned the shower on. It wasn't a bad idea—Gwyn had shoved my head into dirty creek water a few hours earlier. Had I completely misread the tone of our night together? Was he one of those assholes who lost interest the moment a person slept with him?

Or maybe he was just kidnapped by a sadistic faerie, reason pointed out. Collith didn't have any visible wounds, but that meant nothing. Maybe Gwyn had indulged the side of herself that Jassin had been so obsessed with. The thought made me feel sick.

Needing to move, I stood up and walked over to the dishwasher. I put my glass inside, next to Collith's, and pushed the door shut. Collith was still showering, so I walked down the hall and into my room. For a moment, I stood with my back against the door, staring at my neat bed. Emma must've been in here—there was no way I'd done that.

Sleep. I should get some sleep.

It felt like my veins were buzzing now. Like I'd touched an electrified wire or just gotten an injection of adrenaline. *Shock,* I thought faintly, taking off my shirt. Unzipping my jeans, dragging them down, then kicking them off. *You're in shock.*

I told myself that didn't make sense, since Gwyn had killed me hours ago. But as I crawled into bed, my teeth started chattering. I pulled the comforter around me and curled into myself. After a moment, I rolled over, and my gaze landed on the alarm clock. The bright, glowing numbers felt like an anchor. I fought through the wave of panic and held onto them. I watched the shapes change, over and over, until another hour had gone by. The roaring in my ears slowly abated. My breathing calmed.

At that point, Collith had long since finished showering. I left the sweaty bed—I seriously needed to invest in a second set of sheets—and took my towel off the closet door handle.

Another fifteen minutes later, I was returning to my room, water dripping from my hair and streaming down my legs. I put on an oversized T-shirt, dragged a spare blanket off the chair in the corner, and laid down on top of the comforter. *Go to sleep. Go to sleep.* I squeezed my eyes shut and blocked the events of the day by picturing a bunch of fluffy sheep hopping over a fence.

For what felt like hours, I shifted positions endlessly. When Oliver's face loomed in my mind, his blue eyes bright with pain, I let out a breath and opened my eyes. Sleeping was overrated, anyway.

I'd just darted another frustrated glance at the clock when something brushed against the wall guarding my mind. I froze in surprise.

The presence made no effort to avoid catching my notice. As soon as I moved closer and got a taste of its power, I knew exactly who it was. Before I could react, she sent a taunting image of the exterior of Cyrus's house. My eyes widened with realization.

She was outside.

Adrenaline coursed through me again. I wrenched the bedspread aside and grabbed a pair of jeans lying abandoned on the floor. After I'd yanked them on, I opened the top drawer of the nightstand, sending a squeaking sound into the stillness. I removed a hunting knife and the Glock—the blade and bullets were regularly doused in holy water—and tucked both in hiding spots beneath my clothing.

In the entryway, I yanked on my coat and my boots. Then I switched the Glock to the coat pocket, where it would be more accessible. It felt like I could hear the blood in my own veins, rushing like a waterfall. I paused with one hand on the doorknob, double-checking that I hadn't imagined the presence. It floated there, at the boundary of my mind and the yard itself.

Her proximity to my family sent a jolt of fury through me. I yanked the door open and rushed into the cold to confront her.

Later I would blame exhaustion or remnants of shock, but at that moment, it didn't occur to me to wake or summon anyone.

When I reached the bottom of the porch steps, I slowed and searched those distant trees. It was another dark night, as though even the stars were cowering. The wind had died down and fat, white flakes fell to the earth in silence. My breath billowed through the air. I walked forward a few steps, every sense was on high alert. My fingers twitched, longing to reach for the Glock. *Where are you?*

"I made you a promise." Arcaena's voice cut through the air like a dull knife hacking at raw meat. I turned around, and there she stood, looking more like a ghost than a living thing. She could probably hear the cadence of my heart, loud and uneven, as if I were a frightened rabbit instead of fear itself.

As the faerie came toward me, I saw that she was not beautiful anymore. Her hair was short and slicked back, which made her sharp features all the more prominent. She was too pale and her skin did not possess one wrinkle. It almost looked as if someone had taken the sides of her face and pulled back, stretched it tight over her cheekbones. As usual, her clothing was archaic. She wore no coat, despite the relentless cold, and her dress was made of black lace. Thin, pale toes poked out from beneath the hem.

It took another moment for her words to register. At first, I frowned in confusion, trying to remember what promise she was talking about. It came to me a few seconds later. *I'm coming for you, Fortuna Sworn. I will make you scream.*

"How refreshing," I remarked, shoving my hands into my pockets. My knuckles brushed the cool plastic of the Glock. "A faerie that keeps their word."

Arcaena stopped a few feet away and studied me as if I were an odd, slightly distasteful insect she'd discovered on the ground. "What is it about you that affects them so strongly? I can understand how you have those two idiotic kings wrapped around your finger—every male thinks with his dick first, his intelligence second. But the huntress puzzles me. Why would she break centuries of tradition to spare your life? Do you have a magic cunt?"

The question was rhetorical, most likely, but I answered it anyway. "It has nothing to do with my cunt," I said flatly, "and everything to do with what I am. My face, my voice, the way I move—it all caters to your perfect idea of beauty. Even the strongest minds find that difficult to resist."

"How do you know, then, who loves you and not the face they see?" Arcaena questioned.

I kept my face devoid of all expression. "I don't."

"What a tragic life. Perhaps it's a mercy that I'm here to relieve you of it," she added. Every muscle in my body went rigid and I wrapped my fingers around the handle of the Glock, but Arcaena didn't move. She was still watching me, staring at me, as if I were something she'd never seen before. "I supposed I should be grateful that incompetent bitch didn't kill you. Now I get to experience the pleasure of it myself."

The bitterness in her tone seemed personal, and there was frustration written in her frown. It felt like a light turned on inside me. "You're the one who paid Gwyn's fee," I said slowly. "You put the Wild Hunt on me."

Lyari and Nuvian had both known it was a possibility, of course, that Arcaena hired Gwyn, but she'd been so careful to stay in her rooms all this time. For every one of Nuvian's weekly reports, he maintained there was no proof of her involvement. *She's had no visitors. She hasn't spoken to anyone.*

Any word on her missing twin? I would ask next.

This always made Nuvian pause, and the air ripened with suspicion. For some reason, though, he had never questioned me about Ayduin's disappearance. *Nothing.*

Now, in response to my accusation, Arcaena smiled. It didn't look comfortable on her face, as though her mouth had wanted to do something else. Like the bad wolf had been forced to lick Red Riding Hood's cheek instead of tear into it. "I may be just a mortal now, but I've walked this earth for centuries. I know where to find power," she informed me.

Manic, I thought suddenly. That was how to describe the light in her eyes. "So the cherubim were your doing, too, I take it?" I asked casually, resisting the urge to take a step back.

Arcaena cocked her head, and there was something reptilian about the movement. "Cherubim, you say? They are the mongrels of the underworld. You have made some powerful enemies, little Nightmare, if cherubim are after you. Unfortunately for them, I'm not interested in sharing."

Standing barefoot in the snow, her lacy dress flapping in the wind, she truly looked like a creature from one of my recent nightmares. It was obvious only one of us was going to walk out of this field. Fear pulsed in my throat, but I forced myself to take stock of the ancient faerie like she was any other opponent. Arcaena had the ability to lower inhibitions, I knew that. But what else lurked behind that alien face? What other powers did she contain within her sickly-looking skin? I had to be ready, because she could move faster than—

Arcaena came at me like a bullet. All I could do was dive out of the way and try to hit the ground rolling. Snow clung to me as I shot back to my feet. I instinctively lowered myself into a squat, one arm raised toward Arcaena while the other yanked out the Glock. It all happened within two seconds, but even this was too slow—she slammed into me with such force that the air left my lungs. This time, I landed on my spine. A wheezing sound left me, and I stared up at Arcaena, helpless as her hand came down to tear out my throat.

The blow never landed. Instead, there was a horrible squelching sound. Arcaena's face slackened and her eyes went dull. She crumpled to the ground... and revealed the Seelie King.

Or the faerie who used to be the Seelie King.

It took a few seconds to speak. "Why did you do that?" I asked, sitting up. Adrenaline was still pumping through me.

Laurie allowed Arcaena's heart to roll off his fingers and hit the ground. When he raised his eyes to mine, internal alarm bells clanged. In all the time I'd known him, Laurie had been careful to wear a mask of civility. Seeing him now, with blood covering his hand and wrist, was a stark reminder of what I'd allowed myself to forget. Yet his voice was pleasant as he answered, "So you wouldn't have to."

"You've been doing that a lot lately." I didn't think before saying the words, and my heart quickened when I realized that I'd just opened a door between us. I stood up, careful not to touch Arcaena's body, and studiously avoided Laurie's gaze. We hadn't truly spoken since Gwyn killed me. Since Laurie had sacrificed everything to open the tomb and it became impossible to deny his feelings for me.

And my feelings for him. Whatever the hell they were.

Laurie opened his mouth to respond, but I beat him to it. Now was *not* the time for a heart-to-heart. "I better go now," I blurted.

Seeing the wariness in my eyes, Laurie smiled. It reminded me of Arcaena's smile, just a few minutes ago, when she'd had a heart in her chest. I looked down to where she lay at my feet like a wilted flower. I couldn't bring myself to feel any guilt or sorrow from her death. "Why do you need to leave?" I heard Laurie ask.

"Well, despite *that* mental image"—I swallowed and nodded at the heart on the ground—"I should probably get some sleep. Believe it or not, dying and coming back to life really takes it out of you."

The faerie looked at me for a long moment. His silver eyes were too sharp, too perceptive, and I fought to make my breathing steady and deep. If Laurie knew I was trying to make him leave to avoid a conversation, he'd stay and manipulate the truth out of me, just because he could.

"Quite right," he said finally, looking dissatisfied by what he'd found. Or the lack of it.

Relief rushed through me, but all Laurie saw was a look of concentration on my face as I pulled out my phone. "Oh, will you do something with... that?" I added, glancing down at Arcaena's body again.

Looking more like himself, Laurie knelt carefully in the grass and put his hand on her arm. "I'll have her buried next to her twin. Kind of cute, isn't it?"

I processed Laurie's question and frowned. No one knew where Ayduin's body was—no one except whoever had removed it from the bedchamber. The thought made my gaze fly to his, but he was already vanishing with Arcaena.

"*You* were the one who helped me?" I demanded. At the back of my mind, I had always wondered what happened to Ayduin's body and the recording of me leaving their rooms. As time went on, I'd assumed it was Lyari's doing. I should've known Laurie was behind it—he was behind *everything*.

The thought sparked another realization. My gaze snapped back to Laurie's. "You're the one who got that chair, aren't you? The chair in Naevys's room?"

The faerie just kept fading. "See you soon, Firecracker."

"Laurie, wait!" Half-faded, he raised his eyebrow in a silent question. But I wasn't entirely sure why I'd stopped him. Anything I wanted to say would provoke that conversation I didn't want to have; I knew exactly why Laurie had buried Ayduin for me. It was the same reason he'd opened the tomb and killed Arcaena. I searched for a safe question and eventually mumbled, "I've been dying to ask... why are you so afraid of Dracula?"

Laurie's laugh sounded in my ears like a spirit. "Afraid? I'm not *afraid* of that self-righteous parasite! I just owe him money from a card game he won back in '69, and I have no intention of paying up. He almost certainly cheated."

Dracula didn't seem like the cheating type to me, but I kept this opinion to myself as Laurie went off to do whatever he usually did while we were apart.

As I walked back toward to the house, I thought I felt phantom lips brush against my cheek.

CHAPTER NINETEEN

*C*ollith was back in the barn.

I stood in my room, staring at those brightened windows. I had a white-knuckled grip on the curtains. It wasn't sleep deprivation that had me in such a foul mood—for once, I felt well-rested. After my long night, which involved not only dying but also watching Arcaena get her heart ripped out, I'd managed to fall asleep for a few hours. A dreamless sleep, free of bad memories or tormented best friends.

Now an entire day had gone by and Collith still hadn't talked to me. Hadn't even been in the same room as me. Maybe it felt like a step backward, after I thought we were finally moving forward. But what had I expected, really? For us to date like a normal couple? For our complicated past to stop mattering?

Yeah. Yeah, I had. I *still* wanted those things.

Resolve turned my heart to stone. Suddenly it didn't matter if he rejected me, or if he didn't want me back. I swung away from the window and hurried toward the front door. As I walked past the mudroom, movement drew my gaze. The kitten had spotted me, too, and she froze mid-kick. "It's a litter box, not a Zen garden," I scolded her, eyeing the mess she'd made on the tiles. I'd clean that later.

Right now, I had an Unseelie King to confront.

It was a windy night. Air howled through the trees, moaned over the frozen ground. I walked across the yard and yanked the barn door open without hesitation. My hair billowed around my face, and I whirled to pull the door shut. A bang resounded through the abrupt silence.

All these weeks, I'd been so curious about what he was doing out here. Despite my frustration, I looked around eagerly.

Collith was standing in the middle of a dim room, surrounded by... a barn.

There were stalls along the wall to his right. To the left was a stairway and what looked like an old tack room. Everything was charred, some walls completely burned away, so it was difficult to know for certain. But there was nothing to hint at how Collith filled his time while he was avoiding the house. Avoiding me. For some reason, this only pissed me off more.

"You shouldn't be in here—" he started.

"I'm not leaving until you tell me what's wrong," I said with a downward slash of my hand, cutting him off. My heart had started turning into flesh again, and I willed it back into stone. "Did Gwyn hurt you? Is that what's wrong?"

Collith bent and plucked something off the concrete floor. It was a horseshoe, I saw when he straightened. "Can we do this another time?" he asked, turning it over with his fingers.

I couldn't believe what I was hearing. Even the voice didn't sound like Collith's—cold, bored, with a thin layer of fury in between. Suddenly I realized it was the same voice he used when he was talking to Laurie. "No. We can't," I said past the lump of panic in my throat.

"Fine." Without warning, he turned and threw the horseshoe so hard that it embedded in the wall. Then Collith started walking toward me, and I couldn't stop myself from retreating.

"You haven't been honest with me, Fortuna. I suppose you're not obligated to speak truth, seeing as we're no longer mates, but I should've at least been paid the courtesy of knowing your heart lies elsewhere."

"What are you *talking* about, Collith?" I demanded.

He scoffed. He didn't stop approaching and I kept backing away. "Cease the act, please. If you wanted to cause me pain, you've accomplished it. I beg for mercy."

At last, my back slammed into the wall. Collith's hands flattened on either side of my head. "I have no fucking clue what—" I started.

"*Laurelis.*" He said the name so vehemently that it was almost a hiss. Never, in all the hours, days, weeks of knowing Collith, had he spoken to me that way. His eyes blazed as he ignored my shock and went on. "Laurelis sacrificed his crown for you. Everything he was, everything he's ever given a fuck about, he gave up without demanding anything in return. That is not the Laurelis Dondarte I've always known. That is not something he would do pursuing a casual fuck or to take revenge on me."

"You're asking if he and I are together?" I glared up at him, still trapped between his arms. "After everything we just did to get you back from Gwyn? I thought you were smart, Collith, but maybe you came back from the dead without part of your brain."

"Don't resort to your delightful sarcasm, Fortuna. Not right now."

"Or what?" All at once, I lost my fear of him. I shoved at his chest, and he immediately put space between us. Now I was the one to hunt, stalk, pursue. "What will you do to me, baby? Because I know you don't have it in you to take what you want."

Collith stopped, right there in the middle of the barn, and I found myself glaring up at him again. "If that's true, how did you come to be my wife? If I'm such a spineless coward, how was I the one to claim you, after so many others had failed?" he challenged.

"*Ex*-wife," I snapped. The moment I said the words, regret rushed through my veins, followed immediately by exhaustion. I pinched the bridge of my nose. "Collith, I don't want to fight with you."

He didn't move. "Why not? Because it would require some kind of passion? Because it would remind you what it feels like to be alive again?"

"You're one to talk."

"We're getting off topic," he snarled.

"Your Majesties."

Lyari stood in a shadowed corner. At the same time, we both spun toward her and snarled, *"What?"*

Her expression was solemn. She looked at Collith, and suddenly I knew what she was going to say—I'd seen that look on a policeman's face, once, when he realized he was looking at a child whose parents had just died.

My stomach clenched, and the anger in the air dissipated. I wished there was a way to save Collith from what he was about to experience. Maybe I was wrong. Maybe Lyari was here for something entirely different. *Don't say the words,* I thought helplessly.

But then Lyari said them. "It's Naevys, my liege."

———

The ground had almost finished its consumption of Naevys Sylvyre.

It was impossible to tell where the roots ended and she began. I studied the veins in her eyelids, how her eyelashes looked like black feathers against her pale cheeks. She was still beautiful—the spell hadn't changed that. Collith crossed the room, approaching her without making a sound, as if even his footsteps might harm her.

"Mama," I heard him whisper. He stopped before her, clenching his fists. He'd been about to reach for her. She was too fragile. Too brittle. A single touch could make her shatter.

I stayed near the doorway, feeling like an intruder. Watching Collith, seeing his enraged helplessness, I realized he had never prepared for this moment. He shouldn't have had to. Faeries didn't age. Faeries didn't fade. They were creatures of everything eternal.

"May I have a moment?" Collith asked, turning slightly to direct the words at me. His gaze was averted. His jaw worked, as though he were holding back a scream.

Sorrow clawed at my throat as I nodded. "Of course," I managed.

I left the room without hesitation, making sure to pull the door shut behind me. There was a gathering of Guardians in the passageway, faeries who had guarded Naevys often throughout the years. All of them wore identical expressions of grief, and it struck me, looking at them, that families could form anywhere. Even within the Unseelie Court.

We waited silently. Though I was wearing a thick hoodie, I wrapped my arms around myself. The stillness was so profound that I could hear armor shifting whenever one of the Guardians moved. It came to an abrupt end when Nuvian stalked down the passageway.

"Is it true?" he demanded, his eyes immediately going to me. "Is he here?"

I inclined my head toward Naevys's room. With burning eyes and a tight mouth, Nuvian moved to wait with the rest of us.

Minutes later, Collith re-emerged into the tunnel. "She wants to see you," he said to me, his eyes dark with pain. From the corner of my eye, I could see Nuvian staring—it was the first time he'd seen Collith since he'd vanished.

I nodded again, then followed Collith back into the other room. He stayed near the door, giving us the illusion of privacy, and I went up to Naevys as I had so many times before. Her breath was the weakest I'd ever heard it. The faint wheezes made my heart ache as she struggled to open her eyes and look at me. When she did, I saw that the whites had turned to yellow.

"Have faith in him," the faerie whispered through her cracked lips.

I stepped closer, using my experience as the queen to hide any feeling from my face. "Have faith in Collith?" I asked gently.

She paused. Her throat worked. "Yes. Yes, Collith. He does not always… make the right choices. He needs someone… to have faith."

"Okay," I agreed. I didn't need to think about it. "I promise I'll always try to have faith in your son. He makes it pretty easy, anyway. You did a good job raising him, Naevys."

But she didn't answer.

I witnessed the moment Collith's mother finally let go—her face relaxed, making me realize that it had been rigid with pain all this time. The fingers that were still visible slightly drooped. I looked back at Collith, my heart in my throat.

His face was devoid of all feeling. Without another word, he walked away, his long legs carrying him down the tunnel faster than I could keep up with. Nuvian broke into a jog to keep up with him, and his sword made a clinking sound with every step. Seconds later, the two males were swallowed by the tunnel's black mouth. The other Guardians stayed with me. No one spoke. The silence was broken only by the sound of our shoes crunching over dry earth.

When I reached the surface, greeted by a cold gust of wind in my ears, the Guardians that had accompanied me topside were no longer in the passageway. I stepped into the open and saw there was also no sign of the Unseelie King.

Grief had strange effects on people—I knew that better than anyone—and worry dug a hole in my stomach. I broke into a run, heading in the direction of home. I prayed Collith would be there.

I'd only gotten a few yards into the trees when I spotted him up ahead. Nuvian was probably nearby, as well. Relief made me pause, and I leaned against the closest tree trunk, waiting for my pulse to slow. *Breathe, Fortuna, just breathe.* I was about to emerge from the shadows when Laurie materialized.

He had his back to me, and his moonlight hair gleamed even though there was no light. Something glowed in his hand, as well. "I thought you quit," Collith muttered, making me realize it was a cigarette.

Laurie shifted, allowing me to see his face, and took a long drag. Even now, after the biggest loss of his life, he was the height of fashion. He wore a suit of deep blue, and the handkerchief poking out from the pocket looked like silk. "I did," he answered, tapping the end of his cigarette. "I only indulge myself when the sorrow is too much to bear."

Collith made a bitter sound. "As if you feel sorrow."

"I feel a lot of things, Collith." Laurie's voice was unexpectedly sharp. Collith didn't immediately snap back, which surprised me. They fell silent, standing close to each other, smoke rising into the air.

"Even after you cut up my face, she would ask about you," Collith said. It took me a moment to realize he was talking about Naevys.

"What about after she found out I was the one who gave that spell to Sylvyre?" Laurie asked softly, his lips curved into a bitter smile.

There was another pause, and it became so long it seemed Collith wasn't going to answer. Then he said, "I never told her."

Laurie tossed his cigarette to the ground and stepped on it. Their pain was obvious in every movement. "She was more of a mother to me than my own. I wish I'd been there when she moved on to the next dimension."

There was another stretch where neither of them spoke. I told myself to move forward, make them aware of my presence, but then Collith asked, "Why did you do it?"

Laurie's head turned. "Do what?"

"Give up your throne for her."

At first, Laurie said nothing. I interpreted his silence as surprise, because that was my own reaction to Collith's question. *Really? After his mother just died, this is what he wants to talk about?* But Laurie had apparently decided to humor him, because his answer came a few seconds later.

"This… thing with Fortuna snuck up on me. At first, I only wanted to know her because I was curious about her motives. As time went on, and I learned more, I couldn't get enough. She can be vicious enough to shoot a werewolf in the kneecap, yet compassionate enough to sit with your mother for an entire night. She can face a dragon to save someone she loves, yet tremble in a cruel human's presence. She won't say a word about her own pain, yet she never fails to say something delightfully cutting if someone annoys her. She makes no *sense*, don't you see? And I'm fascinated by her. Utterly fascinated.

"I gave up my throne because creatures like Fortuna Sworn only come along once in a lifetime, and I'm going to make damn certain she stays alive." He faltered. "It's selfish, really. I've reached the point where I don't… enjoy thinking of a world without her in it."

"You love her."

Collith didn't sound angry about it; he said it like a simple truth. Laurie turned his head again, and I saw another smile touch his lips. "So do you," he countered.

They stared at each other, and something moved in the air

between them. After a moment, Collith looked away. "You're wrong about her, you know—Fortuna isn't a puzzle or an enigma. Actually, she was pretty easy to figure out. I used that knowledge to my advantage when we first met."

"And what did you figure out?" Laurie asked.

"It's family. That's all she cares about. She can be selfish sometimes, yes, and she's so stubborn I've wanted to pull my hair out… but at the end of the day, she would die for them. The ones she loves. Once she considers you part of that circle, you're the luckiest bastard alive."

Laurie made a soft sound, and if I didn't know better, I'd say it was a sound of agreement. My face felt hot. I took advantage of the lull in their conversation and finally approached. The faeries faced each other, and they hadn't noticed me yet. "What do the humans say? May the best man win," Laurie murmured.

"Walk me home?" I said to Collith quickly, speaking louder than necessary. Their heads swiveled toward me, and I could tell they were both wondering if I'd heard them. I couldn't deal with it tonight. I walked past the two males, aiming in the direction of home. Collith appeared beside me and Laurie, I assumed, returned to the Seelie Court.

I didn't let myself wonder how he'd been coping with the loss of his throne.

The entire way back, Collith didn't speak, and I didn't make him. The house was full of shadows and silence when we stepped through the front door. Collith secured the locks while I hung my coat and took off my boots. As he moved to do the same, I stood there and waited. I still didn't say anything, because I knew there were no words that could ease his pain.

After a moment, Collith faced me. His features were difficult to see, but he didn't walk away or speak. The quiet was so absolute that we could both hear the heat kick on. Air hummed through the vents. "Want a drink?" I asked finally. Collith nodded, a barely perceptible movement.

I turned around and headed for the kitchen, turning on the light as I went. The liquor was in a cupboard to the right of the sink. No one had restocked it since our night of celebrating—there was only cheap vodka, an unopened bottle of triple sec, and some whiskey. I took out the whiskey and poured it into two glasses, then carried both to the table. I set one down in front of Collith and settled into the chair across from him.

He put his hands around the glass as if it were a warm mug. His expression was perplexed, a line deepened between his eyebrows. "How do I survive this?" he asked.

I couldn't tell if he was actually asking me or thinking out loud. The question sent my thoughts toward those long months after losing Mom and Dad. Most people had fuzzy memories of their childhood, but mine were sharp. Loss and trauma had that effect, like putting a magnifying glass on every day that went by without the person you loved.

"When someone dies, there is no surviving—there is only enduring," I said softly. I took a small drink of the whiskey, and it burned going down my throat. "Everyone is different when it comes to pain. Some are numb. Some deny. Some just break. Me, I walked around feeling like there was this huge hole in my chest. I could only focus on that moment, then the next one, and the one after that. Enduring each one until the hole started to close and the sharp pain became a dull ache."

It was similar to what Damon had said about scars, I thought. Maybe, no matter where the pain came from, creatures of every species experienced healing in a similar way.

Collith didn't respond for a long time. He sat in his chair, staring at the table. The heat clicked off and the silence returned. He downed the rest of the whiskey, set the glass aside, and stood up. His eyes met mine and he said, "I need you, Fortuna. Right now."

I arched my neck back. The answer was easy. "Okay."

He held my gaze for another moment, as if he was giving me

a chance to change my mind. When I didn't utter another word, Collith lifted me into his arms and carried me into my bedroom. He dropped me onto the bed and turned to close the door. Then, with silence ringing around us, he came back and started to remove my clothing. My jeans, sweater, bra, underwear, and socks became a pile on the floor. Within a minute, I was completely naked.

There was no chance to feel self-conscious, because Collith pulled his shirt off. Light slipping beneath the door allowed me to admire the detailed lines of his chest and stomach, the defined V that vanished inside his jeans. His hair fell over one eye as he undid the zipper. I watched him finish undressing, and seeing his body made my own ignite. Without thinking, I reached forward and slid my hand up his shaft. Collith froze. I started to move my hand up and down, enjoying his reaction to every stroke. Seeing evidence of the power I had over him made me bold.

Without a word, I stood up and pushed Collith onto the bed. He didn't argue—he propped himself up on his elbows and watched me. When I bent over and took his cock into my mouth, he sucked in a breath, as if he hadn't been expecting it. I swirled my tongue around the tip, loving the sounds he made. Those sounds, combined with the way he was still looking at me, sent a rush of power through my veins.

Following my instincts, I pulled away and crawled onto the bed. Still completely naked, I put my legs on either side of Collith and effectively straddled him. I felt his hands grip my hips. His eyes devoured me as if I was the most beautiful thing he'd ever seen. Heat and desire pumped through me, and I kissed him again, grinding instinctively against the hard length beneath me. Just as Collith opened his mouth to say something, I sank down onto his cock.

"*Fuck,*" he groaned.

I started moving in a circular motion and coaxed more

sounds from him, liking how they made me feel. After a few minutes of this, Collith sat up, adjusting me so I was in his lap. Our rhythm only broke for a moment. Then I was moving again, riding him with one hand tangled in his hair and the other braced on his shoulder. His mouth closed around one of my nipples, and the sensation made me gasp. A drop of sweat slid down the small of my back.

"I'm close," Collith growled, finding my clitoris with his fingertips. "I want to watch you come. Come for me, Fortuna."

I arched my head back, eyes closed in ecstasy. The combination of his fingers and his body beneath mine was too heady, and within seconds, it pushed me over the edge. I fell and fell, crying out as I went.

As his own climax came to an end, Collith rolled onto his back. I draped my leg across his thighs and tucked my arm around his ribcage. We stayed like that for a while. I didn't want to speak until Collith did. My mind began to wander, and I realized that we hadn't used any protection this time—I'd have to buy a morning-after pill tomorrow.

Then something wet touched my cheek, and when I raised my head, I saw that tears glittered on Collith's face. All thoughts about contraception vanished.

"Oh, Collith." My heart broke for him. I murmured meaningless things into his hair, holding him even tighter, while Collith's body shook with soundless sobs. It took several minutes to notice tears streaming down my cheeks, too. Sniffling, I raked his hair back and whispered, "You should know. I didn't save you because it was the right thing to do; I saved you because I could no longer imagine a world without you in it."

It was the same thing Laurie had said about me. I watched Collith's eyes flicker as he realized this. "I love you, too," he said softly.

There was something terrifying about hearing the words out loud. "Collith…" I couldn't go on.

He touched my cheek. "It's okay. You don't need to say it back."

I wanted to. It would be the truth, and there shouldn't have been anything to stop me from saying the words back. Maybe I was still subconsciously waiting for the other shoe to drop. But all of that was behind me now. Wasn't it?

Not a huge priority right now, I reminded myself as Collith rolled away to stand up. He gave me a reassuring smile, but there was a shadow in his eyes I worried I was partially responsible for. "I'm going to hop in the shower. Join me?" he asked.

The answer to that one was easy, too.

CHAPTER TWENTY

$\mathcal{I}$ woke with a kitten curled on my chest. Her purring filled my ears as I turned, wanting to see Collith beside me, needing the reassurance that I hadn't dreamed getting him back.

But the other side of the bed was empty again.

Images from my dreams lingered, making it difficult to separate them from reality. My mother's slumped body. A goblin peering at me through the bars of a cage. Steam rising from water as the Leviathan's body sank far, far below. Jassin's catlike eyes smiling into mine. Blood running from Collith's nose as he crashed face-first onto the ground.

Every bad memory and every terrifying experience I'd accumulated over the course of my life. Oliver had been the stopper, the gatekeeper, and now that he was gone they were free to flood my mind each night.

A moment later, my alarm sounded. *Damn it.* I was supposed to be at Bea's in an hour. If I wanted to make it, and avoid another angry rant from Angela, it was time to leave this warm bed. When I sat up, a chill raced over my skin and the kitten made a mewling sound.

"How the hell am I supposed to deny that face?" I muttered, sinking back down. She tucked her oversized head into the crook beneath my chin.

For a few minutes, I slipped in and out of darkness, trying to keep track of the numbers on the clock. A sound woke me, and I stirred at the same time Collith opened the curtains. Luminosity flooded the room. I covered my face instinctively, peeking through my fingers to admire Collith's shirtless torso. Morning light streamed in around him like a halo. He came toward me, and the kitten took advantage of the open door.

A moment later, I felt Collith grasp my wrists and tug at them. That ridged chest was a breath away from my face, and I gave in to the urge to lean forward and kiss it. Collith made a sound in his throat, deep and interested, and tilted my face toward his.

"Wait, morning breath—" I started to protest. Collith kissed me with a mouth that was thorough and patient. I forgot to be embarrassed or self-conscious. He pulled away to put those lips on my jaw, my collarbone, the inside of my elbow and my wrist, then each of my upturned fingertips. Goosebumps rose along my skin and I was already aching for him again.

"Tempted as I am to finish this," Collith murmured, his lips moving against me, "don't you have to work soon?"

I was distracted by his zipper and didn't answer. I'd started to drag it down when Collith retreated. The zipper slipped from my grasp. I tried to pull him back, but Collith was reaching for something on the nightstand. "I can be late," I argued. "Angela will be so unhappy if she doesn't have something to complain about all day."

Ignoring this, Collith pressed a coffee mug into my hands. "I like Bea. I don't want her to be short a staff member."

"You made me coffee," I said stupidly, staring down into the mug. There was a strange feeling in my stomach, as though something had been torn up by the roots to make room for something new. Liquid sloshed precariously against the sides, and I sat up to avoid spilling it over the bedspread.

"With enough cream to make me vomit," Collith agreed, perching on the edge of the mattress.

I took a drink, savored it for a moment, then smiled. "He can make a perfect cup of coffee, too. It's a good thing I have excellent self-esteem, or I'd be feeling inadequate right now."

"Sometimes the things you say…" He smiled and shook his head. "Besides the obvious reasons, I understand why Laurelis fell so hard for you. You're a lot alike."

I wasn't smiling anymore. "Take that back. Right now."

"It's not entirely a bad thing, you know. I wouldn't have fallen for him if he didn't have some good qualities," Collith said. It was the first time he'd talked about Laurie without darkness in his eyes, and in spite of how much it unnerved me, I was curious.

"Good qualities? Like what?"

In an absent movement, Collith brushed strands of my hair away from my neck. "Like… the way he throws himself into whatever he does. You could ask him to paint a bedroom, or go with you on a trip to Spain, and he'd be at your side every step of the way. Making his insufferable jokes and acting like it was the best time of his life."

Collith smiled faintly, shaking his head, and something about the look in his eyes bothered me.

Time to change the subject.

"How bad is it?" I asked, thinking about the previous night. Collith gave me a questioning look. "The pain. I can call Bea and tell her what's going on, if you don't want to spend the day alone."

Understanding filled his eyes. Collith shifted on the bed, frowning now. "My mother is at peace, Fortuna. I watched her fade, day by day, and we both knew this was coming. She prepared me for it, even when I refused to listen."

He fell silent. Wishing I could take that pain away, I leaned forward and kissed him, soft and brief. He kissed me back. The taste of him lingered on my tongue as I pressed our foreheads together. After a moment, Collith took my coffee and put it on the nightstand. Once we were both laying down, he curled around me as if I was all that mattered. A heart behind ribs, the pit in a peach, the chorus in the middle of a song. I turned around and rested my forehead against his chest, pretending the clock behind us didn't exist. We still had a little time, anyway.

"Collith?" I said softly, sounding uncertain, even to my own ears.

"Yes?"

I swallowed. "It always sounds inadequate, but I know that, for me, hearing the words did help sometimes. I'm sorry that you lost your mother. I'm so sorry."

There was another beat of silence. Then Collith shifted both of us so that his body was resting on mine. He propped himself on his elbows, keeping his full weight off me, and searched my eyes. Whatever he found made his frown deepen.

"Fortuna," Collith began. He paused, as if mulling over his words. I waited, suddenly tense. The sound of my name on his lips terrified me. There was something so raw in his voice, a hint of loss and want and a promise of more to come. Something was about to happen, something important about to be said, and I wasn't sure I was prepared for it.

He pursed his lips, a determined glint in his eye. When he spoke, his voice was urgent, almost breathless, "Fortuna, I need to tell you something—"

There came the sound of nails clicking on the floor. Just as I sat up, Finn's whine drifted through the door.

Something is wrong, my instincts whispered. I hurried to get dressed and open it. The werewolf stood in the hallway, looking more like a shadow than reality. But his eyes caught the light, which streamed from behind me, and put a spotlight on the worry lurking in those yellow depths.

Wearing only his boxer briefs, Collith had gone to the window. He held the curtain back with one hand, and sunlight streamed across his bare torso. "I believe Finn is concerned for Emma," the faerie said.

That was all I needed to hear. Finn led me down the hallway and, once I'd donned a coat and boots, through the front door. I saw her immediately, looking smaller than usual, sitting on the porch steps. Emma's thin arms were wrapped around her legs, and I spotted a joint between her fingers.

I creaked my way over to her and sank onto a step just below hers. She studied me for a moment, smiling the slightest of smiles, and turned her head to look toward the brightening horizon. The air smelled like marijuana. Finn sneezed as he went to lay at the other end of the porch.

"You've been getting high a lot lately," I ventured, my voice soft and hesitant. Her grief was so powerful that I imagined I could feel it on the air.

"It's just a way to feel better, sweet pea." Sighing, Emma stretched her legs out. Bones audibly creaked and cracked. She fixed her gaze back on the sky and added, "I had a dream about Fred last night. It felt so real, but then I woke up and saw his side of the bed. I had to remember all over again—that wonderful man went and died on me."

Guilt had me by the throat, and I knew no amount of therapy would alleviate it. I may not have been the one to end Fred's life, but I'd certainly played a role in making it possible. "I'm sorry."

"You have nothing to be sorry for," Emma said with a small, dismissive gesture. Her wrist looked so brittle that the movement should've broken it.

Swallowing, I scooted closer and rested my head on her shoulder. She was wearing pajamas and a thick coat that smelled like a campfire, so there was no danger of touching her skin. We didn't say anything after that. There was no need to, really—Collith had cracked a window open and sounds drifted to us. Clattering dishes and voices blaring from his phone. I'd recently learned that the Unseelie King liked listening to podcasts and audiobooks, and the normalcy of this fact still threw me off guard.

The unfamiliar voices were the soundtrack to my and Emma's shared pain. To our sad wordlessness. For a few minutes, we spoke in a language only people like us could learn. Soon, the day would begin, and we'd hold the pain back. For now, though, we let it take its course. Like falling asleep after a long day, or kicking off shoes that had been hurting for hours.

"Ready to face the day?" Emma asked me at last.

I took a breath. I'd learned that no one was ever ready, and if I waited for the feeling, all I'd do was waste time. And I'd already wasted so much of it.

"Ready," I said.

My shift was a blur.

For the first time, I understood what people meant when they used the phrase *walking on air*. I smiled as I wrote down orders. I tried not to skip as I delivered plates to tables. It took effort not to hum as I printed off checks. Apparently joy was infectious, because it wasn't long before Gretchen and Ariel were smiling, too. It was my first time working with Ariel since discovering the truth about her, but she acted no differently than she had as a supposed human, and her glamour was back in place. After a few hours I stopped thinking about it completely.

At the end of my shift, I didn't even consider stopping at Adam's for a training session; I was too eager to get back home.

I knew I was acting like one of those ridiculous girls in a romance movie, but I didn't care.

I broke the speed limit during the drive. It felt strange not to have Finn in the passenger seat, but now that Gwyn was gone and he knew I was protected at Bea's, he'd relaxed somewhat in his self-imposed guard duties—*somewhat* being a relative term. I'd take what I could get.

I tried not to run out once I'd parked the van. I trailed up the walkway, calm and composed, and opened the door.

As soon as I stepped inside, a burst of music came at me, an eager twisting of beats and wails. Who the hell was listening to *that*?

Stanley, who'd been napping on the couch, dropped to the floor and moved to greet me, his nails clicking on the hardwood. I set my bag down on the bottom stair and patted his head absently. Then I took off my tennis shoes and padded toward the source of the music. I heard the couch springs creak as Stanley returned to his spot.

My kitten shot out of the kitchen and latched onto my sock, attacking it ferociously with teeth and claws. "Hey, there," I said, smiling. I picked her up and tried to rub her stomach, but she clawed at my hands. I set the tiny animal back down and she bolted.

Was Collith in his room?

When I reached the hallway, I discovered the air was thick with hairspray. The bathroom door was open and light poured out. Probably hearing my footsteps, Emma popped into view, a curling iron tangled in her hair. Her lips parted into a cherry-red smile. She reached to turn the volume down on her phone. "Fortuna!" she exclaimed.

"Where are you going?" I asked her, refraining from commenting on her sequined outfit.

"I'm going out with some ladies from town," Emma

informed me with a wink. She pulled the curling iron free and a tight ringlet bobbed up and down.

I watched her for another moment. After our conversation on the porch, it was comforting to see her smiling again. "Well, have fun."

Emma blew me a kiss and reached for another strand of straight hair. I turned away with a smile of my own. That smile immediately shriveled when I lifted my head and realized Lyari stood before me. "No," I told her sternly. "No Court stuff today."

"You'd better come now," she said, ignoring this. "There's a… disturbance in the throne room."

I let out a breath. I thought about asking for details, but Emma might be listening. I didn't want to worry her any more than I already had. Collith should know about it, though. Maybe he would even want to come with. "Fine. I just need a minute to—"

"There's no time." Lyari walked out of view, probably heading for the front door. I grumbled and rushed after her. She wouldn't slow long enough for me to check the barn, either.

Twenty minutes later, we swept into the throne room. Lyari had explained everything during our trek to the entrance. We hadn't even stopped at Collith's rooms so I could change—as my eyes roamed over the gathered crowd, I was wearing the same clothes I'd driven to Bea's in. I found her within moments.

Savannah Simonson moved amongst the fae.

They regarded her with distaste or disinterest. One even shook her off when she touched his sleeve. It was obvious in one glance that she was unwell. Her arms were so frail that someone could snap them with one gentle tug. Her cheekbones were prominent, her actual cheeks nonexistent. Her hair was a dull shade that hung over her shoulders in clumps. It didn't seem possible that she could be on her feet. Her cheeks were hollows and darkness filled the skin below her eyes.

"What are you doing here?" I asked, my voice slicing through the air. Everyone within earshot turned.

Savannah just stared blankly for a moment. Then, all at once, she was rushing toward me. Lyari reached for her sword, along with every other Guardian around us, but I shook my head at her. Lyari still swung her arm out and stopped Savannah from reaching me.

"I came to warn you," the witch hissed, her face etched with fury. Her nails dug into Lyari's bare arm, but the faerie didn't even flinch. "You thought I was talking about Gwyn. No, no, I wasn't. *Someone is still coming.* The aura is closer now. That night, you opened a door that shouldn't have been opened, Fortuna. Do you have any idea what you've done? My son will be—"

"Why don't we take this somewhere more private?" I asked pointedly. One of the faeries watching us made a tittering sound. Savannah followed my gaze. She stared at one of them, and slowly, her expression gave way to confusion.

Her voice was small as she said, "Who are you people? Where is my son?"

"Okay. Let's get out of here." Despite how much touching the witch made my skin crawl, I wrapped my arm around Savannah to steer her toward the doors. At least her necromancer abilities were in no danger of being activated here—the fae burned their dead.

Without warning, Savannah wrenched herself free, and the force of it sent her tumbling. I moved to grab her, annoyed by the spectacle, but she scrambled across the flagstones.

"I see it everywhere now," she whimpered, grasping a faerie's tulle skirt to pull herself up. The room was so quiet, so still, that her voice seemed to echo. By this time, I'd closed the space between us again. She heard me coming and spun to grab me by the forearms. "The aura. It's so dark. Endless dark. It's coming,

Fortuna. I see pain and death riding on its coattails! No, let go of me, *let go!*"

Other Guardians had come forward and peeled Savannah away.

"Do we have any rooms that lock from the outside? *Not* the dungeons," I said to Lyari under my breath. Keeping her focus on the witch, she nodded. I took a breath. "Okay. Take her there, please. Do you know how to contact Zara?"

Surprise flickered in her eyes. "Yes. His Majesty made sure that we all have her number saved in our phones."

"Excellent. Send her a message when you get the chance."

In the meantime, I needed to get my phone. I didn't know Mercy's number by heart, but it was saved in my contact list. She should be informed that her niece had been found.

Lyari moved to obey my orders, and I left for home, where my phone would be waiting on the entryway table. We'd left so quickly—and there was no signal down here, anyway—that I hadn't bothered grabbing it.

Two Guardians followed me through the door. They didn't make a sound or try to walk ahead of me, making it easy to forget them in my haste. I hadn't gotten far when I noticed a dim figure farther down the passageway. Though I stopped, she kept coming, and soon the torches revealed Mercy's face. Some of the tension eased from me.

"I was just on my way to text you," I said. My voice sounded harsh in the stillness.

"I tracked my niece here. She led me on a merry chase all over the mountains, only to end up back where we started. Where is Savannah?" the witch asked. Her expression was pleasant. Neutral. But I knew it could change in an instant, if the wrong words came out of my mouth. Maybe she was worried I'd killed Savannah.

I could feel Mercy's power rumbling in the air, and I'd already died once this week. I wasn't eager to repeat the experience. I spoke slowly, my voice equivalent to the act of walking along a tightrope. "Savannah is with a healer. She came here tonight, of her own volition, talking about auras and death. I had my guards take her somewhere quiet and contact Zara. She's healed me before and I trust her. She should be here soon, if she's not already."

Mercy looked at me for another long moment. "Thank you for helping my family," she said eventually. "It will not be forgotten."

With that, the witch walked past, and I was tempted to throw an insult at her back—she'd abandoned us the night Gwyn killed me. Laurie had lost his throne for nothing. Mercy Wardwell had never atoned for breaking her word.

Tonight, my self-preservation was stronger than my anger. I let Mercy walk away and, with a weary sigh, continued on down the tunnel. I heard the creak of leather and knew the Guardians were still behind me.

At the surface, though, they hung back. I suspected there were Guardians waiting amongst the trees.

I made the journey home, and it felt like I was alone. I enjoyed the brief time of solidarity, taking energy from the serene silence. Whatever monsters lurked in the night didn't come looking for me.

That serenity evaporated the moment I lifted my head and saw Gwyn.

"It's been a long day," I called, halting. "Can we do a raincheck on this?"

She stood between two trees, and the rest of the Wild Hunt seemed to be elsewhere this time. When I stayed where I was, she crossed the distance between us, her elbows swinging. "I'm glad you decided to live," the faerie said once she was close enough.

She was talking about the night she'd shoved my head into

that icy water and held it there. So much had happened since then and it already felt like a distant memory.

But that didn't mean I wasn't still pissed about it.

"*I* didn't decide anything," I said tightly. "You did."

"That's true," she admitted. "I hadn't actually decided yet, whether or not I would try to save you. Then you said that line about my goodness, and all that rot. Naevys said the same thing, when I went on my 'killing spree,' as you put it."

A sarcastic response rose in my throat, but I swallowed it. Gwyn could still change her mind about killing me, and I had no desire to go back to that in-between place. "Well, one good thing came from that night—I'm glad Creiddylad isn't suffering anymore."

"Once again, you mean what you say. How strange." She paused. Her expression didn't change as she added, "I heard that Naevys died. Is it true?"

"Yes." I didn't hesitate or say it gently. Gwyn didn't deserve my sympathy.

The huntress didn't seem to be seeking it. Her eyes were distant, the sign of someone whose mind was in the past. "She was my best friend, once," she said. "I wanted it to be more, but Naevys was in love with that fool Sylvyre. Shortly after she rejected me, I met Creiddylad. I was so happy with her. It made me seek peace between me and Naevys. She betrayed me instead, by stealing my love and hiding her away."

The huntress paused, probably waiting for a response. I looked at her with unveiled contempt. I'd read about this in one of Kindreth's journals. "I think you're forgetting the part where you went on a murderous rampage and the fae had to stop you. Naevys felt responsible for those deaths—that's why she contributed her blood for the spell to seal the tomb. It was her atonement."

I knew a thing or two about atonement.

Once again, Gwyn cocked her head and searched my face, as

if it were a puzzle and she was trying to figure out where the pieces went. "For what it's worth, I didn't enjoy killing you as much as I thought I would," she remarked.

Something about the way she said it made me believe her. Proving once again that I'd spent too much time with the fae, my mind immediately rushed to think of how I could use her regret. Play off any guilt she might feel. Casually I said, "Well, I know a way you can make it up to me."

An amused smile hovered about Gwyn's lips. "You have my attention."

She waited for me to go on, but I hesitated. If I voiced the question hovering at the back of my head, was I putting a friend in danger? Did I truly need to know more about him?

An image rose in my mind. The barn sitting on Cyrus's lawn, charred and abandoned. Nothing more than a painful memory fast fading into nothing. I thought of Cyrus's terror every time he saw a flame larger than his burners. Yes, I decided. I needed to know more. Not only to protect my family, but Cyrus himself.

Finally I said, "Tell me what you know of dragons."

"Your little town is becoming more fascinating by the second." Gwyn didn't try to hide the surprise in her eyes. Her expression became speculative and she began to circle me, exactly as she had the night we met. "It's been centuries since I've encountered a dragon—I thought they'd died out. Their species was feared even more than Nightmares. Like your kind, they were hunted. Not for their scales, though there's value in them, too, but for their abilities. Dragons were a threat to all Fallen."

I frowned at the last part. *A threat.* I wanted to see her face as she spoke, but I resisted the urge to move. It would feel too much like an admission of fear. By keeping my back turned, I was telling Gwyn that I wasn't worried about not being able to see her. "Why? Just because they could breathe fire?" I asked.

She stopped in front of me. Her hands were folded behind her back, and there was some space between us. Usually, she stood so close that our breath intermingled in the air. She was making a notable effort not to appear intimidating, I thought. "No, darling," Gwyn said, her dark eyes unexpectedly solemn. "Because their fire burns away our immortality."

Ice crept over my heart. *Holy shit.* My mind raced at the ramifications. If anyone in the supernatural world were to learn of Cyrus, he'd be dead faster than I could utter a single scream. He was Fallenkind's nuclear bomb. He was an end to the way of life as we knew it. There were some who believed none of the species should exist—radicals, they liked to think of themselves. If they caught wind there was a weapon to render us human, they'd do more than talk. Then there were the Fallen hunters. I didn't want to imagine the possibility of them obtaining a dragon.

I forced myself to calm. Cyrus had no family left, and those he called friends would lay down their lives for him. There was no one to expose him and his secret would remain hidden with those who did know. He was safe...

The thought dangled in my mind, unfinished, when I remembered that someone did know. *Dracula.* He was the one who'd told me about Cyrus, for chrissakes.

I was about to curse when Gwyn added, "Ride with me, Fortuna Sworn."

There was something in her voice that caught my attention —a note of sincerity I hadn't heard her use before. I met her star-bright gaze, this beautiful, ferocious creature of legend, and I couldn't deny that I was tempted. Tempted by her and the thought of experiencing such magic every day. The ends of her hair lifted in a breeze, long and feathery, carrying the impossible scents of moonlight and exotic places.

But, eventually, I shook my head. "There are still things I want to do here," I told her softly.

The huntress sighed and stepped back. "I suspected as much. Can't blame me for trying, of course."

"Goodbye, Gwyn." I met her gaze squarely, and even now, looking at her sent a quake of fear through me. It was instinctive, the natural impulse of any creature standing before death itself. Gwyn's nostrils flared. She moved past me and, before I could turn, whispered into my ear.

"You smell like him. I never really stood a chance, did I?" She nipped the back of my neck and chuckled when I shivered. "Come find me when you get bored, my queen. A creature like you won't be sustained by his type for long."

The jab at Collith made some of my regret fade. Still facing forward, I raised my eyebrows and countered, "Want to bet?"

"I shall go against my very nature to spare you from making yet another disastrous bargain. Consider it my parting gift." There was another smile in the faerie's voice.

I opened my mouth to respond, but apparently Gwyn wasn't one for goodbyes. Between one blink and the next, she was gone, my hair stirring in a whisper of air. I stared through the trees, snowflakes drifting from a swiftly darkening sky.

For the first time in weeks, the night felt... serene. Kind. Safe. Like it used to. Smiling faintly, I bowed my head and watched my feet crunch over a thin layer of snow. I started in the direction that would take me back home. Back to my family.

Back to Collith.

CHAPTER TWENTY-ONE

*N*o *time like the present.* That had been one of my mother's favorite sayings.

Instead of going inside, where it was warm, I sat on the porch steps and waited. Truth be told, I had almost reached my room—and the warm bed I was sharing with Collith—when Mom's words popped into my head. *No time like the present.*

My final conversation with Gwyn wouldn't leave me alone. Cyrus might be in danger, and I couldn't let myself rest until everyone I loved was safe.

I sent a brief text to the phone number Dracula had given me, then prepared to wait. Every few seconds, I glanced down at the screen. My weapons were a solid weight against me. I touched one of them every time I realized I'd summoned an ancient vampire to my home. But I didn't contact Lyari or Finn for backup; no one else I cared about was dying this week. I'd handle this without endangering them more than I already had.

I wasn't sure how I expected Dracula to arrive. In the form of a bat, if Hollywood had gotten anything right. Or maybe on horseback, riding a dark stallion with as much grace and deadliness he possessed in ancient wars and bloody battles.

I didn't expect him to arrive in a parade of black SUVs.

The air filled with the sound of running engines. I stood up and watched as the doors opened and a host of vampires gathered on the driveway—thank God Cyrus and Emma were gone, and the others were probably in their rooms. Dracula came forward, wearing a bomber jacket and leather boots. He looked, I thought reluctantly, ridiculously hot.

"Queen Fortuna. Why have you requested this meeting?"

I'd already thought about how I would answer. I couldn't very well tell him that I needed to kill him. "I've been thinking about your offer," I said.

Dracula leaned close. I couldn't tell if he was smelling my blood or listening to my heartbeat, but both possibilities set me on edge. "Why are you lying, Your Majesty?" the vampire whispered.

He stood close enough that, if I moved fast, I could drive my knife through his heart. It had been soaked in holy water a few days ago. *This could be my only chance,* I thought. The thought should've revived the adrenaline in my veins, but I was standing on that blue mat in Adam's garage, learning beneath his stern tutelage. There was no room for emotions or fear when I was facing an opponent.

And yet, as always, Collith's voice found a way to reach me. *Choose mercy, Fortuna.*

I remembered that burst of pain when he died. That slow dawning of horror and self-loathing when I realized I was responsible for it. No, I told myself. Dracula was not a victim. He was a threat to someone I cared about.

Then why couldn't I take out my knife and plunge it into his heart?

I watched the window of opportunity close as Dracula moved back. I couldn't do it, not even for Cyrus. Resignation burrowed in my stomach, making it feel heavy. "How much would it take for you to tell no one about the dragon living in

Granby?" I asked wearily, trying to remember how much I had in my bank account.

There was a pause. Then Dracula said, "What dragon? The only person of interest I met during my time in America was a young queen. The sort of creature who didn't kill me when my back was turned, which is rare, indeed."

The words were thick with meaning, and I realized Dracula had known exactly why I'd texted him, lured him here. He'd even provided me the opportunity to do it by pretending to be distracted. It had been a test. What if I'd failed?

Choosing mercy had probably saved my life.

I couldn't tell Collith he'd been right, for once, or he would get a big head. Tucking these thoughts away, for now, I raised my eyebrows at Dracula. "If you're surprised by someone not stabbing you in the back, you need new friends."

"Perhaps you're right. Also, I did make inquiries regarding your ancestry." Here Dracula paused for my reaction, probably expecting some kind of excitement or hope. After another moment, the vampire continued. "Most of what my contacts know about Nightmares comes from stories that have been passed down. But there was one who said he'd be willing to speak with you—he was married to a Nightmare, many years ago, until she was killed."

Before I could ask for more information, he slipped a card from his pocket and held it out to me. A name and a phone number were written in an elegant hand. *Jacob Goldmann.* I didn't recognize the area code. I raised my gaze back to Dracula's.

"Thank you," I said, giving myself no time to hesitate over the words. The only way to stop myself from becoming a faerie was to do everything they wouldn't, like expressing gratitude to someone when they'd done you a kindness. A kindness I hadn't expected to find in the world's most darkly infamous vampire.

Maybe this thought showed in my expression, because as the

seconds ticked by, Dracula's demeanor shifted. He stared down at me with a hunger in his eyes that I knew all-too well. "I've half a mind to make you my wife."

I gave him a sad smile. "You don't love me, Mr. Okafor. You just want my power."

Amusement shone from the vampire's eyes now. He extended his hand and remarked, "Love. Power. What's the difference?"

Since we'd already touched, I took it. His skin was overly warm, a reminder of the choice he'd made all those years ago on a starry battlefield. The flavor of his single greatest fear—to fail at the purpose he'd found for his immortal life—coated my tongue. Dirt. It tasted like dirt, as if he'd crawled out of a grave and now his veins were full of it. "Hundreds of years on this planet and you still have so much to learn. Goodbye, Dracula," I said, taking my hand back.

"Until next time, Your Majesty." The vampire said it as if he truly thought there would be a next time. With another bow, he turned and strode back to his army of supernatural soldiers. By some unspoken signal, they all blurred into motion, and suddenly everyone was sitting in the vehicles. Showoffs.

There was the roaring sound of a half dozen engines coming to life. The night flooded with headlights. I watched the fleet of SUVs drive into the darkness, off to visit other parts of the world where mischievous fallen angels needed to be fought. The red taillights faded, winking out like a dying fire.

As I turned away, I couldn't help but hope there would never be a next time.

A knock echoed through the house.

My eyes snapped open, and my first thought was that Gwyn had returned. But the huntress's goodbye had felt final. I sat up and frowned at Collith, wondering why he hadn't stirred. It was almost seven a.m. His bare chest rose and fell steadily. His eyes moved beneath his eyelids. He was the picture of someone in a pleasant dream, and I was loath to disturb him, especially knowing he might wake soon from nightmares, anyway.

But I wasn't a teenager in a horror movie. No, I was queen to things that go bump in the night, and I wasn't about to open that door without backup. Not again, at least. I liked to learn from my mistakes.

"Collith," I whispered, touching his shoulder. He didn't react. I grasped Collith's arm and gave him a none-too-gentle shake. "Hey, wake up. There's someone outside."

Still, the faerie king didn't open his eyes. Fear whispered down my spine as I realized he'd either been drugged or bespelled—there was nothing normal about how hard he was sleeping. When panic threatened to grab me by the throat, I reminded myself Finn would be waiting. It simply wasn't possible for a wolf to sleep through that knocking.

Despite a sense of urgency in the air, my gaze lingered on Collith. Seeing him like this was a reminder of the endless night I'd sat in the kitchen, by his side, waiting for his return. Terrified that we'd had our last conversation and even more petrified to think about why it mattered so much.

Gritting my teeth against the memory, I left the warm bed and opened the top drawer of the nightstand. My Glock rested on a bible that had been here when we moved in. It was one of many hints, throughout the house, that Cyrus was a religious person. I wasn't sure why it surprised me, the first time I saw the wooden cross hanging in his room. He was certainly more private than I'd thought—in all the years we'd worked together, Cyrus had never once mentioned his beliefs.

I was trying to distract myself, and it worked until another knock fractured the stillness. I jumped, swore under my breath, and snatched up the gun. When I turned, my gaze flicked to the window, drawn to the faint light pouring through. It occurred to me that I could get a Guardian's attention—there had to be one of two lurking in the trees. Hell, I could call for Lyari, too. I muttered her name as I rushed across the room. "Lyari, Lyari, Lyari…"

The world was painted in shades of gray. Pressing my fingers against the frosty glass, I searched the yard and beyond. Nothing moved in the shadows or trees. Maybe if I could look through the screen instead… I tried to undo the latch. It wouldn't budge. I gritted my teeth and tried again, putting more strength into it, but the piece of plastic held fast. This time, a trickle of panic broke through, and I almost slapped the glass. It would draw the attention of whatever else was out there, though. Where was Lyari?

If she couldn't hear me, Laurie probably couldn't, either.

My heart hammered as I whirled around and flew to the door. The instant I opened it, I saw Finn's furry body blocking the way. I nudged him with my foot, stupidly hoping I was wrong about the unnatural sleep, but he didn't move. It confirmed whoever was waiting outside wasn't a friend—friends didn't put friends into comas. I briefly considered checking on the others, but if they weren't in the same condition, I'd run out of people I was willing to endanger. At least faeries and werewolves could heal from most injuries.

What about Cyrus? a voice asked from the back of my head. I didn't acknowledge the small, vicious thought. Cyrus avoided conflict of any kind, and whatever his abilities, dragging him into a supernatural fight would be catastrophic. I wouldn't do that to him just to protect myself.

Calling the police was out of the question—it was an instinct that ran deeper than bone for every Fallen creature. Protect the secret. Protect ourselves. Humans could never know about our existence, or we'd share the same fate as the dinosaurs. An extinct species. Too big, too powerful for the world we'd found ourselves in.

Not to mention there was a band of supernatural warriors, led by the world's deadliest vampire, who would kill to make sure that didn't happen.

I was on my own.

Breathing raggedly, I crept down the hall. Shadows quivered everywhere I looked, each one a potential threat. I didn't see anyone through the wide window overlooking the yard, but that didn't mean much—if my visitor was standing directly in front of the door, they'd be out of sight. I hugged the wall and instinctively avoided the floorboards that would emit those tell-tale creaks. It took a full minute to reach the entryway.

Once I'd put on the closest pair of shoes—they were so big, they had to be Finn's—I raised the Glock. My fingers trembled as I rocked the slide back to check the chamber, making sure the round was loaded and ready to go. In the next breath, without giving myself a chance to hesitate, I opened the door and pointed the gun.

Mercy Wardwell stood on the front porch.

"My apologies for the dramatics," she said, lowering the hood of her coat. I blinked at her in shock. "I wanted to speak with you privately. Don't worry, your loved ones are all right. It's only temporary."

Normally, my mind would go alive with rage or suspicion. This woman had put a spell on my entire family and, if Lyari's continuing absence was any indication, on the house itself. But Mercy must've performed several spells before she came today, because the sight of her had a calming effect. I lowered the gun and studied her. *This is a person I can trust*, I thought.

It didn't feel like my own.

It was a good thing I had learned not to act on every emotion or whim—instead of inviting her inside, I thought of the vulnerable people around us, trapped in an enchanted sleep and unable to defend themselves.

I stepped into the morning and closed the door firmly behind me. The action spoke loud and clear, though I said nothing out loud—if she tried to go inside, I would stop her. As I faced the witch, I crossed my arms for warmth. It was cold enough that even I was bothered. "How is she?" I asked by way of greeting.

A frown pulled at my mouth. No, wait, I'd meant to order the witch to take her fucking claws out of my family.

Unaware of the enraged thoughts going through my head, Mercy gave me a polite smile. She didn't need to ask who I meant. "Savannah is resilient. For now, I've done what I can and she's agreed to come stay with me. But that's not why I'm here, Queen Fortuna. You helped my niece, when you had every reason to throw her to the wolves. In my family, we don't waste time thanking someone—we return the favor as soon as possible."

"Return the favor?" I repeated, wariness weaving through my voice now. Witches. Magic. Spells. I had learned that, more often than not, these things carried darkness with them.

Mercy nodded, her gaze distant. "The future is constantly changing. Even the small choices we make, like whether to stop for coffee or kiss that cute boy from school, affect the path. Keep that in mind, for after."

After? I thought blankly.

Before I could form a response, she moved. Later, I would put together that she'd raised her hand and thrown the ingredients of a spell at my face. As a cloud of herbs assaulted me, her palms came to a rest on either side of my head. A croak escaped my throat. I stared into Mercy's blue eyes, drowning in them. She muttered in a language made of music and power. Some part of me remembered it was Enochian.

It felt like I was running a fever, or experiencing a bad high. I hunched over and squeezed my eyes shut, waiting for the feeling to pass. It ebbed and flowed, the pain shrinking and expanding in bursts. After a few minutes, I straightened slowly, hoping to avoid vomiting all over Mercy Wardwell. Not that she didn't deserve it.

But Mercy wasn't standing in front of me anymore.

My eyes darted in every direction. Confusion and fear surged through my veins—I didn't recognize the room I stood in. The walls were a pale yellow, like a fading sunflower, and there was a crib to my left. Turning, I glanced over a changing table and a rocking chair. Everything was aglow with the soft light of dusk. *Where the hell am I? What is this?*

I was on the verge of screaming Mercy's name when the door opened. A familiar figure came through, walking backward, but I would recognize him anywhere. Relief rushed through me, followed immediately by alarm.

"Collith," I said sharply, hurrying toward him. "There was a witch here. She did something—"

"Someone has been asking for you," he cut in, acting as if I hadn't spoken. I frowned at Collith, puzzled—he looked different, somehow—but then he turned. There was something in his arms.

As my eyes fell upon it, I forgot everything.

When he spoke again, it felt like Collith's voice floated to me from a vast distance. "Would you like to hold your daughter?"

"Sorry, what did you say?" I asked faintly. All I could see, beyond the pink blanket covered in yellow stars, was a tiny fist. But something about that fist affected me in a way I didn't understand.

He laughed. "I asked if you'd like to hold her."

I nodded mutely, not trusting myself to speak. Collith crossed the room and carefully settled the baby in my arms.

I handled her as though she were made of something even more breakable than glass. The face peering up at me was pink and scrunched. Her eyes were half-slits as she hovered between waking and peaceful slumber. She did not yet know the nature of the world she had been forced into. I touched the baby's cheek wonderingly, thrilling at the softness of it. "Hello, there," I whispered.

I knew her. She was barely a person yet—she had no memories, no thoughts, and none of the experiences that formed someone, like skinned knees and first kisses—but I knew her. My body knew her. For nine months I had fed her, protected her, waited for her. She was part of me, regardless of whether she still lived inside me. The love I felt for this tiny being had no limits or boundaries.

"I never knew it could be like this," I whispered, running the tip of my finger down her nose. Her dimpled arms reached for the ceiling. "She has your eyes."

I didn't look away from her, not even for a second. Collith's temple brushed against mine. He touched the blanket, his wedding ring glinting, and pressed a kiss to that downy head. Watching the two of them, I felt something happening inside of me. A lock turning, a wall crumbling, clouds parting.

This was the reason. This moment was why we endured so many other bleak, terrible moments in life. Every heartbreak, every night we cried ourselves to sleep, every broken bone—it was worth it, because now I was here.

Minutes or hours later, I noticed that the light shifted, and I reluctantly pulled my gaze from the baby to investigate. Outside, the sun had set. Shadows stretched across the floor. Emma was probably working on supper. I told myself to move, but I made the mistake of looking down again. The child's eyes fluttered as she succumbed to sleep. I watched, riveted, long after her breathing deepened.

Suddenly her delicate face started to blur. *What's happening? No!* I frowned and blinked rapidly in an attempt to clear it. It only worsened, until the blur evolved into a pounding headache. I stumbled away from the crib, crying out, and rammed into something cold and hard.

When my vision cleared again and I was able to look up, I saw Mercy standing on the other side of the porch. I was holding onto the railing for balance—that must've been what I collided into. It felt like my heart was in my throat as I realized there was no baby, no rosy glow over everything, no sense of elation. The day was just beginning, rather than coming to an end. My mind fought to realign with reality.

The weight of loss was so crushing that, for an instant, it felt like I'd had the wind knocked out of me. "What was that?" I managed.

The witch met my gaze without any trace of remorse or concern. "Your future, Queen Fortuna. Or one of them, at least. I apologize for startling you, but the spell only works if your mind is unguarded."

With that, she bowed and went down the steps. Smart woman—she was probably moving quickly to avoid retaliation. Mercy slipped into the dark morning like she was made of shadows, and it finally hit me that she was leaving.

"Wait! We're not finished," I snapped, rankled at the knowledge that she'd done such an intimate spell without my permission. Not to mention that I'd never gotten the chance to tell her off for being a no show at the tomb. Because of her, Gwyn had killed me and gone free. My shoes made hollow sounds against the steps as I ran after Mercy. "Hey, do you know what Savannah was talking about? When she mentioned a door being opened?"

There were other things I wanted to ask, of course—all of them surrounding the vision she'd just summoned—but this one was the most pressing. If my family was in danger, I needed to be prepared for it.

The question made Mercy halt. She faced me and shook her frizzy head. Keys glinted in her hand. "No. I might be able to learn something, though, if you're willing to open your mind to me."

She raised her eyebrows in a wordless question. I started to agree, but something stopped me. The person I'd once been would not have hesitated—she'd let this witch do anything to get what she wanted. The one I had become, though, would not give anyone her trust so blindly. No matter how good Mercy seemed to be.

"Maybe next time," was all I said, wanting to scream in frustration. Too many enemies, too many threats. It felt like I was always putting my family in danger.

Mercy didn't look surprised by this response. She simply nodded and finished walking to her car. I followed, debating whether or not to force the issue, and then it was too late— Mercy opened the door and got in. I was about to walk away when I heard the whir of a window coming down. Wary of another trick, I turned back cautiously.

"I will do my best to find out from Savannah. It might take some time. I'll send you a message, if I succeed," Mercy told me. Her tone was distracted, and she seemed to be searching for something in the passenger seat.

The debt between us was paid; Mercy Wardwell had nothing to gain from making this offer. I wavered between gratitude and suspicion as I replied, "I appreciate it."

"One more thing." She shoved a pair of sunglasses on top of her head, the item she'd been rummaging for, evidently. Their purpose was unclear, since there wasn't exactly any sunlight. Mercy looked me in the eye and gripped the steering wheel with both hands. Her fingernails gleamed red. "When I performed the spell, we became one for the briefest of moments. I saw what *you* fear most. You should know that you are not a monster, Fortuna Sworn."

Something painful and nameless swelled in my throat. It

took several attempts to speak. "What makes you so certain?" I asked finally.

The witch gave me a faint, solemn smile. A smile that said she had her own fair share of nightmares and bad memories. "A true monster doesn't care whether they've become one. Until next time, Your Majesty."

The window closed between us, and I saw my reflection in the glass. As always, I looked tired and... scared. God, I was scared all the fucking time. I dropped my gaze and stepped back as Mercy started her car. Her headlights shone at the garage door. The beams of light revealed flecks of snow rushing past. At some point during our conversation, it had started coming down from the sky.

Once Mercy's taillights had disappeared from sight, I ducked my head and ran inside. Snowflakes rushed past the window like flour being poured from a bag. For a moment, I just stood on the other side of the door, staring out at winter's tears. But my thoughts inevitably returned to the faerie king waiting for me. For the first time since our bond tore in two, it felt like we were connected by a string again, the other end tugging me toward him. I put my back to the pretty snow and padded down the hall.

I stopped in Collith's bedroom doorway and found him immediately. He sat on the floor, cross-legged, hands resting limply in his lap. He wasn't wearing a shirt again. I leaned my hip against the wall and watched him. Enjoyed the grace of his simple movements. Admired the curve of his jaw and how a lock of hair fell over one pointed ear. Then, without warning, I thought of Mercy's vision. My heart trembled when I remembered how Collith had looked at our daughter.

"I can feel you staring at me," the Unseelie King said without opening his eyes. "It's very distracting."

"Sorry," I said, sounding entirely unrepentant.

Collith unfolded his long legs and stood. He retrieved his

shirt from the floor and faced me as he shrugged it on. I dragged my attention away from his hard stomach. "I want to show you something, anyway. Will you come outside with me?" he asked.

I smiled into Collith's eyes. "Sure."

He laced his fingers through mine and pulled me out of the room. We approached the front door and put on our coats and boots. I caught sight of Finn's glowing eyes from the hallway, but he retreated a moment later, probably reassured of my safety when he saw I was with Collith.

Once we were ready, the faerie took my hand again, and we exchanged light and warmth for darkness and cold. He led me across the yard. I frowned when he stopped to pull the barn door open—whatever I'd been expecting, it wasn't this. Collith held the door open for me, and I hurried inside to escape the wind.

My senses were immediately assailed by the scents of wood and paint. I raised my gaze, expecting to see the blackened remains again. Instead, it was a garage. The walls were white and pristine, the floor sealed concrete. Along one wall, rows of new tools gleamed. "But... but I was just in here, and it didn't look like this," I said, frowning as I looked around.

"An illusion," Collith admitted. "I didn't want to spoil the surprise."

His answer only made my frown deepen. "Wait, how did you—"

"Not that way, Fortuna." Collith radiated tension as he latched the door shut and walked toward a flight of stairs, tucked in a space that probably once held horse tack. He waited for me at the bottom, holding out his hand, and I felt an inexplicable twinge of apprehension. But I still curled my fingers around Collith's and followed him upward.

At the top, he touched a switch, and the entire space lit up. I froze in the doorway. I could feel Collith's eyes on me, but I couldn't reassure him. Not yet—I was still taking it in.

"Happy birthday," I heard Collith say. "This was supposed to be your gift, but I wasn't able to finish in time. Hopefully it's worth the wait."

The loft had been utterly transformed. The floors and trim were the same rich, knotty wood, and the walls were a neutral shade similar to how I drank my coffee. To our left, there was a state-of-the-art kitchen, the silver appliances and marble counter-tops gleaming. To our right, Collith had set up a living room similar to Cyrus's, but the leather sectional and matching tables were obvi-ously new. An enormous flatscreen television hung over a mantel, and below this, a wood-burning fireplace awaited. There were also accents everywhere I looked—bookshelves, plants, framed images that Collith must've gotten off my phone—which effectively made the space look like a home, instead of a vacation rental.

Slowly, I left my place near the stairs and began to wander. After a moment, Collith followed. "I might've overcompensated with the bathrooms," I heard him say. "There's one at each end of the hall, and the master bedroom has one, too. Damon takes longer showers than anyone I've ever met—frankly, it gets very annoying when others need to use the facilities."

His tone made my mouth twitch. I soon discovered there were four bedrooms total. In the last one, which was bigger than the rest, I finally refocused on Collith. My eyes were wide with wonder. "You did this? All by yourself?" I asked. It was the first thing I'd said since he turned the light on.

Collith's eyes were fastened to my face, as though to reassure himself that my reaction was genuine. "Well, not entirely by myself. A contractor helped me install the appliances, and the furniture delivery guys carried everything in."

"How did I miss all that happening?"

"Believe it or not, you're not around much, Miss Sworn,"

Collith said dryly. I made a face at him and turned away again, wanting to see the bathroom. It matched the rest of the loft—elegant and warm. There were two sinks that looked like hammered copper. Behind a wide glass door, there was a shower made of gray stone. Beside this was a free-standing bathtub, its faucets shining like something that had never been touched. Collith's voice floated from the bedroom. "Cyrus sold me the land this barn is standing on. There are enough rooms for all of us. Damon and Matthew won't have to share anymore. Well, unless…"

"Unless what?" I prompted.

Collith pursed his lips. Standing there, hands shoved in his pockets, there was something vulnerable about him. But there was nothing fragile in the way his eyes met mine and he said, "Unless you'd prefer we didn't share a room."

Share a room? I thought, nonplussed. A few seconds later, comprehension shocked me like a punch to the face. At last, I understood Collith's trepidation. He'd meant this gift, this home he had spent so much time building, to be the start of something new. The start of *us*.

It felt like there was a bird trapped in my stomach, anxiously fluttering its wings. As Collith waited for my response, I reassessed the room we stood in. It was obviously the master, judging from its size. One of the walls was covered entirely in bookshelves. I moved closer and saw a row of mystery novels. But, just like his house in the mountains, there were also selections meant for me. More veterinarian textbooks and history books on the fae. He'd been paying attention to my nightly reading.

I knew Collith was still waiting for an answer, but even now I didn't say anything. Instead, I left the room and drifted down the hallway. Once again, his footsteps sounded behind me, soft and uncertain. With every doorway I passed, a scene filled my mind. There were Damon and Matthew, playing with some toys on the floor. There was Emma, tucked into her bed with a book in one hand and reading glasses perched on her nose. There was the living room, where we all gathered around a Christmas tree, exchanging gifts wrapped in bright paper. We were a family. We were everything I'd dreamed of since arriving at my first foster home and those lonely, empty walls had stared back at me.

And next to the imaginary tree, those colorful lights dancing over our skin, Collith and I sat next to each other. My head rested on his shoulder as though it were the most natural thing in the world. For the first time since I could remember, I looked... happy.

When I reached the kitchen, I finally stopped. There was a blueprint on the island, its edges curled and faded, as though someone had handled this piece of paper every single day. I touched the place where it said *Collith and Fortuna* within one of the squares.

"What about your other house?" I asked, finally glancing up at the person standing across from me. The person who had been silent all this time, but whose presence I felt at every moment, no matter how much pain and distance I put between us. "The one you showed me in a dream? Between living here and the Unseelie Court, you'd never get to spend time there."

Collith searched my expression. I didn't need to share a bond with him to sense his hesitation. "My home is wherever you are. If you'll have me," he added softly.

Why did those words strike such a chord of fear in my heart? Why did it feel like I was being torn in half by the urge to run and the urge to press myself against him? Silence swelled, filling the air like water. It was difficult to breathe as my mind raced. It came to a jarring halt when I thought of the biggest factor of all.

"What about them?" I asked, my voice tainted with a desperation I didn't fully understand. "Your people, I mean. You can't have both."

Collith was standing very, very still, as if any sudden movements would send me running. "Why not? Why can't we have both?"

A dozen arguments rose to my lips, but I couldn't bring myself to say them. I'd forgotten that the Unseelie King was a dreamer. Above all else, Collith *hoped*, and not even Hell had taken that from him. He looked at corruption and saw potential. He looked at me and saw a future. Being near him, seeing the world through his eyes, made me want to hope, too. After all, every nightmare had an ending. Every bad dream had the potential to become more. Why couldn't the same be said for us?

Feeling the need to move, I walked out of the kitchen. My footsteps echoed through the still space. My eyes flitted over the elegant furniture that Collith had so painstakingly chosen. The wooden floor gleamed from the lights overhead, and I thought of the hours he had spent on his knees, creating something beautiful out of something damaged. After a few seconds, I came to the hallway and faced the rows of doors. I didn't see them, not really—my mind was too busy, too full.

But none of it mattered. Not when I already knew what I wanted. What I'd been wanting for weeks now, and hadn't been able to acknowledge, because being a Nightmare didn't make me immune to fears. And this was probably the most terrifying thing I'd ever done.

With a deep breath, I turned back to Collith and held out my hand. "Would you like to lay down in our bed? Maybe get a little more sleep?"

His eyes flickered at those words. *Our bed*. The Unseelie King didn't answer, but his fingers curled around mine. Once again, I was surprised by their roughness. I had always viewed faeries as a useless species, too arrogant or disciplined enough to work with their hands. Collith was proof that I'd been wrong.

Wrong about everything.

As we went down the hallway together, my heart beat so

loudly I knew he could hear it. Collith's hazel eyes kept flicking between mine, but I couldn't read his expression. It was impossible to think when it felt like I had touched a live wire, and every part of me was electrified. I walked backward into the room Collith had made for us. He released one of my hands to close the door. The sound it made seemed to rival the noise of my heart. He ran his palms down my arms, and a shiver wracked my entire body.

Before it had finished its course, Collith lowered his head and kissed me. It was a gentle, questioning kiss. I answered by opening my mouth to his. He made a surprised, pleased sound deep in his throat that my body instantly responded to.

Consumed by the taste of him, my hand crept down his body. I found what I was looking for and stroked it through the denim. Collith pulled away and groaned. His forehead rested on my shoulder. Tension shivered around us. Slowly, he turned and pressed his mouth against the side of my neck. For a few seconds, his lips sucked and teased, stoking the flames inside me.

Then he bit me, hard, into the tender flesh where shoulder and neck met. I gasped with pleasure. It shouldn't have surprised me, really—however good he was, at his core, Collith was still fae. He'd always have a streak of wickedness.

When he first kissed me, I'd wanted to take our time. Explore each other and reveal ourselves slowly. But as soon as Collith's teeth marked me, those intentions dissipated like smoke.

The moment our mouths met, I consumed him as thoroughly as he'd consumed me. His taste drove me wild. I reached down with both hands and undid the button and zipper of his jeans. Collith responded by pulling my shirt up, and we parted for an instant as it went over my head. His lips came down on mine again, and we walked toward the bed, moving in perfect tandem. Somehow, his shirt came off, too. My core tightened at the sensation of his cool, bare skin beneath my palms. Another pair of jeans joined the ones on the floor. Our heavy breathing filled the stillness. My hands tugged at Collith's briefs while he unclasped my bra.

It was the feel of his hands on my breasts that made me pull away. I stared up at him and struggled against the memory edging in like a knife.

Despite my obvious fear, Collith didn't say anything. He kept his eyes on my face as he sank to the bed and leaned back on his elbows. A slant of light fell across him. Every thought I had quieted, like the hush of an awed crowd. For a moment or two, I just stood there, unabashedly staring at his ridged stomach and his long, hard length. He was the epitome of male beauty... and he was *mine*.

At some point during my admiring, the fear had gone away. I moved onto the bed and put my knees on either side of him, taking control again. Collith looked up at me, his gaze dark with desire. My core throbbed in response. I watched his lips part as I sank down and he slid completely inside. Slowly, I started rolling my hips. Collith's groan sent a rush of heat through me, and I went faster.

In the midst of our rhythm, I felt Collith's calloused hands cup my backside, but he didn't guide me or change the pace I'd set. As always, this was my choice. I was calling the shots. I was about to throw my head back when the tip of Collith's cock brushed against the perfect spot. A breathy moan left me, and I moved my hips even harder. A familiar sensation began to build in my lower stomach. My cries became guttural, like he'd awakened something feral in me, something that could no longer be caged. Collith hit that spot, again and again, stoking the flames. They spread through me. An instant after I reached my climax, so did he. Collith came with a low, male sound that sent more shivers up my spine.

Afterward, we faced each other on the bed, naked and glistening with sweat. Both of us breathed hard. I felt like a mess, my hair a sticky tangle against my neck and cheeks. I desperately wanted to shower. But I wanted to stay more, facing him, admiring the curve of his face lit by lamplight. God, he smelled good. He was glittering with perspiration, yet his scent was intoxicating. It sent a fresh surge of heat through me.

"I'm fairly certain you have the most beautiful smile I've ever seen," Collith said softly, just as I was considering whether or not to climb on top of him again. A lock of hair fell into his eyes, and the way he looked at me made it impossible to move.

Right on cue, my usual cynicism kicked in. *That's just my abilities as a Nightmare affecting you.* I opened my mouth to say the thought out loud, then I remembered that Collith saw my true face. He'd seen it from the very beginning.

Something inside me fluttered. I clutched my pillow tighter. "I didn't realize I was," was all I said.

Collith must have heard something in my voice—a slight line deepened between his brows. He studied me for what felt like the thousandth time, and as always, it felt like he could see every secret as though they were written on my skin. I didn't know what to say, and I was about to escape to the bathroom when he asked, "What makes you happy?"

I frowned. "What do you mean? Like, my hobbies?"

"I want to know what will make you smile again," he clarified.

"Well, there is one thing that always does. Have you ever had a dog rest its head in your hand? That makes me happy." My mind wandered, thinking of other moments that had brought some kind of joy throughout this painful life of mine. A soft smile curved my lips. "Waking up to sunlight, instead of an alarm clock. The feel of a warm coffee mug against my palm. Coming to the end of a long drive. Cuddling with my new cat. Hearing one of my loved ones laugh. And… you. You make me happy."

I spoke this last part softly, feeling yet another pang of apprehension as I said them. Collith was silent. He just stared at me with a light in his eyes that I couldn't define. Dismay? Uncertainty? Pity? Warmth began to spread through my cheeks. "What makes you happy?" I asked quickly, desperate to move past the moment.

Instead of answering, the Unseelie King cupped the back of my neck and pulled me toward him. The taste of his tongue consumed me and cleared my mind, somehow. It had been adoration in his eyes, not uncertainty. Strange how fear could twist reality against you, make you question your own instincts.

And as Collith claimed me with his hands and his mouth, I realized that I'd gotten an answer, after all.

CHAPTER TWENTY-TWO

*T*he following night, my hope was that I'd sleep so hard, I wouldn't have any dreams. It didn't even occur to me that I might return to the dreamscape—without Oliver, it seemed impossible that it would still exist, and I hadn't been back since he left.

But I made the mistake of allowing myself to think as I drifted off. Tossing and turning over Gwyn's prediction, Mercy's vision, the hollowness in Oliver's eyes as he asked me if I'd fucked another man.

Mom used to say that carrying my worries to bed meant I'd carry them right into my dreams, and as with most things, she was right.

I opened my eyes, heavy with reluctance, and my heart sank when I saw where I was. The clouds overhead looked ominous and gray, which happened only when Oliver and I had an urge to dance in the rain. The fact it was happening now, in spite of his absence, seemed unnatural. Like something had broken.

Thunder boomed across the plains. The wind slammed into me, so cold that it felt like the air carried pinpricks of ice. I was wearing what I'd fallen asleep in—yoga pants and a long-sleeved shirt. No socks or shoes. I looked at the cottage, knowing it would be the smart choice. But the thought of being in that space without Oliver was unbearable. I could already imagine the loneliness of it, a place devoid of conversation or the soft sounds of companionship. Instead, I started toward the cliffs, heading right into the danger. It felt like giving Oliver the middle finger. *You're not really gone. You wouldn't just leave like that, and I'll prove it. If you no longer exist in this world, then the lightning has no reason to spare me.*

Thankfully, my feet had gone numb, and I felt no pain as I reached the drop where Oliver had stood so many times. The sea waited below, lapping against the rocks. The water had lost its welcoming loveliness and transformed into something forebodingly beautiful. Like whatever lurked in those depths no longer had to hide.

But the sea didn't hold my attention long—seconds after I stopped at the edge, a strange pattern of light shone across the world. I lifted my head and frowned at the horizon. There were bright, fragmented lines spreading in every direction, breaking up the roiling clouds. I'd never seen them before, here or anywhere else. I tried to come up with a reasonable explanation. There were none.

As I watched the lines spread, revealing a strange blend of galaxies and sunsets on the other side, it became painfully clear this was no storm. *The dreamscape is coming apart,* I realized with a creeping sense of horror. I turned, following the progress of those star-filled fissures.

Something else moved in the distance. A tall, familiar figure with golden hair. He was walking away, his back to me. Joy expanded in my chest and I rushed toward him without thinking, his name rising to my lips. I was on the verge of saying it, hopefully stopping Oliver in his tracks, when a random burst of sunlight fell upon him. I caught sight of a winged shadow on the ground and reared back, a scream hurtling up my throat.

Oliver was wrong. The shadow hadn't left the dreamscape with its maker.

And now I was completely alone with it.

Before I could take another step, the sky cracked open—there was no other way to describe it. Rain hit the ground, almost violent in the din it made. Pieces of colorful twilight fell, crashing to the ground with such force that it exploded. I went flying, and I slammed into the tree that Oliver and I had created countless memories beneath. Pain vibrated down my spine.

There was no time to acknowledge it—the shadow had noticed me now. Its face twisted in dark, naked want. It started running in my direction with the mindless grace of a predator. Breathing hard, I scrambled up and bolted, unintentionally moving away from the cottage and the sea. I didn't have a plan or a single thought in my head, only panic and instinct. Water poured into my eyes and the ground was already slick with mud, but I didn't slow or hesitate.

The shadow moved even faster than last time, and I didn't register it was on me until too late.

It grabbed my arm with iron fingers, and my choices were to swing around or lose the arm. Just as I lost my footing and nearly stumbled into the shadow's chest, I saw something else move in my peripheral vision. Too late, I raised my hand in an attempt to block it—the rock in the shadow's fist collided with my skull.

Pain crackled through me and the ground rushed upward. Everything went dark, then I was blinking at the chaotic mass that used to be a peaceful sky. Lightning flashed, brightening the dreamscape like a strobe light. The shadow's face appeared over mine, etched into an impatient scowl. I couldn't speak or think about anything beyond the throbbing in my head. The shadow bent down and lifted me as though I weighed nothing.

Like a dripping painting, the colors of the dreamscape blended together. An acrid taste filled my mouth. I made a strange sound, something between a groan and a croak, and the shadow shifted in such a way that I knew it was about to throw me over its shoulder.

"No... don't..." I managed just before it did exactly that. Vomit surged through my body and spewed into the grass, leaving a burning sensation in its wake. The shadow didn't even falter.

I was too weak to struggle, even when the creature threw me down. I didn't feel the landing—darkness hovered at the edges of my vision, and I welcomed it. It meant I would wake up on the other side of reality and live to fight another day.

To my dismay, the darkness retreated instead, and the real world danced just out of reach. *Time for Plan B, then.* I pried my eyes open, knowing the shadow was probably near. Nausea immediately rocked through me and I slammed them back shut. I focused on breathing, gradual inhales and deep exhales. Once it was safe to try again, I opened my eyes, more slowly this time.

I was in the cottage. Wind howled against the windows and walls, but they seemed to be holding. There were random objects floating in the air, though, signaling that the dreamscape was still coming undone. An unused paintbrush drifted over me just as the shadow finished securing both my ankles to the bedposts. Why did it keep tying me up?

All at once, I realized what it was trying to do, what it had been trying to do the first chance it got—Oliver's shadow wanted me to stay. Inside this creature's rudimentary mind, if it restrained me, I wouldn't be able to go anywhere. All I had to do was wake myself up and I'd be out of its reach. If that didn't work, I just had to lay here until morning. I'd been through much worse.

But then the shadow reached for my wrist, a rope dangling from its fingers, and my delicate thread of control snapped. I grabbed the back of its neck, tucked my chin, and smashed the shadow's face with the crown of my head. It tumbled to the floor, more surprised than hurt, I thought. Seizing my chance, I dove for the ropes around my ankles and frantically yanked at the knots.

The shadow didn't try to stop me. It got to its feet, swaying slightly, and went into the kitchen. I got my right leg free and started on the left. I could hear the shadow rummaging in cupboards and drawers. *What the hell is it looking for?* The knots felt looser. My efforts grew more frenzied.

The shadow must've found what it was looking for—it went still and stared down into a drawer. I was so panicked that my breath came in gasps. One of the knots wouldn't cooperate. I started scraping at it with my nails, and when that didn't work, I wrenched my leg with whatever strength I had left. The rope came loose as the shadow finally turned around, and something in its hand caught the light. When I realized it was a knife, time seemed to slow.

"You're part of Oliver, so I know you don't want to hurt me," I told the creature calmly, holding out my hands. I spoke in the same tone I'd used with the fox. Low and soft, with a slight lilt. The shadow cocked its head and took a step closer. The movement sent a jolt of panic through me. Without thinking, I moved my legs to the side and stood up. The shadow didn't like that—it hissed and came at me like an enormous bat.

I reacted purely on instinct, throwing my hand out just as Dad taught me when I was eight years old. The shadow collided into it, and I heard something *crunch*. The sound that came out of its mouth, a combination of pain and rage, was far more disarming. The shadow stumbled away, holding its face. Adrenaline coursed through me, pushing out the pain, and suddenly I could think clearly again. This creature felt fear, I'd seen it. I may not have tried Lyari's theory out on Gwyn... but there was nothing to stop me from trying now. There was no time for hesitation. In the next breath, I closed my eyes and delved into its mind.

Silence. Untainted, beautiful silence. I could no longer hear the walls of the cottage, moaning in the wind, or the unnatural shuffling sound the shadow made instead of footsteps. I moved forward, wanting to be in the most hidden part of this thing's mind. The secret places, the dark corners, these were where everyone hid anything worth finding.

It was also where everyone was their most vulnerable.

I'd just stepped into a darker patch of smoke when pain ripped through me. I left the shadow's mind so violently that an instant headache took hold. But I barely noticed it—I was too busy staring down at the knife sticking out of my stomach. Shock roared in my ears. The heat radiating from the wound was like nothing I'd experienced before. It felt like I was on fire.

Slowly, I lifted my head. The shadow and I stared at each other, and I saw my betrayed expression reflected back in those eerily familiar eyes. Oliver had made it seem like his shadow would never harm me. No, that wasn't all he'd told me, was it? I struggled to remember his exact words. *It's like an animal—its instincts are primal*, he had said.

I attacked it, and the shadow had defended itself.

Now I knew that it was willing to draw blood. It was willing to inflict suffering. I wasn't interested in finding out what else Oliver's shadow was capable of.

I was about to run when the room tipped. No, that was me tipping. I fell to the floor in a graceless heap, and the movement made the knife go deeper inside me. I gasped—the pain was a star-bright burst in my head, making me blind to everything else—and reached for the hilt instinctively. *No, wait. You don't want to do that.* If the knife was removed, I would bleed out. I was cold now. Why was I so cold?

The shadow knelt beside me, and once again, ropes materialized in its hands. As it started looping them around my wrists, the rest of my body shook. I knew I needed to wake up. What if I died here? Would I die in my world, too? The rules of the dreamscape were changing, and whatever happened now could affect reality. I wasn't in a gambling mood. Ignoring another burst of pain, I squeezed my eyes shut and willed myself back to consciousness. I felt the shadow securing a rope around my ankles. Just as I had with Oliver, I repeated the words to myself. *Wake up, wake up, wake up.*

The shadow slid its arms beneath my knees and my back. I didn't struggle when it lifted me from the floor—I held onto the silent rhythm I'd built. Two words, two syllables. It felt like a second heartbeat. Like a song in my veins. *Wake up, wake up, wake up.*

It didn't work. I felt the shadow place me on the bed yet again, and the chant deteriorated completely. *Get me out of here!* I thought in a soundless scream. I didn't know who could save me or who I was calling to.

But someone answered.

As the shadow moved away—I heard the whisper-soft sounds it made crossing the room—a presence came out of the darkness. Another mind. At first, I thought it was the shadow's, and a bolt of terror went through me. *Why are you here?* I thought wildly, bracing myself for battle.

I heard you, a young voice said. *You cried out for help.*

Before I could say anything else, the presence drew closer, and I realized she'd given me access to her mind. This was unheard of for any Fallen creature, much less a faerie. I still didn't know who she was, but I could sense the female's immortality, radiating from her like sunlight. *Take it,* I heard her say.

Take what? I was about to say back. But then I felt a power that wasn't mine, easing through my veins like a drug. Suddenly I knew. Though I couldn't see her face, I recognized her essence, somehow—it was the young faerie that had come before me with her father. Daratrine. She'd been raped by an arrogant courtier, and I made sure he would never hurt anyone else. *You're only a victim if you let them break you*, I'd told her that night.

And she hadn't let him—the faerie sharing minds with me was no victim. She was afraid, yes, but this didn't stop her from doing what she thought was right. She wanted to help the beautiful queen that had believed her when few others would.

How was this possible? Hadn't the bond between me and the Unseelie Court broken when Gwyn drowned me?

Right now, none of that mattered. In the way of physical power, Daratrine didn't have much. Even the little she offered, though, was significant when added to mine. Others must've been able to hear her, as well, because it became a chorus in my head. *Take it. Take it. Take it.* Numerous faeries offered up their power to me, filled me up with it, until I felt like a glass overflowing with rich wine. Not all, of course—I could sense my enemies at Court, too, exalting in the pain they sensed in me— but more than I would've expected.

After a few seconds, I came back to myself, heady with the amount of magic in my veins. My eyes felt like saucers as I sat up in the bed.

The shadow was coming toward me again. I didn't know what it had been doing—its hands were empty—but there was intention in its eyes. Dark, dark intention. I knew I was supposed to be frightened. It was difficult to think about anything beyond the delicious haze of euphoria, invincibility, and power. God, the power. No wonder He cast us out when we tried to take some of His for ourselves. I didn't want to part with this, not even for a moment. Already I mourned the inevitable end of my Court's generosity.

Is this what heroin feels like? I wondered distantly as I struggled to focus.

The bedsprings didn't make a sound as the shadow started crawling toward me. This small, almost insignificant detail shone like a beacon, shining through the fog in my mind. In that moment, I knew why my abilities hadn't slowed the shadow down the night I tried to frighten it with water. *Fortuna, you fool.* My certainty was so overwhelming that it crowded out any revulsion or fear. Moving with the speed of the fae, I grabbed the shadow's head, bunching its golden hair between my fingers.

The shadow had broken free of my compulsion because I'd been wrong—the opposite of smoke wasn't water. It was stone. Solid, touchable, corporal stone, while everything of smoke slipped through your fingers and into the air. Fresh with energy and resolve, I filled my mind with the image of a boulder.

The borrowed power, still filling me like the most blissful of highs, responded eagerly. *Stone, stone, stone*, I chanted. No longer trying to escape, no longer running, but finding something. Accepting it. Learning how to use it. God, it felt so good, as though I'd been fighting a shadow of my own and now, at long last, the war was over.

Thankfully, Oliver's shadow was not so strong—the second I entered its psyche, it went still between my hands. *Stone, stone, stone*, I thought, almost dreamily. Daratrine took up the rhythm, even if she had no way of understanding its purpose. I heard others, too. There was so much power flowing between us, it felt like a deep, rushing river. One misstep and I could get swept away. But, like drifting to death within a siren's arms, I would drown smiling.

As the chorus and the river went on, my sense of self utterly faded. *Stone, stone, stone.* The world became blinding, searing power. I was stone and stone was me. It spread through my limbs and my hand. Covered my skin like ice over water.

When I opened my eyes, slowly, feeling drunk on the magic, I found myself staring at a statue.

It was chilling, seeing my best friend's face frozen in an expression of such desire and fury. Cracks ran through its soundless scream. Despite this, it still looked *alive*. Sitting there, our faces inches apart, I hardly dared to breathe. Doubt trickled in. What if it didn't work? What if the shadow broke free again?

Maybe, as an extra precaution, I should put more power into the shadow. Reenforce the cage we'd put it in. *Daratrine*, I thought. There was an eagerness in my voice that startled me. I ignored it and tried to feel for her in my head. *Where are you?*

But her presence was gone. Her voice didn't sound through the darkness. I was about to try again when a new, inexplicable pain shot up my arm. Before I could react, the dreamscape fell away in a colorful *whoosh*.

I opened my eyes in the real world and instantly saw the source of what had woken me—Finn stared with his bright, golden eyes, his face so close to mine that I could see the delicate lines in his irises. His teeth were buried in my hand. Not hard enough to draw blood, but enough that it was uncomfortable. There was a strange light in his eyes, and it took me another beat to comprehend that it was a reflection of my own.

They were shining bright, bright red.

"It's okay, I'm okay," I said. But my voice was weak and there was doubt in Finn's gaze. Still, he released his hold on me, revealing the indents his teeth had left in my skin.

It felt like part of me was still trapped in the dreamscape. To reassure myself, I glanced down at my stomach, where there was no knife jutting out, then around the room. Everything was solid and familiar. There was no sign of Collith, though—maybe he'd had a nightmare of his own.

I sat up, pressing against the mattress for leverage, and realized the sheets were drenched in sweat. I cringed and eased down the bed, into a spot that was cool and dry. Finn watched me, his eyes tracking every single movement, and there was something about his silence that felt expectant. Finn didn't ask questions, but he was asking now. Maybe he could smell my terror, sense how real it was. This had been no ordinary nightmare.

To my surprise, I wanted to tell him. We may not have known each other long, but in that short time, we'd become friends. And something told me there was nothing I could say to Finn that would change that. I tangled my fingers together and took a brief, fortifying breath. "When my parents—"

"Fortuna? Is everything all right?"

The door creaked open and Collith filled the doorway. He held a glass of water in his hand. Finn took this as a cue to slip away, moving quietly for something so large. Collith approached the bed, but instead of sliding between the sheets, he stopped and studied me. I put my hand on my throat in an instinctive gesture, protecting myself, guarding the secrets inside me. As always, Collith saw too much. His gaze went to my hand, where there were probably imprints from Finn's teeth, and to my forehead, where beads of sweat had gathered as I slept. As the silence stretched, I thought of the conversation I'd had with Bea on the day of my panic attack, and remembered how freeing it had been to tell her the truth. No more pretending. No more masks.

Are you all right?

No.

Even though Finn had left, it was still going to be a night for the truth. I angled my body toward Collith and let out a breath. "I want to tell you about Oliver."

His expression didn't change. Collith set down his water— the gentle sound it made felt loud in the stillness—and got in bed. Then he looked at me with those hazel eyes and said, "Okay."

I paused to gather courage… and then I told him. I told him all of it. About the first time I'd dreamed of Oliver, about the parade of child psychologists, about the changes in our friendship as time went on, and finally, about the shadow creature that had almost killed me tonight.

Collith just listened. Once in a while, he interjected with a question. There was no judgment in his tone, no hint of disbelief in his face. I tangled my fingers together on the bedspread as I spoke. By the time I finished, it seemed as though hours had gone by. But the sky outside the window was dark. I waited for Collith to react. Was he disgusted I had been in love with someone that wasn't even real? Did he think I was insane? I felt my heartbeat in my throat, a feathery and frantic rhythm, like a hummingbird's wings.

Startling me, Collith pressed a soft kiss to my forehead. As he leaned back, his breath cooled my cheek. "I think you're one of the bravest people I've ever known," he murmured.

There was no hint of judgment in his expression. Was I still asleep? Was Collith another creation I'd dreamed up? It just didn't seem possible he was real. Emotion lodged in my throat. I couldn't speak, even if I wanted to. But I had run out of words anyway, and there were gray smudges beneath Collith's eyes. The demon may have returned his soul into a restored body, but it hadn't done anything to heal Collith's mind. And that mind was slowly killing him with memories of Hell. Faeries were only immortal because they had willed it into being—they could undo it if they were determined enough.

Trying to hide a sudden twinge of fear, I lowered myself to the mattress and tugged at Collith so he'd do the same. As though we'd done it a thousand times before, he laid down and curved his body along mine. His cool skin was a whisper of relief against me, my body still hot with adrenaline from my nightmare. Within minutes, he was asleep. His chest moved against my back in steady, deep breaths. I waited for sleep to come for me, as well, but it didn't.

The moon rose higher and higher. Long into the night, I stayed in the circle of Collith's arms, staring at the wall. I should've been thinking about the Unseelie Court and figuring out how those faeries had been able to help me without a bond. Instead, my mind relived that moment, again and again, when all that power rushed through me. I didn't know if I'd ever be able to forget it.

But there was one thing I did know.

I wanted more.

CHAPTER TWENTY-THREE

I didn't go back to the dreamscape. My mind wasn't overrun by nightmares. Instead, my sleep was dark and dreamless. For the first time in as long as I could remember, I slept like a normal person, and I passed the night nestled contentedly against Collith.

Then, when I woke up, I realized that I had nowhere to be.

No shift at Bea's, no appointment with Consuelo, no dinner or meeting at Court. It meant that I could spend the entire day with Collith, and we could make the sort of memories normal couples had.

I promptly fell back asleep.

An hour later, Collith woke ravenous and declared that he was making pancakes. The kitchen was already fully stocked, of course, because he never did anything halfway. Wearing faded jeans that hung low on his hips, Collith filled a mixing bowl with the confidence of someone who had done it countless times before. Music floated upward from his phone, a folk song that I'd never heard before.

Clad only in the button-up shirt Collith had worn yesterday, I perched on a stool and found myself watching more than helping. There was a window behind the Unseelie King, and sunlight streamed through the glass, landing on his bare skin and sleep-tousled hair. As I stared, he glanced up at me, probably feeling the weight of my gaze. He smiled, flashing perfect teeth, and a dimple deepened in his unscarred cheek. He'd never looked more human.

Three words ballooned in my heart. Three syllables formed on my tongue. They seemed so small, so simple, but I knew they would change me. Collith refocused on his mixing bowl, singing along to the music, and I searched for the courage to say them out loud. A minute passed, then two, and I swallowed the words back down. *Another day,* I told myself. We would have plenty more.

Or so I believed.

As Collith poured the batter onto a griddle, I lazily flicked flour at his face. He looked at me—his eyes were more green than hazel, in the morning light—and went still. "Don't start what you can't finish," he warned, then launched himself at me. I squealed and ran. Our laughter floated through the sun-dappled air and the music from his phone played on.

While light crossed the sky, we filled every hour with each other. We took a shower and explored our bodies beneath the stream of hot water. We watched a movie on Netflix—or, more accurately, turned it on and made out through every important scene. We played a game of pool and, halfway through, shoved the balls aside to make love on top of the table.

And I filled my phone with pictures.

The two of us only parted when I left to collect my belongings from the other house. When I walked past carrying such a large box, Emma's curiosity was piqued. She followed me back to the barn and visited briefly, wanting to see the results of Collith's work, but she was the only one. Not even Lyari or Finn made an appearance. It was as if they'd all agreed to let us be, as if they knew something was changing, and Collith and I needed distance during the transition.

We made tacos and margaritas for dinner. I didn't know if it was the lovemaking or the fact that I'd had an entire day free of terror or scheming, but I ate even more than Collith did. We sat at the brand-new dining table he'd ordered, with enough seats to accommodate eight people, and a Mariachi band played from Collith's phone now. Unlike other meals I'd shared with an attractive male, there wasn't a single awkward pause—Collith never seemed to run out of questions. When we weren't talking about me, my co-ruler displayed a vast array of knowledge I hadn't known he cared about, from human politics to U.S. history. Shakespeare to environmental concerns.

We were both careful not to speak of Naevys or the fact that Collith hadn't yet returned to Court. And I was careful not to wonder about how the Unseelie Court had lent me their power during my confrontation with Oliver's shadow.

At some point toward the end of the evening, I took a sip from my margarita and laughed. Collith raised his eyebrows. "What's so funny?"

I shrugged and took another bite. "I just had the thought, 'I'm eating tacos with the King of the Unseelie Court.' If someone had told me a few months ago..."

My mirth faded as I realized that I hadn't mentioned Mercy's Telling yet. But how accurate was a vision from some ancient spell? Would talking about it somehow change our course? The thought of never holding that baby again... never hearing the soft sounds she made as she slept...

Unaware of the abrupt shift in my mood, Collith made a contemplative sound. He put his plate in the dishwasher, rinsed his hands in the sink, and faced me again. His palms rested flat on the counter. "You're going to be doing other things with the King of the Unseelie Court as soon as you finish that," he informed me, his voice a notch deeper than usual.

And just like that, I was done eating.

Our perfect day came to an end when, later that night, I woke drenched in sweat.

I didn't know what had yanked me back to consciousness—I hadn't gone to the dreamscape and I couldn't remember a nightmare. Swallowing a whimper, I sat up to escape the damp sheets. Beside me, Collith slept on, his eyelashes a dark fringe against his pale cheeks. I stared at him, admiring the curves and planes of his face, and something in my chest loosened. Breathing became easier. I started to lay back down, but just then, something moved beyond the window. I shot upright, hoping it was a tree branch or an animal.

No. There was someone standing in the front yard.

I was getting really, really tired of these mysterious visitors. I knew it wasn't Gwyn or Mercy—the silhouette was unmistakably male. The moonlight wasn't strong enough to make out his face. What if it was another assassin? Or maybe Dracula, coming to say his goodbyes, as well? For a few seconds, I debated whether to wake Collith.

I need to speak with you, a voice said.

I let out a breath and the tension eased from my body—I recognized that severe tone. He'd used the bond between us to communicate, and I felt his presence as I had felt Daratrine's. He radiated resentment and impatience, but not malicious intent. The sense of paranoia clinging to me melted like frost on a window.

Give me a few seconds, I replied. My visitor remained silent.

With painstaking movements, I slid out of Collith's arms and retrieved a sweatshirt from a box of clothes. It smelled like him, a scent akin to a crisp autumn, and as it settled into place I already knew Collith wouldn't be getting it back. I also found a clean pair of jeans in the box. Well, clean enough.

Near the stairwell, my boots lay abandoned in a pool of melted snow. I yanked them on and hurried through the doorway. Downstairs, the lights were on, and yellow light bounced off the concrete floor. Collith had probably left them on intentionally, in the event Finn came to find me.

Gravel crunched under my boots. Within a few steps, the ground changed to snow. I lifted my head, sending swirls of breath through the air, and searched for that dim figure. My visitor was standing under a tree, his face cast into shadow. His dreadlocks had been tied back, as though he were ready for battle, and his arms were bared to the elements.

I knew I sounded exasperated as I started, "Nuvian, what are—"

"Viessa has summoned you," he cut in, keeping his amber eyes fixed on my forehead.

At this, my eyebrows knitted together. I searched Nuvian's expression as if I'd find an explanation in his permanent scowl or hate-filled gaze. "Since when are *you* her messenger boy? What is this?"

"You are in no danger. That's all that matters. Come." The tall faerie stepped aside, casually resting a hand on the hilt of his sword.

I glanced down at it, frowning, then looked over my shoulder. Maybe it was time to wake Finn or Collith. "Fine. Wait here while I—"

"Viessa would like to speak with you alone."

His tone was pointed, indicating he knew exactly what I'd been about to do. Was I that obvious? My eyes narrowed and I took a step back. "I'm not going anywhere without backup," I told him flatly.

"Have I not saved your life a dozen times over?" the faerie demanded. As he spoke, his gaze finally snapped to mine. The clouds shifted, then, and faint moonlight bounced off those dreadlocks now. I could see Nuvian's expression better, too. From the curl of his lip, I'd clearly insulted him again. He *had* saved my life, it was true. But what I found more interesting was that Viessa must've been holding something over his head— the Right Hand of the Unseelie King didn't just run errands for a prisoner from the goodness of his heart.

It was curiosity, and the desire to placate the individual keeping me alive, that made me ignore my misgivings. After a backward glance toward the room where Collith slept, I followed Nuvian into the night.

There were more Guardians waiting near the trees. They fell ahead and behind me, their swords and armor making slight sounds in the quiet. Nuvian remained at my side. Neither of us spoke, and it was a different silence than the one I shared with Lyari—this one was thick and cold, like there was a sheet of ice between us. I thought back to the moment I'd used Nuvian's fears against him, and I wondered if it had been a mistake. Too often, the line between power and decency blurred, and I always seemed to be standing on the wrong side when they solidified again.

Once we arrived at the entrance to the Unseelie Court, I didn't delay or falter, and the darkness welcomed me like an old friend. The deeper we moved into the tunnel, the more I could feel every creature beneath my rule, like faint lights at the edge of my mind—something had changed when they helped me last night. Despite the absence of a bond, some extended greetings in images or thoughts. As the picture of a rose bouquet floated through me, I felt an unexpected rush of fondness toward them. When had I begun to care about these creatures? How had they slipped beneath the steel plates I'd built around my heart? And how the hell could I still feel them?

I was frowning again as we made our way through the maze. Nuvian offered wordless guidance, nodding or gesturing when- ever we came to a fork. We had been traversing the shadows for fifteen minutes, at least, by the time he halted at a familiar gap in the earth. The golden-haired faerie stood back, waiting for me to walk ahead of him. Remembering my last visit, I stopped to remove one of the torches from its sconce. With a grip as tight as I usually gripped the Glock, I held it aloft and began my descent.

Nuvian followed so closely that I could've reached behind and touched him. The rest of the Guardians must have remained in the passageway, because I could only hear my footsteps. Nuvian, of course, moved soundlessly. Within seconds, a smell assailed my senses. It was a combination of urine, shit, and unwashed bodies. I grimaced but continued down the narrow, uneven steps.

At the bottom, I paused to gather my composure. Faint moans drifted up and down the passageway. Someone was sobbing. Though I'd visited the dungeon several times now, I still thought of that terrible night after I'd been whipped by Death Bringer and vowed to despise Collith forever. So much had changed since then—everything had changed. Including me. I lifted my chin and walked past the seemingly endless row of prisoners. This time I needed no help from Nuvian.

I stopped several feet away from the cell, as if distance between us could protect me from what was coming. I faced its murky depths, and I knew this was the right cage, but there was no sign of the would-be assassin. She was playing with me, no doubt. My voice was harsh in my own ears as I snapped, "Well?"

There came the sound of feet shuffling over stone and dirt. A moment later, Viessa stepped into the light.

She looked different from the last time we'd spoken—someone had been feeding her far better. Her bones no longer jutted from her skin and her pupils, such a pale blue they were nearly white, regarded me with bright anticipation. Bare toes peeked out from the hem of a new gown, which clung to her supple frame. Despite the frost that still coated half her face, the faerie's loveliness shone through. It had been there all along, but I'd been distracted by the words coming out of her mouth and the strange manifestation of her abilities. Now I noticed the graceful lines of her nose, jaw, and brows, the perfection of her features like something out of a painting. I could understand why Collith had fallen in love with this creature, and I hoped she didn't detect the stab of jealousy that pierced me.

"I believe you've met my brother," Viessa said without preamble. Her voice was stronger, too.

"Brother?" I repeated blankly. It took me another second to realize she meant Nuvian, who returned my bewildered stare without expression. As I faced Viessa again, I realized that I'd never asked what bloodline she was from.

No wonder Nuvian had protected me so diligently against the assassination attempts, despite his obvious hatred. If Viessa was ever to get her boon, she needed the Unseelie Queen alive. It was also why he'd never asked questions about Ayduin's disappearance—if I was held accountable for murdering a faerie without a tribunal, after he'd broken no laws, I probably wouldn't have held the throne long.

A small, satisfied smile hovered around Viessa's frozen lips. "Yes, of course. He's the one who made certain you were put in the cell next to mine, so we could have our little chat."

What a fool I'd been. What a complete and utter fool. I'd actually thought Viessa was a rare breed of faerie, one who offered honesty and help without some hidden agenda. But she was just like so many others I'd encountered—always tricking and scheming. Lying and using.

"Why did you summon me here?" I asked with barely-suppressed rage. All I wanted to do was throw myself forward, bury my nails into her bare arm, and send her screaming into terror's dark embrace.

"Well, the time has come, Your Majesty." Viessa gripped the bars with her blackened fingers. "All my pieces are in place. I would like to collect the debt owed to me."

"What do you want?" I asked. Wariness joined the anger, now—it hovered beneath the surface of my voice like the dragon I'd slaughtered, its great shape moving through black waters.

Viessa tilted her head and a curtain of red hair fell over her delicate shoulder. "Isn't it obvious? I want the throne. You're going to publicly abdicate and show your support for my rule."

She truly thought I would just hand over the Unseelie Court to her? An incredulous laugh lodged in my throat. "I told you I would only grant a boon that—"

"Unfortunately, you still have much to learn about the fae," she told me matter-of-factly. "You never specified that you'd only grant a boon you were *willing* to. Wording is a tricky art. I'd advise you to master it."

The faerie paused, probably giving me a chance to consider her request, but I didn't need to. *Sorry, Dad,* I thought. This was one promise I couldn't keep. Without another word, I turned to leave. Nuvian didn't move to stop me—he probably recognized the expression on my face.

"Don't you dare walk away from me! That throne is *owed* to us, damn it!" Viessa hissed. When I turned back, I saw that she'd pushed her face against the bars. Ice spread over the metal and glittered in the firelight.

I kept my face expressionless as I asked, "What makes you think you have any right to the throne?"

Viessa drew back and loosened her hold on the bars. It was as though a mask fell over her face. Within seconds, the faerie looking back at me was calm once again. "It was written that in the event of Sylvyre's death, the crown would go to his twin Folduin," she said. "But the bastard snuck in an addendum—he wrote that only his descendants would rule. It was his final 'fuck you' to his brother."

My humorless laugh echoed down the black corridor. "Faeries suck. Welcome to my world. It still isn't enough to make me betray my mate."

"How interesting. My sources inform me he is your mate no

longer, and that he is very much alive. Did you lovebirds miss the 'until death do us part' portion of the vows?"

"Your sources," I echoed faintly. I must've reacted to her comment in some other way, because the other female smiled. I felt hollow as I considered who had known about the broken mating bond. There were only a few possibilities. Who had betrayed me? Betrayed Collith? Viessa was talking again, her dulcet tones floating through the dark, and I forced myself to refocus on her.

"...for the best, of course." Viessa gave a mock shudder. "I'm assuming he told you about his... collection. So parasitic. Like a leech."

Don't take the bait, Fortuna. Don't fall for her tricks. I stood there for a moment, trying to find the strength to walk away. Instead I heard myself ask, "What are you talking about?"

Triumph flashed in her eyes, and I could have kicked myself. Still playing with me like a child with a toy, Viessa arched a brow. "You didn't ask him? No, of course you did. Silly me. Collith excels at dancing around the truth."

"And what is the truth?" I demanded, stepping closer in my impatience. I knew I was giving her exactly what she wanted, damn it, but I couldn't stop myself.

Viessa didn't crook a finger, and it was probably because she knew the gleam in her eyes was just as effective. Her voice lowered, as though she were telling me a delicious secret. "Every time Collith has sex, he takes a piece of his partner," she whispered through the bars. "Just a tiny piece. You hardly would've noticed its absence."

My mind took a beat to process her words, then another laugh rose to my lips. I could already hear it, echoing in the tunnel around us, scornful and dismissive. *Lies. More lies. That's all your kind does.* Slowly, though, the laugh died and the disbelief wavered. Viessa's revelation replayed through memory, then replayed again. I began to consider the unthinkable.

What if she was actually telling the truth?

It felt like someone had shoved their hand through my chest and wrapped their hand around my heart. Tight, too tight. I heard Collith's voice now, entwining with the shadows of his bedroom, claiming me like a spell. *Some faeries have a... specialty. A certain power or ability unique from others.*

What's yours? I had asked.

He never answered.

A new suspicion took root now, and every word I spoke was a drop of water, making it grow and grow. My mind flashed back to that strange moment in the barn.

But I was just in here, and it didn't look like this.

An illusion. I didn't want to spoil the surprise.

An illusion?

Holy shit. The day we'd met, Collith had disappeared in a theatrical gust of leaves. I had just assumed it was a fae trick, but there were limits to what they could do, same as every other species. I should've questioned his abilities then and there.

"That's how he has so much power," I said out loud. "The heavenly fire... Laurie's illusions... the sifting..."

I trailed off as I fit even more pieces together. Suddenly I understood, at long last, why Laurie had tried to kill the Unseelie King, resulting in that jagged scar. *Collith stole his power.* Then, in typical fae fashion, Laurie tried to exact his revenge with a terrible spell. Sylvyre, of course, had double-crossed him and used it on Naevys. Too many tricky faeries. Too many twisted games.

Even if you win, you don't win, Collith had told me once upon a time. At least he'd been truthful about one thing.

It struck me, suddenly, that Collith was a Nightmare now.

Viessa was silent—she'd said all she needed to. I stared at her lovely, glittering face without really seeing it. My insides roiled and now I was the one gripping the bars. It felt as if they were all that held me upright. This was a pain I'd never experienced before. Different from the night I'd looked down at my butchered parents. Different from the morning I realized Damon was missing. Different from the days I'd spent starving and sleepless in the goblins' cabin. Different from the hour I'd been tied to those tree roots and whipped. Different, even, from that pain-drenched night when I'd traded my virginity for Collith's life.

I'd known there was more to his offer of marriage than desire.

And yet... I had chosen to trust him anyway. I allowed myself to fall, even though I'd known the floor was concrete. These past few days, secret daydreams had flitted through my head, visions of a future I'd never dared to hope for before. More mornings with him, filled with freshly-made coffee and making love in slants of sunlight. More evenings with him, sitting next to each other at the kitchen table, aware of every brush of our knees while the rest of the family talked around us. And, eventually, the arrival of the daughter Mercy had shown me in her spell.

It was an entire life. Together.

All of those daydreams shriveled like a dying flower, until nothing remained but dry and colorless petals.

I knew Viessa was watching the parade of emotions march across my face. I forced my mind back to the present, and I realized I was blinking rapidly, as if every torch around us had gone out and we were sitting in the dark. Viessa was offering this information up without anything in return... but that didn't mean it was free. She was a faerie, after all. She wanted to drive a wedge between us. Wanted me to hate him.

Well, it worked. I didn't even care that I was playing right into her hands. I raised my head and met Viessa's pale gaze. My voice was as cold as her skin. "You want the throne? Tell me what to do and I'll do it."

I expected another flash of triumph or a cruel smile. Instead,

I thought I caught a glimpse of pity in her eyes. But there was nothing in her voice as she said, "It's simple. Be at the throne room tomorrow night. Eight o'clock. My followers will assemble the entire Court, and once we have their full attention, I will require a display from you that rejects both Collith and your queenship. Oh, and I will need you to persuade him to join us."

"Does Nuvian have a key for your cell?" I asked dully.

The faerie waved an emaciated hand. "Never mind that. It's all been arranged."

"I do have one condition," I said. Viessa had begun to turn away, and at my words, she paused with a quirked brow. I looked at her and did nothing to hide the ruthlessness that lived in my heart. "Don't undo the only good thing I did as queen. Don't bring back the slave trade."

For a moment, Viessa said nothing. Her expression didn't change, but there was something behind her eyes, a light of calculation and cunning. When I saw that, I knew she would be a powerful queen. Whether or not she would be a good one was yet to be seen. "Very well," she said at last.

"Not good enough, I'm afraid. I would like a blood oath." She inclined her head in silent agreement, and I turned to Nuvian. In the same lifeless tone I asked, "Do you have a knife?"

"You don't need a knife," Viessa interjected. I looked back at her and caught the end of an assessing look, as though I'd surprised her. She thrust her arm through the bars. Icicles grew from her palm like a dozen needles. She watched my face, probably expecting to see hesitation or wariness. But I didn't flinch as I took her hand—this pain was nothing.

The usurper's voice was startlingly sincere as she said the words. "I, Viessa of the bloodline Folduin, swear an oath to keep slaves out of the Unseelie Court for the entirety of my rule."

She tried to pull away once she was finished, but I held on tighter. Viessa's eyes met mine in a soundless question. My chest felt hollow as I told her, "If you try to find a loophole or break your oath, I will come back and slaughter you, along with everyone you love. Am I being clear enough, or shall I provide some imagery?"

Though she tried to hide it, fear crawled into Viessa's eyes. Good. She wasn't a fool, then. "You are perfectly clear," she answered.

With those words, it felt like something inside me shifted. Like I'd turned the final page of a book or the curtains had closed after the last act. I let go of Viessa's icy hand and drifted away. My boots felt heavier, suddenly, and it took all my concentration to lift them, again and again, and get up the stairs.

"Where are you going?" I heard her call after me. The question went unanswered, lingering in the darkness like a restless spirit. The truth was, I didn't know.

Some part of me was aware of Nuvian and the other Guardians following my progress. I wandered through the passageways—the same ones I'd once run through in mindless terror—and stopped in front of a door. The door to Collith's rooms, I realized distantly. It opened with a light push, and the hinges creaked as I shuffled inside. Unlike the first time I stepped into this place, there wasn't a welcoming fire in the grate. It had probably been that way for a while, but I hadn't noticed until now. *No one to start one, I guess.* The thought put a strange smile on my lips. I moved through the cold, alone now, since Nuvian and the others had stayed in the tunnel.

I ended up in Collith's small library. The air smelled like old paper and dust. There was a wistful, forgotten feeling about the furniture, as if the reading chair and the shelves longed for their owner's return. Slowly, I grasped one of the books by its spine and pulled it out. Agatha Christie. I recalled the first time I'd seen these books and realized there was more to the Unseelie King than met the eye.

There was a high-pitched ringing in my ears. Power hummed in my veins. It wanted to get out. It wanted to latch onto someone. It wanted to *feed*.

I didn't linger long in the king's rooms—they held nothing for me but memories and pain. I looked at the bed and saw myself lying there with Collith, beginning to trust him against my better judgment. I saw the wardrobe and thought of all the gowns it housed, costumes for the role I'd been playing all these long weeks to buy Collith more time. I saw the desk, the fireplace, and the chairs and relived the night we'd read together, giving me a glimpse of the life we could've had.

When I entered the passageway again, I started toward the surface more out of habit than any real decision to do so. Torches quivered as I passed. Dry earth crunched underfoot. The Guardians followed at a distance, as if they could sense that hungry power inside me. I stopped at the mouth of the tunnel, and only then did Nuvian dare to approach me. Slowly, I turned to face him. "I want to be alone," I said with a voice that didn't sound like mine.

Strangely enough, the Guardian didn't utter a word of argument. I saw my face reflected in his eyes, and I almost didn't recognize it. The creature looking back at me was void of anything resembling humanity. She was death incarnate and rage personified. I put my back to her, to Nuvian and the others, and moved into the sleeping forest.

I walked for hours. With every step, I gathered the darkness of the Unseelie Court to me. The bond to them was still broken, but that didn't matter—something had crumbled in me, or been unlocked, and now it had overtaken all the rest. I feasted on their anger. Their pain. Their cravings. The sun crested the tree-filled horizon, erroneously radiant and hopeful.

At long last, I arrived at the black market.

During my brief time as queen, I'd thought of this place often. It was a thorn that throbbed during my quiet moments.

Now there was nothing to stop me from doing something about it. As a cherry on top, some of these creatures belonged to *him*. They were his kind and his subjects. His *blood*. Striking out at them, however depraved they may be, would hurt the one who had betrayed me.

I stopped in the center of the clearing.

It didn't take them long to notice my presence. A minute, maybe two. I didn't think about the fact that I hadn't made physical contact with anyone—not as all this power ran through me like I was a live wire. I was invulnerable. Limitless. Slowly, I lifted my arms, and with a single attempt I claimed every mind in the clearing. So many fears, so many flavors, so many memories. It was a rush almost comparable to what I felt when I'd been fighting Oliver's shadow. For a moment or two, I forgot why I'd come. I was a junkie in the grips of a high.

Then, inevitably, I thought of Collith. The euphoria retreated... and the rage returned.

My arms were still raised, and I opened my eyes slowly. I met the gaze of a shapeshifter with a pig snout. He stood in front of a stall full of jars, and the ones I could see held body parts floating in clear liquid. One of those parts was undeniably a baby's hand. I looked back at the shapeshifter. He was frowning. Probably trying to figure out if I was a master or an escaped slave. Just as he started to say something, my own hands closed into fists.

Their fears exploded into existence like fireworks.

Blinded by my illusions, helpless against my will, slavers scrambled to open cages. I saw every species imaginable claim their freedom. Shapeshifters, vampires, witches, warlocks, humans. One of the captives climbed out of the cage closest to me, enormous and thick-limbed. When he straightened, I recognized the horns jutting from his head. I knew that curly dark hair, that angular jaw, and those clear blue eyes.

The goblin from the oubliette.

"You just have some shitty luck, don't you?" I murmured. Before the creature could reply, I gave him a cold smile. "Looks like your luck has finally turned. Leave this place, now, and I will let you live."

My arms dropped to my sides. Now imaginary doors slammed shut, trapping the slavers in rooms with their worst nightmares.

The goblin ran when the screams started. I took no pleasure in their pain, but I didn't relent. Not for a moment. I stared at them, feeling as if I were watching it all through a pane of glass. I was untouchable. The wind howled with the voices of the dying.

After an hour or two, silence reigned in the clearing. The captives I'd freed were long gone, including the goblin. Bodies littered the snow, along with blood and debris—some of the slavers had gotten violent in the grips of their hallucinations.

The urgency in my veins had dissipated. Feeling like a husk of who I once was, I turned in the direction of home.

My eyebrows went up in faint surprise when I saw the kelpie.

It stood by the tree line, and I got the sense that it had been waiting for me, somehow. I'd never seen a kelpie before—they were rare, not because of being hunted, but rather there hadn't been many to begin with—and despite how hollow I felt inside, I took the opportunity to study it.

The creature at the edge of the clearing had come a long way from the heavenly mounts of its ancestry.

Kelpies lived in deep water, where it stood in wait, like a crocodile, and dragged its victims into the darkness to drown and feast upon. Fins stood in place of where a horse's pointed ears would be. Instead of hair, there was a scaly hide. Its eyes held no irises or pupils, only a milky sheen that seemed to be staring right at me, but I knew that was impossible.

Kelpies were blind.

I owe you a debt, a voice said in my head, making me jump in both pain and surprise. The words felt like a ragged fingernail scraping over my brain matter. Before I could react it continued, *Should you ever have need of me, put your blood in the river and I will come.*

The kelpie didn't wait for a response—without another word, it turned and moved into the trees. I stayed where I was, wary that it was a trick. My gaze shot to every stirring leaf and sought each distant sound, but minutes ticked by and the creature didn't reappear. It really had just stayed to repay a debt it believed was owed.

How extraordinary, I thought with a hollow sense of amusement. *A kelpie with a sense of honor.*

Even though the screams had long since stopped, they still echoed in my mind. I had a strange thought that my soul had been painted black by all the blood around me. There was something in my hand, I thought next. I glanced down with a detached sense of curiosity, and I was startled to see that I was still carrying the novel from Collith's library.

A hollow wind moved past. The cold didn't bother me in the slightest. With a vacant expression, I tossed the book and it landed on one of the bodies, pages splayed. Blood began to seep through the paper.

"And then there were none," I whispered.

CHAPTER TWENTY-FOUR

*I*t was a bright, cloudless day.

Any other morning, I would've gone for a run. Any other morning, I would've been stepping onto the porch with warm coffee in hand.

Instead, I stood in front of the barn.

I stared at the door handle, as I had been for several minutes, and considered whether to wrap my hand around it. Silence rang all around me, but inside my head, it felt like a disquieted crowd had gathered. I knew I'd have to face Collith sooner or later, and part of me wanted to. When he lost his crown, he should know why.

There was another part of me that would do anything to avoid him. Put off the inevitable ending. I could go into the house and put it off by a few hours, at least. But if Emma saw me, she'd ask why I was back in my old room. She'd ask if something was wrong. Those questions might shatter the wall of numbness I'd built around myself, and I wasn't ready to face what was on the other side of it.

So I put my hand around that handle and pulled. I stepped inside and my senses were assailed by the now-familiar smell of fresh paint and new wood. The door closed behind me and I stood there for another moment, waiting for the sound of footsteps or something playing on Collith's phone. But there was just more silence. I forced myself to move toward the stairs. It felt like my body temperature increased with every step.

The lights were on in the apartment, but there was no one in the kitchen or living room. None of the showers were running. Was he still sleeping? Feeling bolder, I quickly walked past all the doorways. Each bed was made and every light was off. I stood in the middle of the space, absorbing the stillness, and came to the obvious conclusion.

Collith was gone.

Since leaving the black market, I felt my first emotion—relief. Faint but unadulterated relief. A second later, I heard a trilling sound, and I looked down to see the kitten rushing at me. She immediately started twining around my ankles. "Hello," I said.

The clock on the microwave said that it was almost noon. Not morning, then. It must've taken longer than I thought to walk home. In eight hours, I would go back into the ground and take Collith's throne from him. Right now, though, I needed to sleep. Sleep until the screams in my head faded to echoes and the throbbing in my chest subsided to a dull ache.

Emma, Damon, and Finn hadn't moved in yet, and their rooms stood empty. I chose one at random, closed the blinds, and crawled into bed. I was still wearing Collith's sweatshirt, but it didn't smell like him anymore. I curled into my body, small and tight, like the knot in my stomach. The position made something jab into my thigh. With a tired frown, I pulled a cell phone out of the pocket. *Oh, right. I put it there.*

The screen brightened from my movements. The lock screen showed numerous texts from Lyari and one from Finn. That was surprising—he'd never used the phone I gave him. I had only been gone since last night, and for all they knew I was pulling a shift at Bea's or training at Adam's. My bodyguards were overzealous, though. They'd probably figured out something was wrong.

Some faraway part of me knew it would be unkind not to respond. But I was so heavy. So weary. Even the thought of pressing buttons on a phone seemed daunting. Telling myself that I would reassure them the second I woke up, I put the phone on the nightstand and curled back into myself.

The kitten must've come into the room shortly after I had, because suddenly I felt her press against my ribs, solid and warm. I stroked her soft head as my eyes fluttered shut. The vibrations of the small creature's purring went through me, oddly soothing.

"Fortuna."

That familiar voice yanked me from darkness. I must've only been half-sleeping, because I knew instantly who it belonged to. I sat up and hugged my knees, blinking the drowsiness out of my eyes. In doing so I dislodged the kitten, who yowled in complaint and walked to the end of the bed.

Twilight shone through the window. I reluctantly turned my face toward Collith's. The light was at his back, making his features dim. As the silent tension lingered, he stepped forward. Our gazes met. His eyes were so dark that his pupils were nonexistent. Sweat slid down the small of my back but I didn't shove the blankets away. Somehow, they felt like a defense against him.

"What did you do, Fortuna?" Collith asked finally. The words were hollow. He already knew about the black market, then. I wondered who told him. He probably had a spy or two reporting everything happening in his absence. He could hardly call himself the Unseelie King if he didn't.

Hearing his voice brought back images of all our nights together. They were imprinted on the insides of my eyelids. I saw bare skin, shy smiles, gentle touches. Physical pain I could handle; it was this sort of pain I couldn't endure. Collith Sylvyre had managed to do what no one else had.

He'd completely shattered my heart.

"I know the truth," was all I said.

Something in my voice made him go still. He hadn't been moving, but those tiny movements that made us blend in and seem human—blinking, fidgeting, shifting—those were gone. Collith stood in the middle of the room like some creature from a fairy tale, come to whisk me away into the magic-filled night.

Except this was no fairy tale.

"The truth about what?" he asked at last. More pretending. A faerie, through and through, no matter how easy it had been for me to forget it.

Suddenly I smiled at him. It wasn't a real smile, not when I could feel the pieces of my heart inside me, fragmented and out of place. "No more games, faerie," I said, finally pushing the covers aside. "The real reason you married me. The reason I've always wondered about, no matter how many pretty lies you spout at me."

"Fortuna, I—"

I stood up and walked toward him, every movement slow and deliberate. I felt like something dangerous now. Maybe Collith felt it, too, because a shadow passed over his face. "You looked me in the eye that day I asked if you'd told me every-thing about your abilities. 'That's everything,' you said. You didn't flinch. You didn't blink."

My words confirmed, beyond a shadow of a doubt, what I'd learned about him. Realizing this, Collith's jaw worked. I waited for him to say what I secretly wanted him to say—that I was wrong, I had made a mistake, and he hadn't been lying to me from the moment we met. What followed was the longest silence I had ever experienced. Finally he said, his voice more anguished than I'd ever heard it, "I'm sorry."

His apology rolled off me like a drop of water. All I could

feel was the disappointment, the pain, rushing through my veins and washing away anything good or light.

"God, how stupid could I be?" I asked bleakly, still gazing up at him. "During the story about your feud with Laurie, you said you were 'showing off your abilities' to each other, and that's what led to the fallout. I believed you without question."

Laughter bubbled up and I couldn't contain it. Collith watched me laugh for a minute, then he said tightly, "You aren't stupid."

"It just made me wonder," I continued as if he hadn't spoken, "how far back does it go? Did you have those goblins kidnap me so I'd end up at the black market?"

"*No.*" He pursed his lips. "But I did know of your existence before we met."

"Explain."

"You once asked why I hadn't done anything to help Damon, when I saw him at Court. I told you I did do something, and that was the truth—I went to Nym."

"To Nym? Why?"

As he always did whenever I asked a direct question, Collith hesitated. My control was a swiftly-unraveling thread, though, and he must've been able to sense it, because the Unseelie King dropped all pretense. "Nym has the ability to move through time," he said with an air of finality. "Every journey takes a little more of his sanity, so I rarely ask him to do it."

Move through time? I thought blankly. And with that, another piece of the puzzle clicked into place.

I remembered that night at the Unseelie Court, sitting at my injured brother's bedside, clutching Damon's hand as if holding onto someone tightly enough was all it took to make them stay. Collith had sat in a chair across from me, giving me bits of his secrets like scraps from a table. I asked him why he hadn't helped Damon when he first saw my brother at Court. *It's difficult for me to make significant decisions without knowing something of the outcome. When my conscience wouldn't rest because of Damon Sworn, I sought... counsel. In hopes of discovering what effect taking him from Jassin would have.*

This response had sparked a wildfire of questions. At the time, I'd decided to back down. Let Collith come to me on his own terms. It was all so ironic now. My voice sounded like someone else's as I asked, "What did he find?"

"Nym told me that someone else was coming to save Damon. He began drawing you. For weeks, he was obsessed. Your face covered the walls of that room, and in some of them, you were wearing a crown. That's why I didn't stop you from pursuing the throne—Nym said your brother's survival hinged on it. I had the crown made weeks before we met.

"There must've been some part of me that didn't believe you were real, because that morning, when I saw you at the black market, I thought it was a trick. Some kind of creature that could see your face in my head or a spell that showed what I wanted most. But I had nothing to do with your abduction, I swear it."

I scoffed and shook my head, backing away from him. I sank onto the bed and stared at the wall. "Your word means absolutely nothing. If all you wanted was to get in my pants, you should've just said, instead of forcing me through that farce of a marriage."

Collith stayed where he was, but every muscle in his body tensed as if he'd been about to move forward. "Fortuna, that's *not* why I slept with you or built this home for us—"

"Oh my God," I blurted, my gaze snapping to his. "*That's* why you wouldn't have sex with me, back at the old place. You weren't being noble! You were feeling *guilty*."

His silence told me I was right. More laughter burned in my throat, but it faded as my mind traveled even further back. I remembered standing in the wet darkness of the Levithan's prison, thinking that I was about to die. That night, Collith could see I was terrified. *You will survive this, Fortuna. That I can promise*, my new mate had told me.

Even then, I'd found it strange. *How? How can you promise me that? Can you see the future?*

Another question that had gone unanswered. There was so much I hadn't seen. So much I hadn't known. But I'd ignored my usual instincts, changed who I was because I was falling for the Unseelie King. Ultimately, I only had myself to blame.

"...admit it, after the day Laurie cut my face open and I realized what I was capable of, I made mistakes," Collith was saying. I blinked at him, slow to focus. "It was the darkest time of my life. I hurt and used others for their power, and for a while, I resembled my father more than my mother. But that's not who I am anymore. It hasn't been for a long time."

"I suppose you miraculously had a change of heart?"

"No, I had a mother that loved me," he answered. His throat worked before he went on. "She asked me to dinner one night, and it started like any other. We talked about the other bloodlines and events happening in our old world. Then, out of nowhere, she put down her fork and turned to me. 'Is this it, then? This is who you want to be?' she asked. I'd never seen such disappointment in her eyes."

Even now, Collith flinched at the memory. He stared at the floor for a few seconds, as if he could see his mother's face in the pattern of the wood. It felt like an hour had passed when he refocused on me. "For years, I didn't touch the powers I'd stolen," he said. "Then, of course, my father finally used the spell Laurie had given him. He'd heard a rumor that I was conspiring with a Folduin to overthrow him. He could've used the spell on me, but he didn't want the Court to think he was afraid. It was a taunt. A challenge. He killed my mother with that spell to teach me a lesson."

I felt the beginnings of sympathy, but it died like a grape on a vine when I remembered what he'd done. I shook my head, more to myself than him. It was no use. Everything had changed, and even if we could go back in time...

A line deepened between my eyebrows, and I held my knees tighter. Back in time. The thought brought yet another memory up, like a bubble rising to the water's surface. I saw the two of us, facing each other just as we were now. We'd been at the Unseelie Court, talking about how things could've gone differently, as we always seemed to.

We can't go back in time, can we?

No, we can't, he'd said.

Another lie.

"Now? You tell me this now, when it's too late?" I whispered. Damon was wrong—some wounds didn't heal into a scar. Some wounds just ran too fucking deep, beyond the scope of healing, and all they could do was fester.

Collith must've seen every thought written on my face. His voice was fierce as he said, "It's *not* too late, Fortuna. When I met you, I felt alive in a way I hadn't for years, and it was only when I started to breathe again that I realized how long I'd been suffocating. I wanted you so badly, I would've done anything... and I did. I'm not proud of manipulating you into the mating ceremony, or lying about my ability."

Something inside me cracked. "Then *why did you?*" I screamed.

"Because of this! Because I knew you'd never trust me if you knew!" Collith's eyes were wild. Before I could say anything else, he picked up my phone and put in the passcode. I was so taken aback that I didn't try to stop him. A second later, my own voice floated through the dim room.

Collith started translating when the recording reached his part of our wedding vows. "I know you are afraid of me. I know you don't love me yet. But I vow to do everything within my power to change that. There are many things I cannot promise, because we live in a world of variables. Anything I can promise, though, I do so gladly. My home, my life, my heart. I will never tell you goodbye, because I will never leave you. I will give you a life of hellos, Fortuna Sworn."

The recording ended. Collith tossed the phone back onto the bed, and it landed near my knee. Telling me the truth made him seem pounds lighter, as though each one had been a pound shed. But I felt heavier. Colder. Like a layer of frost had spread over my skin and was creeping into my heart.

"Do you know what I went through to bring you back from the dead? What I sacrificed?" I asked without looking at him. My voice cracked.

"As a matter of fact, I don't." At the edge of my vision, I saw Collith's hands clench. "What did you sacrifice, Fortuna? What happened?"

The question echoed through me. It was the hundredth time he'd asked, but I had never been able to answer before. Ironic that I could finally admit why, now that it didn't matter—I'd been afraid the truth would change how Collith looked at me. Afraid that he'd see I was as unclean as I felt.

At long last, though, he would get his answer. I jerked forward, leaning on my knees. Collith was still standing next to the bed, making it easy to dig my fingers into his scalp. He didn't struggle, and I slammed into his mind without difficulty. Collith staggered from the force of the blow. I barely noticed.

Just as the Unseelie King once showed me his dreams, I showed him my nightmares.

I made certain he experienced everything, down to the tiniest details—the ridges of bark against my palms and the bite of cold air on my skin. Then Collith felt my shock as the demon pushed its way inside me. He felt my horror as it came in a burst of unwelcome warmth. He felt my anguish as I vomited all over that lonely road.

When I opened my eyes, Collith's were bright with tears. I let go of him and wrapped my arms around myself. The air was so still it felt like a blanket of snow covered the room. What could he possibly say?

I had one more thing to give him. One more truth that would drive the knife deep inside his gut. Not about our daughter—that secret I'd take with me to the grave. I wouldn't allow Collith to taint it.

"You should know something," I added bleakly. "When Gwyn killed me, I saw everything. I watched her perform CPR. The most bizarre out-of-body experience you can imagine. Funny thing, though… I had no idea who any of you were. I didn't even know you were faeries. I've thought about it a lot since then, and what I've concluded is that my soul was the one watching you. The one that was standing there in the tomb. Which means when I heard your name and remembered you, I'd recognized you with my innermost self. Kind of sounds like we might've been soulmates, huh?"

A tear dripped off the edge of his jaw. "Please forgive me. Please."

"Enjoy the power you stole, Your Majesty. It'll be something to remember me by." The words felt as though they were torn from my chest, each one leaving a wound that throbbed and bled. *I trusted you. I gave myself to you.*

We both knew there was nothing else to say, nothing else he *could* say, but Collith didn't move. His face looked haggard, as if he'd aged ten years in the time we'd been in this room together. "For me, you were never a Nightmare, Fortuna Sworn—you were a dream come to life."

Tears were streaming down my face now, or maybe I just hadn't noticed them until this moment. Suddenly it felt like I was on the verge of another panic attack. I wanted Collith *gone*.

Blinded by a rush of salt water and pain, I fumbled for the piece of paper on the nightstand. It had been waiting there for days, forgotten until now.

"Come to the throne room at eight," I told the faerie coldly.

Then I whispered the final part of the spell that Laurie had given me, staring hard at Collith's face as I spoke.

He flew backward as if someone had shoved him, right in the chest, and he shattered through the drywall. It was fitting, really—now our home match my heart. Jagged edges and gaping holes. I sat there as my face dried, staring at the hole, wondering distantly how I would explain it to the others. How I would explain anything, really. Finn was probably crossing the yard already, drawn by the racket Collith had made during his exit.

The kitten cautiously returned to me. I closed my eyes and buried my face in her fur. She smelled like naps in the sun, fresh laundry sheets, and... Collith.

I curled my body around her and shook with silent sobs.

I wore another black gown.

Well, if it could be called a gown. The top barely covered my breasts. Thin, dead branches encircled each shoulder. My midriff was bare. The skirt reached for the floor in dark gossamer. Leaves and vines swept through the material. All I wore for jewelry was the necklace Collith had given me. This time, the crown would stay here, tucked away into shadow.

Somewhere else in this underground maze, Viessa was getting ready for her coronation. Rumors were already circulating—her absence from the cells had been noticed. Apparently Nuvian had used this to his advantage. According to Lyari, he'd sent Guardians in search of the escaped prisoner, and it was a safe bet they were the ones who would've stopped the coup. The Folduins had planned their takeover carefully, and a tiny part of me admired the patience and cunning they'd displayed.

Other than Lyari, who believed we were here for a tribunal, the room behind me was empty—I'd left the house without waking Finn, and this time, I felt no guilt about it. Tonight was an event I didn't want him to see.

I squeezed some lotion onto my palm at the same time a knock disturbed the silence, spreading through the air like a ripple in water. "Enter," I called.

The door creaked open, and I watched the Tongue's bulky form appear in the mirror's reflection. "You asked to see me, Your Majesty?" he asked.

His arms were tucked into the drooping sleeves of his robe, lending him a serene air... but there was nothing serene about the stench of his fear. The beads around his neck seemed to quiver more obnoxiously than usual. I turned away from the glass, leisurely rubbing the lotion onto my arms. "Yes. I was just curious," I said without looking up. "Did you start scheming with Viessa before my coronation, or after?"

There was a beat of silence. I raised my gaze and saw the Tongue's baffled frown. Behind him, I also saw Lyari's face twitch with surprise. "I don't know what you're talking about, my queen," the big faerie said, shaking his head.

"Well, *someone* mentioned my broken mating bond and the fact that Collith is alive. I can count on one hand how many people knew the truth. And you were *so* fascinated by our conversation during that council meeting. I bet you just couldn't wait to tell Viessa what you'd learned. Still don't want to talk, huh? Lyari? How long has it been since you've removed someone's head?" I asked curiously.

She was standing next to the door. The Tongue didn't turn around, but his eyes darted to the side. It made me think of a nervous rodent. In the meantime, Lyari's lips twisted with speculation and her eyes went unfocused. She was really thinking about it, I realized with faint amusement.

"Too long," my friend concluded.

Maybe the Tongue saw something in our expressions that made him realize we weren't bluffing. Or maybe he was too much of a coward to take that chance. "How did you know?" he asked past stiff lips.

"I didn't for sure. But now I do," I said coolly. All at once, his terror coated my tongue, flavors of rot and mold. I stood there for a few seconds, letting him fear the worst. Then I added, "Luckily for you, Viessa needs someone with your skills to perform the ceremony."

Lyari was frowning again, and I could practically hear the next thought darting through her mind. *Ceremony?*

I kept my focus on the Tongue. Relief flickered in his small eyes. "I only have the Court's best interest—"

"What's that saying? How do you know a faerie is lying? Because they have a pulse. I think that's it." I lifted my skirt and stepped closer to him. "Actually, I should be thanking you."

The faerie visibly swallowed. "Thanking me?"

"Yes. Before all this, I'd lost my mojo. I felt guilty... doing things like this." My hand flew out, and I grabbed his fleshy face so tightly between my fingers that I drew blood. The Tongue dropped to his knees, whimpering, and stared up at me with horror in his eyes. He wasn't seeing me, though—he was seeing his fear come to life in his mind. I pumped more power into him, plundering his memories like some woodland creature foraging through the earth. I found everything he'd buried and brought it into the light.

Above all, the Tongue was afraid of his mother. She sneered down at him with pure loathing in her eyes. "You disgust me," she hissed.

The Tongue—his true name was Gorwin—blubbered like a child. He spoke in Enochian, but the words were too wet and too quick. I couldn't make them out.

Quick as a snake, I yanked my power out of him again, and the memories vanished. "I'm not surprised. You seem like a mama's boy, Gorwin," I said.

The Tongue's body jerked and he gasped. The glassy sheen

left his eyes and he blinked rapidly, then realized who was standing before him. It was the first time he'd looked at me with true fear. Giving the faerie a sweet smile, I tucked my hand beneath his chin and bent down, putting our faces close enough to kiss.

"Run, little mouse," I whispered. His heavy breathing filled my ears. "Run before I change my mind."

And he did exactly that.

"Time for my second appointment of the evening," I murmured. I went back to the mirror, and I saw Lyari frown in the glass again. Though I waited, giving her a chance to ask why I hadn't told her about the Tongue's betrayal, she didn't speak. I turned around, clasping my hands in front of me to hide how they trembled. "Does anyone know where Tarragon is?"

Lyari stepped away and said something to another Guardian through the open door. "He is visiting Nym, Your Majesty," she told me after a moment.

"Let's go to him, then. It's been too long since I've visited Nym." Lyari nodded and moved into the passageway to update the other Guardians. I lingered by the mirror and controlled my breathing. *Long inhale. Hold. Slow release. Do it one more time.* When Lyari returned, I awaited with a distant expression. The mask of the Unseelie Queen, which I would never have to wear again after tonight. I walked over to her and paused in the doorway, taking in the rooms with a sweeping glance. I knew I wouldn't be back.

Down we went to Nym's rooms.

Upon our arrival, there was no sign of Tarragon, and every room within sight was... destroyed. Books had been torn apart and scattered. Some were half-charred. The walls had been drawn on. Not lovely art like the mural, but actual words scribbled over each surface. Mad, illegible scribbles. There was a hole in one of the earthen walls that hadn't been there before, as if someone had struck it with his fist in a burst of consuming fury or utter desolation.

And not a single clock remained unbroken. That never-ending ticking had actually come to an end. The quiet was jarring.

Something small and brown darted by. Moving so quickly I almost missed it, Nym threw a book at the creature with all his strength. The tiny animal squeaked in alarm, dodging just in time. The faerie went after him, running across the chaotic space. He was only wearing jeans, and the hems were torn and faded, as if he'd been wearing them a long time.

"Nym? What happened here?" I asked loudly. I moved forward and stepped on a piece of glass. The cracking sound burst into the stillness. Nym whirled and spotted me. I could sense Lyari coming into the room.

"Your Majesty! Did you get my message?" he blurted. His voice sounded like a child's.

But, really, there was no way to guess his age. Sometimes he looked ancient, as if he'd seen too much in this world. There were other times, like now, when he appeared young, so lost and desperate. The features of his face were so well-defined, so detailed. He was an artist's dream.

I tried not to sound wary as I said, "What message?"

"I told the king. I saw the storm coming. Your mind was locked shut, so I had to contact someone else." Nym started to smack his head. "I told him, I told him about the Wild Hunt!"

I rushed across the space and grabbed at his hands. A flavor coated my tongue; rosemary. "Yes, Nym! He did pass that along. Thank you so much for the warning."

Nym raised his head and looked at me. His expression was strange—it was as if he was seeing two things at once, and he couldn't decide which reality to grasp and hold onto. It reminded me of an expression I'd seen on Kindreth's face.

I thought of the knife strapped to my thigh and resisted reaching for it.

"Be sober-minded; be watchful. Your adversary the devil prowls around like a roaring lion, seeking someone to devour," Nym whispered.

A shiver went down my spine. I reminded myself of what this creature had endured at the whims of faerie kings.

Before I could say anything else, his demeanor shifted again —suddenly he looked even younger. Nym crouched low to the ground, slipping out of my grasp, and hugged himself with boney arms. His lips puckered in contemplation. He made me think of a child who'd woken from a bad dream and found himself alone in a shadow-filled room.

It was this place. These low ceilings and dirt walls were driving him toward the brink of complete insanity.

This is a bad idea, I thought. Nym was unpredictable, there wasn't a spare bedroom in the loft, and it could go wrong in so many ways. But the words still left my mouth. "Nym... would you like to come live with me?"

The faerie didn't answer. There was a line between his brows, and it looked as if he hadn't understood the question. I started to ask again, but his gaze shifted to something behind me. Tarragon's voice drifted serenely past. "I received word that you wanted to speak, Queen Fortuna."

I turned around, locking away the few emotions that had managed to escape their cages. Lyari moved to occupy the space between me and Nym, now that my back was turned on him. "You told me once that you stand wherever I stand. Was that true?" I asked Tarragon, folding my hands to rest them against my thighs.

If he saw the change in me or heard it in my voice, Tarragon was a master at pretending. Nothing flickered in his eyes. No muscles twitched along his jaw. "It was, Your Majesty," he said simply.

"Excellent. I require you to show support for what's about to happen tonight." I told him the events that would soon unfold. I knew Lyari was listening to every word, and it would be the first time she'd heard Viessa's plan, as well.

Once I was finished, Tarragon still offered no arguments. Lyari, I knew, would be fuming if I looked at her. "May I ask why you're doing this?" was all he said.

I didn't answer right away. Maybe because, this time, the answer truly mattered. Half of a minute went by, and then I met the faerie's dark gaze. My voice was the most certain it had ever been since I'd first stepped foot in the Unseelie Court. "I don't want this. And I don't want Collith to have it, either."

Tarragon studied me for another moment, and I could've sworn there was a tiny smile on his lips. A glimpse of admiration. "I shall see you in the throne room," he murmured with a deep bow. "Until then, I will attend to Sir Nym."

"Sir?" I repeated, turning to watch his approach toward the other faerie.

Tarragon cupped Nym's elbows and helped him to his feet. "Yes. Our Nym was once knighted by Queen Elizabeth II. He's quite brave, you know."

"I do know." I watched them for another second or two, then inclined my head at Lyari. She moved into the tunnel, her hand on that sword hilt. She was probably imagining what it would feel like to behead *me*, since it had been such a long time, after all.

"You can't do this," she hissed the instant we were out of their earshot.

"I can and I am." I chose the passageway that would lead us to the throne room and walked faster. Suddenly I was eager to get this over with. Lyari caught up and opened her mouth. I spun to face her, my skirt twisting around me. "Don't. Just don't, okay? I can't be the queen you dream of, Lyari. It's not who I am, and I won't change into that person. Wouldn't you rather have a ruler who *wants* to be in that chair?"

"It's *because* you don't want that chair that you should be the one to sit in it," Lyari insisted.

I could see the hope in her eyes. The bright, naked hope. It was the same look Collith had in his eyes when he talked about the future of his Court. Lyari could be cold and she was often hard, but it was built on a deep love for her people. Why else would she dedicate her immortal life to being a Guardian?

Unable to face the moment I extinguished that light, I lifted my skirts and ran.

Lyari didn't follow me.

Fortunately, I was familiar enough with the tunnel system to find the throne room on my own. Turn after turn, I kept my emotions in their cages and focused completely on the part I'd play tonight. I was so focused that I didn't hear the courtier until it was too late.

As we bounced off each other in a painful burst, I recognized her—we'd spoken at Olorel. The shock of the crash faded, and I remembered that she was the faerie who'd blown on the back of my neck and worn feathers on her eyelashes. *I wonder why he considered you significant enough to mate, but not to crown?* she'd said to me. Now she was dressed exactly as I'd been at the revel, her golden dress gleaming in the torchlight.

"I'm sorry…" I started, but then I saw a flash of Collith in her mind. Our skin must've made contact in the collision.

The faerie tried to back away. I seized her wrist, digging my nails into her skin, and searched for the image of Collith again. "I just did what I was told!" I heard the female cry.

I gave a bewildered shake of my head. "What the hell are you talking about?"

Her fear led me to it a moment later. A memory, steeped in anxiety, because she'd been worried for so long that I would find it. She was in a passageway identical to the one we stood in now, torches crackling all around. The red-orange glow fell upon the face of the Unseelie King, who stared down at her with a remote expression. I recognized that look—it was the same one he'd given me as Death Bringer removed the flesh off my back with his whip.

"These are the exact words you will use," he said.

No, I thought. The dirt walls were getting closer, somehow, closing in on me even though I hadn't seen them move. *Don't do it. Don't betray me again.*

But he did. I watched as Collith fed her the line that had ultimately led to my claiming of the Unseelie throne. *I wonder why he considered you significant enough to mate, but not to crown?* the female asked, just as she'd been told to do.

He'd planned it. Every step of it. Knowing that my own curiosity would be my downfall, he'd orchestrated it so this random courtier would make me wonder about the queenship. And then Collith would oh-so-reluctantly tell me how to gain the throne so that I could also gain Damon's freedom. The only thing unclear was why. Power, probably—it always came down to power.

I wanted to scream. I wanted the earth to collapse and completely bury this place. Lies. Everything he told me, everything between us, it was all lies. I'd changed myself for him. I'd given pieces of myself.

Any misgivings I might've had about tonight were gone. I extracted myself from the faerie's mind and my vision cleared. She cowered before me, her arm dramatically thrown up over her head. I looked down at her, feeling cold again. Empty. "I just did what I was told," the female repeated, weeping now.

I stepped around her and walked away.

There were two figures standing farther down the tunnel. When I drew close enough to make out their faces, along with the rest of them, I felt my eyebrows rise.

They looked like a king and queen.

Nuvian's dreadlocks looked freshly attended to—they hung in thick, shining ropes over his broad shoulders. He wore a tunic of royal blue, and a silver chain hung from one shoulder to the other. He wore the tight pants and tall boots fae males so seemed to love.

As for Viessa, she was more beautiful, more ethereal than any faerie I'd seen walking the dirt halls of this Court. She wore a dress that celebrated the ice within her veins. The filmy, blue material draped over the pale, fragile-looking lines of her body. Whoever designed it had been strategic in where it clung to Viessa's frame, highlighting the curves she'd managed to regain after her long imprisonment.

I'd never seen Viessa without a layer of grime covering her face and hair. Tonight, she had washed away every year she'd spent down in the dark. Her hair, the color of autumn leaves at their most vibrant, spilled down her back in a waterfall of curls and shining locks.

And resting on top of her head was a crown. A crown the likes of which I'd never seen before. Similar to the sword that always hung at Nuvian's side, it appeared to be made of glass. The base nestled in Viessa's curls, and a dozen spires rose up like an eerie castle that stood in a land of snow and ice.

"My father had it made for me," the new queen said, noticing the direction of my gaze. "He never doubted that I'd take back our throne someday."

My voice was hollow. "It's stunning."

"Yes, it is." Viessa glanced at her brother and elbowed him in the stomach. She must've put some strength behind it, because he couldn't hold back a grimace. Viessa rolled her eyes. "Oh, get over it, Nuv. So she kicked your ass. You should be used to it, growing up with me. Now then, shall we claim our destinies, Fortuna Sworn?"

"We shall," I said. Viessa left Nuvian's side and offered me her arm. I frowned down at it for a moment—I wasn't sure why the gesture surprised me. Then I put my hand through, linking us together. Viessa's skin was as frozen as it looked, but the ice didn't spread to mine as I'd once feared.

We started toward the throne room. I looked up at the mural for the last time, wondering if my likeness would be added to its walls. I'd like that, I decided. At least I had been part of someone's history, and my memory would never fade into the anonymity so many feared.

Maybe Viessa was a little nervous herself, because when we reached that enormous doorway, she didn't wait to be noticed. I'd expected a grand entrance—she had surprised me again. We weaved through the crowd, catching brief snatches of conversation.

My sister said it was a killing field.

Has there been any word on the king?

I heard a rumor that he was spotted here at Court.

The Wild Hunt has gone.

Then word of us began to spread, and within seconds, there was a clear path to the thrones. Viessa had apparently planned a celebration—along the side of the room, there were once again tables laden with food. Most of it, I noted, was dessert. There was even a chocolate fountain.

"Revenge is best served with little cakes and lots of icing," Viessa informed me, her tone playful, as if we were two girls exchanging some gossip.

We reached the bottom of the dais. Once again, she didn't hesitate or slow—the frost-covered faerie went up the steps and turned to face the enormous crowd. She looked completely unafraid. I moved to join her, but my veins buzzed with anxiety. At the same moment I raised my gaze, the room came alive with voices. But it wasn't entirely due to Viessa's presence at my side or the sight of a crown on her head.

Collith had arrived.

At least he's punctual, I thought as he came down the pathway

Viessa and I had created. The Unseelie King wore the most fae clothing I'd ever seen him in, as if he'd known this would be a battle for what he held most dear. A duster coat flared behind him. He wore steel boots and matching gauntlets, and beneath this were tight dark pants and a plate of armor that looked molded to his abdomen. A crown gleamed on his head, and it was almost as bright as the sword at his hip.

Collith slowed when he saw me on the dais, standing beside the person who'd tried to kill him. The entire room was staring at the two of us—we weren't using fists or filling the room with screams, but our pain was obvious just the same.

You broke my heart, I thought in a whisper. *Now I'll shatter yours.*

In a deliberate movement, I took the sapphire off. I turned my hand over and let it fall to the floor. Collith's mouth tightened as the jewel slid across the stone and came to a slow stop. I hoped he couldn't see the wince I suppressed—that necklace had been Naevys's, and without it, my neck felt cold and bare.

I could tell the meaning of the gesture wasn't lost on our audience. A marriage wasn't so easily dissolved, but no one dared question me. Many of them had probably heard rumors that our mating bond was gone.

As promised, Tarragon moved to stand on my other side. I watched the faces in the front row, noting their reactions when they saw that a courtier they respected supported me. I didn't know if he stood to gain anything from our display, but I didn't care. Not anymore.

"What is this?" Collith asked, directing the question at me.

Viessa's voice rang through the room, clear and high. "Your bond with this Court is broken, leaving us vulnerable and exposed. You do not have your Nightmare queen to wield over us. You do not have a Right Hand to rule in your stead. You do not have the Guardians to fight for you. You do not have the support of the bloodlines I've so generously negotiated with over those many years of solitude. The Tongue has agreed to perform the coronation ceremony and finally grant my blood-line the throne it was due. Relinquish the crown to me and I will let you leave this room with your life, Collith of bloodline Sylvyre."

"This is not how it's done," Collith said, and there was no glimpse of the warm male I'd shared a bed with. This was the faerie who'd used his unique ability to gain power from the unaware. This was the creature who'd ended his father's life with the red-hot need for revenge. "I challenge you."

"I reject your challenge. It's time for new laws." Just like that, Viessa dismissed him, raking her gaze over the crowd. "I am also eliminating the council. Everything begins and ends with me."

"Or what?" someone called.

Viessa crooked a brow at me, and I looked out at them again, playing my part perfectly. I no longer had a bond with the Court, but as it turned out, I didn't need it. Using the same blind rage I'd channeled in the black market, I sent a ripple of fear over the entire crowd. As their cries and murmurs rose into the air, one face in particular caught my notice. *The goblin from the black market.* What was he doing here?

"Or you will die, either by terror or by sword," the new queen answered, bringing my attention back to her. Her message was loud and clear—Collith might not have a Night-mare to use anymore, but she did. My jaw clenched before I could stop it.

No one was looking at me, anyway. Collith was moving now, and he stopped once he faced Viessa from the bottom of the stairs. She still stood at the top, and he tipped his head back to look at her. "You don't want to make an enemy of me. We both know I'm more powerful than you."

"Take him," Viessa commanded, finally sitting on the throne that had once been Collith's.

In all the time I'd known him, I had never seen Collith at his most powerful. During the battles we'd shared he had only shown me the heavenly fire, because he couldn't explain other abilities without exposing his secret. But I knew, as Collith planted his feet and every muscle in his body went tense, that I was finally about to.

The usual reserve I'd become so accustomed to had fallen away like a curtain, and his beautiful countenance twisted with ferocity.

Dozens of faeries in the crowd suddenly cried out. They blinked rapidly, as though they'd gone blind, and some held out their arms. It was an illusion, I realized as I watched them. Collith was using the power he'd stolen from Laurie to make the weak-minded believe the lights had gone out. It hadn't worked on everyone, and I instinctively took note of those who were strong enough to withstand such power. Viessa. Tarragon. Nuvian. Chandrelle.

Then Collith slammed his hands together. Viessa dove out of the way, and a bolt of electricity slammed into the throne, its blue light almost blinding. The wooden chair went up in flames. The courtiers that weren't stumbling around the room were fleeing for the doors now. Swords clashed behind me, and I glanced back to see that some Guardians had chosen to fight against Viessa. Nuvian was trying to get to her, help her in the battle with Collith, but Omar—shy, kind, timid Omar— wouldn't let him pass.

The heavenly fire flashed again. I held up a hand, squinting, and tried to keep my eyes on Collith. He looked like a dark, vengeful Zeus. Viessa was fighting back now, an incredibly large stream of ice pouring out of her hands. Their power hissed, screamed, and crackled between them.

But Viessa didn't last long against the heat.

She gave a shout of pain, and the ice vanished. Viessa fell to the stone floor, just barely missing the explosion of fire that shot through the place she'd been standing. Before she could recover, Collith lowered his hands. The fire faded while he unsheathed his sword, stormed forward, and brought his arm back.

There was no time to think—before he could ram the sword through Viessa's chest, I was there, standing between them. His eyes bored into mine, more amber than hazel, as though there was a fire burning inside him. The fighting went on around us. I saw a question within those depths, and it was the same one I asked myself at that moment, as the tip of the sword pierced the material of my dress. *Why are you protecting her?*

For you, I thought.

Despite the lies he'd told, despite the terrible things he'd done, my first thought had been of Collith when he flew at Viessa with that deadly blade. Going to Hell had almost destroyed him. Taking the life of someone he'd once loved... I knew he wouldn't survive it. I almost hadn't, and I had far fewer morals than Collith.

But none of this passed my lips. Instead I glared up at him and spat, "If you want to kill her, you'll have to go through me. Which didn't end well for you last time."

The last word had barely left my mouth when Collith sifted. By the time I spun around, he was already on the other side of us, his fingers wrapped around Viessa's throat. Her hands flew up to stop the downward strike of his sword. I heard them both snarling, and they must have sifted at the same time, because the two of them reappeared farther away. Viessa's back slammed into the wall so hard that trickles of dirt came down. She was losing. I knew all I had to do was reach out and take hold of Collith's mind, but the thought made a memory go off like a bomb. Facing Collith in a field of grass. The line of blood sliding from his nose. My own hoarse screams rising into the air.

I couldn't do it.

Then Collith flattened his palm on her chest, and his body

tensed in a way that had become familiar—he was about to send a lightning bolt through Viessa's body. Not even supernatural healing would be able to save her. I could tell from the expression on his face that the darkness inside had claimed him, just as it had claimed me.

"No!" Nuvian bellowed.

"Collith, stop!" I cried.

A pale face appeared over Collith's shoulder. It felt like every creature in the room held their breath as Laurie whispered in his ear. I watched how his mouth moved, and faint fragments drifted to me. "Is this it, then? This is who you want to be?" he was saying.

They were the same words Naevys said to her son the last time he was on the brink between light and dark. Of course Laurie had been eavesdropping when Collith told me that in confidence.

At first, Collith didn't react. His chest heaved and his focus remained on Viessa. His face was so twisted by fury it seemed impossible this was the same faerie I'd known these past few months, and suddenly the tight leash of control he always kept on himself made sense.

Then, slowly, he came back to us. A muscle ticked in his jaw and a light of resignation began to shine in his eyes. He didn't nod or respond, but after a few seconds, he looked more like the old Collith. The in-control Collith. The Collith who had formed a plan to seduce me in order to gain the power of a Nightmare.

At last, Laurie stepped back. Holding the other faerie's arm with a white-knuckled grip, Collith searched the room. His eyes stopped on mine. Though he said nothing, I felt something pass between us. A promise. I stared back, stone-faced and silent.

To her credit, Viessa's voice didn't tremble as she repeated, "Take him."

I waited for Collith to sift, but he just threw his sword to the flagstones. In the same instant he did that, Laurie vanished.

The king's submission seemed to have a chain reaction, and the Guardians loyal to Viessa began to arrest the ones who'd fought for Collith. None of them tried to resist—they were outnumbered, especially now that some of them had been wounded. My eyes followed as they disappeared through the narrow side door, undoubtedly to the delightful dungeons I'd almost died in, and I made a mental note to negotiate with Viessa for their freedom. She'd probably be in a good mood after the ceremony.

As if she could read my mind, Viessa called for the Tongue. The remaining faeries in the room slowly began to come forward again, and some trickled out of the doorways.

Something glittered on the flagstones, drawing my gaze. While everyone watched Collith being bound and led to the dungeons, I bent and retrieved his mother's necklace. I straightened, my gaze snagging Viessa's. Her expression was knowing in a way that only another female could. *Fine,* I wanted to say. *Yes, I loved him. What good does acknowledging it do?*

My stomach started rolling. Without a word, I turned from Viessa and headed for the exit. It wasn't part of the plan—I was supposed to stay for the entire ceremony—but I couldn't be in that room one more second. No one tried to stop me; I frightened them too much. I was dimly surprised to see that Lyari stood by the doorway. As I passed, she looked at me with undeniable disappointment in her eyes.

"I made a choice," I told her dully. Before she could respond, I plunged into the tunnel, desperate for open air and moonlight.

Once again, she didn't follow, and I knew the friendship between us was over.

For the next few minutes, my mind was occupied by the maze. One wrong turn, and I could end up in a room of redcaps or a cave that housed yet another ancient, fire-breathing beast. But I was grateful for the distraction, because I knew the alternative was to remember the expression on Collith's face when he saw me at Viessa's side. *He had to be punished. Don't think about him, Fortuna. Don't waste another second on him.*

The moment I reached the surface, I broke into a sprint.

It was later than I'd thought—stars shimmered overhead and the forest was dark all around. This didn't slow me down, though. I was forced to stop when my shoes kept snagging the hem of my ridiculous dress. I shouted in frustration, yanked out the knife strapped to my thigh, and hacked at the long skirt, again and again, until there was a long slit in the middle. Once again I ran at full speed, even when my lungs started to burn, pushing myself as if there was a finish line somewhere.

My chest heaved as I opened the barn door. A single light-bulb burned at the base of the stairs—Emma's doing, no doubt. I closed and locked the door behind me, then climbed the stairs. I crossed the shadowy apartment and returned to the room I'd slept in earlier. Still hurting from my run, I removed my clothes gingerly, and something clattered to the floor. I felt numb as I bent to pick up the sapphire. It flashed and gleamed.

My gaze fell on Damon's birthday gift to me. The small, cheap box rested atop the dresser beside a framed picture of Matthew. Another Emma touch. I lifted the lid and dropped Collith's necklace within, then shoved the box into the back of a drawer.

It slammed shut with a sound of finality.

CHAPTER TWENTY-FIVE

I dreamed of them. The ones I'd killed in the clearing.

I was back in the same spot I'd been standing that night, my feet buried in snow, facing the busy market. The masters and sellers were already screaming, trapped under the influence of my power. Males and females alike, it made no difference to me—it was their hearts that mattered. And the creatures trapped in cages or tied to hitching rails like they were animals, they were proof of what lived in my victims' hearts. Darkness. Silent, bottomless darkness.

Just like mine.

But this was a dream. I knew it was a dream, because something was different this time—a broad-shouldered figure appeared amidst the chaos. I noticed her straight away because she was standing so still, while everyone around her trembled or writhed. *Gwyn*. Even though I knew she wasn't real, my breath hitched in fear. She wore an antler helmet and armor made of bones, just like I'd seen in a fae history book I read. One of her hands, encased in a spiked gauntlet, rested on the hilt of her sword. The other casually clutched the heart she'd ripped out of her lover's chest.

"Someday you will know what it is to choose between love and power," she called over the cacophony of pain. "Someday you will be just like me."

I tried to deny it, tell her she was wrong, but I couldn't even open my mouth to say the words. Gwyn's red lips curved into a faint smile. Damn it, the cold-hearted bitch knew. She *knew* she was right.

As if she sensed my despair, the faerie started walking toward me. Despite all the shrieks and sobs, and the freed slaves that were running past us, it felt like the loudest sound in the clearing was her boots through the snow, crunching with every step. She stopped a hairsbreadth away, her chest brushing mine, just the slightest of touches. I stared up at her, fighting against a wave of both revulsion and desire. We both knew she was going to kiss me... and I was going to let her. It would change everything. It would change *me*. There would be no going back.

Just as Gwyn lowered her head, I woke up.

I opened my eyes expecting to see the familiar walls of Cyrus's house. When beige walls looked back, my heart quickened again. I tried to find the memory of how I got here. It took another moment to comprehend that I was in the apartment I'd been meant to share with Collith. This was the barn, the home he'd spent weeks building for us. Looking around at it, I started to have second thoughts about living here.

I sat up, feeling sick, and hugged my knees to my chest. Every part of me was slick with sweat. Shame and guilt poured down my face in the form of tears. The slavers' screams echoed through my mind, but the rest of the world was utterly silent. The dream continued to recede. I watched shadows quiver over the floor. On the other side of the window, a blizzard raged. The ledge was already covered in a layer of snow.

I had to escape this feeling. I couldn't endure it for another second.

Without allowing myself a moment to calm or suppress the

emotions surging through me, I tossed the covers aside. After I yanked on some sweatpants to cover my bare legs, I rushed from the room as though it were filled with monsters. I was so frantic that I didn't see the enormous werewolf stretched across the threshold until it was too late—Finn must've sensed my agitation when I'd gotten back earlier tonight—and I slammed into the opposite wall so hard that it sent pain through both my wrists. I righted myself with a wince, then hurried toward the stairs.

Finn followed close at my heels, and though he didn't whine, tension practically vibrated off him. I didn't offer any explanation or reassurance, because I reached the door a moment later and I was yanking it open without a thought. The wind howled before I even stepped outside. Pain registered, and I looked down at my feet, realizing belatedly that I hadn't put on shoes. Finn waited on the porch as I hurried to find a pair of boots, then a coat as an afterthought. I pulled them on and returned to wind and open sky. The cold latched onto me like a thousand claws as the door slammed shut. Hopefully the sound hadn't woken anyone, I thought distantly.

I stopped in the yard and turned to face Cyrus's house—I wasn't sure why. I didn't know what I was doing. I just stood there, hair blowing across my face, and stared at those darkened windows without truly seeing them. More snow came down, tangling in my eyelashes and slipping inside my unbuttoned coat. With Finn a silent presence nearby, I thought about the past month. I thought about how that throne, far beneath my feet, had affected me. I thought about the choices I'd made and the consequences of those choices. I thought about my parents. I thought about Gwyn and Dracula. I thought about tomorrow.

That was the most terrifying thought of all.

What had I said to the huntress, that morning? *It's not like I go on killing sprees.*

Suddenly I was laughing. There was a frantic edge to it, a

hysterical note that reminded me of Kindreth, but this thought only made me laugh harder. I bent over and clutched my stomach. I couldn't stop. The sound didn't echo—instead, it seemed to be swallowed by the sky. If anyone looked out their window, I probably made a strange picture. Standing in the snowy darkness, chortling like I had just heard the funniest joke. In a way, that's exactly what was happening. All this time, I'd been kidding myself, insisting that faeries were the enemy. They were the problem. They were my greatest fear.

But faeries hadn't murdered the Unseelie King. Faeries hadn't stabbed Ayduin in cold blood. Faeries hadn't walked away from a clearing of dead bodies two days ago.

Suddenly my mirth shriveled, and I forgot why I'd been laughing in the first place. There was nothing funny about this. Nothing. I blinked rapidly, shaking snowflakes loose from my eyelashes. Feeling like I'd just awakened from another dream, I looked over at Finn. His gaze met mine, and I could see a question in those golden depths. *What are you doing?*

Normally, Finn didn't ask questions. That alone told me that tonight was different. Tonight there would be more change. "The world of *magick* is dark, and no one goes into it willingly," I murmured. Only the wind answered, but it sounded like one of those dying slavers' screams.

In that moment, I made a decision.

I refocused on the house, this time with purpose. Once, angels had been messengers. Heralds. Harbingers. I'd never tried to summon someone before—it seemed outside the realm of possibility, and just another way to violate an unprotected mind—but I hadn't had this much power before. I'd already crossed so many other lines. What was one more?

Picturing the one I wanted to summon, I filled my lungs with air and released the longest, loudest scream I ever had in my life. The storm snatched the sound away, removing the danger of waking anyone. I had no way of knowing if it worked.

There was nothing else to do except wait. As I prepared to do exactly that, Finn ran into the woods. I watched him go, faintly surprised that he'd actually left my side. I faced the house again, frowning.

The front door opened within minutes.

Cyrus came out. His eyes were downcast, his shoulders hunched. The faux fur lining the hood of his coat moved in the wind, and his hands were shoved in the pockets. He approached me at a steady pace. His copper head gleamed dully in the light shining from the porch. He came to a complete stop and waited. Wind whistled between us while I gathered the courage to speak.

"Do you know what you are, Cyrus?" I asked. My voice was soft.

The fry cook's expression didn't change. He was either skilled at hiding his emotions or he'd been expecting this. "Yes," Cyrus said simply.

My heart pounded harder. "Do you know what I am?"

"Yes."

It felt like there were bombs going off in my chest. I knew the request I was about to make was the most selfish thing I'd ever do. Once, I never would've thought myself capable of it, or any of the things I had done since meeting the Unseelie King. I released a ragged breath and made myself say it. "Help me, then. Make me mortal."

Cyrus was trembling before the words had fully left my mouth. "I can't."

"Because you're afraid to hurt me?" I demanded. He didn't answer. The wind got stronger, more vicious. "How much can one person endure, Cyrus? How far can they venture into the darkness until there's no turning back? Ridding myself of these powers will give me a *chance* at redemption. A chance at survival."

But Cyrus only shook his head again, his eyes wide and

frightened. He began to retreat, as though the distance would help him escape my words. They were in the air now, traveling between us, slipping inside him. He would never escape or forget, just as I couldn't. *Make me mortal.*

He still walked away. His pace was less steady this time, quickening and slowing in bursts, as if he were trying not to run. The door opened and closed, but the wind snatched the sound away. Light from the entryway flared, then faded.

I stood there long after he was gone, clenching and unclenching my fists. I couldn't bring myself to go inside, despite the cold. As a Nightmare, it shouldn't have bothered me, but right now it was all I could do not to shiver. I knew I couldn't stay out here.

I swung toward the van. The keys were in my pocket.

"Fortuna." The sound of Finn's voice made me freeze with one foot in the van. I turned slowly, reluctant to meet his gaze. But I did, because it was Finn. He stood in only a pair of sweatpants, and there were still bits of torn skin clinging to his torso. There was nothing stoic or removed about his expression this time—he looked back with undisguised fear. "Don't leave me again."

Somehow, I knew he was talking about when I'd gone to the crossroads, in the way that Finn and I always seemed to understand each other. Part of me had never returned that night, and we both knew I might not survive losing another piece.

"I'm sorry," I whispered, my stomach clenching with guilt. Pain glimmered in the werewolf's eyes, but he didn't try to stop me. He watched as I got into the van and drove away.

I didn't look at the clock until I was halfway to town. When I saw the numbers, I swore—it was barely past four a.m. The bar wasn't open and my therapist wouldn't be answering her phone for hours yet. But I didn't want to go back and burden my family any more than I already had.

So I went to the same place I'd gone all those nights ago,

when I'd known everything was about to change. When I'd felt like I was standing at the edge of the abyss, deciding whether to jump, and only someone who knew that choice intimately would be able to understand.

Fifteen minutes later I parked my van in front of Adam's shop, relieved to see light glowing through the windows. While vampires generally preferred to be nocturnal, Adam's occupation required that he be conscious during the day. Maybe I'd just gotten lucky, for once, and tomorrow was his day off.

When I opened the door and stepped inside, I spotted Adam instantly, his muscular frame filling the doorway to his bedroom. *He must've heard the van.*

"Must be nice," I said by way of greeting. I was barely aware of the words leaving my mouth, but I heard how hollow my voice was. "You'll always know when your enemies are trying to sneak up on you. What can you do, though, if the enemy is inside you?"

Something flickered in the vampire's dark eyes. Not pity, exactly. He wore his customary jeans and white T-shirt, although it hadn't been white in a long time. He shoved his hands into his pockets as he searched my expression. Was the unflappable Adam Horstman actually worried about me?

I scanned the rest of the space, searching for signs of his sire, but Dracula seemed to be truly gone.

"I have something for you," Adam said in his monotone way. "It was going to be a gift, for when your training is finished, but I think you better have it now."

He vanished before I could respond. He was back two seconds later, balancing something on his palms. We met in the middle of the room and Adam held the sword out to me. He didn't make any pretty speeches or offer encouragement, but then, that wasn't his way. It was part of the reason why we hadn't worked as a couple. Ironic that now I actually appreciated it.

The blade itself was bare. No markings, no decorations, and no engravings. It had a barbed, twisted cross-guard, which ensured the blade was both balanced and capable of protecting the owner's hands against any sliding sword. I wrapped my fingers around the hilt. When I lifted the sword for the first time, it was lighter than I expected. Almost as though it had been made for me.

I met Adam's gaze. "Does this mean we're going steady?"

"Asshole."

"Takes one to know one." My arm started to ache. I lowered the blade and tilted my head at him. "Why do you think I need this now?"

Adam ran an oil-stained hand over his head, showing a glimpse of the tattoo on his bicep. Usually he sported a buzz cut, but lately, he'd been letting it grow out. The greasy strands glinted beneath the fluorescent lights. "Because you have that look again. Same one you had on when you went to find that demon," he said.

I almost lost my grip on the new sword. My stomach roiled as I stared at him. "How did you—"

"I've been around a long time, Sworn. Can't get much past me." He paused. "Want to do some training, so you can actually use that thing someday? Maybe even give it a name?"

I tightened my grip on the hilt again. Holding it made me feel strong for the first time in weeks. This time, when I looked in Adam's eyes, I didn't flinch. "Hell, yeah."

Cyrus was sitting on the front porch when I pulled into the driveway. It had stopped snowing, so his silhouette stood out starkly against the light behind him.

As the sound of my engine faded, I heard Stanley whining. I got out and pushed the door shut. The dog was already there, his nose nudging my legs. He trailed after me down the sidewalk and continued to investigate the smells on my jeans. Halfway to the steps, I spotted Finn through the living room window. He stood in front of the glass, arms crossed, his eyes like a rumbling storm. When our gazes met, he retreated, and then the window was empty again.

Without a word, I settled on the step next to Cyrus. The air was so quiet, so still, that I knew no one else was awake yet. Finn had probably gone back to bed, considering he'd shifted too quickly tonight. It was just me, Cyrus, and Stanley.

Several minutes went by. My mind started to wander, and it ventured toward the brand-new shower in the loft—I was still sweaty from training with Adam. Then Cyrus lifted his copper head, squinted at the horizon, and finally spoke. All thoughts about the shower vanished.

"I'll do it," he said.

Honestly, I hadn't expected that. I swallowed, fighting off an onslaught of fear and guilt. I clasped my hands together so tightly that they turned white. "What made you change your mind?"

"You're my family now." Cyrus said this with the same tone he used for everyday statements. *Bea was looking for you. It's cold out today.* But his agitation showed in how he ran his hand over Stanley's head, again and again.

I looked down at it, trying to think of another way. *Maybe I should just do the Rites of Thogon and leave Cyrus out of it.* The biggest problem with that, however, was the low survival rate. I also didn't want to repeat Arcaena's outcome, in which I was reduced to a shell of my former self. Feeling my life and my sanity break off in pieces, day by day.

"That may be true. It doesn't mean you don't have a choice," I said faintly.

Cyrus's hand faltered. After a moment, he turned his head. He wasn't quite looking at me, but it still felt like he was. "I've never had a family before. Not like other people," he said. "Until high school, I did have my dad. But he was an angry person—he couldn't keep a job because of it. He always said that anger was our curse. Our cross to bear."

"Because of what you are?" I asked, my voice hesitant. Cyrus nodded and returned his attention to Stanley, stroking the dog's head again. I watched him for a moment, silently marveling at how much he was talking. It was probably because he was so scared; fear had a way of changing people. I remembered that moment at the bar, when flames had reached up from the stove and sent Cyrus into a state of panic. "Did... did your dad ever hurt you, Cy?"

My friend shook his head, and there was nothing in his expression that hinted at a lie. "He just broke or burned things," Cyrus answered. "Then, one night, he lost his temper in the barn. He'd been spending more time out there, because he was between jobs, so he was fixing a friend's car. It happened so fast. Flames shot out of him, bigger than any he'd ever made before. The whole place went up like a tinder box. Dad could've gotten out—there was plenty of time—but he stood there and let himself burn. I think he'd been wanting to die for a long time, and he saw his chance."

Even now, his voice was toneless. I studied Cyrus's profile, thinking about my own parents' deaths. It was a wound that time never healed. That's how I knew he was hiding behind a mask of his own. "How do you know that?" I asked eventually.

There was another pause. Then Cyrus said, "Because I was there."

His façade finally cracked, and I saw his jaw working, as if he were holding something back. He didn't let it out, though. I started to respond, but he stood up and hurried down the steps. I hesitated for a moment, the battle still raging on inside me. When Cyrus didn't stop or slow, I jumped up and went after him.

My pulse was an erratic thing in my chest. I thought about what he'd just told me about his father and considered calling it off. *Never mind, I take it back. I don't want you to use your dragon-fire to purge my soul.*

But those nightmares were waiting for me. Those screams were hovering at the back of my mind, ready to surge forward at any sign of weakness. And further back, deeper in the darkness, there was also hunger. The terrible knowledge that, if the opportunity presented itself, I would grab at any power I could and get so high off it that I felt like a god again.

I remained silent.

Cyrus led me behind the barn, where there were no windows or witnesses. Collith's piles of firewood were still there, now covered in snow. I stopped in the same spot where he'd once stood, shirtless and swinging that ax. I banished the memory and focused on Cyrus. We faced each other like we were on the exercise mat at Adam's, preparing to engage in physical combat. "Have you ever done this before?" I asked, making my voice brisk to hide the terror.

"No." At last, he raised his eyes to mine. "Does that change your mind?"

I hated myself a little more as I said, "No."

Cyrus's muscles bunched and a concentrated expression contorted his face. Any other day, I'd find it comical, but now fear filled my stomach like a dozen butterflies. A few seconds ticked by, and nothing happened. Realizing I'd squeezed my eyes shut, I opened them to see what was wrong. Still standing there, facing me, Cyrus didn't move or speak. I sensed his hesitation. His terror.

"Do it," I breathed, putting everything I felt into those two words. The self-loathing. The pain.

Maybe part of me hadn't expected him to go through with it. When the mild-mannered fry cook made a sound I hadn't known he was capable of, I jumped so violently that it felt like an electric shock. Veins stood out from Cyrus's forehead and throat. His hands were fists, held out at his sides. I stared at him, unable to look away this time.

The fire didn't come from his hands—it came out of his mouth.

As the explosion of heat and light poured from him, hurtling toward me, I saw his eyes change color and scales glitter on his neck. Then I was engulfed in flames.

I thought I'd known pain. Throughout my life, I had endured every kind of it. Physical, mental, emotional. My bones had snapped and my heart had shattered. I'd cried myself to sleep and I'd had my skin stitched shut.

None of it compared to this.

Suddenly it stopped. All of it. The agony, my screams, the crackling of hungry flames, the smell of burning flesh, it ended like someone had touched a light switch. My eyes were still closed, but there was something different about the air against my face. I felt a fleeting sense of curiosity—the only thing that really mattered was the absence of pain. I never wanted to experience it again.

Seconds ticked past, and it didn't return. The sound of my own breathing was too loud. I couldn't hear anything else as I sat up. Too late, I realized this probably wasn't smart. But the movement didn't hurt. I looked down, expecting to see burns, charred skin, tattered clothing. My skin was smooth and unblemished. I wore the clothes I'd trained with Adam in, and there was no sign they'd been on fire.

Had I fallen unconscious? Was this another nightmare? I blinked slowly and turned my attention to the horizon. It was a view I knew better than any other, and when I saw it, it felt like something inside me stood on tiptoe. *Am I really in the dreamscape? Our dreamscape?*

But there was no sign of Oliver in any direction. The cottage and the oak tree were gone, too, which made me less certain this was the place we'd grown up together. I pushed myself up and started walking toward the edge of the world. I felt light-headed, high, and it took considerable effort to put one foot in front of the other. There was a haziness to everything, as if I were seeing the dreamscape through a frost-covered window. Clumps of tall grasses ducked their heads close and whispered to each other. *She thought she could burn it all away,* I heard. *As if it's that easy.*

I sank onto the grass, put my legs over the sea, and stared out at the dying sun. There was nothing violent about its depar-ture—the colors spreading over the water were a serene blend of pink, yellow, and orange. Wisps of clouds hung high above. To the right of the sun, a flock of birds flew, and their wild cries traveled on the air. I kept my eyes on all those flapping wings, trying to avoid looking at the bare patch of earth where Oliver usually sat.

Then I heard the distinct sound of footsteps behind me.

Before I could react, someone dropped to the ground and dangled their legs in the space next to mine. *Ollie.* The rush of emotion was so sudden, so overwhelming, that I had to close my eyes and wait for it to pass. Relief, guilt, sorrow, joy. He'd come back. Despite everything, Oliver hadn't abandoned me.

My hands were fists against my knees. The urge to sob slowly subsided. Once the world was steady again I turned, expecting to see my best friend sitting there.

My father smiled back.

A tuft of his dark hair lifted in a breeze, and the edge of his black-rimmed glasses gleamed in the light. "Hey, kiddo," he said.

It felt like I'd had the wind knocked out of me. I stared at him for two, three, four seconds, my heart rioting inside me. He waited patiently, just as he always had. He looked like he was about to head off for work—being a therapist, his wardrobe was all calm colors and neat lines. "Daddy? Is this real?" I asked finally, sounding like a lost child. A hopeful child.

He lifted his thin shoulders in a shrug. Mom used to tease him for his bony frame, I remembered suddenly. No matter how much he exercised, my father was never able to look formidable. In reality, he'd been a remarkably powerful Nightmare. Or so Mom used to tell me, watching him with a smile so small, so quiet, it was like a secret.

"It is whatever you need it to be, sweetheart. That's why they call it a dream," Dad answered, pulling me out of the memory.

I blinked at him, feeling disoriented again. He waited for me to say something. The silence between us thickened and, eventually, Dad turned to look at the sunset. I knew I was staring, but I was terrified to blink or move. If this was a dream, I wanted to stay in it.

Another playful wind went past, carrying my father's scent to me—it was a combination of cigarettes and laundry detergent. The smell of childhood. All I had to do was close my eyes, and I was there again. Time had taken so many of the details from me.

My voice was slow with reluctance as I asked, "Why are you here? What's happening?"

"You're dying, sweetheart." Dad focused on me again. His expression was compassionate, but he spoke firmly. It was the same way he conducted our self-defense lessons.

I'd known the truth, of course, but hearing someone else say it was jarring. "What?" I said dumbly, my heart stumbling.

Without warning, a voice came from the sky. It sounded distant, muffled, like someone speaking behind that red curtain drawn across the stage.

"Dragonfire isn't just heat and light—it's magic, too," Dad told me, acting as if a voice in the clouds was completely normal. "When Cyrus burned your essence as a Nightmare away, your body went into shock. Now it's time to ask yourself a question, Fortuna."

The shadow in his eyes frightened me, and I forgot about the voice. Whatever this question was, it made him sad. I wanted to avoid it. A seagull shrieked above us, the sound echoing across the horizon, but Dad kept his eyes on mine.

This conversation was a waste of time, I realized suddenly. If I was dying, there wasn't anything we could do about it. Who knew how much longer we'd be here together? I scooted back from the cliffside to stand, then looked down at my father with a wobbly smile. "Dad, please, can't we—"

"Do you want to die?" he interrupted.

The fact that he'd cut me off had me staring again. *No, of course I don't want to die*, I started to say. They were the automatic words, the expected words. But they stuck in my throat. I'd never lied to my father, and this had the taste of one. If we were having our last conversation because I was about to use my one-way ticket to Hell, I wanted it to be something I could hold onto. Something to bring comfort as the demons ripped me apart.

"I don't know," I admitted.

Dad got to his feet, too. He wasn't as tall as I remembered, and I met his gaze without needing to arch my head back. "This isn't the first time you've been at a crossroads, is it?" he asked gently.

That word made me blanch, and I took an involuntary step back. *Crossroads.* No, I told myself. He was talking about death, not about the deal I'd made beneath a flickering streetlight. But how did he know about my other brush with mortality? I hadn't come to this place. We hadn't spoken or seen each other.

I opened my mouth to ask the question out loud... and then I remembered. After Gwyn drowned me, I'd seen a male figure in the doorway of the tomb. I'd chased him into the darkness, my voice echoing through the eerie stillness. *Who are you?*

"That was you?" I blurted.

As if he could see the images in my head, Dad nodded. The movement made sunlight bounce off his glasses. "You only saw me for a moment, because we weren't completely in the same place," he explained. "You were in between places, that night. But at some point, honey, you need to choose one and stay there. Because putting your family through this isn't fair to them."

It always came back down to choices, didn't it? Collith had been so certain we could have it all, but that wasn't life. That was just another dream, and I was fucking tired of dreams. Tired of *everything*. My resolve hardened, and I raised my chin, on the verge of telling Dad that *he* was my family. I wanted to be wherever he was. I ached to see Mom.

When I saw his expression, though, my curiosity was stronger than my longing. "What?" I asked.

"My wild, impulsive girl," he murmured. "Even as a toddler, you were prone to reckless decisions."

His eyes were brighter than they'd been a moment ago, and with a start, I realized it was because there were tears in them. I had never seen Matthew Sworn cry before. *This*, I thought as I committed his face to memory. This was what I wanted to remember, instead of the bleeding, broken body I'd found in their bed that night.

Thinking about that night instantly dimmed the light in my heart. Tears sprang to my eyes, too, but they felt hot and bitter. "How can you be so accepting? Aren't you angry that you didn't get to see me grow up?" I demanded.

"I *have* seen you grow up. Of course I wish I'd been there, Tuna Fish, but life had other plans."

Whatever I'd been about to say faded in my throat—Dad and Damon were so alike that it hurt. They endured the darkest experiences and emerged into the light with an acceptance I'd never felt. If I chose to stay, it would disappoint him. My father's disappointment had always been one of my greatest fears, the dusty box at the back of my head. But I wasn't one who allowed fear to make decisions for me.

If I went back, a mortal body awaited me. I stood there and let the realization sink in. For the first time in my life, the people I interacted with would actually see me. I would be able to walk through a room without getting accosted by images and flavors. And that power—that rich, delicious, intoxicating power—would be gone. The corruption and the temptation wiped away like a fingerprint on glass. I could watch Matthew grow up and be with my family, free of the knowledge that I was endangering them.

That seemed like something worth living for.

And... Cyrus. I hadn't even considered Cyrus, who would be wracked with guilt if I didn't survive his dragonfire.

The voice in the sky spoke again, more urgently now. My name boomed through the pink-tinted clouds. I smiled at my father again, knowing we were out of time. Tears flooded my vision and blurred his face. "I'll do it for you," I said. "For them."

Dad pressed a kiss to my forehead, then wrapped his arms around me. "No, sweetheart. Do it for yourself," his voice rumbled against my ear.

Once again, another voice struck the dreamscape like light-ning—there was a frantic finality to it now—and I stepped away from my father. I wasn't sure how I knew the way to get back, but I did. I held his hand tightly and squeezed my eyes shut, focusing on that voice in the sky, picturing the place where I died. My mind instinctively resisted the memory, but the stakes were too high for weakness. With gritted teeth, I remembered Cyrus's anguished eyes and that wall of flame coming at me.

I didn't have a command or a word pounding through my veins as I relived every second of it—only an intention. Back. I was going back. No matter how tempting it was to stay here, live forever in a place that held so many good memories, my fight wasn't over yet. I still had a part to play. I couldn't do to my family what had been done to me; I would not give them another reason to grieve.

"Goodbye, Fortuna," I heard Dad say.

"Thank you for saving me," I whispered, mustering a smile for him. My guardian angel. I'd put together that he was the mysterious dream figure who led me to Creiddylad—Dad must've been there when Gwyn offered to let me live in exchange for her lover. I should have recognized him in the dream, but that golden hair had thrown me off. Maybe being in two different places altered his coloring, made him look like a stranger.

Time to let go now, Fortuna. I pursed my lips and pulled back.

Somehow, Dad must've seen the memory in my head, because his eyes widened. He grabbed my hands and clasped them against his chest, his grip tight, as if I were about to fly away. "Wait. Fortuna, hold on. That wasn't me, in your dream, do you understand? It was—"

Pain. Oh, God, the pain. Some part of me knew I was back in my body. Dad was gone, along with the incandescent sky, and now there was only darkness and agony. I'd made a mistake. I'd chosen wrong. I tried to take it back, but I didn't know where my mouth was anymore. Words had been reduced to a vague idea.

I must've blacked out for a while. When I could form thoughts again, I recognized the sound of sobbing. Someone was saying my name—the voice was too far away to tell if it was male or female. I couldn't open my eyes. I struggled to answer, but a croak was all I managed. It felt like my jaw might fall off if I tried to speak again.

In an attempt to stop a rising sense of panic, I concentrated on the body I'd reclaimed. There was a hard surface against the back of my head and the air smelled strange. Cool hands pushed my hair back, and then a scent I knew washed over me. It blocked out all the rest. *Zara.*

Suddenly I was frantic. Suddenly I was afraid. It took everything I had to open my eyes into slits, but I did it. The details of

Zara's face sharpened. I grabbed the closest part of her I could reach, which turned out to be her hijab, and pulled her closer. "I want to live," I rasped, hoping she saw the truth in my eyes.

If Zara responded, I didn't hear it.

Laughing, the shadows found me and dragged me back into the depths.

CHAPTER TWENTY-SIX

a voice shot into the stillness like bullets through paper.

It took a minute or two to realize it wasn't coming from inside my head. It took another minute to grasp who I was and that I had a physical body again. I was on my back. There was air against my face. I couldn't open my eyes, but that was okay, because I wasn't ready to yet. Reality kept drifting back in waves, each one carrying a memory on it. Eventually I remembered who I was and what I'd done, then I wished I hadn't.

Every time Collith has sex, he takes a piece of his partner. Just a tiny piece. You hardly would've noticed its absence.

I saw a clearing of writhing bodies. Phantom screams filled my ears. I tasted dozens of flavors on my tongue and the rush of a hundred fears pouring into me. I opened my eyes and saw a witch slapping at her arms, tearing at them, screaming as a swarm of fire ants consumed her. A shapeshifter begged for his life as a pack of lions advanced on him.

Even then, the tide of memory wasn't finished. Suddenly I was standing in the yard at Cyrus's, facing my friend as if there were a battlefield between us. *Help me, Cyrus. Make me mortal.*

Flames hurtled toward me.

My mind recoiled from reliving that explosion of pain, and suddenly the darkness became shapes. Seconds later, they solidified into walls and furniture. A frown pulled down the corners of my mouth as I took in unfamiliar surroundings. There was a window along one wall, and dusk poured through the glass. The floor was tiled, there was a privacy curtain hanging to my right, and the bed I rested in had handles on either side—I was obviously in a hospital. I wore one of those thin, dotted gowns depicted in movies and shows. There was also a clip-like device on one of my fingers. I stared at it, struggling to remember the rest. Hadn't Zara been at the house? Though the images were fragmented, I remembered her face hovering over mine. I'd said something to her, the words faint and slurred. Why would anyone take me here?

Unless... Zara had lent so much of her energy that even she hadn't been able to complete the healing.

As I had the thought, a memory floated back like driftwood, and I realized how extensive the damage had been. *Do you want to die?*

His voice had the haziness of a dream, but I knew my father. He'd been real. He'd found me in death to speak truths I didn't want to hear, just as he had done in life. *Thanks for coming through for me one last time, Daddy.* There was an ache in my heart that had nothing to do with supernatural burns.

I was fully conscious now, and with awareness came agony. Despite the painkillers I was probably on, every part of my body hurt. Dear God, was this how mortals felt every time they were significantly wounded?

You deserve it, a faint voice whispered at the back of my head.

Shame spread through me, swift and lethal as poison. Those unwanted memories breathed down my neck. So much pain. So much death.

But I'd fixed it now. I'd made it impossible for me to use that terrible power ever again.

Grimacing, I focused on colors around the room as a distraction. The minty walls, the yellow stain on the tiled floor, the beige blanket draped over my legs. There was a clock on the wall. Once I noticed it, I couldn't block that sound out. *Tick. Tick. Tick.*

I looked toward the hallway, wondering if I could convince a nurse to take the clock down. The door was slightly ajar, but now that I thought about it, I hadn't seen a single person walk past. The voice that pulled me from oblivion had gone silent. Was something wrong?

My instincts were rousing, speaking to me in insistent whispers, and they all said the same thing—danger was near. Fear took hold, stronger than the pain, and I finally sat up and moved my legs to the side.

"Hello?" I called, mindless of my exposed backside from the gaping hospital gown. A draft of air whispered across my skin, reminding me of the Hunt, and I shivered. "Is anyone out there?"

There was no response. The fear expanded until it felt like there was a balloon in my lung, making it hard to breathe. *Tick. Tick. Tick.* Wheezing and cursing the clock, I stood shakily. I called out again, listening hard. When there was only silence again, I took a few steps and grasped the doorknob. It twisted in my hand, but not from my doing.

"What are you doing out of bed?" a nurse chided, entering carefully. I felt as if she could hear the wild frenzy of my pulse, beating in time with the clock. *Thud. Tick. Thud. Tick.* The nurse put her hand on my shoulder and eased me back into bed. "You're not trying to leave, are you?"

The thought was so ludicrous that a laugh caught in my throat. I didn't let it free, though—even that small movement would hurt too much. I let silence be my answer. If the human was bothered by this, she didn't show it. Her expression was pleasant as she checked the machines beeping next to me. "Happy Thanksgiving, Miss Sworn," I heard her say.

She left the room. I wanted to call after her, but I wanted to avoid the pain more. *Did she say it was Thanksgiving?* I wondered dimly, tension seeping from my muscles as I gave in to darkness again.

Days passed.

Or maybe it was only a few hours. I didn't know and I didn't care. I lay there on sweat-drenched bedsheets, trying not to fall asleep. Nightmares waited for me, I knew, hulking shapes within that hovering darkness. Awareness came rushing back when something cold touched my arm.

My eyes snapped open, and Finn's whiskered face loomed inches away from mine—it must've been his nose I felt. Lyari stood behind him. My first thought was that I'd returned to the dreamscape. But we were still in the hospital room and I could read words on the monitor next to me. I was awake. This was real.

"What are you guys doing here?" I asked when my heart had slightly calmed. More time must've passed than I thought, because it felt like I'd healed; I was able to look up at Lyari without a burst of pain. Or, more likely, I'd gotten a fresh dose of the good drugs. The room *was* glowing, which seemed like further evidence of this theory.

Lyari looked at me as though I were an imbecile. "We're here to protect you, of course."

"You made that oath to your queen, which no longer applies to me," I reminded her in a slurred voice, ignoring another stab of pain. This one had nothing to do with dragonfire, though. "You're free, okay?"

"You're really going to make me say it?" the faerie snapped.

I frowned at her, running an absent hand down Finn's back. "What the hell are you—"

"For fuck's sake, this isn't a romance novel," Lyari snarled, then seemed to rein her temper in. "I've come to the conclusion, Your Majesty, that a throne is not what makes a queen. My oath is no less legitimate because of where you were sitting while I made it."

Her voice was stiff and reluctant. As she spoke, the barest beginnings of a smile tugged at one corner of my mouth. I looked away, my head flopping toward the window, and I stared out into the night. *Two things,* I thought. *Two good things came out of surviving those trials.*

I'd saved my brother... and gained a friend.

Within the hour, or maybe it was a handful of minutes, the pain returned and made me forget everything else. Finn nosed at my arm, as he'd been doing repeatedly over the last few hours. It didn't hurt when he touched me—not anymore, at least —but the warmth of his breath was uncomfortable. I didn't stop him, though, because I knew he was doing it to reassure himself that I was still alive. His fear filled the room like scent from a burning candle.

Being human felt like a hollow shell, I decided. I shared this thought with Lyari, but I wasn't sure if I was actually talking out loud. I also wasn't sure if that was Emma and Damon talking in whispers, or if they were another dream.

When I finally forced myself to leave the bed and creak my way into the bathroom—Finn hovered nearby with every step— I walked on legs that felt like brittle sticks. One misstep, one fall, and they'd crack. I finished my task with success and began the painstaking journey back to bed.

I was staring out the window again, my eyes half-shut in drug-fueled drowsiness, when it shattered.

Glass sprinkled onto the floor. Lyari shouted, but her words were drowned out by the humming in my ears. I struggled to sit up just as something crawled through the jagged hole, clicking like an insect.

The cherubim had returned.

Once again, I didn't know if I was sleeping or awake. If this was a dream or reality. I instinctively fumbled for a weapon in the nightstand. But I was weak from the ordeal with Cyrus and my hand slipped off the small handle. *Fuck.*

Down the hall, someone cried out.

"No, don't hurt anyone," I tried to say. A moan was all that passed my lips.

I was dimly aware that Lyari and Finn were both locked in battle with separate cherubim. But there was a third crawling through the window now, and I met the creature's gaze for exactly one shocked, frozen instant. Then its arm moved—I saw it out of my peripheral vision—and time seemed to slow as I rose my own to block it. Too late.

Something small and hard smashed against my head. It cracked like an egg. In the next moment, the most fetid stench I'd ever experienced filled the room. I recoiled against the plastic headboard, gagging, and tried to plug my nose. It had become even more difficult to move, though. The air itself felt like tar.

"Do you see the ghosts?" I whispered to the cherubim. I must've lost time again, because it was carrying me through the air. The hospital room was gone and cold, black sky surrounded us, filled with spirits and voices. "Do you hear them whispering?"

The creature just made another chattering sound. Its wings looked like smoke. No, blurs. I tossed my head, trying to clear it, but the movement only brought darkness closer. There was a reason I didn't want to sleep, I knew. There was something I needed to do.

One of the ghosts was whispering in my ear, saying something about... a prince. Maybe it was a fairy tale. The urgent task felt less urgent, suddenly, and I closed my eyes to listen. A dreamy smile curved my lips. "Was the prince very beautiful?" I murmured.

"Oh, yes," the ghosts whispered back. "Oh, yes…"

The insides of my eyelids were red. Sunlight. Morning. Everyone else was probably already awake. Emma would be trying to cook an enormous breakfast on her own. *Get up, Fortuna. Just open your eyes. You need to help Emma.*

Reluctantly, I started to obey. But just as my eyes cracked open, everything came roaring back like a tsunami. I remembered waking up in a hospital, after Cyrus had burned the bad parts of me away. Finn and Lyari came to stand guard. Then… breaking glass. A battle. People screaming. The memories became even dimmer after that. A final image whispered through my mind. A glimpse of city lights far below. There was a leathery wing obscuring part of my view.

How much of it had actually happened? Which parts were hallucinations and reality? Were Finn and Lyari all right?

When my vision cleared, the haze of sleep efficiently blinked away, I wasn't surprised to find myself in a strange place. I'd been taken, that much I did know. Whatever the cherubim smashed against my head had caused apparitions and lost time. I still felt the effects of it, a grogginess that wasn't fading as I looked around. The bed was mammoth, with a canopy above, and could easily fit several more people. Tall windows surrounded me, their filmy curtains fluttering in a breeze. The ceilings were vast and the walls gleamed with golden wallpaper. To the right, there was an enormous pair of doors.

When I turned, trying to take in the rest of the room, my gaze met Laurie's.

"Shit!" I jumped so violently that my spine slammed against the ornate headboard, and that was when I finally noticed I was in restraints. Chains rattled from the suddenness of my movement.

The Seelie King sat in a chair beside the bed—no, he wasn't the king anymore, I needed to stop forgetting that—legs crossed, hands resting atop his knees. There was a teapot on the table beside him. My wild heart began to calm. If Laurie was here, I was safe.

My gaze moved over the rest of him now. He wore clothing even more elaborate than usual, a gold and blue slashed doublet coupled with gauntlets. Nestled in his silver hair was a crown I'd never seen him wearing before.

"Where are we? What happened?" I rasped. "Do you know if Lyari and Finn are okay?"

Laurie studied my face as though he'd never seen it before. "Welcome to the Seelie Court, Fortuna Sworn," he said. His voice was strange, too. Higher than it normally was.

My instincts were shrieking like a wounded siren. Once again, my pulse quickened. Somehow I managed to stay still. I gave Laurie a questioning look, waiting for him to offer the inevitable, logical explanation for the restraints. While I'd been unconscious, I had thrashed or lashed out. Maybe I'd even hurt someone.

Instead of doing this, the faerie just quirked a silvery brow at me.

"What's going on, Laurie?" I asked evenly. Even now, I hoped for a valid reason I was strapped to a bed. The beginnings of panic stirred, though, and I couldn't stop myself from tugging at the cuffs.

With an elegant flick of his wrist, my friend checked a Rolex watch I'd also never seen him wear before. "As of... 6:23 this evening, I've laid claim to you," he informed me. "You are no longer the monarch of an opposing Court, so in the eyes of our world, I've merely taken another slave. Albeit a very infamous one."

There was something in the way Laurie looked at me, maybe, or the tight crook of his mouth. Not quite a smile, not quite a smirk. Some terrible thing that hovered between the two. Suddenly I had a flash of intuition, like lightning striking a tree, and I felt the fragments left of my heart cracking even more. "You sent the cherubim," I said flatly. It wasn't a question.

Laurie inclined his head, as though he found my response deeply interesting. His gaze fell, just for an instant, and zeroed in on his knee. His sensuous mouth pursed. His long, pale fingers fussed at a piece of lint I didn't see. "A crude method, I admit, but they don't give my secrets away," he remarked.

"And why," I said through my teeth, using anger to disguise my pain, "did you go through all this trouble? Why 'claim' me?"

That's when Laurie smiled, and the sight sent a chill through my body. It looked nothing like the smile I'd known until now. The smile that, somehow, was always just for me, even when we were surrounded by other people.

"Well, my dear, isn't it obvious?" Laurie asked in a self-satisfied purr, his eyes gleaming like razor-edged diamonds. He reached for a teacup. "I have plans, Fortuna Sworn, and none of those plans will come to fruition while you're human."

For a moment, I just stared at him, wondering if this was a dream. Collith's voice floated through my head like a ghost. Haunting me, appearing to me when I least expected it. *Did you know that you can't read in a dream?* Desperation sliced through me, and I scanned the room again, but there was nothing I could test Collith's theory on.

Laurie's words eventually registered. *While you're human,* he'd said. If my heart had been pounding hard before, it was a mallet now, slamming against the wall of my chest so hard it hurt. I tugged at the restraints and snapped, "I don't understand."

"What's not to understand?" He took a sip of tea, then smacked his lips. The sound was too loud in this eerie stillness. Seeing the complete change in his demeanor, hearing the shift in his voice, I realized that Laurie was a stranger. I didn't truly know him, because the person I'd formed in my mind wasn't the one sitting in that chair. A flash of memory blinded me, and I saw the whites of Savannah's eyes, her face flung back as she tried to shout a warning. *Someone is still coming!*

Her voice was still echoing through my head as Laurie's gaze met mine and he said, those pretty silver depths glinting with cruelty, "I'm going to make you a Nightmare again."

END OF BOOK THREE

ACKNOWLEDGMENTS

What a ride.

I wrote this enormous book during 2020, a year I think we can all agree wasn't conducive for creativity. But, as always, I had an incredible support system every step of the way. Without them, I'm not sure *Deadly Dreams* would exist.

The first individual I want to acknowledge is Jessi Elliott. Over this past year, you've become one of my dearest friends. Without our FaceTime calls, our sprints, our shared passion, 2020 probably would've broken me. I'm so lucky to have you in my life. Thank you for the part you played in this book's creation, and I can't wait to write even more together in 2021!

As always, thank you to the other friends in my life for continuing a relationship with me despite the amount of times I say, "Sorry, can't, I need to work on the book." You know who you are.

My eternal gratitude to my outside readers, Randi Georges and Brianna Stahl. It was no small task, editing a book that clocked in over five hundred pages, but neither of you batted an eye when I asked. How did I get so lucky?

And finally, thank you once again to the *Fortuna Sworn* fans who took the time to message, e-mail, review, and share about this series. Your passion feeds my own and every single post continues to surprise and humble me. From the bottom of my heart, thank you.

ABOUT THE AUTHOR

 K.J. Sutton lives in Minnesota with her two rescue dogs. She has received multiple awards for her work, and she graduated with a master's degree in Creative Writing from Hamline University.

When she's writing, K.J. always has a cup of Vanilla Chai in her hand and despises wearing anything besides pajamas. K.J. Sutton also writes young adult novels as Kelsey Sutton.

Be friends with her on Instagram, Facebook, and Twitter. And don't forget to subscribe to her newsletter so you never miss an update!

CPSIA information can be obtained
at www.ICGtesting.com
Printed in the USA
LVHW042248140822
725928LV00001B/16